W9-BJN-937

THE PRESIDENT'S LADY

The

President's Lady

A NOVEL ABOUT RACHEL AND ANDREW JACKSON

By Irving Stone

DOUBLEDAY & COMPANY, INC., GARDEN CITY, N.Y.

TO JEAN

(for her creative editing)

THIS IS A BIOGRAPHICAL NOVEL; it differs from a historical novel in that it does not introduce fictional characters against a background of history, but instead tells the story through the actual people who lived it and helped make it happen. The history to be found within its pages is as authentic and documented as several years of intensive research, the generous assistance of the historians and librarians in the field, and literally thousands of books, magazines, pamphlets, newspapers, diaries, public records, correspondence and collections of unpublished memoirs and doctoral theses can make it. At the back of the book the interested reader will find a bibliography of some hundred and fifty volumes actually used in the construction of this novel.

The interpretations of character are of course my own; this is not only the novelist's prerogative but his obligation. Much of the dialogue had to be re-created, but every effort has been made to create it on the basis of individual character, personality, temperament, education, idiosyncrasy, as well as recorded conversations and dialogue, memoirs, diaries, letters and published accounts by relatives, friends, associates, even of detractors and enemies. The language of the day was more flowery and formal than our own; I have attempted to tell the story in a simpler English, but I have striven constantly to make certain that the difference is one of words, and never of thought, feeling or meaning.

I wish to acknowledge the constant help afforded me by such Jackson and Tennessee historians as Marquis James, whose definitive and highly readable biography of Andrew Jackson is the authority in the field; Alfred Leland Crabb, who took countless hours away from his double task of teaching and writing to tackle difficult research problems; Gerald W. Johnson, for permission to quote from his life of Jackson; Allan Nevins, who helped guide my attitudes toward the characters in this story; Robert T. Quarles, Tennessee State Archivist, who made a special study for me on the early Tennesse militia; Dr. Dan M. Robison,

Tennessee State Librarian, who helped with the research; and to Paul I. Wellman for stimulating my interest in the Jackson story. Arthur M. Schlesinger, Jr.'s study of the older Jackson was a constant help.

In Tennessee I am indebted to Jordan Stokes III, who introduced me to the Cumberland Valley and looked up many obscure legal records; Stanley F. Horn sent me special material on the Hermitage; Mrs. John Trotwood Moore made available to me many of the Donelson family documents, as did Mary Hooper Donelson Jones. Louis D. Wallace sent me publications of the Tennessee State Department of Agriculture; the Ladies' Hermitage Association, Mrs. Robert F. Jackson, Regent, was helpful in detailing the personal possessions of the Jacksons at the Hermitage, in particular the library. In Los Angeles I am indebted to Dr. Emil J. Krahulik for material on obstetrics in the beginning of the nineteenth century; Dr. George McCollister afforded me information on animal husbandry; Louis M. Brown helped me with a study of the marriage, separation and divorce laws in America at the end of the eighteenth century. In Washington, D.C., Maurice Paris was indispensable in my work among the Jackson papers in the Library of Congress; Brigadier General Eustace M. Peixotto, U.S. Army, Ret., made a study for me at the Library of Congress of the military books that would have been available to Andrew Jackson in 1792.

I am deeply indebted to the Library of Congress and the Carnegie Institute, both of Washington, D.C.; to the Library of the University of California at Los Angeles, which gathered old and rare books for me from all over America; and to the Joint University Library, Nashville, Tennessee; to the libraries of the Universities of Kentucky, Virginia, Minnesota, California, for their co-operation in lending me these books.

IRVING STONE

June 6, 1951

THE PRESIDENT'S LADY

Book ONE

THEY EMERGED from the dark woods and were suddenly in the hot September sunshine. At the bottom of the hill their horses stopped to drink from the shallow stream.

"Would you like to rest for a spell, Rachel, and freshen? We'll be home by sundown."

"I'd rather push on, Samuel, if it's the same to you."

He seemed relieved. Why was her own brother so constrained with her? No matter how serious the charges, she had expected support from her family.

They crossed the bottom lands and made their way up the trail to a timbered knob. She paused for a moment to let the cool wind of the uplands blow through her abundant black hair, refreshing her. For the first time in the four days since they had left Harrodsburg she began to feel clearheaded.

It's strange, she thought, during the long week that it took for my husband's message to reach the Cumberland and for my brother to come for me, I was too wretched to worry about anybody but myself. Yet the moment we were on the trail for home I began to think about Samuel and how hard he has taken my misfortune. If I greet my mother and brothers and sisters with the same stricken face I showed to Samuel, I'll make them all as wretched as I was.

I must think this thing through, come to some sort of understanding with myself before we reach home. Was I really guilty of misconduct? If so, how? If I wasn't guilty, then why has this happened to me? I've got to dig down to the root, no matter how bitter it may be to chew on.

She looked across at her brother, the change in her mood communicating itself to him. She had a mirror in her saddlebag, but she had no need for one at this moment: she and Samuel, who was a year younger, were alike as twins. She saw his warm brown eyes, so quick to pain and hurt, proffering her a tiny tentative smile; the thin, curved black eyebrows; the small but immaculate white teeth, showing between the

1

expressive lips; the thick black hair, worn over the ears, pulled back tight and tied low on the neck with a thong; his contour, inclined to exposed roundness, unprotected against the world. He had not been judging her; his confused and troubled expression had been but a true reflection of her own.

Though she had not seen her family for three years there had never been any question in her mind as to which one of her seven brothers would make the dangerous trip to fetch her. They were the youngest and gayest of the Donelson family; when her father was home he had taught her to read and write, but when he was away on surveying trips or treaty-making with the Indians, she and Samuel had studied together from the leather-bound handwritten arithmetic book in which they learned about division of decimals and the double rule of three. Samuel had been clever with books, and their father, who was an intensely religious man, had imagined that at long last he had a son who would follow in the footsteps of his great-grandfather, the clergyman who had helped to found the first Presbyterian church in America.

"Why has he done this to you, Rachel?" Samuel cried out, released at last to discuss their difficulty. "What was his provocation?"

"Provocation? Well, a letter. Sent from Virginia to Crab Orchard, to be delivered to me secretly. Lewis intercepted it."

"But what could be in such a letter?"

"I never saw it. According to Lewis, a proposal that I elope with Peyton Short to Spanish Territory. Also a credit for me to buy anything I might need for a trip down to New Orleans."

Samuel gazed at her in bewilderment.

"When did all this nonsense start?"

Tears came into her eyes. She said to herself, Samuel is right; perhaps if I could find my way back to the beginning of our troubles . . . When did they start?

Probably at the house-raising bee to which Lewis had taken her at Bardstown, when he had suddenly become enraged because she was laughing heartily at a story told by one of his friends, an amusing fellow who insisted upon keeping his lips close to his listener's ear. Lewis had come to her side, yanked her unceremoniously by the arm and taken her away from the party.

Before their marriage her husband had told her that he loved her for her bubbling good spirits, for the way she came into a room filled with people who were feeling dull or unhappy and by her very warmth and genuine liking for folks somehow made them come alive. Then why had he turned against her?

She shook her head angrily, provoked with herself for being unable to reach disciplined conclusions. But when in her twenty-one years had she needed to be logical and disciplined in her thinking?

It had not been very long after the abrupt withdrawal from the party

2

at Bardstown that Lewis Robards began accusing her of being too friendly with the young men of the neighborhood and with those who frequented the Robards home. Had she smiled too warmly at greeting this one? Her husband had said so in unmistakable terms later that night. Had she danced with too much vivacity at her first anniversary party? Lewis's face had gone purple with rage when he locked the door of their bedroom and turned to accuse her. Had she listened too sympathetically to a newcomer's account of his difficulties in adjusting himself to the rude frontier life in Kentucky? But she had been interested in the young chap and the recounting of his hardships, for he had come from within a few miles of the old Donelson home in Virginia.

After each quarrel she had lain awake saying to herself, If Lewis no longer likes me to be friendly, then I must be more reserved. If he doesn't want me to dance or sing, I will be quiet.

She would mind her resolution for a number of days, then forget herself and be gay with old friends, tell stories and let her laughter ring out . . . and Lewis would join in the funmaking, his arm fondly about her; until a day or a week later, when he would again seize upon some harmless incident to stage a humiliating scene in public.

But her real difficulties had not begun, she remembered, until there were a series of Indian attacks around Harrodsburg, with a half dozen killings. Lewis's mother, who had managed the plantation since her husband's death, decided they had better take in a few young men who were experienced in the ways of defending a stockade.

The first boarder was a plump, florid-faced lawyer from Virginia, impetuous, and with a rather loud voice. Peyton Short was a man who liked to talk, it didn't matter what the subject, and he had chosen Rachel as the object of his monologues. She had not thought him clever, but she understood that talking, even at random, eased his loneliness. On warm summer evenings the Robards family, which now included Lewis's brother George and his wife, sat out on the front porch; Peyton Short usually managed to pull his chair up close to Rachel's to tell of the day's doings. Lewis became uneasy.

"Rachel, couldn't you avoid him? He's so confoundedly . . . present."

"Yes, I'll try."

But she found that Mr. Short was not the kind of man one could easily avoid. One evening Lewis came back from the slave quarters to find them alone on the dark porch; her mother-in-law had just gone inside, and Rachel was looking for an opening in the encircling ring of words. Accusing her of having a tête-à-tête, Lewis went straightway to his mother and demanded that Peyton Short be put out of the house. Mrs. Robards refused to listen to what she called his "patent foolishness." Nor did Lewis feel any need to keep his private affairs to himself; everyone in the neighborhood knew that he was jealous of Peyton Short.

They had little peace until John Overton came to live with them. He

3

was a distant cousin of the Robards, homely in a winsome fashion, a little fellow with straw-colored hair and a pale skin, possessor of a dry sense of humor which for a fair time served as an anodyne to the distressed household.

Then, for Rachel, a new element entered into Lewis's jealousy: now his outbursts seemed to bear no relationship to the immediate goings-on: his most violent attacks came when she had not exchanged ten words with Peyton Short in as many days. Once Short stopped her, when her eyes were red, and said:

"You'll never find happiness with a man like Lewis Robards. He has neither the sense to love you nor the pride to protect you. But not all men are such fools, Mrs. Robards."

She had not understood his words; in truth she had not listened. But a few weeks later, after Peyton Short had gone home to Virginia, Lewis had burst in upon her, thrusting the crumpled Peyton Short letter into her face.

She reined in her horse, feeling ill, as though she were back in her room at the Robards house at the beginning of those days of waiting, waiting for any one of the paralyzing eventualities: news from Virginia that her husband had been killed in the duel to which he had challenged Short; word that her family had received her husband's letter requesting that someone be sent to fetch her, but had decided not to interfere; that she would have to remain unwanted in a house where her husband had renounced her; or that one of her brothers would arrive and take her away, to . . . what?

2

Samuel helped her off the horse. She sat down at the base of a big tree, leaning her head against it. Her brother kneeled in front of her, wiping the perspiration from her brow with his unbleached cotton handkerchief.

"Are you taken bad, Rachel?"

"Just give me a few moments to rest, Samuel."

"Is there something I can do for you? A drink of water, maybe?"

"I'll be all right."

They were now only a few miles from the Donelson stockade. She understood why Samuel had been unable to ask questions or offer sympathy: separation of husband and wife had never happened in their part of the country. On a frontier where all relationships were based on confidence, where men were of necessity away for months at a time and the hospitality of their homes often meant survival to settlers moving westward on the trails, she had been judged unworthy of this basic trust.

Everyone on the Cumberland would know that she had been repudi-

4

ated. How badly had she injured her family? What would be her position among her friends and neighbors? Would she be an outcast?

She could see these uncertainties reflected in Samuel's eyes as he leaned over and smoothed her hair back from her forehead. She simply could not reach home in this state; yet there were just a few more miles before they started climbing down the rim into the Cumberland basin.

Often in the past four days she had imagined that she was thinking her way through to the core of the problem, but it always eluded her. No matter how severe she might be in her self-judgment, blaming herself for each of Peyton Short's poor jokes at which she had laughed, she still could find nothing in her attitude that logically should have led to her present predicament. It almost seemed as though this was something that had happened to her from the outside, and to which she was not a party.

Very well then, if the original cause did not lie in herself, where did it lie? In Peyton Short, surely, for having written such a foolish letter; but hadn't there been two years of intermittent quarrels before Short arrived at the Robards house?

Forcing her mind backward torturously, she compelled herself to remember the times her husband's jealous outbreaks had come when the family had seen no outsiders; how at such times Lewis had simply refetched old accusations. She had wondered why he had brought up these largely forgotten matters; once she had asked him this question specifically. He had not answered.

Now fragments began to fit together, broken bits of action and explanation, basic uneasinesses. One of her husband's characteristics was to go away for a night, giving an offhand reason or excuse. But all along she had had an inkling of the handsome young mulatto who had been a house servant during the years before their marriage; at intervals she had surprised a fleeting smile on the girl's face, had caught something intangible between them as Lewis issued an order and the girl silently accepted it. She realized now she had sensed the bitter truth . . . even though she had rejected the evidence. By the same token, couldn't that be the reason for Lewis's conduct? She relived the scene in her upstairs bedroom, with Lewis shouting, "I've written your mother to send someone to get you out of my house. And I'm leaving tonight for Virginia to kill Peyton Short!"

Mrs. Robards had taken Rachel in her arms and turned to her son with blazing eyes to tell him that he had gone stark mad. Lewis's older sister insisted that Rachel had never given Peyton Short anything but hospitable courtesy. Jack Jouitt, her husband, had tried to calm Lewis by telling him that he was the only one in all Kentucky ludicrous enough to believe that Rachel Donelson Robards could be guilty of any part of this clandestine affair. John Overton had said in his shy manner: "Lewis, I could write you a letter tonight inviting you to join me in

5

horse stealing and murder, but that would hardly make you a horse thief or a murderer." But it was Mrs. George Robards who had said coldly to Lewis, "All this arises from your own improper conduct."

Rachel rose, walked unevenly to where the horses were drinking, and stood with one hand grasping her saddle, the other clenched tight as there rushed into her mind the formerly unrelated evidence: her husband had left her side, sometimes even their bed, to go out to the slave quarters; inevitably when he had returned he had accused her of a crime against their love and marriage . . . transferring to his wife his own capacity for betrayal.

Her hand fell from the saddle and she stood with her head lowered. After a time a feeling of relief came over her: if she could not live with her husband, she could at least live with herself; she could face her family and her neighbors and friends. Her husband had hurt her, hurt her severely, but she had not hurt herself, she had not injured her own dignity or self-respect.

She loosened a strap on the saddlebag, took out her traveling kit and emptied its contents onto the grass: an oblong mirror, a silver-backed comb and brush, a piece of scented soap from Richmond, a clean rough-fibered towel. Glancing down at her brown linsey-woolsey dress she saw that it was soiled from travel. From the saddlebag she took a fresh blue linen dress, then slipped out of the rumpled one, kneeling at the side of the creek in her white petticoat. She was small-boned, barely five feet two in height, with rounded shoulders and firm pear-shaped breasts; her hips were delicately modeled and her waist both slender and short, allowing for unusually fine long legs.

She scrubbed her face, neck and arms, splashing a good deal of the cool water over her bare shoulders, then removed the small combs that held her long black tresses in place, and brushed the cool water through her hair. She gathered the bulk of it low on her neck, tied it with a white ribbon and sat on the bank in the warm afternoon sunshine, gazing into the mirror. Her enormous brown eyes, set wide apart and framed by thin curved black brows, had recovered from their days of weeping and confusion: they were soft and clear. After having been set grimly in a thin line, her mouth was once again full and red-lipped. There was a spot of color high on her ivory-tinted cheeks. Her face, usually a little on the round side, was now slender-cheeked.

It becomes me, she thought. I'm only twenty-one. Surely life can't be over for me?

She put on the dark blue linen dress with the flaring skirt and white collar, wide and V-necked, looking like a bright shawl. Then she called out to her brother, who had borrowed her soap and was washing his hands and face in the creek.

"We can go now, Samuel. I'm feeling much better. I'm really anxious

6

to see Mother and the family again. You haven't told me much about French Lick. Are there a lot of new settlers?"

He helped her into the saddle, mounted his horse and they went swiftly down the trail, the horses sensing their changed spirit and the eagerness to reach home. She turned to look at her brother and saw that he was smiling at her.

"You'll never recognize the old place, Rachel. They've even changed the name to Nashville. There must be about forty new cabins there, with two taverns, a store and a courthouse. It's really quite a big town you're coming home to."

3

Rachel was shocked to learn that her mother was already known throughout the Cumberland as the Widow Donelson. Their joy in this reunion was restrained, for Colonel Donelson had been killed on the trail since they last met; and now the Widow Donelson's youngest daughter and namesake was in trouble. Rachel could perceive little change in her mother in the three years since she had last seen her: about five feet two, a touch on the plump side, her hair a deep brown, her skin, except for the intricate network of lines radiating from the large brown eyes, still as soft in texture as Rachel had remembered it from her childhood. Only the warm bright light that had shown behind her mother's eyes was gone.

Rachel Stockly's family had settled in Virginia sometime before 1609 as original members of the Virginia Company; they had been large land and slave owners, and when seventeen-year-old Rachel Stockly married nineteen-year-old John Donelson and went with him to the western frontier of Virginia she took with her a substantial dowry, education and family tradition. They had come in handy, all three, in clearing the wilderness, raising eleven children, building a prosperous plantation and managing it while her husband served in three terms of the Virginia House of Burgesses.

"Rachel, perhaps you don't want to talk about it yet?"

They were sitting in the big room beneath the oblong porthole windows, sunlight flooding over their faces, so amazingly alike in coloring and bone structure, and in the quality of their unhappiness. Across the room the tall wooden cogwheeled clock sounded the buzzing whir of inside works before clanging out its metallic strokes.

"It seems so strange to me. I remember Lewis as a gay and carefree young man."

"Yes, we all thought so." Rachel's voice was soft and unhurried, with considerable body, as though coming from deep within her; both she and her mother had carried over the musical intonations of Virginia.

7

A familiar step sounded outside the room. Rachel had always been told that she was the prettiest of the Donelson girls, but looking up quickly she realized all over again that her sister Jane was the truly beautiful one of the family: a willowy figure, five feet six in height, halfway between the extremes of tall lean Catherine and short pudgy Mary; with fluffy blond hair that filled a dark room as radiantly as the September sunshine, light green eyes, cool and appraising, a sharp frosty tongue, realistic but not malicious. Jane had waited until she was twenty-six before marrying, an age called middle-yeared on the frontier, insisting that she must have a great man . . . or none at all; and had relentlessly passed by her young admirers, waiting until she found Colonel Robert Hays in Nashville, then knowing instantly that this was her man and this was her love.

Mrs. Donelson watched Rachel and Jane greet each other warmly, for these two younger of her four daughters had grown up as close friends. Rachel had known that Jane would come to her immediately. When their mother was called from the room, Jane asked:

"Rachel, what is wrong?"

Rachel hesitated for a moment; her pride made it difficult for her to speak even though she and Jane had always been confidantes. Then, forthrightly, she told Jane about the quarrels Lewis had precipitated because of his jealousy, of her own bewilderment and unhappiness over them; she described the humiliating scenes Lewis had created at parties and dances; and finally repeated Lewis's denunciation of her in their bedroom the last time she had seen him.

Jane listened attentively, her eyes never leaving her sister's face.

"His mother said he had gone stark mad, his sister and her husband, Jack Jouitt, believe that I have done no wrong, they told him so, but his ears were shut to them. His sister-in-law even accused him . . . Oh, Jane, there's a slave girl . . ."

Her calm left her and she sought refuge in Jane's arms, holding her face against her sister's long graceful neck. Jane stroked her hair.

"Samuel tells me that William is against me?"

"Oh yes, William the Cautious is thoroughly outraged and was dead-set against Samuel going for you." Jane's tone was icily refreshing, her voice a full octave higher than her sister's. "He has told people in the neighborhood that you've just come home for a visit and that you'll be returning to Harrodsburg next month. Johnny is also up in arms about what he calls the insult to our family name."

"It isn't only the humiliation, Jane, or even what William would call the disgrace of being put out of my husband's home; that's bad enough when you consider it has never happened to anyone we ever knew. But what am I to think about the future? Even a widow is better off; at least her position is clear. Do I remain Mrs. Lewis Robards all my life, and yet never lay eyes on my husband again? Jane, I mean to be

8

strong . . . but my husband doesn't want me in his home, my brother doesn't want me here . . ."

"Rachel, why did you ever marry Lewis?"

She pulled away from Jane's embrace, her gentle brown eyes meeting her sister's cool dispassionate green eyes head-on.

"Then you never . . . liked him?"

"Oh, Captain Robards was the best-looking of the young men who took you to parties and dances; he dressed better than anyone else around and seemed to be more exuberant. The men he commanded during the war certainly idolized him . . ."

". . . but none of these things impressed you?"

"No, because I always felt that, inside himself, he was . . . uneasy. He took me to a few parties, you remember, while you were growing up. If he had a unified character, I couldn't find it; I never learned what he really wanted or believed."

"It's still . . . difficult," Rachel admitted slowly.

"Lewis is weak," pronounced Jane, "and you are strong because you're sure inside yourself. You're bright, and Lewis's mind is less active. In short, Rachel, I think you could have married considerable more man."

"I loved him, Jane."

Jane chose her words carefully as she asked the all-important question.

"And what about now, Rachel? Do you still love Lewis? Or perhaps you would rather answer that to yourself?"

Did she still love Lewis? She had suffered at his hands, had lost a great many of her romantic illusions. Now, after three years, she understood her husband in the sense that Jane had understood him from the beginning. This unfocused quality, his unwillingness to relieve his mother as manager of the prosperous Robards plantation, or to involve himself for long in any task; his inability to have confidence in himself . . . or her.

"If only we had children . . ." she replied resolutely. "Perhaps children are what he needs to settle him down, to give him a sense of permanence."

The Widow Donelson's station was some ten miles north of Nashville, just beyond where the Kentucky Road joined the Cumberland Road. The following morning, thinking to divert her, Samuel suggested that they ride into the town of Nashville; there had been only one stockade on the bluff overlooking the river when the Donelsons had abandoned the Cumberland after the disastrous summer of 1780.

Their first stop was Lardner Clark's store, a double-sized log cabin, mud-chinked, the only light coming from the open front door and from the grease lamps hung on the back wall. There were long roughhewn counters on either side; on the left, little piles of clothing and household goods: pans, dishware, candles; on the opposite side, sugar, salt, spices,

9

whisky, smoked meats; and at the back the shelves containing axes, cow bells, a few farming implements, rifles, powder and shot.

There were three families in the store when Rachel and Samuel entered. The first to see them were the John Rainses, who had come to the Cumberland with the Donelsons. They greeted Rachel warmly, expressed their delight at seeing her again and wished her a happy visit with her family. The second group were new acquaintances of Samuel's; when he introduced his sister, the young wife of the couple said:

"You'll come visit us soon as you settle? Sam, you be sure to bring her now, there's so few young people in the station where we live."

Rachel squeezed the young woman's hand. Then she felt a pair of eyes staring at her from the back of the store.

"Why, it's Martha Dinsmore, from Harrodsburg."

She started toward Mrs. Dinsmore, but even in the semi-darkness she saw that the woman's expression was forbidding. Rachel stopped short. Mrs. Dinsmore turned away with no sign of recognition, pushing her wide skirts forward and around her, as though to keep them clear of sin.

The blood rushed to Rachel's head. She thought she heard Mrs. Dinsmore say:

"Where there's smoke there's bound to be fire."

Did I really hear those words, she asked herself, or is it just my imagination? How could the news have come down the trail so quickly? Her father used to say: "Bad news travels fast because it has so many helping hands." If Martha Dinsmore knew and could feel this way, there would be others.

She felt Samuel gripping her arm.

"Rachel, you've turned a sour-apple green. You mustn't pay attention to people like that. There are always a few who get pleasure from believing the worst."

"I'll never expose myself again. I'm going to stay home until it's all over . . . till it's all over . . ."

4

She stepped out onto the hard-bitten earth of the yard, which was enclosed by a high stockade fence sheltering the spacious two-story main house, a large barn and six smaller cabins used for the kitchen, dairy, storehouse, smokehouse, guest cabin, forge and leather shed. It was the first of March, five months since she had come back to the Donelsons'. The sky was a brittle blue, the sun bright but the air cool. She walked to the kitchen to inspect the sides of venison, bear and buffalo that were broiling on their spits, the wild turkeys and geese roasting on their suspended hempen cords, the pigeon pies baking in deep coal beds along with dozens of hoecakes and johnnycakes. It was a double birthday, for

10

her oldest brother Alexander, who was forty, and her youngest, Samuel, exactly half that age. This had always been the gayest day in the Donelsons' year; back in Virginia the entire countryside had been invited in for the feast.

Rachel was the only one of the four daughters now living at home; the Widow Donelson had turned over the household management to her, pretending to want a winter of rest. Rachel had been thankful for the busiest months of her life, supervising the making of the soap and candles, carding and spinning of the wool into yarn, stuffing the new pillows and mattresses.

She stood in the open door of the cabin watching Moll, the deep-bosomed, gray-haired Negress in a dress of drab hunter's cloth who had helped to raise her and had been bequeathed to her in her father's will, along with Moll's husband, George. Inside she saw her brother William, who managed the plantation, drinking a hot toddy with the Reverend Craighead, who had had Christmas dinner at the Donelsons' and routed his circuit riding so that the first of March would see him back in Nashville. William was a heavy-boned slow-moving man; he had never become reconciled to her living away from her husband. In the opposite corner, tightening catgut, sat James Gamble, who traveled from station to station, Bledsoe's to Eaton's to Freeland's to the Donelsons', carrying his fiddle fondly in a sack of soft doeskin, and telling everyone, "I love her, but I never squeeze her so as to break down the bridge or put her out of tune." He took no pay for his fiddling; he and his wife, as he called the violin, entertained at weddings, christenings, holidays, birthdays, logrollings, house-raisings, and were even called in to soothe the pains of the sick and wounded.

She stepped into the kitchen where Moll was spooning the juices out of the low-lying pan and basting the turkeys with them.

"Have we plenty of meat roasting, Moll? It's beginning to look as though I asked the whole Cumberland Valley."

"And about time, Miz Rachel." She spoke quietly so William and the Reverend Craighead would not hear. "I don't take to you lockin' yourself up the whole winter like you done . . . not even one dance or quiltin' bee or house-raisin'."

Rachel let her gaze wander about the kitchen, which had been equipped to cook for a hundred. Almost the entire east wall was a huge stone fireplace; across the top of the room were long poles of dried apples, peppers and pumpkin rings. Strung on the lug pole were her mother's favorite iron pot, weighing some forty pounds, the rotating clock jack for roasting meats, the smaller brassware pots and highly polished copper kettles. On the hearth stood the potato boiler, the dye tub and Dutch oven.

"I haven't been lonely," she murmured, "with ten brothers and sisters. And I really haven't wanted to see . . . outsiders."

11

Moll carefully measured out the precious coffee for the pot of water hanging on the crane over the fire, then turned for a penetrating look at Rachel. They were friends and trusted each other.

"You ha'n't done nothin', Miz Rachel. If you're not married no more, then I seen lots of fine young men come here for militia meetin's and taxes payin', and they's plenty you could have for husband. How long you think you goin' hide that pretty young face of yourn inside the house, even refusin' to go to suppers to Miz Jane's? How long you gonna be like a prisoner?"

Rachel went to the open doorway of the kitchen and stood gazing at the big and prosperous Donelson stockade, at the young apple and peach orchards which her seven brothers had planted, at the plowed fields which the boys would seed with corn, cotton, wheat, indigo and tobacco. Beyond was the pasture with a herd of thirty milk cows and the family's twenty-odd horses. Except for the high pointed palings which surrounded the station, their new home was coming to look more and more like the Virginia plantation they had been obliged to sell back in 1779, when she was twelve years old and her father had suffered reverses through the failure of his infant ironworks, the first to be established in that part of the country. That was when the entire family had set forth on the flatboat *Adventure* for the voyage down the Holston and Tennessee, then up the Ohio and Cumberland rivers, a two-thousand-mile journey through wild country and uncharted waters.

Images floated through her mind of how they had lived in tents on the south side of the Stone River while they felled the trees, broke the fields to the plow, planted cotton, surveyed a six-forty for each of the boys, and combined with their few neighbors to stave off the Indian attacks. She remembered how heartbroken her father had been when their crops had been flooded out and they were forced to take refuge at Mansker's station, spending more of their hours repulsing Indian attacks than working their fields. In the fall, when John Donelson realized he could not establish the legality of their land titles, they had chosen to retreat over the Kentucky Road to Harrodsburg where the family had settled for five years, until shortly after her marriage to Lewis Robards, and had then returned en masse to French Lick, determined that this time they would not be driven out.

And now, after only three years, they had built the most prosperous plantation in the Cumberland Valley. What a pity her father could not have lived to see this; for the settling of the Cumberland had been the last great dream of his life. People had said that the failure of the ironworks had been only an excuse for old Colonel Donelson, that he had the wilderness fever. The colonel had been killed on the Kentucky Road just a few days after he had visited Rachel in Harrodsburg, while returning from a business trip to Virginia. He had always said, "There isn't an Indian alive who can kill me," and for more than forty years had proven his contention by traversing the wilderness, surveying and treaty-making with the Indians for the Virginia government. He had been shot to death not far from Nashville and his brief case rifled; the Donelsons believed that his two companions on the trail, strangers to the frontier, had murdered their father.

She shook her head with a quick dispelling movement as though to unloose these pictures, then started back toward the main house. Suddenly she stopped, seeing a figure framed in the open doorway of the guest cabin. The man had his back to her; he turned and she exclaimed in astonishment:

"Why, it's John Overton!"

Through her mind flashed the thought, He comes from the Robards'. He will have news for me . . . perhaps a letter . . .

Eagerly, she crossed the yard to greet him.

John Overton was a small man, all clashing angles and nervous movements, and though he was only twenty-three years old his almost colorless straw hair barely covered his scalp. His chin was bony and turned up, his nose was bony and turned down, and between them his bloodless lips seemed to be not only overwhelmed but lost; his eyes were such a light vapor gray that half the time they seemed not to be there at all, and you imagined yourself to be looking out the back of his head. Yet after five minutes of talking with him Rachel always forgot that he was ugly, at the end of ten minutes she no longer imagined him to be plain, and at the end of an hour she believed him to be a beautiful human being. Behind Overton's seemingly transparent eyes there was at work a first-rate brain: fast, rangy, disciplined, logical, humorous, yet with the flinty incorruptibility of his Scottish ancestors. Inside himself, where he lived and breathed and fought, he was a big man; only newcomers were deceived by his unlikely shell.

"How good it is to see you again, Rachel. And how well you're looking."

"And you too, John." She hesitated a moment. "Are you passing through our country on business?"

"No, I've decided to settle in Nashville and open my law office here. So of course I came straight to the Donelsons' and asked your mother if she would take me in."

A slow flush crept up Rachel's cheeks: Overton's coming directly to the Donelsons' was an act of faith on his part; he had been a witness to the Peyton Short episode, had even risked Lewis's anger by refuting him. A man of John Overton's rigorously ethical nature would never have come here if he had considered his relative injured; he would have had as little as possible to do with the Donelson clan. And certainly if he had at any time suspected Rachel of wrongdoing he would not have been so indiscreet as to expose her to further gossip. She felt deeply grateful to him.

13

"I'm happy you are going to be part of our family, John. And I know you're going to be a fine lawyer. You have the talent and temperament for it."

His lips pursed while he judiciously weighed in his own mind the possibilities of his becoming a good lawyer. He was a bookish man; the passion in his life was the law, its nature, philosophy, logic and structure.

"All I know, Rachel, is that I have a great love for the law, and if love be sufficient . . ."

"Love is sufficient for nearly everything, John . . ."

She broke off. They stood facing each other in silence, both thinking of Lewis Robards. She had had no word from her husband in the five months since she had returned to Nashville, nor had there been any report on the outcome of his duel with Peyton Short. From the timbre of the silence she knew she had been right in assuming that Overton brought news from Harrodsburg, yet she sensed that he would never so much as mention Lewis Robards until she gave him permission to do so.

She gazed at him for a moment longer in silence. Was his news good or bad? And for that matter, how would she differentiate between the two when she herself hardly knew what she wanted from the future? John Overton's reticent expression confided little. And she knew that she did not want to, could not, in fact, hear his news now. Perhaps when the party was over.

"I must finish my tour of inspection," she said abruptly. "Once again, John, the heartiest of welcomes."

5

It was night, the children had been awakened from sleep and bundled up, the guests had departed. Her family had retired, exhausted from the day-long festivities. She could still hear the happy sound of the hundred or more voices, the singing, the heart-warming laughter and gaiety.

But now everything was quiet in the big room, the last of the candles extinguished, the lamps snuffed, the fire banked and cooling; behind her the tall clock made its buzzing whir, then clanged out twelve strokes.

She stood at the porthole, slipped a wooden bolt and opened the heavy wooden shutter, gazing up at the lone star in the March night. She tried to warm herself by pulling more compactly into the yellow wool dress, crossing her arms on her chest and holding the long sleeves tightly, pressing so hard against the bleached bone buttons that she felt them dig into her flesh. Her heart felt as cold in her bosom as the star up in the chill sky. She felt lonely and sad; the Donelsons had done everything they could to make her feel welcome, yet as she stood trembling at the window she felt not only unwanted but rejected. During these months she had recoiled emotionally from all serious thinking about her husband, but with John Overton at hand she must try to determine her feelings about Lewis. Then, when she heard Overton's news, she would be prepared, she would know how to deal with it.

She had loved Lewis Robards; he had seemed to her the handsomest, most romantic figure she had met, one of the most admired of the war heroes in Kentucky. He had wooed her with ardor and impetuousness. She had loved him during the first peaceful year of their marriage.

And now? Did she love him still? Did she think of him harshly? Or did she pity him, think of him as ill? That had been the way his mother had explained his rages. Mrs. Robards had said:

"It's something the war did to Lewis. He was so happy during the years we were fighting: life was a great adventure for him then. He liked the hardships, the dangers, the command of his men, the forced marches and swift attacks. He was living hard and bright and true, every minute of it. But when the war ended . . . when he came home to . . . inaction . . . overseeing the spring planting . . . he felt as though the best part of his life had already been lived. He became bored, morose, irritable. That was why I thanked God for you, Rachel; I was sure that with you he would find a new life and new happiness."

Yes, she felt sorry for Lewis, in the way she would for a child who was forever stumbling in the dark and hurting himself. Had he been in the room now she would have cradled his head on her breast and wept for him, for his twisted unhappy life.

She murmured half aloud to the dark room and to the lone light in the sky, All my dreams and plans and hopes are tied up in my marriage. Without it I am nothing, I have no place, no hearth, no future. I am a woman dispossessed. I want my husband back and a home of my own . . .

She watched the sun rise. When it was well above the horizon and she heard the first stirrings throughout the house, she walked across the yard to speak to John Overton. Spring had broken early that year: the jonquils were banked thick as butter on the slopes leading down to the river, running clear again after its cargo of mud; the cardinals, silent all winter, were singing in the tall yellow poplars. While she tried to slow down the beating of her heart she counted the sparrows, chickadees and woodpeckers exchanging perches on the highest limbs of oaks, beeches and sycamores. In a corner of a freshly furrowed field she heard an old cock quail calling bobwhite. The earliest violets were showing through the fresh vernal grass and across the river a young peach orchard had begun to show its pink blossoms. She felt quieter now.

"John, I feel that Lewis has asked you to bring a message to me. I appreciate your not saying anything until I was ready . . ."

Overton bowed slightly, took his silver-rimmed spectacles from an inside coat pocket and slipped them on. For a moment Rachel thought he was going to read her a paper of some sort, then she remembered that John used his glasses not to see more clearly the print in front of his eyes, but rather the thoughts behind them.

"Rachel, Lewis has cleared you completely. I've heard him tell his friends in Harrodsburg that he has been the blindest fool."

A long soughing breath escaped from her, one that seemed to have been held in pent-up suspense since the day her husband had written to the Donelsons to come and take their daughter away.

"Your husband assured me of how much he regretted your separation; he told me that he was convinced his suspicions were unfounded, that he loves you and wishes to live with you again. He requested that I 'use my exertions to restore harmony.'"

"You can imagine how happy I am to hear this, John. And the duel with Peyton Short? Neither of them was hurt?"

The flow of communication was suddenly shut off. She saw John's jaw set a little, as though he had locked his back teeth.

"There were no serious results."

The silence fell again. Rachel perceived that she would have to make the next move; there was something unpleasant here, something in which Overton had been offended.

"Please go on, John," she said softly.

"I told Lewis that I would undertake to restore harmony, providing he would put down his jealousy and treat you kindly as other men treat their wives. For I would not like this to happen to you again, Rachel."

His sympathy broke through the structure of her constraint.

"Oh, John, I felt so . . . degraded."

"Lewis says that if you will come back to him he will never again cause you unhappiness."

She tried to separate her tumultuous feelings, not the least of which was the fact that she would be vindicated in the eyes of the world. Now that her husband had declared his confidence in her, she would go back to him, of course; for when had she ever wanted to be apart? But could she feel secure in Harrodsburg where Lewis had humiliated her so often and so abjectly by his torrential scenes? Could she return to the Robards home where that young girl would be in daily evidence? Above all, how could that same unfocused life for the two of them, with Lewis unwilling or unable to take the responsibility of running the plantation, passing his days in hunting and long stretches of idleness, ever breed anything but the same unhappiness she had already known?

Her face was averted while she was thinking; John Overton left her in peace, disturbing her neither with words spoken nor with words thought. Now she turned back to him. She had a forthright manner, with little that was complex or devious in her nature; her gaze was direct, she looked people straight in the eye the instant they met and continued to hold this personal contact as long as they spoke together: she was

16

entirely willing that others should know what she was thinking, since there was rarely anything harsh, hidden or condemnatory in her thoughts. Nor did she have any inner protective veil with which to shield her eyes and their mirrorings.

"John, there is nothing I want more than to be with my husband again. I'm convinced that our problems at the Robards home make it impossible for us to live there happily. My father registered a fine piece of land for us just a few miles from this station, a square-mile pre-emption that can be turned into a good plantation. Would you be so kind as to write to Lewis and tell him that I reciprocate his feelings, but that I feel we have a far greater chance of success if he will come here to Nashville where we can build a house on our land and start an entirely new life for ourselves?"

6

She heard a hammering on the iron front-door knocker, gentle at first, then insistent. When no one answered, she left her bedroom on the second floor and came down the rough plank stairs. She opened the door and saw a tall young man with a thick mop of sandy-red hair. Apparently he had grown a little discouraged, for he was half turned, looking toward the heavy log gate which had been barred behind him. She was glad he had turned away momentarily, for it gave her a chance to study this odd-looking creature in the ill-fitting black homespun suit. He seemed the tallest man she had ever laid eyes on, surely some six and a half feet, she thought; and with a thinness to match his height.

The back of his head seemed disproportionately massive to the slender features which she could see in profile, with the high forehead and flat-ridged nose; but then everything about him seemed a little disproportionate: the incredibly long face, the long thin neck which appeared too delicate to support such a heavy head; the oblong torso and the gangling arms and legs. He looked like a youth whose figure had stretched to its outermost limits and would now require a full decade to fill out; yet in spite of this sense of physical immaturity he held himself rigidly erect, and there was a suggestion of power, as though this scraggly body were having difficulty containing its own force.

The man felt her presence; he wheeled sharply. She found herself gazing up into the largest and most brilliant pair of blue eyes she had ever encountered, vibrant and piercing in their quality. He seemed to be towering at least three heads above her, yet there was nothing formidable about him; rather she felt a warm glow and discovered to her astonishment that both she and the young stranger were smiling at each other amusedly.

"Please forgive my intrusion, ma'am, but I am Andrew Jackson of Nashville, a friend of John Overton's."

"But of course, Mr. Jackson. We've been hearing tales of your exploits ever since you came here. I am Mrs. Lewis Robards."

He bowed slowly from the waist, acknowledging the introduction; and everything about him, not only his courtly gesture, but the angular tilt of his big head, the opening of his sensitive, slightly moist lips, the smile in his brilliant blue eyes, all of these bespoke a deep, ingrained courtesy. She noted a scar on the left side of his forehead, saber-thin, arcing from his hairline down to the thick undisciplined eyebrow.

"Then you'd be Widow Donelson's daughter from Kentucky?"

Rachel felt the color rise to her cheeks. Had he heard of her difficulties?

"I've come to ask a favor, Mrs. Robards. Since I reached Nashville, beginning of last November, I've been living at the inns. John Overton tells me there's room in the cabin he's occupying. Do you think your mother would take me in? I am a crack shot with a rifle and have had considerable experience in fighting the Indians."

He blushes like a schoolboy, she thought. But then he is a boy. Surely he can't be over twenty?

"I would consider it a great honor to be able to join this family," she heard him saying. "Oh, Mrs. Robards, if you could know how tired I am of the brawling and drinking and the greasy eatables at the Red Heifer!"

"Well, Mr. Jackson, we certainly are glad to have all the protection we can get. Our neighbor Captain Hunter was killed last week by some Creeks and when our men pursued them, they killed Major Kirkpatrick." She hesitated for a moment. "But I am not the mistress of this station. My mother and my brother William are in Nashville for the day."

She saw him turn and gaze wistfully at the full saddlebags on his horse; he had brought all his possessions with him. He was a bold man, sure enough, with a lean scrawny sense of independence, but she also felt that he was a little lonely.

"You said that John Overton is willing to share his cabin with you?"

"Oh yes, we have just formed a partnership, the long of the law I guess you'd call it: I'm long on height and he's long on the law. He said we could hold our office right here."

"But aren't you attached to the court? An officer . . . ?"

"Indeed I am, ma'am; Judge McNairy and I brought that court with us from North Carolina. I carry the hifalutin title of attorney general; that only means I prosecute criminals where and as I find them. Rest of the time I'm just like all other lawyers, looking mighty hard for cases."

Again that queer combination of strength: the lawbreaker would be caught and prosecuted, his voice left no doubt about that: and humility, the young lawyer hopefully awaiting clients.

18

Rachel felt certain that her mother and William would welcome this young man, in fact they had spoken several times of bringing someone in to share the cabin with Overton; yet she had no authority to give him assent. Neither could she turn him away.

"In any event, you must stay to supper with us, Mr. Jackson. The family will want to meet you."

"Thank you, Mrs. Robards, I was frankly hoping you would invite me."

"Why not take your things out of the saddlebags and bring them over to the cabin in the meanwhile? Then you can turn your horse out in the canebrake."

He did as he had been bidden. Rachel walked across the yard with him while he supported the bulging bags on his bony shoulders, a rifle nursed under each arm. She pushed open the door to the cabin. The log house was fourteen by twenty-two feet inside, with a small sleeping room at the back containing a big double bed, a stand, a pitcher and a bowl of water. The front room was about fourteen by twelve with two good-sized porthole windows and a fireplace with a shelf above it on which John Overton kept the volumes of his law library. There was a heavy walnut table, two chairs made of hickory, a rude cupboard in which Overton's extra suit and shirts were stored, deerhorn racks on which were hung one rifle, two pistols and several buckhorns for powder, and an iron grease lamp suspended from the wall.

Andrew Jackson stood in the middle of the room, the top of his massive red hair barely an inch beneath the crossbeams which held up the roof, gazing at the fieldstone fireplace, then at Overton's books, at the pistols and powder horns and colorful striped cotton curtains at the windows.

"This is about the prettiest cabin I've been in," he said softly. "Are you superstitious, Mrs Robards? I am. For instance, I like to start new ventures on a Tuesday, like today, but I'll never begin anything on a Friday."

"That wouldn't be the Irish in you, by chance?"

He grinned, rubbing the freckles that ran like a speckled band straight across his nose and high cheekbones. There was an openness, a guilelessness about his smile that was like her own: suggesting to her a man who had little to conceal, and even less temperament with which to conceal it. His mouth was large, the teeth strong, compact.

"My mother always said I carried two things that gave away Carrickfergus on me: my face and my temper."

He went down on his haunches beside his bags, took out a half dozen books including Matthew Bacon's *Abridgment of the Law*, packets of ammunition, tea, tobacco and salt, two blankets and some spare clothing, which he hung in the cupboard.

"I'll just unpack a few little possessions and put them away. Then if your mother or your brother should say no, I'll come over quietly, get my things and slip them into my saddlebags."

Rachel watched his quick, awkward movements which somehow had considerable grace in them; and she was aware of a tiny smile, not on her lips, but somewhere inside her head.

At that instant the young man turned, rose, stood towering above her. They gazed at each other in silence, even as they had in that first surprised moment at the front door of the Donelson home.

7

She had refused all invitations to parties in the neighborhood, even when they were held in the homes of old friends, fearful lest people misunderstand if they found her dancing and enjoying herself. She had not wanted anyone to think that she was flouting her husband, or that she did not grasp the true implication of her situation. But John's good news spread over the Cumberland Valley, abetted, she knew, by her brothers who had informed the countryside of Lewis Robards' impending arrival and of his public acknowledgment that he had been wrong.

Now she felt free again and happy.

Sunday was gathering day for the Donelson clan. At the head of the polished split-log table sat Mrs. Donelson, and at the foot Rachel's oldest sister Mary, the plump pigeon of the family, fat-cheeked, cheerful, homey, a magnificent cook, whose twelve children went up in regular steps like rungs of the ladder to a hayloft, and whose oldest child was almost Rachel's age. Next to Mary sat her husband, John Caffrey, who had wanted to add on rooms or build new cabins as his progeny increased year by year; but Mary had refused, insisting that she wanted her children under her feet. Across from John Caffrey sat the next sister, Catherine, tall, stringy, gray, unrelentingly vocal at home with her nine children, but always silent at these family reunions. With her was her husband, Thomas Hutchings, a quiet but sympathetic man.

In the first seat on the right sat John, Jr., not because he was the oldest; Alexander, the first-born and perennial bachelor of the sharp yellow teeth and migratory feet, had gladly given up this place of ascendancy to Johnny who, because he bore his father's name, had become the titular head of the family. Opposite Johnny sat Alexander, next to him, William the Cautious, and then Samuel. Rachel's regular seat was next to Samuel's. Across from her were Robert and Jane Hays, and immediately next to Jane was Stockly, the sometime lawyer and politician of the family. John Overton sat next to Rachel with Andrew Jackson across from him, next to Stockly. The two last seats at the bottom of the board were occupied by Leven, who was two years older than Rachel but still an immature boy, and Severn, who was the ill member of the family, hollow-cheeked and with a severe cough.

Rachel noticed Jane watching Andrew Jackson intently, for the spring term of the Davidson County court was to open the following morning, and Samuel, who was fascinated by the two young boarders, was asking endless questions about the law. Andrew Jackson had been circuit riding up in Sumner County just before joining the Donelsons, and he had amusing tales to tell about Joshua Baldwin, who had been indicted by the Grand Jury for altering his name to Joshua Campbell; of William Pillows, who had been convicted of biting off the upper end of Abram Denton's ear; and of John Irwin, who had been sentenced to declare publicly that the "rascally and scandalous report I have raised and reported concerned Miss Polly McFadin is false and groundless, and I had no right, reason or cause to believe the same."

Samuel had been drifting aimlessly during the months since Rachel had been at home, not knowing whether he wanted to be a teacher or preacher or perhaps surveyor; he had taken on a new vitality since the lawyers had entered the family circle. Further to stimulate his interest, Rachel too began asking questions about court procedure. John Overton said:

"Samuel, I heard your mother say that you were riding up to Nashville in the morning to do some shopping at Lardner Clark's. Mr. Jackson and I have a number of interesting cases to try, so why don't you bring your mother and sister to court?"

"Won't Judge McNairy be upset at having lady visitors?" asked Rachel.

"Surprised, perhaps," replied Overton, "but on the pleasurable side. Besides, my partner is an officer of the court and I'm sure he'd be glad to intercede for you."

The next morning Rachel and her mother donned their severe black wool riding dresses which best resisted the dust of the ten-mile ride into town. In Mr. Clark's general store they bought a loaf of sugar, some whole spices to be ground at home and a bolt of unbleached muslin. Several of the women greeted Rachel, hugging her and saying how well she was looking. Then they walked up the rutted street to where a large number of horses were hitched to the stocks and whipping posts in front of the courthouse, which was built of hewn logs, chinked with a dried mortar-like mud. On the south side was a twelve-foot porch crowded with men who had ridden many miles to watch the day's litigation. They were dressed in buckskin trousers, leather leggings, buffalo-hide moccasins and the long deerskin hunting shirt with the uneven knife-cut fringes over the shoulders. Rachel saw a number of friends among them, bowed and exchanged greetings.

Samuel took each of the women by an arm. As they went toward the open door Rachel drew back with an instinctive shudder of distaste: for the interior was filthy, with mud, dirt and dust over everything,

21

tobacco spittle in the corners, the two doors askew, the window shutters sagging, the entire place reeking of neglect. At the end of the small room was a long table behind which sat a young man of twenty-six, John McNairy, the first judge to have been appointed by the legislature of North Carolina for this Western District. There were also a number of split-log benches for the spectators and litigants, who now turned to gape at the two ladies standing in the doorway.

"I think we had better go," said Rachel, feeling self-conscious.

At that moment Jackson and Overton came from the end of the court-room where they had been discussing the calendar with Judge McNairy, the only three men in the courtroom dressed in store suits and white shirts.

"Here, let me make you comfortable," said Jackson.

He pulled a bench into line, wiping it vigorously with an enormous colored handkerchief. Samuel sat down, his eyes bright and his hands clasped tightly in his lap. Neither Rachel nor her mother moved. Rachel's eyes continued to study the courthouse. Finally she turned to the two men and said:

"Yesterday when you were discussing the law I commented to myself on what a great respect both of you have for your profession. Then I come into this . . . forgive me . . . pigsty. How can you work here? How can you establish any dignity? How can anyone respect the law, or lawyers, or any decision that the judge might make?"

The men looked at each other for a moment in blank silence.

"Mrs. Robards is completely right," said Jackson, as though seeing the interior for the first time. "Why didn't we think of it for ourselves?"

"I am just a fresh-baked lawyer, Rachel," Overton said, "but our friend Mr. Jackson here is the attorney general. Anything he says the court will have to take under advisement."

Rachel turned to Jackson expectantly, but he ducked one shoulder, grinning.

"Mr. Overton," he said, "I hereby appoint you special counsel for the city of Nashville to plead the case of this neglected courthouse."

John's silver spectacles moved up and down on his nose as his decision fluctuated. After a moment he walked ceremoniously up the crooked center aisle.

"Your Honor, it is a rule of equity," he said in his slow, meticulous voice, "that every suitor shall come into court with a clean shirttail. Without unnecessary offense to the majesty of the law, the ermine of judges or the purity of anybody, I defy suitor or advocate, much more this honorable court, to maintain pure thoughts and white linen in such a pigsty."

Rachel shrank; she had used the descriptive term for private rather than public consumption. Judge McNairy's eyes circled the courtroom slowly from left to right, then he too said in a slow drawl:

22

"Counselor is right. Is David Hay in court? Mr. Hay, I herewith order you to repair the courthouse by making two doors well fixed and hung, with three window shutters well hung, and the benches repaired. Each day that the court meets you shall see that it is sweeped, washed and cleansed, compensation to be arranged when this court adjourns."

She saw Jackson and John exchange an exaggerated wink. She and her mother sat down beside Samuel, who was chuckling. At that moment Hugh McGary burst into the courtroom, his face hard-set with anger.

"Andrew, I'm not going to need you for that case against Casper Mansker. I'm going to kill him right here in the courthouse and take possession of that slave. We had a written agreement, then he goes and loses the bill of sale on purpose."

Jackson rose, put a long-fingered hand on McGary's shoulder and said in a placating voice:

"Now, Hugh, I think this can be settled peaceably. Casper Mansker is one of the oldest settlers around here and everybody says his word is better than a bushel of salt."

A voice behind Rachel called, "Did I hear someone ask for me?"

"Yes, Hugh McGary and I were looking for you, Mr. Mansker," Jackson replied quickly. "My client and I have just been thinking we ought to find a friendly compromise. Let's go sun ourselves on the south porch, gentlemen, then we'll really be settling this matter out of court."

Rachel saw Jackson link his arms through old Mr. Mansker's and McGary's, and take them not so much by physical force as by force of will out of the court's jurisdiction.

"He isn't at all like the stories they tell about him," commented Mrs. Donelson. "He's really quite gentle."

"What kind of stories have you been hearing, Mother?" asked Rachel.

"Well, there's the story of that bully in Sumner County who purposely stepped on his foot in the public square, and then came back to step on it a second time just to make sure Mr. Jackson knew it was on purpose."

"And what did our peaceable Mr. Jackson do?"

"Why, he picked up a rail from the top of a fence and knocked the man down."

They heard a tremendous clatter of hoofs and the noise of a shouting band. By turning her head Rachel could see a group of men in filthy buckskin shirts carrying rifles, their faces grimy, hair uncombed. She watched while they sprang off their horses, several of them picking quarrels with men standing on the porch.

Samuel asked if something couldn't be done. She had not noticed that Andrew Jackson had returned to the courtroom.

"If I was an officer of the court a few minutes ago," he replied slowly, "making jokes about appointing John as special counsel to get the place

23

cleaned up, then I guess I am still the attorney general when Spill Cimberlin heaves into sight."

He extracted a court citation from a sheaf of papers he was holding in his left hand, walked to the door and cried in a strong voice:

"First case on the docket is the State versus Spill Cimberlin, charged with theft, disturbing the peace, assault and contempt of the court."

Rachel rose so that she could see through the doorway to the crowd beyond. Spill Cimberlin shifted his rifle to a more comfortable position under his arm, came within a few inches of Jackson and stuck his face forward so that his nose was almost touching the younger man's.

"There ain't no damned court on this whole frontier that's man enough to try me."

"That's no way to speak about your own courts, Spill," replied Jackson. "The law is here to protect you as well as to punish you. If you've done wrong, then by gumshun you're going to be punished."

"And who's going to punish me, a skinny green saplin' like you?"

There was a silence during which Rachel watched the muscles in Jackson's jaw work up and down. He turned, went a short distance to his saddlebags, pulled out his own two pistols and cocked them as he whirled about. He walked straight at Spill Cimberlin, the guns aimed at the man's head. Rachel went cold; Cimberlin's rifle needed only the slightest bit of raising. When Andrew got within three feet of Cimberlin he said in a voice that carried the length of the main street of Nashville:

"Step up to the bar of justice and be tried by His Honor, or I'll blow your meager brains out."

There was an insucking hush. If Cimberlin was going to do anything, this was the second when he must fire. But the man slowly sagged at the shoulders. Excited talk broke out; Rachel turned to her mother.

"Would Mr. Jackson really have shot him?"

"Mr. Cimberlin seemed to think so," replied Mrs. Donelson with a smile.

Judge McNairy banged his gavel.

"By the way, Mother," Rachel asked, "what has happened to your picture of our new boarder as a peaceful man?"

As they were leaving court after adjournment, Jackson fell in step beside Rachel.

"Weren't you frightened?" she queried. "Mr. Cimberlin could have killed you awful dead."

"Oh, I was just showing off," he replied, pleased with himself. "Besides, I like to graze danger."

8

That evening at supper, while thundershowers pounded down inter-

24

mittently on the roof, they lingered at the table with the light of the pine knots and logs on their faces. Mrs. Donelson asked:

"Don't you have any family of your own here in the West, Mr. Jackson?"

"No, Mrs. Donelson, I'm an orphan. Have been since I was fourteen. My father died a few days before I was born, hurt himself trying to lift a whole tree log up at our place in the Waxhaws. I had two brothers; Hugh, the oldest, he died after the battle at Stono Ferry. My mother rescued my younger brother Robert and me from the British military prison at Camden, but Robert died two days after we got home, of infected wounds and smallpox."

He stopped abruptly; his long expressive face lost its pallor and became suddenly very red while the livid scar on his forehead stood out like a silver scimitar.

"When I pulled through the smallpox, my mother heard that my cousins, Joseph and William Crawford, had been taken by the British and were lying sick in a prison ship off Charleston, so she gathered up all the medicine she could find and made the journey with two other women. I don't know how many days she spent in that prisonhold trying to cure the boys, but she contracted ship's fever too and didn't get very far on the way home, just a couple of miles out of Charleston. I don't even know where she is buried. It's an unmarked grave in an open plain. I've searched several times, but nobody seems to know."

His voice trailed off, the enormous head was lowered, the heavy lids closed. Rachel had never heard him speak this way before; for the first time she sensed the tenderness in the man and his overpowering need for love. When he looked up again there were tears in his eyes.

"That's why, Mrs. Donelson, I think the greatest thing in the world any man can have is a family, the bigger the better."

"I wish I had another daughter for you."

"Seeing as how there are no more Donelson girls," said Rachel, "as soon as my husband and I are settled in our new house we'll scour the countryside and give a lot of wonderful parties. Unless there is some girl waiting for you back in Jonesboro or Salisbury?"

He gazed at her for a moment from across the hearth, then answered in a bantering tone:

"Oh, sure, ma'am, dozens of them, whole jury panels full."

"What are their names?"

"Names? Oh yes." He ran his thin tapering fingers through the mass of red hair, pulling some of it down over his forehead. "Let's see, there was . . . why, of course, Susan Smart, in the Waxhaws, used to tell me I had agreeable eyes and that I was a leaning-forward fellow. Then there was Nancy Jarret in Salisbury. Pretty girl, Nancy. Could ride a horse as fast as a March wind. But her mother didn't approve of me, said I drank and gambled too much."

"And did you?"

"Oh, I suppose so. I was a wild lad as a student. But there wasn't much else to do when taverns were the only place a man could find to live. When I was sixteen and my grandfather left me a legacy of three hundred pounds, I went to Charleston and lost that money on the racing ponies so fast my head is still spinning. But since joining the Donelson family I've become a sober, responsible citizen. Don't even gamble any more, and won't . . . until I can build me the finest stable of racing horses on the frontier."

But it was from John Overton that the Donelson family got its real grasp of Andrew Jackson's character. John commented quietly:

"He towers over all other men I've ever known. You've noticed that scar on his forehead, of course."

There was a general nodding of heads.

"Back in 1781, it was, Andrew and his two brothers were fighting under their uncle, Major Crawford, against the British Dragoons who had invaded the Waxhaws. The Dragoons attacked our men in the local church, setting it on fire. Andrew and his young cousin Thomas Crawford managed to escape but they were overtaken and Crawford was made a prisoner. The next morning when Andrew made his way back to the Crawford home to tell them what had happened to their son, a company of Dragoons surprised the family. The British officer commanded Andrew to clean his high jack boots, which were splashed and crusted with mud. Andrew was only fourteen and just about came up to the middle button of the officer's red coat, but he cried out: 'Sir, I am a prisoner of war and claim to be treated as such!' "

"I can just hear the tone of voice in which he said it," commented Samuel.

"The commanding officer lifted his sword and swung it down on Andrew's head. Andrew threw up his arm, which was gashed to the bone; that's how he saved his life, but the tip of the sword cut his forehead."

There was silence while the seven brothers went back into their memories; they had all fought in the War for Independence.

"What did Mr. Jackson do about that?" Rachel asked, which brought a quick laugh, for her tone suggested that Andrew Jackson would somehow take command of the situation and avenge himself.

"Just what you would expect: the British officer ordered him to lead them to the home of a Waxhaw fighter, a man by the name of Thompson. Andrew avoided the regular road and led the British through a winding path and across an open field; Thompson could see them from half a mile away and escaped. Somehow the English officer didn't like that any better than he liked Andrew's refusal to polish his boots. He made Andrew march forty miles to the British military prison at Camden without allowing him even a drink of water."

26

Rachel gazed into the fire, observing to herself that she too would have need of such stamina.

9

It was a magnificent May afternoon with the red haw and forsythia in bloom, the late-arriving purple martins and the wrens chattering in the trees, the air filled with the fragrance of honeysuckle, when Rachel saw a party of traders come down the trail with Lewis Robards leading three heavily laden pack horses. She watched him from the porthole of the big room, sitting his horse with easy, almost arrogant grace. He appeared heavier, and from the lines in his face rather older than the passage of months should have indicated.

In the weeks since she had received the letter from her husband telling her that he would be happy to wind up his affairs in Harrodsburg and come to the Cumberland to live, she had looked forward to this moment when he would reach the station. She ran quickly to the door to welcome him.

The bulging panniers on either side of Lewis's pack horses had been filled not with his personal possessions, but with expensive and carefully selected gifts for each member of the family: a sapphire ring for herself, a French dressing mirror for her mother, a boxed compass for Alexander, a set of tools for William, one of the new Youmans rifles for John, Jr., the complete works of Shakespeare for Samuel, a wallet for Stockly, the money-maker of the clan, a hunting knife for Leven, an illuminated Bible for Severn, and for John Overton, out of gratitude for this reconciliation, a leather-bound set of lawbooks with his name tooled on the backstrap.

Lewis was greeted warmly by everyone except Samuel, who could not wipe from his mind the picture of his sister's tear-streaked face when he had taken her out of the Robards home eight months before. But as the day progressed Rachel saw with a kind of gnawing anxiety that her husband was very uncertain of himself. After supper the men fell to talking about land values, the difficulties of clearing titles farther out in the wilderness.

"Speaking of titles," said Overton, "I've checked that six-forty of yours, Lewis, in Clover Bottom. Rachel asked me to make sure the records were clean and legal. They are."

"Thank you, John, but I wasn't as much concerned over the title to the land as I am the amount of Indian raids. It's still pretty wild country, isn't it?"

William replied gravely, "Yes, there have been several attacks out that way in the past month. Mrs. Hargart and her two children were killed."

27

"Then it would hardly be safe to expose Rachel to such danger, would it?"

There was an uncomfortable silence. Rachel trembled as she felt old misgivings sweep over her. Yet she knew that none of her brothers considered Lewis a coward. The silence came because no man could tell any other how deep he should go into Indian country, or what attitude he should take toward the omnipresent threat of attack; yet all of them had lived on the frontier, all of them had been attacked and had fought the Indians. She knew what her brothers would be thinking: if nobody pushed out the frontier, risking Indian attacks, then this land would always be sparsely settled and unsafe.

"If you will permit me an opinion, Captain Robards," she heard Andrew Jackson say, "I've always felt that the Indians never attack where they know a man is fast with his rifle. Your presence would be all the protection Mrs. Robards would need."

Lewis flushed with pleasure at the compliment. Rachel felt her own anxiety ease. Now she sat back quietly as Lewis told the first news of George Washington's inauguration as President a couple of weeks before on April 30, 1789, in New York; this brought double pleasure to the Donelsons because Washington had been their friend in Virginia.

"After Mr. Washington took the oath, the chancellor of New York cried, 'Long live George Washington, President of the United States,' and the crowd thundered back, 'Long live George Washington, President of the United States.' "

"Sounds too much like 'Long live the King' to me," growled Jackson. "We're a new country and a new government, with a new kind of elected executive. Why don't we make up our own saying?"

No one took his grumbling seriously. Instead they asked each other whether the establishment of the new government might at last bring them some paid militia and some permanent protection against the Indians, a job which their mother state, North Carolina, had been unwilling to continue since it was obvious that these Cumberland people would soon be forming a state of their own. They spoke of agitating to have North Carolina cede this territory to the Federal government so they could be set up as a territory, for they were in desperate need of roads, a mail service and trading routes for merchandise from the East.

There was also the difficulty of knowing what kind of money was going to be legal tender. English sterling was still acceptable but it had almost disappeared from circulation; the Spanish gold florins which had found their way up the Natchez Trace from New Orleans were considered reliable, but the immediate need was for a standard form of money so that men could be paid for their services in hard cash instead of goods.

"I've been practicing law here in Nashville for half a year," said Jackson, "and if all the square miles I've received as fees could be strung to-

28

gether there'd be enough to make a whole county. If I don't get paid in land they give me mink skins, linsey, rye whisky, tallow, beeswax, cured bacon, peach brandy, beaver, otter, raccoon and fox furs. I ought to open a trading post."

Rachel was surprised to find what a wonderful background for thinking could be provided by men discussing with all seriousness the trying problems of the day; how strange it was that she could hear them clearly, take in and understand what they were saying, yet at the same time push her own thoughts forward step by step.

Her husband was attached to John Overton; they had remained friends at the Robards home even after Overton had defended her. Andrew Jackson and her husband had gotten off to an excellent start, for Mr. Jackson's compliment was something that Lewis would cherish for a considerable time. However, they were all going to live together here in fairly close quarters, until the new Robards home and plantation had been begun. She resolved to give up the robust relationship she had enjoyed with the young lawyers during the past months. Every life had to be lived inside its own boundaries; and if her husband's nature formed the palings which closed them in, then she would try to live happily and securely inside that fence.

10

During the next weeks Rachel and Lewis rode out to their land, studying it with a view to clearing, planting, putting in orchards and choosing a site for their cabin. They saw the family only at dinner. She greeted John Overton and Andrew Jackson formally when they met, then moved on to whatever chore she was doing.

Late one afternoon she was crossing the yard from the dairy cabin where she had been preparing buttermilk for bleaching linen thread, when Andrew Jackson rode in. She didn't know how he accomplished it so quickly but before she had gone three steps he stood directly in her path, his long thin shoulders hunched over toward her, his eyes searching hers.

"Mrs Robards, have I said or done something to offend you? If so, I assure you I never meant it. You know that I have only the deepest . . ."

She hastened to reassure him.

"No, no, it's nothing you've done, Mr. Jackson. It's just . . . that since my husband's return I've been so busy . . ."

As she raised her head she saw in his eyes an expression that was rather like Moll's the day she had told Rachel she was living like a prisoner. Jackson quickly veiled his feelings, said, "Please forgive me for embarrassing you, Mrs Robards," and was gone.

At dinner she no longer listened with interest to the legal discussions,

29

even though the law firm of Overton and Jackson had converted the Donelson cabin into the most active law office west of the Blue Ridge. Samuel's problems had been solved: he was now reading law in the guest cabin, where he had moved everything but his bed. When it came time for Colonel Donelson's will to be probated it seemed only natural that John Overton should handle it. When Stockly needed money for a new business venture and mentioned this at the dinner table, it seemed only friendly for Andrew Jackson to volunteer the loan; when Overton and Jackson rode circuit and were paid in barter for their services, paid such things as woolen cloth, good flax linen, country-made sugar or tobacco, they brought the stuff home to the Donelsons to be thrown into the family larder.

With seven brothers, each engaging in a dozen different activities, there were bound to be unending discussions, councilings and group enterprises participated in by the Donelsons and their two paying guests. Only Lewis refrained. He was as clever and as educated as the rest, but he had no interest in the growth of Nashville or the hundred ways in which the Donelson clan was planning and working to establish the frontier and to make money.

It was two months after his coming to the Donelsons' that he told Rachel he had decided against developing the land at Clover Bottom.

"But Lewis, you promised in your letter . . ."

"What do I need another plantation for?" he demanded. "I've already got one back in Harrodsburg."

"Don't you really want to start the way everyone else does, and build your own life?"

"I would if I had to, but I can't see much sense in going through all that work when I already have what it would take us ten years to build here."

"Then what do you want to do?"

"Why must I do something? You like this house, don't you? You're comfortable. And I've been hunting; I've also made a few profitable land swaps in Nashville. Would you think it more important if I went around blabbering like those two walking lawbooks you're so attached to?"

Rachel pulled back.

"I'm sorry, Lewis, I didn't mean to hurt your feelings."

"Why don't they move into Nashville and build themselves an office there? It surely can't be convenient for them to ride ten miles into town and back every day."

"But they're both alone, Lewis, and they're happy here with us."

His skin grew dark; for a moment it seemed as though he would hold back, but the temptation was too strong.

"And you're happy with them."

Rachel took a deep breath. It was so painfully familiar.

"Oh, Lewis, let's start the cabin at Clover Bottom."

30

"So now you want to run away?" His voice had grown louder with every passing sentence. "Well, I'm not going to let Andrew Jackson drive me out of here."

Rachel was shocked. There was a knock at the door. It was Mrs. Donelson.

"Lewis, for shame!" she exclaimed as she entered the room. "You've been shouting so loud that everybody downstairs has heard you."

Lewis stormed out of the house, jumped on one of his horses and rode off at a killing pace. A few hours later he was back, contrite. He asked, "Am I forgiven?" and Rachel replied, "Yes, of course." To avoid further trouble she stopped eating in the dining room with the rest of the family.

The peace lasted for two, almost three weeks. Then one noon, when she was in the kitchen with her mother and Moll, making a meat and vegetable hotchpot, Lewis burst in, shouting:

"I won't stand him around here any more. You get that fellow off this place or I'll run him off myself!"

Rachel could only stammer: ". . . what man . . . are you talking about?"

He waited until Moll had left, her step unhurried, reluctant.

"You know perfectly well who I mean. Andrew Jackson. He insulted me. If it had been my home I would have shot him dead!"

"Mr. Jackson? But how? Mr. Jackson admires you, he wouldn't insult . . ."

"He admires my wife, not me. He's trying to make me look ridiculous so he can get you away from me."

She sank onto the log bench alongside of Moll's sand-scrubbed workboard, saddened. She caught only fragments of her mother's questions and of Lewis's loud replies. Apparently Andrew had made a generalization about some absentee land cases and Lewis had taken the remark personally. She did not know when Lewis left but when she turned around from the fireplace she saw John Overton standing in the doorway; it was a warm summer day and he was in his shirt sleeves, the cuffs turned back, his writing fingers stained with ink. She felt exposed; she had no way of concealing her emotions except to go into a room and close the door behind her. So many people were able to mask their feelings; if only she could!

"Forgive me for intruding, but I heard the . . . the commotion. Is Lewis at it again?"

Mrs. Donelson nodded with grim hopelessness, then left the kitchen.

Rachel spoke. "John, I must ask you to do something dreadful."

"You want us to go?"

"No . . . not you . . . just Mr. Jackson."

"We'll both go, Rachel." He put his hand out and covered hers where it lay clasped on the table, her thumb clenched under her fingers. "But

31

I am reluctant to do this: Lewis Robards is probably the only man on the frontier who doesn't understand the implications of insulting Andrew Jackson, of accusing him unjustly."

He began pacing up and down the kitchen. Rachel had never seen him thoroughly angry before; his eyes had the solidity of gray marble.

"In another month Andrew and I start on circuit. No one in Nashville will think it strange if we don't come back to the Donelsons'. But if we are obliged suddenly to move out people are bound to ask 'Why?' I shall ask Lewis to let things go along until we leave for the next court session at Jonesboro."

It took only a few moments for them to reach the Robards' bedroom.

"John, I've always trusted you," cried Lewis, "and now you are turning against me."

"As your cousin," interrupted Overton, "I feel it my duty to hit you over the head with a tree trunk. But as your attorney I'm going to give you some advice."

"I don't want your advice," snapped Robards.

"Lewis, when I left your home to come to Nashville I agreed to serve as your emissary because I thought you had learned your lesson. And now you are behaving in the same unmanly fashion. When you have quieted down you will realize that there has not been an untoward word or gesture between your wife and Andrew Jackson. I eat and sleep and work and travel and spend every moment of my life with that man; I know his character. If you drive him out of here you will have to go around again as you did at Harrodsburg, apologizing and explaining that it was nothing more than your feverish imagination."

"You may interpret it that way," replied Lewis, his voice dry and harsh. "I'm beginning to think that maybe I was right about Peyton Short, after all."

Rachel sat stunned and sickened.

"I beg your forgiveness, Rachel," said John, "for everything that has happened. I influenced you to let your husband come back; I sent Andrew Jackson here. My intervention today has caused Lewis to reopen old wounds and insult you again. I will tell Andrew tonight and we will be gone in the morning."

She slept fitfully. When she awakened the sun was already bright. She drew the curtains and saw John Overton standing between his horse and Jackson's, both laden with heavy saddlebags. Her eyes traveled to the fence by the orchard and there they found her husband and Andrew Jackson. Lewis had his fist raised as though to strike Jackson; Jackson drew back several steps. Her husband lowered his arm. Andrew Jackson turned and walked to the horses. He and John mounted and disappeared out the gate.

She dressed hurriedly, scooped cold water onto her face from the bowl and ran quickly into the yard.

"Your chivalrous Mr. Jackson!" snorted Lewis. "He said he apologized if he had done anything to offend me, but that he couldn't leave without first telling me that you had done nothing to warrant my anger. The man is a coward, Rachel; I offered to thrash him and he refused to fight."

Rachel turned toward the house. Andrew Jackson knew that if he and Lewis Robards rolled on the ground like a couple of drunken brawlers the whole of Nashville would hear about it by nightfall. Mr. Jackson had afforded her a protection her husband had not cared to provide.

Quiet descended on the Donelson station, but it was the wrong kind of quiet. By a tacit agreement the outlying Donelsons, Jane and Robert Hays, Catherine and Thomas Hutchings, Mary and John Caffrey, Johnny and his wife Mary, were remaining away from the parental stockade. Alexander and Leven and Stockly, even William, were avoiding Lewis; Samuel was seething with resentment.

"How could you put John and Andrew out of our home?" he demanded of his mother. "If Father were alive he never would have allowed this."

Mother and son turned to look at Rachel. Samuel fumbled with an apology.

"I'm sorry, Rachel. I didn't mean to make you any further unhappiness."

She knew what she would have to do.

"You happen to be right, Samuel. Lewis and I have spoiled everything here. I can't have the family staying away from the house. We'll start building our cabin at Clover Bottom."

After several days of argument with Lewis, Rachel was forced to say firmly:

"Lewis, I cannot feel comfortable here any longer. I am a married woman and am entitled to live under my own roof. Everybody will help us make a clearing and erect our cabin."

"I don't need their charity," he replied; "I've got the means to build a home. I'll hire my own workmen. I'll pay for what I get and be beholden to no one."

He bought two husky Negroes in Nashville and hired the town's carpenter to see that the cabin was built to Rachel's specifications. Once they were installed he set the slaves to cutting down trees in a wide circle about the cabin for protection against the Indians, then plotted the fields and slopes to determine which sections of the land could best be used for crops. While Rachel was busy furnishing her first home, Lewis hunted, molded bullets, cleared the thickets. When winter came on and darkness fell early he spent the long afternoons sitting by the fire, staring at the flames.

Finally they were shot at. Lewis stacked large piles of bullets beneath

33

each porthole, stayed awake nights with his guns loaded and cocked, grew thin and jumpy. During the first heavy snowstorm he caught cold and came down with fever. Rachel sent for Samuel, who rode out to the clearing, wrapped Lewis in bearskins and carried him to the Donelsons'.

New Year's Day of 1790 dawned clear and bright. The family gathered for a dinner of roast wild turkey and suckling pig. Lewis had made a good recovery, but remained in bed. Rachel sensed that the day he was completely well would be a difficult one for them both. At first she had imagined that his lethargy was part of his convalescence; now she began to perceive that the spirit had gone out of the man.

In early April he informed her that he had to go back to Harrodsburg. She was puzzled both by the offhand way in which he spoke and by his choice of words.

"You *have to,* Lewis? Is something wrong?"

". . . well, Mother hasn't been feeling well . . . and there are a number of business matters that have to be settled: some slaves to be sold, there have been good offers for our outlying land that we never put under cultivation . . ."

The family took Lewis's announcement calmly. Moll laundered his linen, packing it neatly in one of the saddlebags; George groomed his horses and repaired their hoofs; Rachel supervised the preparation of enough food to carry him comfortably.

On the morning of his departure Rachel and Mrs. Donelson had breakfast with him and then walked him down to the front gate where Thomas Crutcher, an old friend, was waiting to start out with him for Harrodsburg. Lewis kissed them both on the cheek, thanked them for their hospitality and rode off.

Rachel leaned heavily against the log gate. While this was infinitely less unpleasant than being put out of her husband's home, Lewis's smile and farewell embrace could not conceal from her the fact that she once again was caught in the halfway point between being married and unmarried. In Harrodsburg she had been convinced by her husband's attitude that their marriage was over; difficult as it had been to face that hard fact, it was something definite that one could grasp and somehow grapple with. How did she endure this new kind of void, with no part of the future that she could either predict or control?

11

Two weeks had passed when John Overton came to call. The two lawyers were again holding forth in the April session of the court in Nashville, and were promptly invited for Sunday dinner. John managed to get a few minutes alone with Rachel.

34

"Rachel, do you know what Lewis's plans are?"

"No."

"Then I'd better tell you what I heard. On their second night out Lewis and Crutcher camped on the Barrens, and Lewis's saddle horse strayed off. The next day he was depressed about the loss. Crutcher tried to cheer him by saying that some hunter would find the horse and take him back to Nashville where Lewis could claim him. Lewis said he'd be damned if he'd be seen in the Cumberland again, that he hated the valley, the people and the life there. Crutcher is convinced he never intends coming back to Nashville."

She thanked him and slipped away to her bedroom. There was no shock to her in the story Overton had brought, only the confirmation of what she had suspected. There was a knock on the door. It was Moll to tell her that dinner was ready. She bathed her eyes in cold water, put on a too bright smile and went down to the dining room.

There were half a dozen excited conversations going on simultaneously around the table, for the Cumberland had at last secured its freedom from North Carolina and become a territory of the Federal government. Rachel seated herself between Samuel and Alexander, noting idly that her mother had ordered their finest linen board cover and napkins for the occasion. For the moment the pewter plates stood empty; Rachel looked down the long table at the chattering guests; only Andrew Jackson seemed constrained, silent. Then her brother John said grace and George and Benjamin, the best of the serving men, came from the kitchen with huge chargers of roasted meats and fresh vegetables in heaping basins. She asked Samuel to pour her some milk from the great jug of heavy leather sitting in the center of the board. Its coolness steadied her nerves. She heard her mother ask from her position at the head of the table:

"John, how are you and Mr. Jackson getting along over at Casper Mansker's?"

"Well, the Manskers are giving us every courtesy but we have no room for our office, we are practicing law across the bedcover."

"I don't mind that so much," said Jackson, "I can practice law in a hayloft. But the cooking is bad. John and I lay awake nights thinking of Sunday dinners like this."

"We haven't had any tenants in your cabin since you left," said William blandly. "Wouldn't you like to move back into your old office?"

"I think it's a wonderful idea," said Stockly. "I still owe Andrew some money and I think he ought to be around to protect his investment."

"And I could continue my studies," cried Samuel.

"There's nothing Andrew or I would like better," said Overton. "But is it . . . wise?"

"For my part," replied Mrs. Donelson quietly, "I can tell you that I was heartily against your moving out in the first place. However the

35

question of what is wise or unwise in this particular case must rest with Rachel."

All eyes turned on her. She thought with an inner grimace that during the past year she had had to grow used to doing her thinking in public. But there was no fumbling or hesitation in her mind. Was there any reason why some twenty Donelsons should be controlled by one absent and hostile Robards? She turned to the two lawyers who were sitting up-table from her.

"I know of no reason why you shouldn't come back. Move into your cabin again, gentlemen. We enjoy having you here."

After dinner a number of them walked into the orchard to see the first blossoms on the peach trees. They had gone only a few steps beyond the fence when Andrew Jackson fell into step beside her.

"I want to thank you for your kind invitation, Mrs. Robards, but I just can't move back here. There's never been any young woman whose friendship has meant so much to me. That's why I was so distressed at causing you trouble."

"You didn't cause the trouble, Mr. Jackson. You just got caught in it, same as I did."

"Do you know what I am denying myself?" he cried out. Then, lowering his voice, he continued more calmly, "I will keep office in the cabin with John; but for the time being I think I had better continue living at Mansker's. I feel that I must do this to protect you, Mrs. Robards."

Rachel turned an unsmiling face up to him. "I don't think you need concern yourself about Lewis Robards."

He studied her, perplexed, his lips a little parted. She thought how peculiar it was that one could look at a man's face every day for two months as she had the year before and not really know its detail until a moment of crisis when one's vision was sharpened by the tautness of emotion. It was not a symmetrical structure: the high arched forehead was too narrow, his right eye was larger and somewhat more deeply recessed than the left, the left side of his lips seemed slightly fuller than the right, and his long jutting nose slashed across from the right eye to the left corner of his mouth. All these things she saw vividly, certain that they were not the ingredients of handsomeness; then why did it seem to her the most attractive face she had ever known? Her questioning was cut short as he managed to speak.

"I don't understand."

"I don't believe he's ever coming back to Nashville . . ."

It was the most beautiful spring anyone could remember in the ten years of the Cumberland settlement. The magnolia tulips were in bloom and the early scent of lilac was already in the air. The small flowering redbud and dogwood trees showed pink and white among the ferns on the green hillsides; throughout the woods the wild grapevines were

36

climbing among the tree trunks, the grass was already high and pastel green, and the yellow jasmine was rich with summerlike fragrance.

Rachel found her naturally buoyant spirits coming back in full force, and a tremendous need to be gay, to sing and make jokes, to be happy over the simple fact that she was twenty-two and alive in a beautiful springtime. She went to the neighborhood dances; on Sundays the Donelsons and their friends packed picnic lunches and rode along the river, finding quiet shallows where the water was caught in a winding bend, and where they could wade in the coolness. Once she joined John and Andrew Jackson and the pretty daughter of a settler who had just arrived in Nashville, walking along the river road with the warm sun streaming onto their faces. She liked to walk; her gait was easy and unhurried as she moved through space with her own compact graceful rhythm; her head was set a little too low on her shoulders for complete effortlessness, but her long slim legs kept pace with Andrew's tempered stride.

John and the pretty blond girl were up ahead. Rachel and Andrew Jackson talked about what they wanted out of life. For Rachel this was not difficult to tell, though it had been so difficult to achieve: a husband with whom she could live in love and peace; children; a home up here on the bluff overlooking the lazy green Cumberland.

It seemed that Mr. Jackson had no desire to become a great lawyer.

"I haven't the talent for the law that John has," he said. "Oh, I do well enough, but the law isn't something I've wanted all of my life, it was just the field that happened to be open to young fellows with spirit. What I really want to be is a planter. That was what my father wanted back in the Waxhaws. I'd like to put hundreds of acres under cultivation, see the crops grow clean and strong in the sun. And I'd like to raise blooded horses."

"But the law is an open door to politics," protested Rachel. "Stockly says we're going to become a state within a few years. Would you like to be a congressman, or a governor, perhaps?"

"No," he said quickly. "I have no political ambitions. I even surveyed a beautiful site down near Natchez in the Spanish territory when I was there on business last year." He turned to gaze headlong at her. "But now I just want to live here in the Cumberland."

A party of traders came in from Harrodsburg; they carried a packet of letters for Mrs. Lewis Robards. Rachel sat in the big chair beneath her window and arranged them chronologically by glancing at the opening lines in each letter, then read them through swiftly, almost without thinking or feeling, before going back to let each sentence carry its own weight.

First, Lewis assured her that being home again had brought a complete return of his energies; that his mother's illness had left her feeble and he had taken over the management of the plantation; that he was now employing two soldiers who had fought with him in the war to help

37

him work the plantation and defend it; and that he had sold a number of slaves, male and female. He apologized for having caused her anxiety, assured her that he loved her, and wouldn't she come to Harrodsburg as quickly as possible?

She sank deep into reverie; how cleverly the letters had been put together, how carefully they had been designed to dispel her fears. The subject of the young slave had never been discussed between them, yet apparently he had sensed her knowledge of the relationship and was assuring her that the girl had been sold; he was assuring her too that since his new employees were trained fighters there would be no more boarders over whom he could become jealous. Lastly, he was making it clear that he had assumed the management of the plantation and would now be responsible and occupied.

In all of her days of determination not to return to Harrodsburg she had never once imagined that her husband would use this approach. She was glad that Lewis still loved her; she was grateful to him for being willing to reconstruct his life so that they might have a chance to live well together. Just how great that chance was she did not know. She was no longer eighteen years old, no longer able to give herself over to daydreams. She had been happy during this past month, yet what would happen to her over the months and years of being a woman without a defined status or position? Where was her chance for a home of her own, for children?

She must try again.

12

She packed her belongings and waited for news of a trading party that would be going down the Kentucky trail to Harrodsburg. The Donelson clan gathered to see her off, but was reluctant to have her leave.

She reached the Robards home late in the afternoon with the bright June sun lighting up the rambling stone house. She had anticipated being met by Lewis at Crow's station where she branched off the Kentucky Road, but no one had been there to greet her. The leader of the trading party insisted upon escorting her directly to the Harrodsburg house, but there was no sign of welcome here, either. She tied her horse to the hitching post, walked up the four broad log steps and knocked on the iron knocker.

She was escorted to the library, the door closed behind her. There sat Lewis, sprawled across a chair in a perspiration-soaked linen shirt and wrinkled woolen trousers, his booted legs stretched straight in front of him, crushing the striped nankeen coat which lay beneath them. His eyes were bleary and his face red from drinking. She stood with

38

her back squared against the door, gazing at her husband in bewilderment. He made no effort to rise.

"It didn't take you very long, did it?"

"Take me . . . long? Five days, instead of four; there was a sick woman traveling with the party."

"I was no sooner out of sight than you invited him back to the blockhouse."

All of her expectancy had crashed at the first sight of her husband's unfocused eyes. Now her hope went along with it.

"Lewis, what are you saying?"

"Don't play the innocent with me."

"Do you mind if I sit down?"

"Friend of mine came in from Nashville, told me that Andrew Jackson was living at your house again."

"Mr. Jackson is not living at our station, Lewis. We invited him to return but he refused."

"Refused? When he's there every day?"

"John is living with us again, but Mr. Jackson comes only on his free days. He said he thought it would be better if he did not live there since you had once demanded that he leave."

Lewis pulled himself heavily out of the chair and stood with his face close to hers. "Then you admit that you invited him back?"

"It's not a matter of admitting, Lewis. Mother wanted him and so did the boys. After all, it is their house; he is like a member of our family."

"Yes," replied Lewis with an insinuative leer, "an intimate member."

She was too sick at heart to search deeply the implications of what her husband had said, but she sensed that for the first time he was accusing her directly of infidelity. She hung her head in shame: shame for herself and shame for Lewis. Then she turned, went out into the hall and up the stairs to her mother-in-law's bedroom.

She needed only one look at the thin face framed in the nightcap on the pillow to know that Mrs. Robards was seriously ill. She went to her side and kissed her. Mrs. Robards cupped Rachel's face in her hands. The long-sleeved gown with the ribbons tied at the wrist concealed her thinness, but her voice was strong.

"Rachel, my dear, there's nothing in the world I've wanted more than to have you become mistress of this house."

"Yes, darling, I know that."

"Lewis was a good boy, we loved him devotedly, my husband and I . . . but there can be no life for you . . ."

"You mustn't exhaust yourself. I'm going to stay here and help nurse you . . ."

"No, Rachel," the older woman interrupted. "We must get you back home . . . at once." She closed her eyes for a moment, then whispered,

39

"He promised me he would sell the girl, but he brought her back yesterday. He has been doing nothing but drinking and shouting. I'm frightened for him. You must write to your family at once. I will see that the message goes to Nashville with the first party to leave. You can stay in that little room yonder."

During the long warm days Rachel nursed Mrs. Robards, feeding her, at the doctor's orders, chicken broth and a medicinal tea brewed from bloodroot and wild ginger. She saw nothing of Lewis except at a distance, when she sat in her little room at the square window with wooden inside shutters and watched him riding to Harrodsburg or returning late at night slumped in his saddle. Her hope for her marriage was gone.

She slept little, only for an hour or two at a time; in the middle of the night she would rise, open the shutter and gaze out into the phosphorescent full-moon night. There was time and stillness in which to think back over her life. In a sense she would be free, free from pain, from humiliation, from falsely raised hopes. The years stretched ahead; but she had neither the will nor the clarity to face them. She would live one day at a time, find a moment or a task or a sight in each to warm her and bring her a reason for living.

Suddenly she blinked her eyes hard for she saw a figure on horseback come up the road, riding fast, and sitting his horse with ungainly ease . . . looking for all the world like Andrew Jackson! She leaned out the window, studying the figure that was coming toward her. Her letter to her family saying that she was leaving Lewis forever had gone from Harrodsburg ten days ago; she had expected that someone would arrive for her; but surely it would have been Alexander or Samuel or Stockly? Surely they would not have sent Andrew Jackson? Lewis would take this for a personal affront, an insult deliberately administered by the Donelson family. How could they have done this, she asked herself over and over again, when I have so many brothers?

But it was Andrew, there could no longer be any doubt about that, dressed in tight-fitting buckskin trousers and a leather hunting jacket. He dismounted with a quick sliding motion that enabled him to reach the ground at the same instant that the horse drew up before the porch. He pounded on the door with his fists, and it was as though that pounding were coming from her heart.

Except for necessities, her possessions had never been unpacked. She went quickly into her mother-in-law's room to bid her farewell, telling her that it was Mr. Jackson who had come for her, and that she wanted to get away before Lewis could return, that she dreaded the thought of a public quarrel and, still worse, of another duel.

"You need have no fear of that, my dear," replied the old woman; there was a quality in her voice that not only brought Rachel up short but put an end to her nervousness. The tone, rather than the words, brought

40

back to her the scene with John Overton when she had asked him about Lewis's duel with Peyton Short, and he had evaded a direct answer. Gropingly she said:

"But Lewis fought a duel with Peyton Short."

Mrs. Robards turned her head slightly on the pillow. She had been a proud woman and a high-spirited one all her life. She could look neither at Rachel nor herself in this painful moment.

"This is a sad thing for a mother to have to reveal about her son. But you are entitled to know." She turned her head on the pillow; her eyes met Rachel's. "When Lewis found Peyton Short in Richmond, Mr. Short asked Lewis if he insisted on fighting a duel or if he would accept a money settlement."

"A money set . . . But for what?"

"For damages done to Lewis's feelings because of that letter. Lewis said he would consider a settlement. Mr. Short paid him a thousand dollars in sterling at Gault's Tavern."

Rachel felt her face flame. How could a man so insanely jealous that he would banish his wife accept money from the other man?

Tears welled in Mrs. Robards' eyes. Rachel kissed her mother-in-law's cheek, hard, and fled from the room.

This then was what had offended John, and what he had kept from her. This was why even William the Cautious had withdrawn his opposition to her remaining at the Donelsons'. Her whole family must have known, and thought to spare her further humiliation. But what difference could it have made if she had known? Where was there a pattern for separation or divorce that she could take refuge in? What else could she have done but send for her husband?

Alongside this news all concern about Andrew Jackson's having come for her was forgotten. By the time she reached the front door her chestnut mare had been saddled and brought up from the stable to the front of the blockhouse. She and Jackson exchanged a quick glance of greeting; it was not until they were several miles on their way to the Kentucky Road that he first addressed her.

"Shall we light straight out for Nashville or wait for the next party? There has been some Indian activity along the road during the past few weeks."

"How did you come?"

"Alone."

"Then that's the way we'll go back."

It appeared to be the answer he had expected; he made no comment.

"Besides, I'd like to get distance between us and Harrodsburg as quickly as we can. Lewis will return soon, and I'm sure he will follow us."

"Follow?" He wheeled his horse sharply so that he was facing her. "For what purpose? We understood from your letter . . ."

41

"He won't be coming in pursuit of me, he'll be coming after you. That was why I had to write home . . ."

It was a little before sundown when they reached the Boar's Head where they were provided with an excellent supper of fresh baked bread and butter, chicken fricassee, apple dumplings and coffee. Rachel had a room to herself, with a candle on the night stand, clean muslin sheets, a huge feather mattress and a goose-down patchwork quilt. Andrew had to share the last available bed with two other men. She was sure she would not so much as close her eyes because of all that had happened to her that day, but she had no more than put her head on the soft feather pillow than she heard Mr. Jackson's voice calling to her that the sun would be up soon and to dress quickly.

She put on the light blue calico summer gown which had only a moderate amount of material in the skirt to make it comfortable for side-saddle riding, and with the sleeves cut just below the elbows for coolness. It was the most austere dress she had ever sewn, with a high neckline but no collar. She slipped into moccasins, a short doeskin cloak, and left her room in the first ash-gray light of dawn. A hot breakfast was waiting on the downstairs board.

They were on the road again by the time the top curve of the sun pushed itself over the horizon. Their horses too were rested and they made good time as they streaked across the open meadows with the mist drying on the grasses. They stopped when the sun was perpendicular and hot, washed themselves in a cool stream, gave the horses a drink and had some of the bread and cheese from their saddlebags. In the afternoon the horses tired, and for the first time she realized how seriously Jackson was on guard, his whole being cocked at every tree and bush as they went through a copse of cedars. Suddenly he pulled in his horse.

"Can you shoot straight?"

"Sometimes."

"Then take this pistol. A group of Indians, I can't tell how many, perhaps only three of four, have been paralleling our course through the woods. They've just pulled out ahead of us to get to that spot up above. Do you see that fallen tree about twenty yards this side of the open space?"

"Yes."

"I'm going to pull off the road just beyond that log."

He started his horse at a medium pace. She followed behind him. When he passed the big cedar log he gave his horse the spur and dashed into the woods. She came behind him as quickly as she could. He fired his rifle, then called to her, "Use your spur!" and in an instant they were out of the clearing and back onto the trail.

"I missed," he said, "but it served the same purpose. They'll leave us alone from now on." He turned to her. "Were you scared?"

42

"No, I didn't see anything. Besides, I was too interested in watching you. If I'd been an Indian I'd have been sure there was a whole militia regiment behind you."

"That's the best tactic," he replied, pleased. "It will bring you out unscathed nearly every time."

She joined his laughter at the use of the word "nearly"; and the laughter dissipated the tension between them.

13

That night they stayed at the cabin of a family which had come over the Wilderness Trail with Daniel Boone in 1776. It was a one-room log cabin with a divided loft for sleeping rooms, chickens and dogs in the hard-packed-earth yard, hogs around the corncribs and children running in and out of the open door. There was cold broiled ham, milk and hoecake for supper served on a tree stump in the yard. Rachel shared a bed with several daughters of the family on the ground floor while Andrew climbed up the roughhewn ladder to the loft, where he wrapped himself in a blanket and slept with his head on a pillow of straw. In the middle of the night Rachel was awakened by the tossing of the children. She got her huge bearskin, spread it on the floor as a mattress and slept soundly the rest of the night.

On the third day the Indian danger was past and so was the threat of Lewis Robards catching up with them. They let the horses set their own pace, riding side by side. The day was soft and warm; they listened to the sounds of the wild life about them, feeling a sense of peacefulness and of companionship.

"You aren't frightened by the wilderness, are you?" he asked.

"I was brought up with it. All of us Donelsons were. We made that trip with Father on the *Adventure,* you know."

"I had forgotten. You couldn't have been very old?"

"Just twelve. But there were many children younger than me. In fact, one of them was born on the trip."

"That *Adventure* voyage was the most amazing ever made on the western frontier."

"Father and the boys built the *Adventure* on the Holston River, up near Fort Patrick Henry. It had a hull of squared logs and sides well bulwarked against gunfire, with a roof over a considerable part of the hull, bunks for sleeping and a stone hearth for cooking. We launched it the first of November 1779. There were thirty boats altogether, most of them flatboats, with a few pirogues. I guess about two hundred folks started the journey; there must have been more than fifty of us on our boat."

Colonel James Robertson, Donelson's partner in the venture, had left

43

earlier in the fall with the best Indian fighters, heads of the families and considerable livestock to take an unexplored overland route through the Cumberland Gap and the Kentucky Trace. Colonel Donelson was to bring the women and children, and about thirty able-bodied men to handle and defend the boats on the longer but comparatively safer river journey, using the big flatboats to transport household goods, supplies, farm implements, sacks of seed, tools, slaves and building material.

"Father and Colonel Robertson were going to found a whole new community, maybe a whole new state . . . like Virginia. But the truth is Father had a bad case of 'wilderness fever.' I can still remember the excitement in his voice when he described rolling green valleys and broad rivers flowing through them which no white man had ever seen, let alone settled."

They left Fort Patrick Henry three days before Christmas, but could go only three miles the first day to the mouth of Reedy Creek because there was already ice on the water.

"For two months we had to live on our boats, and in tents in the snow. At the end of February we started again, but within a matter of hours the *Adventure* got stuck on Poor Valley Shoals. So did two of the other boats. We finally had to jump into the icy water holding sacks of food and tools in our arms to lighten the boats. Mother entrusted me with the monogrammed family silver, our most valuable possession."

As she talked the sun lighted her eyes with specks of hazel; there was a smile of nostalgia on her lips. Jackson watched her as her hands played with the reins, and admired the easy poise with which she sat her horse.

It had been rainy and blustery all through the early days of March as the *Adventure* floated down the great valley of the Tennessee. Gray sedge grass sprinkled with young trees and growths of brier and bramble covered the open savannas near the river; back of it all they could see through the streamers of rain clouds the great mountain ranges they were leaving behind them.

"Hardly an hour passed without some kind of accident somewhere along the line. Mr. Henry's boat was capsized by the force of the current. We all had to stop to rescue the little children and snatch floating articles as they went by."

By the time they had passed the mouth of the Clinch they were in hostile Indian country. The cold was still great. Colonel Donelson put into the mouth of South Chickamauga Creek where one of the Dragging Canoe's towns had stood, and here Mrs. Ephraim Peyton gave birth to a child. The next day the flotilla ran the gantlet of the Chickamauga towns. The boats were fired on, and Mr. Payne was killed from ambush on Moccasin Bend.

"Most of the upsets and hardships had been fun for us kids. Then we had a real tragedy: when Thomas Stuart's flatboat broke out with smallpox Father ordered the boat to keep at a distance. The Indians captured

44

it and killed the whole party, twenty-eight people. We could hear their cries, but there was nothing we could do to help them."

When the *Adventure* flotilla approached the entrance to the Suck they could see bands of warriors along the rocky paths parallel with the river. The boys stood with their rifles trained on the shore while the older men guided the boats through the whirlpools and crosscurrents of the narrow gorge. Rachel had fired as many shots as any of the younger boys, but she wasn't sure she had ever hit anything.

"Some of the men in Abel Gower's boat were wounded. Young Nancy Gower, she was my age, seized the rudder and steered until the men reorganized. When the flotilla got under way again Mrs. Gower saw that Nancy's skirt was stained with blood. She had been shot through the thigh but she didn't tell anybody about it. Now there's a girl I've always admired."

Jackson smiled gently in the darkness. They rode in silence for a few minutes, the trees and the dusk closing them in like walls of a room.

The Indians continued to harass the *Adventure* until it emerged from the narrows and entered the Great Bend of the Tennessee. They thought they had lost Jonathan Jennings and his boat, but it had been grounded on a reef and had been submitted to a galling fire by the Indians.

"Worst of all, Mrs. Peyton, who had had to help unload the boat and pull it off the reef, lost her newborn baby in the confusion. Mother practically carried Mrs. Peyton in her arms for the rest of the trip."

At last spring broke through. In a week they floated two hundred and fifty miles to the junction of the Tennessee and Ohio rivers; the weather turned fair and the young green began showing in sheltered places beyond the cane thickets and gaunt white sycamores that fringed the banks. They poled the boats up the uncharted Ohio River against high and rapid currents. Their provisions were exhausted, most of the men were wounded or ill and the families discouraged because they did not know how many miles were still left to the journey.

"My father held most of the flotilla together through sheer will power, hoisting sails when there was wind, shooting buffalo and wild swan to live on. At the end of April, when we reached French Lick and the blockhouses that Colonel Robertson had built, we had lost thirty-three people. Father wanted to be out by himself. He moved us eight miles farther up on the Cumberland and another couple of miles up Stone River to Clover Bottom. I should have thought Mother would have had enough of the wilderness, but she made no objection whatever, saying that the land was richer on Stone River.

"Our first station consisted of tents; we put in cotton and corn, but just about everything went wrong: the river overflowed and drowned our crops, the Indians scarcely let a day go by without attacking; another Indian treaty would have to be made before we could perfect our land title. Father had to move us over this very road to Harrodsburg. It took him four years to get back to French Lick . . . it has taken me just as long . . ."

She stopped abruptly. Jackson was silent; he spurred his horse, stepping out along the path in front of her.

She thought, We Donelsons have had difficulties before, plenty of them, and we've always managed to survive. Father used to say, "If you can't solve a problem you just have to outlive it." But those other hardships, when she was young, they had been easy to bear because they were all in it together. This new trouble had happened to her apart. Perhaps that's what growing up meant: your troubles were yours alone and you had to overcome them by yourself.

She was glad she had told the story of the *Adventure*; thinking about the past had heartened her for the present.

14

Jackson had brought her an invitation to stay at the blockhouse of her sister Jane and Colonel Robert Hays in Haysboro, the community of stations that had been founded by Robert, his parents and his brothers. Their plantation was in rather wilder country than her mother's house; there were grapes, cherries and ripe blackberries in the forest to be picked. Rachel was glad to be returning here instead of to the Donelsons'. Jane's offhand manner would have a remedial effect upon her. Mr. Jackson turned her over to Jane, waved aside their efforts to thank him and rode off for Nashville.

Rachel's sanctuary lasted two days, long enough for Lewis Robards to reach the Hays plantation. He came along the dogtrot, chatting in an amiable voice with Jane.

"You have company, Rachel," called Jane, as though an acquaintance had just ridden out from Nashville. Her lids were raised the tiniest fraction over her Cumberland-green eyes, a signal for, I'll be close by. She's looking unusually lovely, Rachel thought; if only I could have her coolness and detachment.

"Aren't you going to welcome your husband after he's ridden more than two hundred miles to see you?"

Lewis's voice was low, charming. He had stopped somewhere for a bath and a shave and had changed into a smartly fashioned corduroy suit, a bit on the warm side for the first of July, she mused idly, with a spotless white silk shirt and polished black boots.

"The kind of welcome I had expected when I reached Harrodsburg?"

"I behaved badly, Rachel. I had been inflamed by the stories I'd heard."

"What kind of man believes every chance story that gossips may care to repeat about his wife?"

"My kind of man, I guess: a little stupid, a little hysterical."

46

"And you don't take it amiss that it was Andrew Jackson who brought me here?" asked Rachel bluntly.

"Certainly not," he replied. "If it was more convenient for your mother to send Jackson, then there is no reason why he shouldn't have come.' He went to her impulsively, with one of his tenderest smiles. "I trust you, I love you, and I want you to come back with me. We'll leave for home in the morning."

"No, Lewis."

"No? But there are no more doubts in my mind. It won't ever happen again, my dear. I give you my word of honor."

"You've broken your word many times before."

"But there must be some way I can convince you . . ."

"It would do no good."

He peered at her intently, as though there were some explanation that might not be contained in her words.

"No good?"

"I no longer love you."

"That's a lie!"

"I bear you no ill will, Lewis, but I have no affection left for you, none at all. Under these conditions I could never live with you again."

The placating manner vanished.

"I don't believe you! Besides, it has no importance. You are my wife and you must do as I say. We will return to Harrodsburg in the morning."

His voice had risen. She replied with a firmness he had never before heard.

"Lewis, I never intend to see you again."

There could be no mistaking the finality in her voice. He stood close to her, his fist clenched in front of her face.

"Then it was true."

"What was true, Lewis?"

"My suspicions of you and Andrew Jackson! The fact that he came to Harrodsburg for you clinches the case!"

"But it's only a few moments since you told me that there was nothing wrong in Mr. Jackson's coming for me."

"That was before I knew."

"Knew what?"

"That you were in love with Andrew Jackson."

She had never realized that a few spoken words could have the solid substance of a physical object: that they could be a splinter under your fingernail, a fence rail that hit you over the head . . . or a sharp knife that penetrated deep into your bosom.

Did she love Andrew Jackson?

A hundred images of him revolved quickly on the screen behind her eyes: Andrew standing at the front door on the first day of his arrival, tall and skinny as a split log, looking lonely and forlorn, as though he

47

had no homeplace; Andrew in the courtroom facing the bully and his guns, with "Shoot!" in his eyes; Andrew dancing at a party, indefatigable as a windmill, and similar in style. Andrew refusing to polish the British officer's boots. Andrew riding on the trail down from Harrodsburg, his whole being glued to both sides of the road. He was a man among men, she knew that, a fearless one and a leader like her father; strong, reliable, teeming with energy and ambition, and at the same time gentle and sympathetic. But as for love . . . How could she love anyone when she had been so badly hurt by love?

She turned her back on Robards.

"Please go now, Lewis."

"You are my wife and I'm going to stay right here until you are ready to return to Harrodsburg. Colonel Hays would never put me out."

To that extent Lewis was right: Colonel Hays refused her entreaties to ask Lewis to leave.

"I can't do that, my dear. He is still a member of our family, and I can't have it said that I refused hospitality."

She saw that she was embarrassing her brother-in-law.

"Forgive me, Robert, you are right. Would you be so kind as to ride me over to Mother's house?"

"No, Rachel, I think that's just as wrong as putting Lewis out. If your mind is fully made up, then in a few days Lewis will become discouraged and leave of his own accord. In the meantime you are perfectly safe here with us."

She spent the next days in the house with Jane, spinning and embroidering, going out in the evening for a breath of cool air under the thick-leafed oak trees.

"I'm uneasy about your berrypicking party tomorrow," she told her sister as they sat before Jane's large dressing table brushing their hair before retiring. Jane had loaned her a muslin nightdress and a bottle-green twill robe. "You and Robert invited Mr. Jackson, remember?"

"I'm sure we can rely on Mr. Jackson," said Jane soothingly, braiding her hair into two thick blond plaits. "And you'll come too," she added doggedly. "You always loved to eat the berries right off the bush, with the hot sun on them."

But in the morning their mother arrived, upright, corseted, in a light yellow cotton dress and ruffled white linen cap. Leven had brought her from church. Rachel remained in the cool log house to tell her what had happened at Harrodsburg.

"It's really the end, then," said Mrs. Donelson with a sigh of finality. "But how are you going to get free of Lewis?"

"I am free of him. In my mind, I mean, and that's the most important place. He can never hurt me again."

"Yes, my dear, but life consists of something more than not being hurt."

48

They heard a clatter of hoofs. Rachel went to the window, pushed aside the printed India chintz curtains which concealed the omnipresent board coverings and saw Robert Hays jump off his horse with unaccustomed haste, toss the reins to a yard boy and storm into the house. Samuel, who had ridden in with him, remained in the yard, mopping his forehead with a big muslin handkerchief.

Colonel Hays was white-faced. "Your way would have been the lesser of two evils, Rachel."

"Then it was Lewis. What has he done?"

"Made some nasty remarks about you . . . and Andrew Jackson, loud enough for the whole party to hear. I've come to the end of my patience. He'll have to be gone from here before dark."

Mrs. Donelson had moved past her daughter and son-in-law, and was gazing out the front door of the house.

"If they don't bury him in the blackberry patch," she interjected with a grim smile. "There goes Andrew to find him; he's just been talking to Samuel."

By nightfall Lewis was gone, leaving the countryside in an uproar. Rachel put the story together from garbled and conflicting reports: a young girl who had been berrypicking related that Andrew Jackson had said to Lewis, "If you ever connect my name with Mrs. Robards in that way again, I will cut the ears out of your head, and I am tempted to do it anyhow!" One of the more excitable boys said that Lewis had ridden to the nearest magistrate, secured a peace warrant against Andrew and had it served by two deputies. Still another version was that Lewis had run into the cane, with Jackson in pursuit.

She did not see Andrew Jackson after the quarrel, but she knew that in any event he would have refused to discuss the matter with her. By now she realized that the whole affair had degenerated into a distasteful farce. But it was blunt, untactful Leven who really upset her. He caught her alone in the yard under the oak tree.

"I have a word for you from your husband. He said, 'You can tell Rachel for me that I shall haunt her.' Can you imagine a man being willing to die just for the pleasure of keeping his wife unhappy?"

That's not what he meant, Rachel said to herself. He meant that I'll never see the end of all this trouble.

15

She lived like a bird on the wing that sharp blustery fall, with no permanent place of abode, visiting back and forth among her sisters and brothers to be with their children, particularly the newborn whom she helped usher into the world and took care of until their mothers came back to full strength. The youngsters awaited her visits eagerly

49

and talked about Aunt Rachel so much that her family took to calling her, as though it had settled her peculiar status: Aunt Rachel. When the children were ill she nursed them, sitting by their bed during the day and night; if they got into trouble or needed a confidante, she performed that service too. If the man of the family had to go away she moved in with sister or sister-in-law to keep her company and offer added protection.

"You're a circuit rider now," teased John Overton one raw mid-November day when he and Jackson had picked her up at her brother John's and were taking her to her mother's, "the same as Andrew and I."

"A circuit-riding aunt," she said with a laugh. Her cheeks were a bright red from the cold, though she was snugly warm in the fur-trimmed bonnet and boots, and the heavy wool dress fastened securely under her chin.

Overton was amused, but Jackson was not.

"I'm sorry, but I don't happen to like that Aunt Rachel title. It has the implication of a middle-aged lady."

They arrived at Mrs. Donelson's stockade at sundown. Jackson was still living at Mansker's, but was invited to stay for supper. They went into the main house, removing their heavy coats, wool caps and mufflers.

"I think it's nonsense that you don't move back here altogether, Mr. Jackson," said Rachel as they stood in front of the fire, rubbing their hands before the flames. "I am not here more than one day a week, if that's what is keeping you out."

"I'm not going to give anybody a chance to do any more talking." His voice was determined.

"We are all still living our lives under the dark shadow of Lewis Robards," she replied a little sadly.

There had been no direct word from Lewis during the fall months, only news that came indirectly as a result of unguarded conversations around Harrodsburg. At first the threats did not disturb her: the talk about his legal rights, that he would come to Nashville and claim her. One day she found Overton alone in his office.

"I know he can't do that, John," she said, "but I'd feel so much better if I were completely free. Isn't there any possibility of a court action or a divorce?"

Overton, who was writing a brief from voluminous notes, moved his papers and iron inkpot to another corner of the desk, began taking down thick volumes and running through the passages he had annotated in anticipation of this inevitable question.

"Practically none, Rachel. Our law here derives from the English law, and even in London a man has to get an act through Parliament before he can have what's known as a legal separation. Each state makes its own laws about divorce; if you and Lewis had been married in Pennsylvania, he might conceivably have secured a divorce. New York does not allow court action for a divorce, and in Virginia the legislature has to grant each divorce separately. To the best of my knowledge it is impossible for a woman to secure a divorce in this country. In fact, it's almost impossible for her to get into a law court at all, except as a spectator."

"Then there's nowhere I can go, nothing I can do, to make sure Lewis will have no right to disturb me again?"

Overton rose, put a chopped log into the small fireplace and watched the flames catch the peeling bark.

"Well, there is one possible way: you might be able to secure a separation down in the Spanish territory, say at New Orleans or Natchez. But that would never be considered legal up here; if you should ever marry again you would be considered guilty of bigamy. And if you had children . . ."

The hope drained out of her face. "I see."

"However, if you were to remain in the Spanish territory, and remarried down there, any second marriage might be considered legal."

Shortly before Thanksgiving a letter reached Rachel informing her that Lewis had apparently convinced a segment of the Harrodsburg folk that the Donelsons were keeping his wife away from him against her will, and that he was organizing a band of his cronies to swoop down on the Cumberland and take her back with him by force.

The news was brought to Rachel on a blustery autumn morning when she was at home with her mother making pies and candies for Thanksgiving. Samuel went over to the guest cottage to summon John and Andrew. Each of the three men read the letter in turn.

"Can he really do this?" she asked of no one in particular.

"He can try."

"What do you mean by that, Mr. Jackson?"

"He can ride in with some armed men and start shooting; unless they took you by surprise and unprotected, they couldn't capture you . . ."

"But there is always the chance?"

"There is always the chance."

"The men around Nashville can shoot just as fast as the ones from Harrodsburg," said Samuel bitterly.

Tears came into her eyes. "I must go away, far away."

"But where would you go, Rachel?" her mother asked.

"It doesn't matter, Mother, just so long as there are thousands of miles between Lewis Robards and me."

"Colonel Stark is leaving for Natchez soon," said Alexander as he entered the room. "I've seen him outfitting his boat. Perhaps he would take Rachel along. She could stay there with Tom or Abner Green's family."

"Yes, you would be welcome there," said Mrs. Donelson with excited relief. "The Green boys have been asking us to come down and see the beautiful estates they've built."

51

"That's a mighty dangerous voyage," commented Jackson; "almost two thousand miles down the Cumberland, the Ohio and the Mississippi rivers, much of it inhabited by hostile Indians."

"It won't be any worse than our trip on the *Adventure*," said Rachel.

"You had ample protection then; your father was a great expedition leader. Colonel Stark is an elderly man. Unless there are experienced Indian fighters along . . ."

She stood with her feet planted firmly, digging her toes into her thin-soled shoes and the floor beneath them, arching upward from her slender hips, her shoulders thrown back, every line of her face and figure stoutly determined.

"I'm going!"

She and Samuel found Colonel Stark at the landing, smoking a smelly ancient pipe, coonskin cap covering his cold ears, supervising the loading of barrels of salt, bales of cotton and hogsheads of whisky onto the boat. It was a twenty-foot-wide, one-hundred-foot-long, broad-bottomed structure, some two thirds of which was covered by a round roof, with carefully carpentered side walls containing cutouts for windows. He stopped in the midst of his labors and knocked the ashes from his pipe. The river was muddy, but a sharp current kept it covered with whitecaps. Two other flatboats were also loading, as part of the flotilla.

"Now, Miss Rachel, you know I'd do anything for you I could. But I simply can't shoulder the responsibility."

"Why not, Colonel Stark? You're taking your wife."

"We have risked our lives before, moving on to new country. But if anything happened to you . . ."

"Colonel, we'll take full responsibility," said Samuel. "Rachel's simply got to get away."

"Tell you what I'll do, Miss Rachel: there's a young fellow in this town who's a real Indian fighter. I was with him when we lifted the siege last year on Robertson's station. He can smell an Indian a hundred miles away with the wind blowing in the wrong direction. I'm referring to Andy Jackson, of course."

There was nothing in the old colonel's voice except admiration for young Jackson.

"But Colonel, that's simply out of the question! I can't ask Mr. Jackson to make this trip."

"Why not?"

"Well, a hundred reasons: he has his law practice, he's an officer of the court. John Overton says that Mr. Jackson is going to appear in fifty cases that are coming up for trial here in Nashville in the next few months."

"He's young, he'll have thousands of law cases."

"No, Colonel, I simply could not ask him. However, I will sell my possessions and hire a couple of good militiamen to come along."

52

"Better ask Andy Jackson, Miss Rachel; he might be awful hurt if you don't give him first chance."

Two days later, having made inquiries about engaging the riflemen to make the trip under Colonel Stark's command, Rachel went back to the dock. She was surprised to have the colonel greet her with a broad smile.

"It's all arranged, Miss Rachel, you can come along, and my wife will be mighty proud to have you."

"Then you've changed your mind . . . ?"

"Gettin' too old to change my mind, Miss Rachel. When you left here I simply went down to the courthouse and put the proposition up to Andy Jackson."

"You didn't!"

"Certainly did. Told him I wouldn't take you unless he came along. He seemed mighty upset. Said he'd need a couple days to mull it over. Wasn't more than an hour ago that he told me he'd come along, and when did we leave?"

She wondered whether there would ever come a time when she would again feel some single and unified emotion over what was happening to her. She was glad that Andrew Jackson was coming along, she was touched by this tribute to their friendship; but what obligations to each other were they undertaking by this move? And what would Nashville say?

Arriving home late in the afternoon, she made straight for the law cabin. John Overton was alone, immersed in a batch of documents. It was a dark, gloomy, dirty-gray day, and he had lighted not only the candles on his desk but the grease lamps on the walls as well.

"John, do you know what Andrew Jackson has done?"

"Yes, he's turned all his cases over to me and he's going down to Natchez with Colonel Stark."

"I came to tell him I couldn't allow it; but from your tone of voice, it would seem that you approve."

"Yes, I must say I do. Andrew paced this cabin for two days and nights with that long chin of his on that bony bosom. I finally asked, 'What the devil is eating you?' He told me that he was the unhappiest of men, that he believed you to be the finest woman he had ever known, and that he had unintentionally been the cause of your troubles for the past two years. He feels that he must get you safely out of Nashville and installed with your friends in Natchez, and then he will have done everything he could and should."

She cried in a hurt tone, "Kindly tell your law partner that he has no further obligation to me! I'm hiring a couple of militiamen. Besides, the family would never approve of his going."

"I think they will."

"What makes you so sure, John?"

53

"Because I think your mother, and Samuel and Jane at least, are now convinced that you and Andrew Jackson belong together."

She dropped onto the log bench reserved for clients and thought back to the time five months before when Lewis Robards had accused her of being in love with Andrew Jackson. It had been untrue then. But now, since she had terminated her relationship with Lewis . . . yes, now it was true. She loved Andrew Jackson. She had known for some time, but the occasion had never arisen for her to face the fact. Did he love her? They had never discussed love or their own personal relationship; her strange position had made this a subject which they both wanted to avoid. But now at least there was no need to conceal it from herself: she loved Andrew Jackson with all her heart.

She looked up at John, wondering how much she could tell him. If Andrew did not share her love, then she must never embarrass him by an expression of it. John's back was to her, as though he wished to afford her the opportunity of thinking in private. Now he turned, sensing that she was ready to continue.

"Have no fears, my dear Rachel," he said softly, "nor any misgivings. Andrew loves you too. He has told me so."

There was a long but gentle silence between them, so unlike the hostile and violent silences she had come to know these past years. She felt hollow and weak at what had been revealed. Unconsciously she pushed back her long black cloak that was trailing the floor, and ran her fingers through the ridges of her dark red corduroy skirt. Her hair suddenly felt too tight on her head, as though imprisoning her thoughts. She untied the dark red ribbon that held the heavy black tresses in place. Instantly she felt released, able to speak.

"Then don't you see, John, that's all the more reason why he must not go along on this trip."

"I would say all the more reason for him to accompany you. Every man has the right to protect the woman he loves."

"You won't tell him of anything that's been said here?"

"No, Rachel, nor would I have told you of his feelings if I had not considered it necessary to your future well-being. This is a secret I think you are going to have to keep from each other for a considerable time. That will make it possible for you to travel on this long journey together as friends, friends who would do nothing to compromise each other's good name or position. It is not in the character of either of you to make Lewis Robards look as though he had been right in his accusations!"

16

The morning of January 20, 1791, was cold and leaden-skied. Samuel took her to the landing with her two heavy portmanteaus strapped on a

54

pack horse, one containing woolen clothes for the journey down-river, the other her light summer linens and lawn dresses. She picked up her skirts as she walked along the muddy bank, then across a plank and onto the boxlike boat which had been built of green timber sawed from the forests immediately behind the river and put together with wooden pins. She stood irresolutely for a moment until Andrew, stooping low, came through the door of the cabin. It was the first time she had seen him in the heavy buckskin shirt and breeches since their trip home from Harrodsburg the summer before. He greeted her with a pleasant but casual smile, assured Samuel that he would watch over her and then, when she kissed her brother good-by, picked up her two cases and led her toward the prow.

She stepped over the sill and found herself in the front portion of the cabin where Mrs. Stark, in a huge leather apron over her cotton dress, was directing her serving couple in the preparation of the noonday dinner. She turned toward Rachel with an open-armed gesture; she was a big shapeless bustling woman who moved about with astonishing speed in a pair of floppy buffalo moccasins; her greatest need, as Rachel was to learn over the ensuing weeks, was for talk.

"Well, now, welcome, Rachel. The colonel has dragged me up and down rivers and trails so much of our lives that whenever I land anyplace, even a flatboat, I hang up my pots and curtains and make believe it's a permanent home."

She took Rachel by the arm, leading her through the middle compartment of the flatboat in which were stored the bales of cotton, barrels of salt and smoked venison, buffalo and pork, which had to be protected from the weather, into the rear third of the cabin, which constituted the sleeping quarters. There were two bunks fastened to the log wall with leather hinges. A thick curtain of buffalo hide was pegged to the rafters; it fell heavily over the doorway.

"You and I will live here, child; it will give us good privacy."

It was still early in the morning when they shoved off the Nashville landing into fog and heavy rain, the two other flatboats following. Rachel remained in her little compartment; out the square hull window she could see that a group had assembled to say good-by to the Starks. She had made no attempt to conceal her own departure for Natchez; that would have been just as impossible as it would have been to conceal the reason for her flight.

The rain and cold continued for a full week. Rachel rarely left her quarters, reading, sewing, helping Mrs. Stark make a pair of intricate bedcovers. In addition to the Starks and Andrew there were five traders on board, spelling each other at the sweeps which kept the boat away from the banks and from collision with boulders. Colonel Stark did most of the steering himself, clinging hour after hour to a board fastened to a long pole.

55

The meals were simple, roast saddle of venison or buffalo, corn bread, stews and preserved dried fruits, strong draughts of whisky for the men when they came in after the long hours in the cold. They ate in two shifts, Rachel sitting with Mrs. Stark, the colonel and one or two of the traders, Andrew relieving Colonel Stark at the steering rudder. There wasn't much talk; the dark skies and penetrating cold dissipated any will toward conviviality.

During the first week they tied up at various settlements and at Fort Massac, bringing the settlers much-needed salt, coffee and sugar from Pittsburgh, taking in exchange packets of furs which would be sold down-river. The Starks and the traders from the three boats went ashore to deliver letters and exchange news with the people in the forts. Rachel and Andrew sat at the scrubbed plank table in front of the blazing log fire, his red hair plastered down from the many hours under a heavy wool cap. He spent his leisure studying his briefs and the lawbooks which John Overton had loaned him. The Andrew Jackson she had known, the man with the teeming energy and radiating inner force, the sparkling eyes and the deeply emotional nature, had remained in Nashville; the uncommunicative young man sitting opposite her needed but a pair of silver-rimmed spectacles to be John Overton. These periods of quiet, almost of solitude, were their only moments alone together.

It took them ten days to navigate the Cumberland and Ohio rivers. On the eleventh morning she awakened to find that their tiny flotilla was already several miles along the Mississippi, with the sun shining brightly overhead. As the days passed and they drifted swiftly down the swollen river the weather grew warmer and once again, just as she had from the decks of the *Adventure,* she saw spring grass and flowering shrubs on the banks to tell them that they were moving southward into a radiant spring. The next day at noon, when Colonel Stark came in for his dinner, Rachel went out to the stern of the boat and stood beside Andrew. He had donned a clean doeskin shirt which was open at the throat, letting the sun beat on his lean face and neck. She had packed her heavy winter woolens and was wearing a yellow linen dress, light enough for the warm days ahead, yet sturdy and suitable for life aboard the flatboat. The wind blew her hair and rippled through the open-work collar.

"I feel as though I'd been dead," she murmured, "and have suddenly been reborn."

His fingers gripped the steering pole as he moved the craft to avoid a floating log. She watched the muscles in his arms and shoulders work smoothly under the soft shirt: he was not a powerfully built man, not even a strong man, for there was little flesh on his frame.

"Not dead," he answered. "Just dormant, like those sycamores that have been standing bare and now are beginning to leaf."

Straight ahead it seemed as though the river were coming to an abrupt

56

end, but it was only making a sharp turn. After a moment he spoke to her again.

"I think you'll like the South, Rachel; the air is warm and fragrant, the land is fertile, the whole countryside seems friendly and soft. Natchez isn't very big yet, only about twenty or thirty houses, but quite a few Americans have built plantations up and down the river. The forests are tremendously deep: cottonwood, willow, giant oaks. The sky over the river at sunset is crimson, or indigo; there are herons and pelicans and forests full of deer."

They had been attacked twice by Indians, once from a high bluff when they had steered too close to the bank and another time from an island thicket which had looked innocent enough as they approached. There were a number of bullet holes in the superstructure, but only one man had been injured, slightly, by an already spent bullet.

Then late one February afternoon they became separated from the other two boats and were obliged to tie up to an abandoned landing at the foot of a dense forest. Andrew pointed out to Colonel Stark how close the cypress trees came down to the shore, how the bank made a lagoon so that the Indians could surround them on three sides and subject them to a murderous crossfire. However, the colonel was unwilling to risk the river currents in the impenetrable darkness. Andrew took the youngest of the traders onshore with him. Colonel Stark tried to dissuade them from going.

"I want every man to remain on board so we have our fullest fighting strength."

"You've got to have advance warning, Colonel, and the only way you can get it is for us to go ashore."

He cleaned his rifle, filled his shot pouch, picked a flint, summoned his companion, who had been molding bullets, and the two men slipped noiselessly onto the old timbers of the landing, leaving orders for one of the traders to remain awake with an ax in hand, ready to cut the tie rope at the first sound of a shot. Rachel followed him to the edge of the railing.

"But how will you get back on board if we cut this rope?" she asked. "The current will sweep us out into the river."

"Don't worry about us," he murmured. "Just stay under cover."

She watched him until he had disappeared into the darkness, then went to her cabin, pulled the bunk from the wall and lay down fully clothed. After a time Mrs. Stark came in, undressed, pushed her own bunk down on its supporting legs, methodically folding the bedspread. She then got under the covers and began to talk, quietly and pleasantly, of other trips, other alarms. Rachel listened with only one ear, for the other was listening for sounds on the outside; even so she could hear everything Mrs. Stark said, could even answer, and tell stories of her

57

own. An alligator lying along the bank was putting up a tremendous howling and bellowing.

Suddenly in the middle of one of her own sentences Mrs. Stark fell fast asleep. Rachel rose quietly and went out on deck to find the sky black, with no vestige of a moon. The guard was asleep. She stood peering into the darkness. The night was now still except for the call of some swamp birds. Then she saw the flash of a gun on the beach, followed by a burst of fire. The sleeping traders on the deck were awake at once. The guard grabbed the ax, but Rachel was waiting and seized his arm.

"Don't touch that rope."

"But Jackson gave orders . . ."

"I don't care what orders he gave. Here, give me that ax. I'll cut this rope the instant those two men are on board, and not before."

He stared at her, hearing the ring in her voice, shrugged, handed her the ax and picked up his rifle. Two more shots were fired, then she saw Andrew and his companion move swiftly up the plank and drop onto the deck. She brought the ax down sharply. The flatboat edged out into the river.

She and Andrew stood at the prow watching the currents, with Colonel Stark steering as best he could. She heard Andrew chuckling to himself.

"Tell me the joke," she said, "I should like to laugh."

Without turning his head, he replied, "So you refused to let them cut that tie line, eh? Don't you know you could have been massacred?"

"I like to graze danger," she said, mimicking his tone. "I might ask the same question of you."

"Fighting Indians is a bigger part of the circuit rider's job than trying law cases."

"Even so, how could we have left you on the beach and pulled away to safety?"

"From the evidence before this court, I would say you couldn't."

He put his arm about her in a slow encircling movement, holding her with his long sinewy fingers, crushing her shoulder against his in a momentary grip of avowal. Then, almost before she knew it had happened, he moved away.

17

Thomas Marston Green's home, Springfield, was the most luxurious Rachel had ever seen, bringing to mind the stories her father had told her about George Washington's Mount Vernon. It was a sturdy structure of red brick with six majestic pillars across the front, each standing on a solid rectangular base, deep shade galleries hung with vines to insure coolness, a lacelike wooden balustrade protecting the second-floor porch;

58

long narrow windows and tall green shutters, everything else painted a soft white. The social rooms were high-ceilinged, with carved cornices, hand-trimmed mantels, glistening crystal chandeliers, a side-lighted central doorway and an elegant foyer paneled in wood. The house had been built high above the murky swamps, was wind-swept, and stood framed at the end of a row of magnificent oaks.

The Greens quickly assembled all the Americans in the neighborhood for a welcoming dinner party. When Rachel saw the turquoise gown and the satin slippers which young Tom Green's wife was planning to wear, she knew there was nothing in her portmanteau that would stand comparison. Mrs. Green loaned her a lace-trimmed pale blue satin with a delicate lace cap; it required only a moderate amount of alteration to make it fit quite well. When she walked into the dining room on old Colonel Thomas Green's arm she found a hundred candles in the chandelier throwing a glow of light on the silver, crystal goblets and polished wood.

"You've transplanted the very best of Virginia down here in the South," she exclaimed breathlessly.

The old colonel was pleased; he turned to Andrew, who was just behind them, his black Nashville suit set off by a fine linen shirt with a lace jabot and lace cuffs which made him feel almost as elegant as the handsomely attired men about him.

"Every man carries his home with him no matter how far he travels. Isn't that true, Jackson? Of course we have a few things extra down here: mosquitoes, alligators, swamps, heat, but we take the bad with the good."

Colonel Thomas Green had been a friend of her father's in Virginia. He was a heavy-set man of about seventy with a magnificent splurge of white hair topping a leathery tan face. The unquestioned leader of the American colony in Louisiana, he had suffered greatly in his efforts to split off this region from Spanish ownership, set up a new county called Bourbon and attach it to the state of Georgia. The Georgia legislature had authorized Green's acts, but the coup had failed and Thomas Green had been thrown into prison in New Orleans. His wife had died of shock and grief. The Spaniards had pardoned him after this tragedy but he had been obliged to transfer all of his property to his young sons, not only this plantation at Springfield but also the Villa Gayoso, some eight miles south on Cole's Creek which he had previously bought from the Spanish governor of Natchez and where Abner, the second of his two sons, now lived.

"Too bad your father didn't live to see Springfield, Rachel," said the old colonel, "he would have moved down here and built a house just like it."

Rachel knew that her father had loved the Cumberland deeply, and that nothing could have persuaded him to move again; but she did not think it necessary to tell Colonel Green this. His son Tom at the head of the long mahogany table said:

"Since we can't have Colonel Donelson, perhaps we can have his daughter. How about it, Rachel?"

Tom Green's young wife nodded her agreement. "We feel as though we have scored a victory every time another American family joins us."

The elder Green lifted a goblet of Spanish madeira as he turned to Andrew, who had been handling a number of involved cases in Nashville for all three members of the Green family. The servants were bringing in bottles of light wine from the cool cellar and silver bowls of oranges, bananas, melons and grapes.

"You're staying this time, aren't you, Jackson? That's a fine piece of land you have over at Bayou Pierre, and you can have just as much more of it as you are willing to pay the survey costs on. We'd like to have you with us when we start our next revolt against the Spaniards."

The men plunged into a discussion of the comparative onerousness of being ruled by the Spanish or English. The Greens hated the Spanish as much as Andrew did the English, and so the race ended in a dead heat: how many years was it going to take to persuade the government at Philadelphia that Louisiana was a natural and contiguous part of the mainland? that the United States would have to acquire it in order to assure free navigation on the Mississippi, and to keep open the now-Spanish ports of Natchez and New Orleans? that it wouldn't require more than a few hundred men with rifles to chase the Spanish out forever? Surely Spain was farther away than England, and had even less business here on this American continent?

Rachel was disturbed by the suggestion of the Greens that she and Andrew remain in Natchez and establish another American family. Just how much were they assuming? They had asked no questions, in fact had treated them as guests who had arrived simultaneously but from opposite directions. Yet love was difficult to conceal; put a man and a woman who loved each other into even as spacious a room as this, and as large an assemblage; place them at opposite ends of the table, and still everyone would be sure to know.

She saw little of Andrew, for he spent a number of days in Natchez, some thirty miles down-river from Springfield, where he was discussing the settlement of cases with the clients he had acquired a year and a half before, and taking on new claims for men who had left land or other business assets behind them when they had come down the Mississippi. After that one fleeting moment at the prow of the boat in the seclusion of the dark Mississippi night there had been no intimate word or gesture between them.

Then early on a bright, fragrant Sunday morning they rode the two miles to Bayou Pierre to see Andrew's tract of land on the bluff overlooking the river. Rachel dressed in sheer pink lawn over her several billowing pink petticoats, with a wide velvet ribbon at the waist and a matching ribbon on her wide-brimmed bonnet. Looking into the mirror of her dressing table, she decided that she was beginning to look well again. Poor Andrew, he would have to carry all his life that scar on his forehead from the officer's saber; how fortunate that one's inner scars could not be seen every time one looked into a mirror; for, not being seen, they could be forgotten, and perhaps vanish completely.

They made their way to the small log cabin that Andrew had built and saw the outlines of the racecourse he had staked out. They stood before the door of the little house looking over the wide, slow-moving waters and the vast forest of cypress and oaks rolling horizonward to merge with the pastel sky. It was a beautiful spot, almost too beautiful; it gave her a poignant feeling of nostalgia.

"You will have to be going back soon, won't you, Andrew?"

"Yes. The spring court in Nashville opens on April twelfth."

"How long will it take you to go up the Chickasaw Trace?"

"A year and a half ago, about twenty days. There's a group of boatmen starting back at midweek. I'll travel with them. I'll carry a supply of imported silks and satins, some spices and Spanish segars."

His voice fell off; he stood gazing over the river for a moment. There was no breeze and the sun glared hotly on the water; in the distance wild birds were calling. When he turned his eyes were unguarded and full of his love for her. He untied the strings of her bonnet, took it off her head and ran his fingers through her hair.

"Rachel, I don't have to go back at all. We can stay right here together, the two of us."

"But how, Andrew?"

"I've been asking in Natchez: you could get an annulment there from the Spanish authorities. It would be legal."

"Not really legal, just a way around the law is what John called it. You took your oath to the United States government when they installed you as attorney general of the territory; I can't let you go back on your word. And you have the biggest law practice there, even John says so."

"I couldn't be a lawyer, perhaps. I couldn't hold public office, and I'd have to become a Spanish subject, but I can do just as well down here." There was a tiny edge to his voice. "Look about you. Isn't it proof I had this whole Bayou Pierre plantation staked out?" He rushed on, not wanting to give her a chance to answer. "The main house was to be over on the edge of the bluff; straight across I was going to build stables. The land is good for cotton, tobacco, indigo. There's money to be made, tremendous sums of money. One day we'd have a plantation as lovely as Springfield."

She slipped into his embrace, held herself against him.

"Yes, you can do all that. You can do it anywhere, Nashville, Natchez, or the moon; but my dear, how could you ever be happy as a subject of

Spain? You'd have no voice here, and no vote. You're an independent man . . ."

"It wouldn't be for long; this country will be American. I wouldn't mind helping the Greens bring it into the Union. I could go back to Nashville, take care of my cases, sell my lands and load everything movable on a flatboat."

"No, Andrew, I can't take the responsibility. If you ever became unhappy down here, or if somehow we failed . . . one morning you might wake up to find you had wasted your life in Louisiana. Oh, you'd never reproach me, you'd do your best to keep your feelings hidden even from yourself; but I can't put this burden on our marriage. Our love is right and good; our marriage must be right and good too, from the first instant."

His eyes, ordinarily so clear and penetrating, were confused and hurt. She drew back.

"But what are we going to do?" he cried, as though the volume of his voice could knock down the walls which enclosed them. "We are caught. We are helpless. Robards holds all the weapons."

"No, Andrew, that isn't true. He stands empty-handed. We have the only weapon that counts: love."

"Rachel dear, I am not a fickle man, I have never loved before, and I'll not love again. Only you. Always you."

"Thank you, my darling."

He put his arms about her and kissed her full on the mouth.

"We would have to believe in miracles," he murmured.

She cupped his face in her hands, kissing him on one cheek and then the other.

"I do believe in miracles, Andrew. The fact that we have found each other, that we are standing here together, that you have your arms about me, that I can kiss you, so, all this is proof that miracles can happen."

18

After six weeks with the colonel and the Tom Greens she was invited to visit down-river at Villa Gayoso, surrounded by huge oaks which dripped gray moss. Mrs. Abner Green was a woman of thirty, soft-spoken, but an exacting mistress of her household; it was the better part of her kindness which soon made Rachel see that she was not to live here as a guest, but rather as a part of the family, with her own daily chores, participating in the spinning and weaving, training the servants in the making of colored candles and scented soap for which her mother had given her a recipe.

There was no word from Andrew, nor from any of the Donelsons; southward movement over the Natchez Trace was practically unknown,

62

and with the coming of summer the boat traffic on the Mississippi ceased. The weeks passed and she felt her strength and sense of well-being, of joy in life, return in full measure. The tinkling of the fountain, the enclosed patio so deeply shaded by vines of wild grapes, the twittering of small birds, the heavy scent of the magnolias, the deep colorings of the surrounding country, these were the only pleasures she needed. And as the slow, lazy, hot days of summer drifted by her eyes became bright and luminous, her step became buoyant.

"My dear, you are lovely," commented Mrs. Green as they sat on the broad gallery beneath deep roofs where Rachel sang softly and played the harpsichord.

Whatever she had suffered from Lewis Robards and her disillusionment, from the harassment of the past years, had been expunged by these months of tranquil living, a tranquillity which took so strong a hold that she felt she could wait out the rest of her life here.

Two months later she was sitting at the window of her bedroom having a tumbler of milk from the springs in which the dairy products were kept cool all summer, and watching a rust-colored sunset. She heard hoofbeats coming up the main road. Horsemen came and went all day, and she'd heard perhaps half a dozen in the past hour, but there was only one horseman who rode like this, who changed the rhythm of the horse to fit his own, so that no matter what its peculiar gait or tempo it must move precisely as Andrew Jackson moved through space: headlong, almost cyclonic, and always knowing its destination.

She picked up the skirts of her crisp white cotton dress and ran down the winding staircase. There stood Andrew in the doorway, hot, disheveled, in wrinkled buckskins, his boots white with dust, and wearing a three weeks' beard. As she went forward to greet him she saw that something crucial had happened, something that would change their lives. She led him toward the dark oak-paneled library, with its tall narrow windows open to the pungent fragrance of the tropical garden, resolved not to think or feel or even to fear until he had told her the purpose of his visit. He closed the door securely behind him.

They met in the center of the room. She felt his lips, dry and cracked from the long days on the trail, bruising her own. He held her securely for several moments, then blurted out:

"There's news . . ."

"About . . . Lewis."

"Yes. He has divorced you."

She gasped, felt a sharp pain in her chest.

"Divorced me? But how?"

"The Virginia legislature. He persuaded his brother-in-law, Jack Jouitt, to introduce a bill. The legislature passed it."

Her eyes widened, and a question began to formulate itself on her lips. He spoke quickly.

63

"You're free now, my dear. We can be married as soon as you are ready."

She had not been diverted.

"The Virginia legislature gave him a divorce? But on what grounds?"

". . . well . . . desertion."

She gazed at him, unable to get breath into her lungs.

"And what else, Andrew? The Virginia laws don't allow divorce merely for desertion."

"That's what the bill says."

How badly he lies, she thought. Aloud, she said, "Tell me the rest. I must know."

". . . *adultery*."

She felt as though she had been struck across the face. She tasted blood on her lips, not knowing she had bitten through the skin. The only voice she could muster was so faint that she imagined she was saying the words inside her own head.

"Adultery! But . . . with whom . . . ?"

He enveloped her in his long arms and held her rigidly as though fearing she might fall.

"With me."

". . . you . . . but when . . . ?"

"When we . . . 'eloped' . . . the bill calls it. From the Robards home."

"Eloped? But the family sent you. Lewis knows that. When he came to my sister Jane's and tried to persuade me to go back home with him, he said there had been nothing wrong in your coming for me. He never would have come for me if he had believed for a single instant . . ."

She burst into tears, hot scalding tears, while he stroked her hair and kissed her temples and spoke soft words to comfort her. After a time she looked up, her eyes wet, the tears still on her cheeks.

"I had expected he would try to kill me. This is worse."

"Only in the sense that still another injustice has been done. But let's look at it from our point of view: he could have kept us from each other for years; we might never have been able to marry or to have each other's love. Don't you see, dearest, this is the end of our troubles. A bitter end, I grant you that, but it means that we can have our life together. We can have a home and children and never be separated again."

There was a constriction about her heart which she thought must burst it.

"How could Jack Jouitt do a thing like that to me? He was my friend. He fought for me when Lewis was making trouble over Peyton Short. He believed in me during all those early years, had faith in me, but if now he is convinced . . ."

"I don't believe Jack has lost any faith in you. Perhaps he introduced

64

the bill because he knows this is the only way you can ever get your freedom. It could have been an act of kindness . . ."

"To label me an adulteress!"

He dropped his eyes, unable to face her blazing indignation.

"Do they know what they have convicted me of? Does the charge of adultery mean the same to a man as it does to a woman? It can't, or they wouldn't have sat so calmly in their seats and voted . . . without even giving me a chance to appear and defend myself, voted me guilty of the vulgarest of all sins! By what majority did they decide that I am a liar, a cheat, a fraud . . . ?"

He put his hand lightly over her lips.

"What they have accused you of, they have accused me of. We are together in this . . . as we will always be in everything that happens to us."

Her anger was spent now; she sat limply on a chair, her head lowered, unable to face him, seeing only the waxed and polished stone floor. After a moment she whispered:

"Half of those men have known me since I was a child. Father sat with them in the House of Burgesses; they've been guests in our home, watched me grow up. They know that the Donelsons have never been . . . low . . . And John Overton, what does he think of this?"

"When I first heard that the legislature had granted Robards that divorce I wanted to go out and shoot him. I would have too, except that John stopped me. He said, 'Let's look at these facts calmly, as lawyers should. The divorce on these terms is Robards' final act of indignity. Nevertheless it opens the heavily barred door to your future. Now you and Rachel can be married. We would all wish it to be under different circumstances; but these are the circumstances Providence has seen fit to impose. Forget the bad part of it and think only that you and Rachel can begin your lives together.'"

She sighed deeply. "John is right; he's always right." She hesitated for a moment. "How did you learn all this?"

"Your family heard about it first. Probably half a dozen men brought in word from Richmond."

"Was it published in a paper?"

"No, I think not. It reached the Cumberland the way most news does, by word of mouth."

"Then everybody . . . knows . . . in Nashville . . . ?"

It was his turn to be angry now; the harshness in his voice brought her head up abruptly.

"Everyone knows that Robards has secured his divorce. But there's not a soul in the Cumberland Valley who could believe you guilty of anything more than having married an insanely jealous man. Everyone also knows that I came down here for our wedding. We are going to have a fine home and a fine life together, Rachel, and that will be the last we

65

will ever hear of this wretched affair. None of our friends or neighbors can believe us guilty of duplicity. And if any enemy should ever raise his voice to accuse us, or to injure your name, I shall know how to deal with him."

She rose and walked to the window. She stared out into the darkness of the garden, hearing the water of the fountain and the croaking of frogs in the still evening air. Andrew walked to the candelabrum above the fireplace and lighted a single candle.

"Our marriage will give them more food for talk," murmured Rachel. "It will look as though Lewis was right after all, and that the Virginia legislature was justified in giving him his divorce."

She leaned her hot cheek against the dark oak panel of the window frame. She did not hear him come near, but suddenly she was whirled about and shaken rudely by the shoulders.

"All this has nothing to do with us! We can't let that kind of thinking keep us from our love." He released his grip on her shoulders and stood quietly, his face pale. "You do love me?"

She saw now that he was suffering as greatly as she. In her compassion she lifted her face to his, kissed him.

"Yes, Andrew. I will always love you."

"Then that is all we need. We can live at peace with ourselves. Our love will be a fortress that no amount of hostility or cruelty from the outside can ever penetrate."

"Yes, my darling, you are right."

"We will honeymoon here in my cabin at Bayou Pierre. It is so beautiful, overlooking the river. Tom Green will provide anything we need, and we can be utterly alone, perhaps more alone than we will ever be again in our lives."

"Give me a few days. I want to have a wedding gown made, so that you will be proud of me, and think me beautiful."

They stood together, silent in the dark room, holding tightly to each other.

This we will always have, she thought: our love. It will brighten our lives and sustain us through hardships. But Andrew, my dearest, you are wrong when you say this is the end of our troubles.

66

Book TWO

THEY SPENT a languorous two months in the stillness of Bayou Pierre, where the gray moss dripped from the huge live oaks and the air was heavily perfumed. Then they set out on the thousand-mile trip up the dangerous Natchez Trace, reaching Nashville on the first of October.

On the morning after their arrival at the Donelsons' Andrew rode into town with John Overton to rent for their law office a newly erected cabin immediately across from the courthouse. Andrew kissed her goodby with special tenderness.

"This will be the first time we've been separated in three months." He turned to Overton, who was waiting for him, grinning impishly. "John, we're looking for a homesite. Got a likely piece you'd care to sell us?"

"You can have any parcel I own as a wedding present, but those six-forties of ours are out in the wilderness with tepees sitting all over them."

By midmorning the five Donelson women had foregathered in the big room around cups of coffee.

"Thank goodness the last of my daughters is securely married," commented Mrs. Donelson with so much relief in her voice that her daughters laughed.

"There are times when I think it was you who arranged for Mr. Jackson to rescue me from Harrodsburg," replied Rachel, blushing. "And I wouldn't be at all surprised if it was you who first gave Colonel Stark the idea of insisting that Mr. Jackson make the trip to Natchez."

"I'm neither admitting nor denying," replied her mother; "I say all's well that ends well."

Mary, the plump, romantic sister, said, "Tell us about the wedding and your honeymoon, Rachel. Is it beautiful down there in Louisiana?"

Rachel sat quietly for a moment, her hands clasped in the lap of the deep blue Spanish silk robe which Andrew had bought her in Natchez. Her eyes were glowing.

"The ceremony was held in Tom Green's drawing room under a heavy

67

cut-glass chandelier, with a hundred lighted candles. I can remember looking up several times and praying, 'Dear God, don't let that chandelier fall, I'm just about to begin to be happy.'"

"There was nothing to worry about," commented Jane matter-of-factly; "Andrew would have caught it before it hit you."

Rachel nodded her head.

"You're right, Jane, I should have waited all these years for Andrew Jackson, just as you did for Robert Hays."

"That's foolish backwards talk," observed Mrs. Donelson tartly. "You should thank Almighty God, instead of indulging in regrets."

"Now you three stop arguing," cried Mary, "I want to know about the wedding party, and what Bayou Pierre is like."

"Like heaven; the air is so soft you feel you can reach out and take a handful, as though it were silk, and sew yourself a gown. We danced cotillions for hours, then Andrew and I slipped away and rode over to Bayou Pierre. There was a full moon, and the Mississippi was so light you could see every drop of water separately. The nights are just as soft and warm as the day . . ."

"It must be a wonderful place to be in love," interrupted Mary dreamily.

"Any place is a good place to be in love," snapped Catherine; she had spent thirty years being embarrassed by her older sister's unabashed romanticism.

"You're right, Cathy, love is a place," replied Rachel. "It has its own foliage and trails and houses, even its own sun and moon and stars. Nashville looked just as beautiful to me yesterday as Natchez did; the air was as fragrant and the sun as warm."

"I hear you had some trouble coming up the Trace," said Jane, whose station in Haysboro was a clearinghouse for frontier news. "Indians, or those bands of no-good whites?"

"Neither, really. Andrew has a trouble-repellent manner: he peers so hard at the woods and the trail that he sends out a signal which says, 'Better keep away, we're prepared for you.' The only quarrel was with Hugh McGary."

"I'm sorry to hear that," said Mrs. Donelson. "Remember that first day we saw Andrew in court, Rachel; he persuaded Hugh to settle peaceably with Casper Mansker."

"Andrew says that Hugh has never forgiven him for that; it's the only time he's ever recommended compromise rather than fight, and look what it got him."

"Stop going down side paths," chided Jane, "and tell us precisely what did happen."

"Well, when we were about to cross the Tennessee River, Andrew and Hugh decided the Indians were going to attack that night. Hugh picked a camp spot, reasoning it would be better to entrench ourselves

68

and greet the first Indian shots with a good round volley. Andrew said he wasn't going to get shot at like a sitting goose; he wanted to push ahead in the dark. Hugh claimed that only made us better targets; Andrew insisted the Indians never attacked a party going at top speed. The men voted to move out under cover of dark and leave the fires burning behind them as a decoy. We traveled all night and there was no attack. That proved Andrew right, but of course Hugh might have been able to beat them off with one volley . . . or they might never have attacked at all. Anyway, from that moment on the men looked to Andrew for their orders. Hugh resented it. He didn't exchange a single word with either of us for the last two weeks of the trip; when we parted in Nashville he walked away without saying good-by."

"Andrew knew the McGarys back in the Waxhaws, didn't he?" asked Mrs. Donelson.

"Yes, they are related: Hugh's brother Martin married Andrew's cousin. I did what I could to prevent the quarrel, even suggested that possibly Hugh was right. Andrew said, 'Possibly he is, but I'm not taking the one chance in a thousand that a British bullet in one of those guns should hit you.'"

"The McGarys are an unforgiving lot," said Mrs. Donelson.

"My husband can take care of himself," replied Rachel. It was the first time she had said *my husband* of Andrew Jackson. And here in the Donelson big room with her sisters around her, the words sounded good.

They had been back in Nashville only a few days when Andrew greeted her in a fever of excitement.

"Rachel, what do you suppose has happened?"

"You've been appointed governor of the territory!"

"Even better. I've been elected a trustee of Davidson Academy."

She kissed him soundly.

"Congratulations, my darling." And even while she held her lips to his, a number of tensions suddenly relaxed. She had not known that she was worrying about the kind of reception their marriage would receive in Nashville; for hers had been the first divorce in the Cumberland Valley. She had been accused before the Virginia legislature of eloping with Andrew Jackson. All Nashville knew this. By their marriage they had apparently proven the action of the legislature to have been right. She would not have been surprised if some of the families had resented this. Several nights on the Natchez Trace she had lain awake wondering whether Andrew's swift flight to Natchez and their immediate marriage might not be held against them.

Now they had no sooner returned than General James Robertson, her father's partner in the founding of Nashville, the Reverend Thomas B. Craighead, head of the Davidson Academy and the only clergyman in the community, Lardner Clark, who owned the supply store, General Daniel Smith, Revolutionary War hero and second-in-command under

Governor Blount of the territory, Anthony Bledsoe, brother of Isaac Bledsoe, who with Casper Mansker had first explored the Cumberland Valley in 1771 . . . these most important men in the territory had by their gesture pushed aside potential criticism, and made it known that Andrew was one of theirs.

She had imagined that her husband's pleasure derived from the same source as her own. To her astonishment his exultation was on an entirely different level.

"Forgive me if I gloat, my dear, but that's just the last position I would have imagined I would ever be elected to. One of the heads of the academy! Do you know how much formal schooling I've had? A month or two at Queen's Museum at Charlotte. Oh, I went for a few years to an old-field school in the Waxhaws, it was just a one-room place, built among the stumps of a field that had been worked over and abandoned. Even taught readin' and writin' in one of them for a short spell when I was sixteen. All I've learned I've had to hew out of the few books I stumbled across. But that Davidson Academy, I'm going to pitch in and help make it one of the best schools this side of the Blue Ridge Mountains. Then our youngsters will be able to get themselves a real education."

"Amen," said Rachel under her breath.

The following Sunday they visited her brother Johnny to see the new daughter, and Rachel's namesake, who had been born while Rachel was in Natchez. Johnny was thirty-six, with Jane's green eyes, fluffy blond hair and slender face. He had married Mary Purnell when she was sixteen years old, taking her on the *Adventure* trip as a honeymoon. Their first child had been born in the open camp of Clover Bottom in 1780, but had not survived the difficulties of that first rude settlement. Little Rachel, now four months old, had three brothers and a sister, all healthy and vigorous.

Johnny owned some three hundred and thirty acres of Jones Bend, a snug and fertile peninsula bounded on three sides by the slow-moving green Cumberland and across the river from the Widow Donelson's station. The constant danger and death of the *Adventure* trip had had opposite effects on Johnny and Mary: of Johnny it had made a wanderer, a man who enjoyed staking out a new claim, clearing it, building a home, birthing a child and then moving on to the next six-forty. Mary detested not only change but movement itself. On the death of her first-born she had promised God that if He would give her children who would stay alive she would never cease thanking Him. Over the household hung a fervent religious spirit, for whenever Mary could spare a few minutes from her family duties she went into the lean-to sanctuary Johnny had built for her, fell on her knees and fulfilled her promise to God.

Dinner was ample, both with victuals and noise, for the four older

70

children were propped up at the puncheon table. Johnny caught a quizzical expression on Andrew's face.

"They're forever talking and scratching and bawling, Andrew, but wait till you have five of your own, it'll sound like a heavenly chorus."

"I'll take twice as many as your five," replied Andrew, "and a hundred times the bawling."

After dinner Rachel, Andrew and Johnny walked down to the river. The woods were a blaze of glorious October colors: reds, russets and purples, light greens fading into dark greens. As they walked over the fields they tried to count the different kinds of trees and shrubs: beech, maple, hickory, ash, hackberry, mulberry, walnut, sweet gum, haw, poplar, redbud, dogwood, sycamore.

"You're going to have a fine plantation here in a couple of years, Johnny."

"No, I'm not, Andrew."

Rachel stopped in her tracks, holding back on her brother's arm.

"Johnny, surely you're not going to . . ."

"Yes, I am. I'm posting notice that it's for sale."

"Isn't the soil good?" asked Andrew.

"Nothing wrong with the place; it's me. I want to move on. I know a place about three miles from here, bigger. It can be more prosperous. No reason why a man shouldn't rise in the world."

"Now, Johnny, don't try to pull the woolsey over my eyes," said Rachel. "You don't care at all about moving upward, you just want to move sideways."

Johnny grinned. They walked in silence until they came to the river, then half slid down the trail. The river was not wide here, in the horseshoe bend, but it was deep, of a superb jade green. Andrew was the first to speak.

"How much are you asking for the place?"

"One hundred pounds. Know somebody who might be interested?"

"Might. However, I'm not helping put Mary on the move. The minute you get an offer, let me know about it. I'll see if my client won't better the price."

"You know what I like about this place, Andrew?" murmured Rachel as they walked across the path to their horses.

"What?"

"It's almost an island, surrounded on three sides by the river. If someone wanted to build a good stout fence across the back . . ."

She saw by his expression that he knew what she meant. He reached out encircling arms.

"It could be our first home," he said softly. His eyes roamed the acreage. "You don't think it's too isolated, Rachel? I have to be away so much, circuit riding to Jonesboro and Sumner County. The Creeks are still harassing these isolated spots."

"Surely you wouldn't counsel Andrew Jackson's wife to run away from a few Indians?"

2

Love was not only a place, but a time. She had no need for the kind of calendar that Andrew kept in his office in Nashville. Every waking moment was intensified, every look, every thought, every feeling was stamped sharply upon her mind; and yet filled as the days were, they sped by so fast that it was impossible to retain them.

Yes, and love was a climate too. It was deep into winter now, there was snow on the ground, the trees were bare, the overcast skies the color of the copper pots that the new smithy was fashioning at the end of the public square. Yet in her happiness she did not know that it was winter: the snow was warm, the heavy skies were brilliant, the raw wind was gentle and invigorating. True, there was a tornado, but that tornado was her husband. They were not to take over Johnny's place until spring, but already Andrew was building a barn for the livestock, adding a small kitchen to the main room so that Moll could spend part of the day with her, throwing up cabins for the Negroes, erecting stout fences across the back of the property, burning off the cane and undergrowth, grubbing the small trees, belting the larger ones to make way for productive fields; and at the same time riding circuit, hundreds of miles over wilderness trails to serve in Jonesboro, Gallatin and Clarksville as prosecuting attorney for the territory, and then as civil attorney for the hundreds of clients throughout the district who wanted him to speak the legal language for them in the courts.

The affection of the Donelson family for Andrew served as a cohesive which brought the eleven brothers and sisters together at every possible opportunity. Robert Hays formed a partnership with him on a land deal; Samuel read law with him and had been promised a partnership; Stockly was selling much of the goods which Andrew received in lieu of cash for his services; they had fun together on the snowy winter afternoons and evenings, convoking mock court around the blazing fire with Rachel, Johnny, William, Severn and Mrs. Donelson as audience, while Judges Jackson and Hays appointed neophyte Samuel as Lord Chief Joker and General Humbugger of North America.

She had once heard the adage that "the proper study of mankind is man." Then wasn't it doubly true that the proper study for a wife was her husband? There were men in Nashville who said that Andrew Jackson was quarrelsome, that he had an uncontrollable temper. Yet how could this be when he was so gentle with her? Sometimes he would come home angry or disgruntled, he would tell her of what some scalawag had done, his voice would rise, the blood pound into the pale scar on his forehead, and soon he would be pacing up and down the room as though it were a court of law, trying the offender before her. Yet she had only to speak a few quiet words, put a finger on his sleeve placatingly, and he would stop short, shake his head, say:

"I'll meet thousands just like him in my lifetime. How foolish of me to take him seriously. But thanks for letting me unboosom myself."

She had perceived that her husband suffered from a raw sensitivity. Slowly she learned the reasons why: he had grown so fast that he could not always control his gangling frame, and the other children had called him awkward. As an outsized boy of ten he had tried to run with the fifteen- and sixteen-year-olds, but he had not had the physical stamina to stand up with them. His mouth had been too large for his face, his desire to express himself greater than his ability to control the moisture that gathered in either corner of his lips; but if any of his friends laughed at him or so much as mentioned the word "slobbering" in his presence, he found himself involved in a fight. One of the young men who had grown up with him in the Waxhaws told her:

"I could throw Andrew three times out of four, but he would never stay throwed!"

Once his playmates had secretly loaded a gun to the muzzle and given it to him to fire so that they could watch it kick him over. The recoil had knocked young Andrew several feet through the air; but their pleasure had been short-lived for he had sprung up from the ground and cried:

"By God, if one of you laughs, I'll kill him."

Nobody had doubted it.

Andrew's mother had wanted him to become a preacher because he had been the bookish one of her three sons, having taught himself to read and write at the age of five; and also because Dr. Richardson of the Waxhaw Church had been able to acquire a prosperous plantation, a two-story manse and the finest library on the frontier. Andrew had taken his turn as the public reader in the Waxhaws, where a large proportion of the men and women could neither read nor write. When the weekly folio arrived from Charleston, or the Philadelphia newspapers came in once a month, the community would gather at the house of his uncle, Squire Robert Crawford, to hear the news. Andrew read regularly to some forty assembled people in a shrill and penetrating voice, never growing hoarse, going straight through his assigned articles without stopping to spell out the words.

Yes, it was fascinating to learn, slowly, all there was to know about a man; and to possess that knowledge in the warm, bright light of love. Yet when she thought of his sensitive, tempestuous nature, and of their troubled past, she trembled for him . . . and for herself.

On the first of May they moved into Poplar Grove. Their nine Negroes were established in well-chinked cabins, the stock had a stout barn and the fields had been planted with tobacco and corn. Rachel took from home the walnut secretary her father had willed her; her mother gave her a liberal share of the Donelson silverware which had come on the *Adventure*, and promised her the big clock. Her sisters and sisters-in-law had been weaving and spinning a good part of the winter and now presented her with quilts stuffed with soft down, pillows and mattresses; rugs, fine linen board covers and napkins; bedcovers; yards of cotton, striped and plain; ticking; dressed doeskins, soft and pliable, and lengths of bleached and unbleached muslin. Andrew had Lardner Clark send to Philadelphia for the largest canopied bed he could find; it completely filled Mary Donelson's former prayer room. They stood in the center of the cabin, which Moll and George had scrubbed with lye, holding hands.

"It's our first home, and I love it," said Rachel emphatically.

"Part of the chinking has come loose," replied Andrew. "I'll start redoing it in the morning. And it's much too dark; Mary must have made John cut those portholes that small."

They went out into the fields and walked the boundaries of their land, ". . . beginning at sugar tree, red oak and elm on the bank of the river, the lower end of the tract running thence north sixty degrees . . ."; they listened to the cardinals, starlings, coveys of sparrows, redheaded woodpeckers, quail. On the bluff overlooking the river they enumerated the flowers and plants that had burst into bloom: jonquils, red haw as golden as the forsythia was yellow, the magnolia tulips, lilacs, green willows, privet, violets. Andrew sketched for her the disposition of their acreage: these fields would be for cotton, these for corn, these for tobacco, these for indigo, these for orchards, here the canebrake would be left for the cattle to graze in, and here they would have a corral for their horses and colts.

"We will put the place on a paying basis just as soon as possible," he said. "Then when we are ready we will be able to sell it for a good price."

"Oh, darling, please don't move us out so soon. We haven't even spent our first night here."

"But this is not our final home, Rachel," he protested. "It's just one step on the way up."

"Where is up from being happy?" she asked. "So long as we love each other, it won't matter where we are."

He kissed her anxious mouth.

"You are a sentimentalist, and I love you for it, but there's no reason why we can't love each other just as much in a big house and on a large plantation as we can here in Johnny's rather crudely built cabin. Because you see, my dear, I am ambitious for us: I want to accumulate land: miles and miles of land, great herds of cattle and horses, and raise fine crops for market. I want us to be secure."

"All I want is to be secure in our love."

74

Had she spoken too softly? Hadn't he heard? Probably not, for his eyes were glazed and his mouth set.

"I want us to be rich, very rich. The one thing I never want to see is the ugly face of poverty."

She slipped her hand softly into his, thinking, I was wrong to imagine that unseen scars vanish; sometimes they stay with us all our lives.

"We are never going to be poor, darling," she said reassuringly. "How could we be with your energies and talents? But I could sleep on a straw pallet in front of the fire and eat our meat off the stick it'd been broiled on, and it wouldn't frighten me. I have no faith in *things*: they come and go so fast."

"That's true," he said a little impatiently, "but I promise that you will have the best of everything . . . whatever else may happen to you because you married hotheaded Andrew Jackson."

3

She remarked the arrival of new seasons not so much by the changing weather or foliage as by the fact that during January, April, July and October Andrew attended court sessions in Nashville. While he was riding to the quarter sessions at Jonesboro, Gallatin and Clarksville one of her bachelor brothers came to stay. Her sisters visited frequently with their children. Jane, whose station at Haysboro almost adjoined Poplar Grove, spent one full day a week. As Jane watched her younger sister go about the endless tasks of a self-sustaining plantation, she commented:

"You're happy now, Rachel, aren't you?"

"Yes, completely . . . or I will be, when I have children."

"No hope yet?"

". . . none. Is there a special prayer?"

"Not that I know of. For some women they come a little too fast, and for others a little too slow, but we Donelsons all seem to get our share."

"I keep remembering that."

Time went quickly; she and Andrew had been married a full year. They were sitting on the front porch watching the moon arch upward across the stars. Andrew had taken to smoking a pipe since they had moved to Poplar Grove; he slowly consumed one bowl of tobacco, knocked out the powder-gray ash against his boot heel and turned to her with a touch of amusement in his eyes.

"Well, my dear, I've brought you home a first-anniversary present. You are now married to a judge advocate."

"You mean like Judge McNairy?"

"No, not a judge at all, really. It's just that I am now the lawyer for our county militia. Last year I sent a plan to Governor Blount for the

75

organization of our militia system; he liked it so well he forwarded it to the Secretary of War. I guess that's why they gave me the appointment. Anyway, I am now a captain."

"May I kiss you, Captain Jackson?"

"I'll take that kiss, thank you, ma'am, but you can leave off the title. Nobody is going to call me captain just because I straighten out a few warrants or contracts. I'll use the title of captain when I've earned it, fighting the Indians and the British."

With Andrew away almost half the time the responsibility of running the plantation was hers: in June there was the corn to be cultivated, the flax to be pulled, tied in stacks and arranged for drying; the hemp sowed; in July the wheat and timothy hay had to be harvested, the turnips planted; August was the best month to preserve the fruits and vegetables and also to clear new lands. In the early fall all buildings had to be repaired and chinked against the oncoming winter, meat had to be butchered and stored; there was the winter supply of candles to be made from the fats that had accumulated over the summer.

Her mother had been an expert in this difficult task and had trained each of her four daughters diligently. Before dawn the coals in the kitchen fireplace were stirred and a good fire started under the two huge iron kettles which hung on the lug pole; the melted tallow was given two scaldings and skimmings and put into the half-filled pots of boiling water. Two long poles were laid from chair to chair and across these were placed, like the rungs of a ladder, eighteen-inch candle rods which had been used in the Donelson family since Rachel was a child. Each rod had eight straight candlewicks with double-twisted wicking. The rods were dipped into the hot tallow in the pot at regular intervals and given sufficient time to cool and harden between dips so that they could grow steadily. For Rachel this had always been the most exciting operation of the year: she used everyone at the station to keep the fires high, the tallow pots constantly replenished, large sections of bark underneath the rods to protect the scoured floors from the drippings. At the end of the process the candles were packed into compartments of candle boxes, covered over carefully and stored where they would neither melt nor discolor.

The presence of Moll was a comfort to her. No one knew how old Moll was, least of all Moll herself. Her fine black skin was smooth in texture and a colorful contrast against the soft white of her hair; she went about her duties tirelessly, humming spirituals under her breath, knowing the tunes to dozens of these hymns but not one complete line from any of them. She was an inexhaustible mine of information, for as well as Rachel had been trained by her mother, this was the first actual opportunity she had had to function as a plantation wife. So many of the tiny details had escaped her: the recipe for making red dye out of logwood; the exact moment when the lye was strong enough for making soap; the right combination of woods and the degree of warmth for the smokehouse; how to make bayberry-bush candles which burned more slowly and gave off a pleasant scent.

Each day she loved Andrew so deeply that she knew there could be no going beyond it either in the depth of her emotion or the joy of loving completely, and being loved. Yet always the next day was infinitely sweeter, their love heightened and more complete: for did not each new morning promise still another day of wonderful memories to feed and grow upon?

It was a late December afternoon with the snow up to the doorsill when Andrew and John Overton returned from their fall circuit. They had a hilarious time unloading the bags on the saddle horses.

"I am going to have to open a general store," said Andrew. "Look what we've got here: bags of salt, cow bells, axes, loaves of sugar, bridles, a saddle, sacks of corn meal, bear and beaver hides, beeswax, smoked hams and venison, two rifles with horns full of powder, lead for bullets, and a bolt of bright calico for Moll. I was also paid with one cow, two horses, five pigs and eight sheep; I kept the horses and swapped the cow and sheep for land warrants."

But most important there was a pearl brooch for her, as a coming-home gift. She dressed for supper that night, brushing her hair until it gleamed in the candlelight, then piling it high on her head. She put on her long-sleeved red wool dress, its collar framing her tanned throat, the low neckline of the bodice a perfect setting for the new brooch on its silver chain. Her husband told her that she was beautiful. At dinner they held hands under the table.

"When I see you two together," said John, "I feel a little sorry about being a bachelor."

"But John, why should you stay a bachelor? There are a lot of nice young girls in the Cumberland looking for husbands."

John raised his hand before his face as though in self-defense. After a moment he said without emotion, as though it were a question of law:

"What woman could love me, Rachel, when I'm so homely?"

She rose and put her arm about his shoulders.

"John Overton, how can you be so kind to everyone else and so cruel to yourself? One day a woman is going to look at your gentle, sympathetic eyes and she will think you beautiful . . ."

John and Andrew gazed at each other in astonishment, then burst into hearty laughter.

"Now, Rachel, even my mother didn't think I was beautiful."

"Well, I'm not beautiful either," said Andrew, still laughing. "My face is as long as a pony's . . ."

"Oh, Andrew, stop; our faces are as God made them. A woman doesn't love a man because of the amount of hair on his head or the shape of

77

his nose; she loves him because of some inner quality: strength, perhaps . . . or integrity."

The law practice of Andrew Jackson and John Overton was growing so fast that for the term of April 1793, in which there were a hundred and fifty-five cases docketed in Nashville, Andrew had been retained as counsel on seventy-two of them, while John had a considerable portion of the remainder.

"Rachel, why don't we build a guest cabin for John? We could set it up as an alternate office with a supply of lawbooks, and then I'd be home more."

"Good. I'll build it in the spring, while you're away."

Rachel and the Donelsons set to work at once to make the necessary bedframe, desk and chairs. As her own contribution Rachel loomed a bed coverlet of indigo-dyed hard-twisted wool in the intricate design known as Bachelor's Fancy. She asked her brother Samuel if he would stay with her for the two months that the men would be away. Samuel accepted at once.

"It's a wonderful opportunity for me. I'll have those lawbooks all to myself."

Andrew had been gone only a week when there began a series of Indian attacks the like of which Rachel could not remember. The son of Colonel Bledsoe and his friend were killed opposite Nashville, and on February 17 another son of Bledsoe was fired on and pursued by Indians to within fifty yards of his stockade. Five days later two sons of Colonel Saunders were scalped; a couple of days after, Captain Samuel Hays, brother of Robert, was killed near the front door of John Donelson's new house. General Robertson issued orders that every home, stockade and group of men working in a clearing were to keep night and day guard.

Rachel was caught in a dilemma: she could not go to her mother's and leave her hands at the mercy of the Indians, but if she took their Negroes with her the Indians would burn the station to the ground.

"I'm not letting my husband come home to a mess of charred embers," she declared.

"No," said Samuel, "but you can't let him come home to a scalped wife, either. Maybe Mother can spare us Alexander or Leven for the night watch."

Andrew and John returned home on April 9, the day Colonel Isaac Bledsoe was killed while working in the fields. Andrew's relief at seeing Rachel safe found its outlet in a torrential denunciation of all Indians. When he finally exhausted himself, John said in his driest legal tone:

"Surely you will admit that the Indians have a case too?"

"Sure, a case of whisky from the British and a case of rifles from the Spanish."

John said, "Pun me no puns," then added, "Bad as the Creeks and

78

Cherokees have behaved, they can't hold a candle to us. The history of this country can be told in terms of the white man moving onto the Indian's lands, killing off his game, cutting down his forests and tilling his fields. We have bribed them, corrupted them and broken practically every treaty."

Rachel felt Andrew's gorge rise. He jumped up from his chair, shouting:

"By God, John, I'll not have you taking the side of the Indians against me in my own house! Furthermore, I just heard that the Federal government wants everybody to celebrate the Fourth of July this year. What are we supposed to bottom our celebration on?"

"On our independence," replied John. "The thing you got that scar for, remember?"

"What independence?" cried Andrew belligerently. "Do we have a vote? Do we have representation in Congress? Does the government build us roads or deliver our mail or provide us with troops to police the frontier?"

This was the Jackson temper she had heard about. She went to Andrew, put her finger on his arm. He gazed at her hand for a moment and dropped heavily into his chair, rubbing the back of his hand over his eyes.

"I think it's a wonderful idea," she said. "We could have a big party here; I've never given a party all by myself. Besides, it's most time for our second anniversary. We could plan an outdoor dinner for the Fourth of July, then anyone who doesn't want to celebrate the day politically can celebrate our anniversary."

More than a hundred adults and uncountable swarms of children came to their Fourth of July party. In the cool of the morning they went berrypicking in the woods and when the sun got hot the youngsters splashed in the river. On a smooth piece of ground under a shade oak some of the men were gambling over rattle and snap, with jugs of cool spring water to mix with their whisky; another group of men were down at the corral racing their horses for good-sized wagers. On the north side of the house, where the grass was the coolest, three fiddlers led by James Gamble provided untiring music for the contradance and the jig.

She made her way from group to group to be sure that everyone had all he wanted of food and drink and company and fun. Every once in a while she would go looking for Andrew just to exchange the bright pleased smile of hosts who know that their guests are enjoying themselves. John Rains sat in the shade of the doorstep and gathered listeners. The year before he had raised a bumper crop of tobacco, built a flatboat and carried his cargo down to New Orleans where tobacco prices were high, but the Spaniards had confiscated not only his crop but the logs out of which he had built his boat; and he had had to walk all the way up the Natchez Trace, empty-handed.

"Sometimes it beats me why we bother to stay here at all, friends. Certainly those white-wigged New Englanders don't want us to be part of the United States. It was our own government gave the Spanish control of that Mississippi."

Looking about her, Rachel saw that every one of these men had fought against the British. Andrew spoke for them when he said:

"Our Congress said we're too young and too weak to quarrel with the Spaniards, and the mouth of the Mississippi wasn't important anyway, so they give Spain control over the navigation on the Mississippi for twenty years. The English are still occupying forts in the Northwest, Detroit and Maumee, that they agreed to get out of ten years ago. But does our government force them out? No, we are too young and too weak. We watch them incite the Indians against the settlers and send them on the warpath against us. We're going to have to fight that war for independence all over again; but next time, by God, we'll make it stick."

John Overton sighed, then said, "Now, Andrew, a baby has to crawl before it can walk. If Spain had begun a war with us over the Louisianas our government might have collapsed. It's going to take years for us to grow strong enough to put the British out of those northern forts. We can't risk brawling with every nation that wants to quarrel with us."

"No wonder everybody despises us," growled Andrew.

When the blazing hot July sun finally settled itself onto the western horizon the guests started home.

"Was my party a success?" asked Rachel when they were alone. "People become so angry when they get involved in politics."

Andrew was astonished. "Why darling, everyone had a wonderful time! Political arguments are one of the treats."

Rachel glanced at her husband quizzically. Maybe so, but for herself she liked the way people had called her Mrs. Jackson, ma'am; she liked the feel of the name, it had a solidity for her, and so did the attitude of the guests that this Jackson marriage and this Jackson love and this Jackson home were permanent.

4

It was a melancholy gray-black day, with the fall sky as heavy as the timbered roof over her head when she heard him coming heavily homeward. Was it possible that she could know from the gait of the horse that something was wrong with the rider? Alarm fragments flashed through her mind: he was ill, he had been wounded, something had gone wrong in court . . . These past two months since he had gone away had been difficult ones: Catherine's nine children had been desperately ill from eating spoiled meat, and Rachel had spent two weeks getting them back on their feet; her sister Mary had gone down with neuralgia, Rachel taking over the management of her brood of twelve; only two days before Jane's station had been attacked by Indians and two of the men defenders killed. And now Andrew . . .

She was slow in getting out of her chair, in opening the door and moving into the yard. One piercing look at her husband's expression and she was almost felled by the instinctive blow that whatever was wrong concerned them: Rachel and Andrew Jackson. He slid off his horse, unsmiling, did not speak or kiss her, but held his cheek against hers so that she could not see his eyes. She bruised her skin on the rough stubble of his cheek in bringing her mouth round to his, felt his reluctant lips hard.

They made their way into the house. The big room was cheerful, logs crackling in the fire, the wall lamps lighted against his return. He slumped into his chair by the fire while she went past the wide stone chimney into the small kitchen, returning in a few moments with hot coffee. When he had gulped down most of it, and spots of color had risen on his cheeks, she sat herself at his feet.

"What has gone wrong, my dear?"

He stared at her almost blankly for a moment, as though the thing that had happened was a nightmare of the road, having no possible reality here in their home with the fire crackling and the lamps spreading a bright glow. He tried several times to form words and get breath behind them before he finally garnered the strength.

". . . it's . . . what you might expect. Robards."

"Lewis? But how?"

"He's . . . done something."

"But what could he do? We're safe, we're married . . ."

She stopped short, her body frozen. Could it be possible . . . had Andrew shaken his head? Or had it been the way he had blinked his eyes and swallowed?

"Andrew, what are you trying to say, that we're not . . . ?"

"No, no!"

He pulled himself out of the chair and sank to his knees in front of her, his long arms clasped passionately about her as she sat immobile on the hard hooked rug.

"We're married. We always have been. We always will be."

In a hoarse voice she said, "Lewis is trying to make trouble. He's challenged our marriage in Natchez . . ."

"No."

". . . everyone said it was legal, the only way we could be married down there."

"It's not that. I only wish it was." He picked himself up, walked blindly about the room for a moment, then returned to her. The words

81

came out in a rush. "He is only now starting suit for a divorce! The report that he got a divorce from the Virginia legislature was not true. They refused his petition. When I rode down the Trace to bring you the news, in July of '91, and we were married . . ."

She pulled back, gazing at him with terror-stricken eyes.

"I was still married to Lewis Robards!"

Her head began to spin. Andrew caught her, his fingers digging into her shoulders.

"I'll kill any man who even dares question . . ."

She did not hear his words, only his tone. She thought, At last Lewis Robards has had his way. He has made me an adulteress.

As she walked into the Donelson dining room and found the family assembled in their ritualistic places around the long table, she saw with stark clarity the character expression on each face; it was like a recapitulation of all the crises in the Donelson family.

At the head of the table sat her mother, with an expression which said, I'm hurt by this, but I still think that no price is too high to have paid for Andrew Jackson. In her father's place at the head of the table sat Johnny, whose expression intimated that at the moment he was more concerned about what was happening to the Donelson name than he was about what had happened to the Jackson marriage. Opposite him sat Alexander, who had no interest in women, love or marriage, and whose expression said, What can you expect if you are foolish enough to marry? At the second seat on the left she saw William the Cautious, sorry that his sister was in trouble, but remembering that he had told her to stay with Lewis Robards. Next to William sat Samuel, his usually creamy skin now mottled with anger, his soft brown eyes deeply hurt: a complete and authentic replica of herself, had she looked in a mirror.

Her regular seat was next to Samuel's. She dropped into it. Andrew sat beside her. She glanced across the table and saw Jane seated next to Alexander, Jane, who was recalling even now, with a gesture of distaste, the scene caused by Lewis at the Hays home. Next to Jane was Stockly, the former lawyer, too busy trying to figure out the legal complexities of this affair to be concerned over his sister's suffering. Coming back to her own side of the table, she saw Colonel Robert Hays reaching a hand in front of Andrew to clasp hers reassuringly. He was the most dazed one at this table, for he was a genuinely good and tender man, a fighter, second-in-command of the militia under General Robertson, yet a person of such utter decency that he could not conceive of any other human being behaving this way. Next to Robert Hays sat her brother Severn, hollow-cheeked, who rarely gathered at the family conferences any more; and across from him was Leven, without experience or responsibility, whose puzzled look inquired, What are you all so upset about? At the end seats on their side of the table were her two brothers-in-law, John Caffrey and Thomas Hutchings, married to Mary and Catherine. They nodded to her sympathetically, but their expressions said, This is a Donelson affair; we'd be glad to do anything we could to help, but for the time being we'll remain silent. At the end of the table, facing their mother and Johnny, were her two sisters, Mary and Catherine, Mary who had grown plumper and jollier with the arrival of each of her dozen children, and Catherine, who had grown more wiry, and who still sat through these Donelson conclaves in silence.

She felt there was someone missing, yet all of her ten brothers and sisters were here, as well as her four in-laws. Then the door opened and John Overton came in, the water running from his broad-brimmed hat. He took off his sodden boots, slipping into his accustomed place alongside of Leven. Now her family was complete. The council of war could begin.

Stockly was the first one in voice.

"For heaven's sake, Andrew, what has happened? We can't make it out."

Andrew nodded his head down-table to John Overton.

"I guess we'd better let John start. He's the one found out about it."

All eyes traveled down the long table to Overton. When he spoke it was as though he were placing the words one by one in a bowl in the center of the table, for people to help themselves.

"When Andrew and I started for Jonesboro, I learned that the divorce was scheduled to be heard at the Court of Quarter Sessions at Harrodsburg."

Everyone sat waiting quietly. Then Stockly asked:

"What was the matter with the divorce granted by the Virginia legislature?"

John Overton looked steadfastly across at Andrew. He nodded to John to continue.

"We were misinformed. The legislature refused Robards' petition for a divorce. What they actually passed was what we call an enabling act, which merely gave Robards the right to plead his case before a judge and jury."

"But he didn't do it at that time?" inquired Mrs. Donelson sternly.

"No, he waited until April of this year. The court wouldn't hear his case then, and it was put over until this September."

Robert Hays leaned forward across the table, his hands clasped before him. His disciplined mind insisted upon getting at the core of matters.

"How could we have believed there was a divorce in the spring of 1791? Who was responsible for spreading that report?"

"I heard it myself from three or four different sources," said Johnny, "men who came from Harrodsburg and Richmond."

"We accepted rumor as truth," replied Andrew bitterly.

83

"There was more substance than word-of-mouth, Andrew," said Overton. "While you were in Natchez I stopped with the Robards family for several days. It was the assumption of everyone in that family that Lewis and Rachel were divorced. Mrs. Robards told me she was happy that Rachel was free."

These were the first words Rachel had really heard. She looked across at John, blinking her eyes at him as though this might bring further understanding.

"Mrs. Robards said that we were divorced?"

"Yes, and so did her daughter, Jack Jouitt's wife."

"They wouldn't . . . misrepresent," said Rachel tonelessly. "They have always liked me."

"Robards deceived them too," cried Samuel.

"Now, Sam, that may be a little harsh," said Robert Hays. He reached into his coat, took out a letter and unfolded it on the table. "It was only a month or two after the so-called divorce that I got this letter from Robards asking me to sell his land and send him his half of Rachel's inheritance from her father." He placed the letter in the center of the board and pointed out the sentences:

I shall depend on you and Mr. Overton that there is no advantage taken of me in my absence. You will please to write by the first Opportunity if the Estate is divided as I may get my Right. If there is any Opportunity offered of selling my land you will please to let Me know.

Her mind shut out the voices that beat like the rain against the shutters. She lived again through her wedding under the exquisite chandelier at Springfield, through the happy weeks of honeymooning at Bayou Pierre. Should they have stayed in the Spanish territory after all, where this kind of trouble could never have reached them? But that was being disloyal to the happiness she and Andrew had had these past two years. Inside her head an agonized voice was crying: Why? Why has this happened to me? What sins have I committed that this brand should be burned forever into my living flesh? I was only a girl when I met Lewis Robards. I never knowingly hurt him. I tried to be a good wife. If I had done something wrong, then I could understand that I should suffer, and do penance. But of what, Almighty God, am I guilty? For what am I being punished?

She heard John Overton speaking quietly, heard each tiny sound in the room, the very breathing and murmuring of the seventeen people around the table, with a terrifying distinctness.

"Robert is right about the letter," commented Overton; "since Lewis asks for his division of the land he owned here and his half of Rachel's legacy from her father, that can only indicate that he believed he was already divorced."

84

"But how can all this be?"

Rachel had not been watching the table and did not know who had cried out in such naked pain. Suddenly, from the fact that everyone had turned and was looking at her with pity in their eyes, she realized that it had been her own voice and her own pain. She felt Andrew's hand reach over to take hers. Everyone waited for him to speak, but he could not. John Overton assumed the burden.

"Perhaps it's because the whole subject of . . . divorce . . . is so new. Lewis's petition for a divorce was only the second that had come before the Virginia legislature. When the legislature passed the Enabling Act, I think nobody except a few lawyers knew what it really meant; everyone else appears to have assumed that the bill actually granted the divorce, instead of merely the right to go into court to prove the charges."

"And now the case is to be tried. In Harrodsburg!" cried Rachel in anguish.

There was a silence which Andrew broke into, his voice hoarse with self-reproach.

". . . the fault is mine. No one else's. I'm a lawyer. Or supposed to be a lawyer. What right had I to accept the report of the divorce, regardless of how many people repeated it? My first duty to Rachel, to all of you, was to get a copy of the Virginia bill. I should never have gone to Natchez without it."

"Now, Andrew, there's no call for you to castigate yourself," said Stockly. "I used to be a lawyer too, and it never occurred to me that there could be anything wrong. That trip to Richmond would have taken you months . . ."

". . . and we were the first to tell you that the divorce had been granted," broke in Mrs. Donelson; "we had heard it while you were on your way up the Trace after taking Rachel down to Natchez with Colonel Stark."

"Wait a bit," said Alexander in his lazy, loose-jointed way, "I'm just remembering. That spring of '91 I was staying in General Smith's house for a spell; one day he pointed to a Richmond paper and told me he read a notice of the Robards divorce."

But Rachel saw from the way Andrew had his jaw set that no one would ever acquit him to himself.

"I got back here in April and didn't leave until the latter part of July. I could have sent a messenger to Richond to bring back a copy; I could have gone myself between court sessions if I had taken enough horses and ridden hard . . . I was guilty of the worst kind of stupidity and carelessness. If I served my clients as badly as I served my wife, they would never let me practice law."

Jane Hays had been listening carefully.

"I don't think these post-mortems and soul-searchings are going to help us a bit." Her voice had an astringency which dried up their emo-

85

tion. "You said, John, that Robards asked for a divorce trial in April of this year. How does it happen that none of us heard about it when there is so much travel back and forth between here and Harrodsburg? And why is Robards trying again now?"

Overton replied, "Early this year Lewis Robards met a woman by the name of Hannah Winn. When he decided he wanted to marry her, he went into court to get a divorce."

"Then he knew all along he was not divorced!" This was Samuel's explosion again. "For two years he let Rachel live . . . implicating herself . . ."

"I don't know about that, Sam. Let's give Robards the benefit of the doubt. Let's assume that when he went for a marriage license he found he couldn't get one . . . because he was not divorced. Or let's assume that his intended father-in-law insisted upon a thorough search of the records. Under the provisions of the Enabling Act, Robards was obliged to advertise eight weeks consecutively in a Kentucky newspaper so that the defendant, in this case Rachel, could learn about the impending suit and enter her defense."

"We get all the papers from Kentucky," said William. "We never saw any such notice. Nobody in the Cumberland ever told us about having seen it."

"No," agreed Overton. "The notice was never published in the papers. I checked on that in Harrodsburg."

"On what grounds will he seek his divorce?" persisted Jane.

"Through fraud!" It was Andrew who had answered tangentially, his face blazing. "His petition to the legislature charged that Rachel had eloped with me from his home in July of 1790, and that we had lived together thereafter. He lied, and he knew he lied, because he followed us to your home and begged Rachel to come back with him."

"That was my fault," cried Samuel. "I had gone for Rachel once, I could have gone a second time."

"Yes," agreed Severn grimly; "there are a lot of us who should have gone. But there seemed such good reasons at the time to stay home."

"If there is any blame to be taken here, I will take it," announced Mrs. Donelson. "Andrew was like one of my sons. We didn't know that Lewis was quarreling over him again. There was no conceivable reason why he shouldn't have gone."

"We can defend . . ." shouted Stockly, but John waved his hand quietly to interrupt.

"There is no need. Robards is no longer bringing that Harrodsburg trip into the case. The divorce papers state that Robards will introduce evidence that Rachel and Andrew lived as a married couple a year later, on the way up the Natchez Trace in September of 1791."

"But that was after we were married!" Rachel was aghast.

"He can't do that!" cried Stockly.

86

"You are right, Stockly; his original petition to the Virginia legislature charged that Rachel had eloped with Andrew from his home in July of 1790, and it is on that basis that the legislature gave him permission to sue for a divorce. It is that charge he must prove. He has also failed to provide the necessary eight-day notice to the defendant. We can go into that court in Harrodsburg and demonstrate that the divorce will be fraudulently secured; but the more effectively we defend ourselves in Harrodsburg . . . the more surely we throw out Rachel's marriage to Andrew."

There were commingled gasps around the table.

"We've got to stay out of the case," snapped Jane.

Rachel buried her head in her arms, her body shaking convulsively; for how could one do anything but weep when one was trapped as she was trapped? If she did not defend herself in Harrodsburg, if she did not take this opportunity to go into court and establish her innocence, was that not proof, eternal and indisputable, that she admitted her guilt?

"Do you know who will testify against Rachel at the trial?" It was Johnny, wanting to identify the enemies of the Donelson family. "I think we ought to know."

"Hugh McGary. He testified that he had observed Rachel Robards and Andrew Jackson sleeping under the same blanket on the journey north. The jury will accept that as proof of the charges. It is our misfortune that . . . adultery . . . is the sole grounds on which a divorce can be granted."

Andrew jumped up from the bench and strode out the door into the rain. Rachel raised her head, stared after him, saying, "There is no marriage. It was never legal. It is not legal now; it won't be legal even after Lewis's divorce . . ."

Johnny asked Overton, "Are those records in Harrodsburg permanent?"

"Permanent?"

"Do they stay there forever, or are they thrown out at the end of, say, a court year?"

"Records are never thrown out."

"We could always burn down the courthouse," observed Alexander dryly.

"But it's totally unfair," cried Samuel. He turned to his sister, his eyes blazing. "Rachel, we've got to go into court and defend you. We can prove fraud against Robards, and falsehood as well. The jury will acquit you of the charges. You will be vindicated."

There was a heavy silence, a silence filled with frustration. Mary came in from the kitchen with pots of coffee and milk, followed by two servants with chargers of food. She would take no part in this discussion, but she would keep a supply of food coming in, maintaining, "Even the worst looks better when you have something hot in your stomach."

Mrs. Donelson handed Rachel a cup of coffee. Rachel drank slowly,

87

the hot fluid scorching her throat. John Overton turned to her, his eyes deeply sympathetic.

"We must not defend you against those charges in the Harrodsburg court, Rachel. If Lewis can't get a divorce to marry his Miss Winn . . . neither will you be able to marry Andrew!"

5

It was pitch-black and raining harder than ever when they started for home. Moll, waiting in the little kitchen, gave them hot toddies against the chill, then retired to her own cabin. Overton bade them good night, went to the door, then hesitated.

"Perhaps we ought to look on the more constructive side of this tangle," he suggested blandly. "Suppose Lewis Robards had not wanted to marry Hannah Winn. It might then have been five or ten years before you found out that there never had been an actual divorce. That might really have had serious implications."

"You mean . . . if he should have gone seeking a divorce . . . after children had been born?"

"Yes, Rachel."

He turned his head slightly so that he was focusing on Andrew. "I think Lewis means to keep this trial as quiet as possible. Uncontested, the divorce will be over in a few hours. Robert Hays and I will sign your marriage bond for a new ceremony. That ceremony can also be short and quiet."

"As something we are ashamed of, eh?" Andrew broke in.

"John's trying to help us."

"We're married." Andrew's jaw was set. "We've been married since August 1791."

"Neither of you has ever told me the details of your marriage at Natchez," said Overton a little sternly. "If the Virginia legislature had granted the divorce in 1791 there may never have been any reason to question that Spanish territory ceremony. But now that we're in the middle of a hotchpot . . ."

Rachel stared at him dully. She saw Andrew clenching and unclenching his fists in black anger. He was a fighter: to strike out when he believed himself right was as natural as breathing; but how could he expose her to the battle? No matter how quiet the trial might be, the whole countryside would be twattling again, reviewing her story, embellishing it with these newest, delectable morsels.

Overton put a hand on Andrew's shoulder.

"Andrew, you have no choice; you must get a Nashville license and be married according to the American law."

Rachel stood before him supplicatingly.

88

"John is right. We must be married again."

Andrew walked away from her, went to the hearth and stood staring wildly into the fire, his hands clasped behind him, pushing roughly against the small of his back, talking into the flames:

"You are wrong, both of you. Terribly wrong. Don't you see what this means . . . we publicly admit that we have not been married these past two years. We plead guilty to the charges thrown against us in that Harrodsburg court, forever exposed to any enemy or scoundrel who wants to plague us with the record." He walked to the door. "Good night, John."

When John was gone he gazed for a moment into the dark night, then turned to Rachel. The anger had drained from his face; in its place came hurt pride.

"In our own eyes we are married, and so are we in the eyes of our family and friends. No one else matters. We've got to stand firm on this one base: that no purpose is served by going through a second ceremony when the first one was legal and adequate."

And now his expression told her why he was so adamant: he was taking upon himself all the blame for allowing her name to be thrown into a public courtroom in Harrodsburg, where her former friends and relatives could hear her character maligned; for everything she was suffering now and everything she would suffer in the future because, together, they had been convicted of adultery. And because she understood this, she knew how to quiet her husband and gain his consent.

She stood with her back to the fire, letting the heat burn in warmth and renewed strength. Andrew remained at the door, avoiding her eyes, sunk deep in his own injured feelings and even deeper in his remorse. She waited patiently until at last he came to her, took her in his arms and now, just as he had tasted the salt of her tears on his lips earlier that day, she felt his tears damp on her cheek. In the whole defeated cast of his body she saw his horror of this trial, the frustration of not being able to contest it, the terrible things they would be forced to admit thereby, and yet the total lack of any other course.

"There's so little we'd need do to stop Robards. Courts don't like to give divorces; the slightest intimation from us of irregularity and it would be all over . . . We have every right and every weapon to defend ourselves; and yet we have to let him appear as the injured party, to paint us black as he pleases; there is not one word we can utter in our own defense. Do you know how hard it is for me to take that?"

"Yes, my dear, as hard as it was for me to take the news you brought to the Villa Gayoso. You quieted me then, and comforted me with your love, by showing me that at last we were free: free to love and free to marry. It was a bitter price to pay for that freedom, Andrew, but you were right. No price is too great if we can spend our lives together. So now it is I who must tell you not to weep, not to storm, and not to defend us.

We must not dwell on the injustice, but think only of our two years of wonderful happiness, and all the years of happiness that are to come."

She put her index finger lightly across his lips as he opened them to protest, then took it away and kissed him

"Do it for me, my darling. Even though you may be right, and I may be wrong, even though you don't want to, and it galls you, do it for my sake, because I want it, because it will help me. Do it because you love me and because . . . when our children come . . . there must be no question, no man must ever be able to hurt them because of something we refused to do before they were born."

"Yes, Rachel, I'll do it for you. I'll do anything you want . . . always."

Book THREE

THE BLEATING had turned from the plaintive to the urgent; they quickened their steps, leaning forward against the lateral wind which swept the big flakes downward.

"How did it get out of the barn?" She turned her face full to Andrew in order that the wind would not carry away the words.

"I don't know; George and I locked everything secure last night when this snow began."

A leafless poplar loomed up ahead. At the base in trampled snow they found one of their ewes, licking the moisture off a newly born lamb. Even as Rachel and Andrew reached her side the ewe weakened, began to stiffen in the snow. Andrew went to his knees to examine the animals.

"Is the little one still alive?" She dropped to the ground beside him, pushing the wool hood back off her head so she could see better.

"Just barely."

"Then let's get it up to the house quickly."

Andrew stripped off the long leather coat which he wore over a buckskin shirt and spread it on the snow, lifting the lamb onto its thick warmth. He looked over at the sheep.

"I'm sorry to lose her; she was a stouthearted renegade: broke out of the pasture to mate, and then out of the barn to lamb."

"Isn't that the fate of all renegades?"

Andrew rose with the lamb in his arms. "Only those who don't plan their uprisings for the proper season."

She ran ahead, her black leather boots making holes in the snow, cried out to Moll to bring in warm milk, and spread a plaid wool blanket before the blazing log fire. Moll came quickly with a tumbler of milk.

"Should we put in a drop of whisky?" asked Andrew. He was brushing snow off his hunting shirt, making damp spots on the floor.

"Yes, in you. Moll, please get Mr. Jackson a hot toddy."

They sat in silence, Andrew in his big chair, the soles of his boots exposed to the fire, sipping his drink. She was on the edge of the hearth,

91

her cape tossed aside and her full wool skirt crushed under her as she concentrated on getting the warm milk between the lamb's lips. She caught a curious expression in Andrew's eyes, and said softly, "How precious all life is, even that of a stray lamb we didn't know existed a few moments ago."

Andrew lit his pipe while Rachel stroked the lamb's curly white wool. When his pipe was half ash, he said quietly:

"Rachel, I'm thinking of opening a store."

She looked up at him in astonishment.

"A store? You mean like Lardner Clark's . . . ?"

"Yes, but out here in the country. Even in the raw weather of these past weeks there must have been a full hundred families come over the Cumberland Gap in their Conestoga wagons, and a lot of them are settling out this way. There's a desperate need for goods."

She made no attempt to hide her amazement.

"But Andrew, why? You are attorney general for the territory, the most popular young lawyer . . ."

"Because I want cash money!" His voice sounded doubly loud because he rarely interrupted. "As a lawyer I'm still getting paid in land and livestock, but people will pay cash for what they buy in a store, three times what I can buy the merchandise for in Philadelphia."

The lamb stirred; she moved it gently so that she could nestle its head between her breasts.

"Andrew, how long before we'll know whether it will live?"

"If it's on its feet by nightfall. Now what I'd like to do is gather up all our lands, John will throw in with me, go to Philadelphia, sell them for cash and use that cash to buy stock for the store. Then, when we take our cash profits from the store, we can buy even bigger tracts of land . . ."

". . . to sell in Philadelphia?"

"Yes. The land companies will buy up everything you've got."

"But isn't that going around in a circle?"

"So does the sun. Look at your brother Stockly: he's accumulated hundreds of thousands of acres. Rachel, this is going to become the greatest trading center of the West, the meeting place for goods coming down from Philadelphia and up the Mississippi from New Orleans. The man who opens a trading post here will become the richest man on the frontier."

"It's hard for me to think of you as a shopkeeper, Andrew. Do you have the special kind of shrewdness that has made Lardner Clark so successful?" She noted that the lamb had only its lower teeth at birth, and that its eyes were a light blue behind the nearly shut lids. "Sooner or later you will make just as much money out of your law."

He moved in his chair with a restless gesture, crossing one booted foot over the other.

92

"It's not that I'm getting tired of the law, but the cases are so alike: conflicting land claims, disputes over the sale of goods, who started a quarrel and who finished it. I've never concealed from you the fact that with me the law is only a means . . ."

Moll bustled in from the kitchen in her gray cotton dress and black apron to see how the lamb was faring. Andrew walked to the window to stare out into the snow. His red hair shone in the brilliant firelight. Though it was not yet four in the afternoon, darkness had fallen.

"I've got it all figured out: together John and I own about fifty thousand acres, and I have thirty thousand in my own name. They've cost us about ten cents an acre; I can get a dollar in Philadelphia. The round trip will take me about two months. There's a cabin on the main road I can buy cheap. Two or three trips to Philadelphia, then we'll be able to open stores up and down the Cumberland Valley, with trading posts in Natchez and New Orleans."

He was pacing the main room of the cabin now, showering off enough sparks to shock the lamb into life.

"But what about your cases, and your attorney general work?"

"John will handle the cases on circuit, Sam can do the paper work in the office. As far as the attorney generalship is concerned, you know the court is delinquent in its pay to me, five years delinquent, ever since we became a territory. So I guess I can be delinquent for one quarter session . . ."

Strange man, she thought: he has this tremendous hunger to accumulate wealth, and yet he can work for five long years without receiving a cent of pay, and never let it be known.

"It'll only be a matter of a few years, Rachel, and then we can have the great plantation I've always dreamed of. I want the finest in the Cumberland for you . . . the finest in all the world. Then we'll be at the top. No one will ever be able to climb up high enough to attack us."

She lowered her head until her chin nestled on the softness of the lamb's head. For a full year now, since they had been remarried, she had known that he was determined to have . . . wealth, power. The higher he rises in the world, she thought, the more untouchable he thinks we will be. For herself, the need for seclusion, for the ability to live her days without being the focus of strange eyes and strange ears and, even worse, strange tongues, now seemed uppermost. It was not that she wanted to shut herself up, but only to live behind an impenetrable privacy. It was a hunger greater than she had ever known for food or drink or sleep, or even laughter.

They had been happy at Poplar Grove until . . . that news from Harrodsburg. During those first two years Andrew had been content: the land was good, they could live comfortably off its yield, it was in no way different or better than twenty others in the neighborhood. Folks still referred to it as the John Donelson station, which meant added ano-

93

nymity . . . until people had forgotten, until she and Andrew had established themselves. Yet these things which brought her comfort and protection had become increasingly galling and unacceptable to Andrew. It is odd, she thought, that the need for that second ceremony has influenced no one but Andrew and myself. It's going to drive him on relentlessly. If I try to keep him as small and inconspicuous as I want to be, it would kill him.

She raised her head. Her voice was clear.

"I'm sure the store will be a success, Andrew. I'll help all I can."

She felt a slow movement against her bosom. It was the lamb raising its head, the slim legs twitching.

"Look, darling, his eyes are open."

The animal gave a little bleat or two and shook itself.

"You can set him on his own feet now, my dear," said Andrew. "He wants to walk."

She put the lamb down gingerly, holding him just beyond her skirts. He stood there for a moment weakly, looked about the room, backed away in fright from the fire, then suddenly ran straight-legged down to the other end of the cabin and back to Rachel.

2

She rarely left Poplar Grove, even for a brief trip into Nashville. She had developed a sixth sense about people and could tell at the first piercing glance whether her story was so close to the top of their minds that its edges spilled over into their eyes. She feared the probing glances, the guarded talk, the repetitions of the tale: all invasions of her intimate life. She flinched from meeting strangers, even when she encountered them in the homes of her sisters and knew them to be friends of the family. She was no longer always able to keep her gaze steadfast; at the subtlest intimation of prying, querying, her eyes fled in confusion and pain. In her own home, on her own grounds, she had a lulling sense of security. She was happy to have people come to her, for anyone who took the trouble to make the long ride must be a friend, uncritical and accepting; surely only well-wishers broke bread at your board?

She had need of her calm, for the messages from Andrew were disturbing. Owing to a depression that had settled over the East the arrangements he had made by correspondence for the sale of his lands had fallen through by the time he reached Philadelphia. The land he had planned to sell at one dollar an acre he had brought down by slow degrees to twenty cents, and still no takers. At the end of three weeks of vexation he wrote:

Through difficulties such as I never experienced before, they put

94

me in the Dam'st situation ever man was placed in. I would not undertake the same business again for all the lands . . .

Samuel and John Overton frequently came to Poplar Grove to have supper with her; John had recently moved to his own cabin, which he had named Travellers Rest, about five miles south of Nashville. He read the message without his glasses, then put on his specs to see more clearly what he was thinking.

"I told him we ought to keep our land and sell it parcel by parcel to settlers as they came through," said John. "But he was so anxious to go to Philadelphia . . ."

With her husband away she lived in a suspended world in which she filled every hour with endless tasks, making infant gowns for the new baby expected by Johnny and Mary, knitting coarse oversocks for the winter and white hosiery with clocking, sewing a broadcloth riding habit for herself and a fine linen shirt with a double pleated frill of woven linen cambric for Andrew . . . all of her feelings stored against the hour of his return. The Nickajack Expedition of the militia had driven away the hostile Indians and for the first time since coming to the Cumberland she could walk her fields without fear of attack, could plant a rose garden and vegetable patch behind the house. She kept the lamb by her side as a pet. In the first bright April sunshine she directed the field hands in the plowing and planting of the crops, striding across the furrows in her high boots and long skirt of heavy cotton twill, a large straw hat shading her face. By mid-May the rows were showing fresh green lines, and the ewes and cows and horses began dropping their young. There were going to be good crops to harvest, plenty of livestock for food, tallow, wool and leather. She too felt young and vital and fecund; at night her loins ached for her husband, and the child she might carry.

She was prepared to find Andrew disgruntled and upset, but there had been no way to prepare herself for the sight she encountered when she came up from the barn in the heat of a scorching June day to find him sitting slumped in the saddle in front of their cabin. This was hardly the same person who had started out so hopefully three and a half months before; his eyes were sunk in their sockets, his cheeks gray and hollow; the wrinkled brown clothes hung on his body as though he were made of cross-sticks.

She led him into the house, saw to it that he had a bath with plenty of hot water and soap, then got him into a clean white linen sleeping gown and tucked him into bed. He ate lightly, squeezed her hand and fell into a sleep of exhaustion. She let the dark bear-skin blind fall over the window to shut out the sunlight, then gently closed behind her the door of Mary Donelson's former prayer room.

When he awakened he wanted to get up at once.

"Right now I'm stronger than you are," she replied resolutely. She

95

stood with her hands on her hips, her apron berry-stained from making preserves, her brown eyes reflecting her happiness at having him home. "You are going to stay in bed for several days."

When they took their first walk across the fields to the river he was delighted with everything he saw.

"You're a wonderful manager, darling, you do a better job than I do."

They slid down the bank to the water's edge. Rachel took off her moccasins and waded at the edge of the shore, her skirts held above her knees. Andrew caught catfish and told her what had happened in Philadelphia. He had been on the verge of leaving the city without a sale of any of the land, and consequently without any merchandise for the store he wanted to open, but rather than admit defeat had sold their holdings to David Allison, a former Nashville lawyer who had gone east and become wealthy buying and selling western lands.

"Only trouble was I had to take Allison's personal notes. We went to Meeker and Cochran where I bought forty-eight hundred dollars' worth of goods, then Allison took me to Evans and Company where they sold me another sixteen hundred dollars' worth on his paper."

His greatest excitement seemed to center about the packet of books he had toted all the way from Philadelphia: Comte Maurice de Saxe's *Memories on the Art of War*, Frederick William von Steuben's *Regulations for the Order and Discipline of the Troops of the United States*, and Vegetius's *De Re Militari*, known as the military bible.

"By the way, my love, I don't think I've ever told you," he said *sotto voce*, "I intend to become major general of our militia."

She threw back her head, laughed heartily, shook loose the long black hair that had been held up by only one small comb. She put her arms about his neck and made him pull her up until their lips were on a level.

"Do I detect a note of disbelief in that laughter?"

"No, General Jackson; it was pure joy. Now I know you are well again."

3

On the Fourth of July, before the heat rose, they walked their horses to the old log cabin Andrew had purchased as his store. The interior was black, with tiny portholes and smoked walls, everything saturated with dust, cobwebs, ashes and the grease that had run down from the wall lamps.

Rachel grimaced. "I'll bring George over this afternoon with a bucket of lye water, also a saw to cut some window holes. By the way, who's going to sell your goods? Surely you're not planning to stand behind the counter?"

"I wouldn't mind. I like the feel of goods and money changing hands.

96

But I've got to ride the circuit again in September, and if Governor Blount's count of our population goes over sixty thousand we'll have a constitutional convention and form ourselves into a state."

She caught the eagerness in his voice. "Apparently you think we are going to have sixty thousand people? And even more apparently, you intend to go to the convention. I thought you weren't interested in politics?"

"Answering your questions, madam, in the backwards order of their presentation: making an independent state of this territory is not politics: we've got to become a state in order to have representatives in Congress. If you saw some of those nabobs in Philadelphia, with their green silk breeches and powdered hair . . . it's hard for me to understand why those aristocrats ever broke away from England when they spend their whole lives aping everything British."

"Now, Andrew . . ."

He smiled. "All right, I won't fight them today. Answering your other question, I certainly do hope to be elected to that convention. Governor Blount told me in Knoxville that he's going to put my name in nomination. I've got a lot of ideas about how this new state should be set up. As far as population is concerned . . ." he chuckled, "there's not a citizen of this territory so mean-spirited that he wouldn't step up and be counted at least three times."

On August 1, Samuel, who had brought Andrew's merchandise by flatboat from Limestone, Kentucky, arrived in Nashville. It took several days to move the goods onto the shelves: nails, axes, cooking utensils, nankeens, striped calicoes, a few bolts of satins and laces, shoes, hats, stationery, pepper, tobacco. Three weeks later they were paying their first visit to John Overton's Travellers Rest, and inspecting the young apple and peach orchard he had just set out, when Samuel arrived with a letter for Andrew which a trader had brought in from Philadelphia. It was marked *Important*.

It was a short message, but from the way the blood drained out of Andrew's face Rachel could see that it was too long at any length.

He looked up, his eyes dazed, his mouth for the moment wide and uncontrolled.

"It's from Meeker and Cochran in Philadelphia. David Allison is in trouble. His notes

". . . now falling due are not generally or regularly paid. We take this early opportunity to make known to you that we have little or no expectation of getting paid from him, and that we shall have to get our money from you, which we shall expect at maturity."

She stood on the garden path listening half to the low hum of conversation among the three men and half to her own insistent voice. Andrew owed Meeker and Cochran forty-eight hundred dollars, half of

97

which he would have to pay on December 1. How were they going to sell enough of the stock to get the cash?

"I'll find a market somewhere," announced Andrew grimly.

"You can't, there isn't that much 'ready' in the entire Cumberland Valley," said John.

"The whole fault is mine, John: I promise you won't lose on it."

Rachel watched John Overton weigh this promise carefully.

"Whatever we manage to collect from Allison we'll divide half and half. Money can squeeze the life out of a friendship quicker than a grizzly bear."

She was saddened not by the loss of the money, which could be earned again, but by Andrew's suffering. It would be a blow to his pride: the fact that he had been defrauded, his judgment proven unsound, his working capital wiped out. He was not the kind of man to indulge in regrets, but to what new ends would he drive himself to reach that state of affluence which appeared to be his primary need?

They rode up the winding path that led to the top of Hunter's Hill, the highest eminence in the countryside, overlooking the Cumberland and Stone rivers. They reached the crest at about noon. Andrew spread a blanket on the lee side of the hill; they could hear the wind above them blowing away the few remaining autumnal leaves.

"We should have brought Lamb with us," said Rachel. "He would have liked to gambol up here."

"You are taking a gambol every time you let him out of the house. You seem to forget that the lamb is now a sheep. One day he'll be jumping the fence to join his kind."

"You could have made a double pun by spelling that last word with an *e* instead of a *d,* and it wouldn't have been any worse than the first one."

After lunch they stretched out side by side in the center of the blanket, her head nestled comfortably on his shoulder. He wrapped the rest of the blanket around them, then began speaking in a light, jocular tone.

"I brought you up here under false pretenses. I really wasn't so anxious for the picnic I dunned you into."

"Oh?"

"It's just that I have a story to tell you and I thought you would like to be sitting on top of the world when you heard it."

"Wherever you are is the top of the world."

"Thank you." He paused. "I've sold the store."

"For enough to meet the Meeker and Cochran note?"

"No, there's no one with cash who'll buy; Elijah Robertson's paying me with thirty-three thousand acres of good land worth a quarter an acre. The Philadelphia people will give me time to sell. We won't come

98

out too badly once I've sold the land. I don't like failure, no man does. But I've learned a lot; I'll not make those mistakes next time . . ."

He lay quietly, looking down at her and stroking the hair back from her forehead, tracing the high arch of her brows with his fingers. Then he said, "Governor Blount sent me word yesterday that the population count is finished. He wants me to help write the new constitution."

She thought, This is what he really came up here to tell me.

"Good. You'll be helping to set up the state that Father dreamed about when he brought us all to the Cumberland. I'd like to see you at the convention speaking to all those men."

"Then it's done! You'll come with me."

She rose from the blanket, walked a little distance and gazed below her at the smoke rising from piles of burning underbrush, at the fences and groves of trees and the creeks and branches shining in the sun.

"Oh, I didn't really mean watch you in the flesh; I meant that I'll read the accounts in the *Intelligencer* and picture you standing there."

She did not hear him come up behind her.

"It's a magnificent view, isn't it?" he asked.

"The finest I've ever seen."

"Could you be happy here?"

"One would live above so much of the . . . struggle . . . that goes on below."

"I'm mighty relieved to hear you say that."

She turned about swiftly.

"Andrew, what do you mean?"

"My dear, you've been picnicking on your own land. I bought Hunter's Hill."

"But how could you? We've been so strapped . . ."

"I'm going to build you the finest home in the whole new state, Rachel. It's going to be the first house of cut lumber in the Cumberland Valley. I brought nails and glass back from Philadelphia and have kept them hidden away. And wait until you see the furniture: beautiful brocade settees, walnut tables, French wallpapers . . ."

"With what, darling? We've just failed in our first business venture. You say the new land is worth twenty-five cents an acre, but you may only get ten cents, or five."

In his excitement he was towering over her like a slender cypress trunk.

"Ah, my dear, that's the time you must dare to pull yourself up to the heights, when you have failed and everyone thinks you are on the road down. Then you yourself, and only yourself, can reverse that trend! You must search out the highest peak in the landscape, climb it and claim it as your own. Then when people see you, as they'll see us at the top of Hunter's Hill in a magnificent home, they'll look up to us. Rachel, the whole world will come to your door . . ."

She slipped her hand into his. "Whatever you want, Andrew, I know you can do."

4

The day before he was to leave for the Constitutional Convention in Knoxville Andrew announced he was posting notice that Poplar Grove was for sale.

"Oh, Andrew, must we sell?"

The words had escaped her. They had lived nearly four years at Poplar Grove: a woman didn't trade a home and happy memories quite as easily as a man did. She added quietly, "Couldn't we just rent, to Samuel, for instance? He's going to propose to Polly Smith any day now."

"We need cash money for the cut lumber from the mill. That's for labor, and they won't take personal notes."

He had instructed her to show the place. The first family or two of prospective buyers were not difficult for her, they were brought by friends and she could pretend it was a social visit. But by the middle of January when complete strangers began drawing up before her door in their wagons, with big-eyed children peering out from under the canvas and the fathers saying from a hunched-over position on the hard wagon seat, "You Miz Jackson, ma'am? We hear tell this place is for sale. We're look-ing for a likely place, now," she packed her portmanteau and fled across the river to her mother's house.

"You want we should make it look bad, Miz Rachel?" Moll asked. "George and me, we can heap the furniture like a shambles . . ."

"But how we gonna make that sweet earth and the fat animals look bad?" demanded George tartly.

Rachel found herself laughing for the first time in days.

Once she reached the Donelson station she felt brighter, for there was always activity and people here: slow-moving, slow-speaking William the Cautious had fallen in love with young Charity Dickinson and was court-ing her with all the fast-moving, fast-talking ardor of a seventeen-year-old. There was no regular mail service from Knoxville but the steady flow of travelers brought news each day. Andrew and Judge McNairy had been selected as the two local delegates to help design the government, and Andrew was working fourteen hours a day to create what he called a Jeffersonian constitution: two legislative houses instead of one; the right of all men to vote after six months' residence; only a two-hundred-acre ownership necessary for election to the legislature. Rachel read the newspaper report of Andrew's speech when proposals had been offered to name the new state after George Washington or Benjamin Franklin:

Georgia was named after a King, the Carolinas, Virginia and

100

Maryland after Queens, Pennsylvania after a colonial proprietor, Delaware after a Lord; and New York after a Royal Duke. Since Independence there is no reason for copying anything from England in our new geography. We should adopt for our new state the Indian name of The Great Crooked River, Tennessee, *a word that has as sweet a flavor on the tongue as hot corncakes and honey.*

She returned to Poplar Grove the day before Andrew was due.

"I see you practically worked yourself to the bone trying to sell Poplar Grove before I got back," he commented.

"I hope everybody hates it."

"Vain hope. I've got a buyer, your brother Alexander. Met up with him in Knoxville. He's paying five hundred thirty pounds . . . in cash, enough for me to order my cut lumber and other coin-on-the-barrelhead items to start building Hunter's Hill."

John Overton came to spend the evening. "Do I start calling you congressman now?" he asked Andrew.

"Congressman! I'm not interested in politics."

"Then you can put those military books away, General, because you're evidently not interested in the militia, either. That army is going to evaporate unless Congress repays the thousands of dollars spent for the Nickajack Expedition."

Andrew shook his head in despair.

"Now there's a choice assignment! The War Department forbade us to go out on that expedition against the Indians. General Robertson has had to resign because of his row with Secretary of War Pickering over the battles we fought. The Federal government has declared the whole expedition illegal, null, void . . . and now all you want me to do is to get the Congress to pay for it!"

Rachel found that Andrew's prophecy about Hunter's Hill proved sound: he no sooner started construction of the house, which attracted visitors from all over the Cumberland, than people began to speak of his tremendous success. He acknowledged their accolade by starting on a land-buying spree that surpassed anything he had ever done before: each day he brought home new titles: on March 11, a thousand outlying acres for two hundred and fifty dollars; on April 18, another five thousand acres for four hundred dollars; on April 19, a six-forty for twenty cents an acre; on May 9, three separate purchases: twenty-five hundred acres for two thousand dollars, three thousand acres for three thousand dollars, one thousand acres for one thousand dollars; on May 14, five thousand acres . . .

When she added up the books she found that he had bought some twenty-six thousand acres and spent more than sixteen thousand dollars . . . all on his personal notes. He sometimes sold land too; in her strongbox Rachel held signed papers from at least a dozen men in the Cumberland. Each man's credit was as good as his reputation; but let any one fail, man or reputation, and the whole structure would collapse. Rachel was convinced that this was a pure gambling game, like rattle and snap, played more for excitement and fun than for profit.

Both the excitement and the fun drained out when she learned that Andrew was contemplating buying the six-forty on which she had lived with Lewis Robards. This land, which was part of Clover Bottom, had been sold by Lewis to a Mr. Shannon who was now offering it to Andrew. She was amazed at the ardency with which she did not want to own that land again.

"The fields are innocent . . . and fertile," said John Overton; for at the last moment Andrew, unable to bring Robards' name past his teeth, had asked John to discuss the purchase with Rachel. "It adjoins Hunter's Hill. That particular piece will be indistinguishable from all the rest."

"Then you think I ought to approve?" she asked, swallowing so hard that her audible gulp filled the momentary silence.

"No . . . But is it worth making an issue of?"

"I see." She blinked several times, as though clearing cobwebs from her mind. "Well, I'll get over this feeling. We'll run the furrow straight down from Hunter's Hill to the river."

As soon as word got around that the Jacksons had bought the former Robards six-forty to add to their holdings, a wave of argument swept the valley. It had not occurred to Rachel that it would cause a controversy, with everyone taking sides and resurrecting the Robards-Jackson affair for the many newcomers of the region. She had imagined her reluctance to be something private and personal, and now here she was the center of discussion again, her past revealed and distorted. As far as she could gather, half of the people condemned them for bad judgment: this land could bring nothing but ill luck; the other half accused them of bad taste in wanting to show the world that they had been victorious over Lewis Robards and had thus symbolically absorbed him.

But she did not sense the extent of the argument until she learned that John Overton, who abhorred all forms of physical violence, had actually been involved in a fight in Nashville, and had had his eye blacked for his trouble. When he reached the Jacksons' at Rachel's urgent request, the lid over his right eye was still highly discolored, the bridge of his nose too tender to support his spectacles.

"That's the first time in my life I ever tried to knock a man down," he admitted sheepishly. "Of course I missed by a country mile."

"I don't know whether to be ashamed of you or proud." Then, no longer able to sustain her effort at humor, she cried, "Oh, John, how long will this go on? It's been five years since Andrew and I were first married, and three since that . . . divorce."

"I don't know," he replied grimly; "I thought so much time had elapsed and Andrew had become so important in the state that the whole affair would be forgotten."

"But it's never going to be, is it?"

They moved into Hunter's Hill on a Tuesday toward the end of May; it was the day of the week on which Andrew liked to begin new ventures. The house seemed enormous to Rachel, with its parlor and dining room on either side of the entrance hall, and Moll's kitchen to the left beyond a porte-cochere. The furniture Andrew had selected in Philadelphia was installed in the parlor: a settee and upholstered chairs covered in double damask with flowered figures standing out from the satin background, and on the floor a sixteenth-century Tabriz animal carpet he had purchased at an estate auction.

Behind the two front rooms was a music room, completely empty, and Andrew's study in which he reverentially placed her father's wide walnut desk, then lined the fireplace wall with bookshelves. He took the four big outside drawers of the desk for his papers, and gave Rachel the eight smaller enclosed drawers with the brass knobs, for her household bills and account books. Upstairs there were four bedrooms fitted precisely over the four downstairs rooms, but only their own bedroom had furniture in it, the four-poster which they brought from Poplar Grove. The half-empty rooms doubled her sense of hollowness. Even as the small cabin at Poplar Grove had seemed to hold her close, to protect her, so the vast areas of Hunter's Hill seemed to expose her on all sides. Her husband might find the eminence of Hunter's Hill dominating and powerful; she felt it only made them the more vulnerable.

That summer Andrew worked in the fields to raise the small crop that had been planted in the spring. On July 30 the Tennessee legislature voted him his five years' back pay as attorney general. He used the money to build a road up the hill to the front door, while Rachel supervised the erection of a dairy, smokehouse, storehouse, stable and log cabins for the Negro families.

"We've come to the end of our troubles," he declared with satisfaction. "If I could get back to Philadelphia . . ."

She hated the thought of another separation, but kept all emotion out of her voice.

"You'd really like to be our first congressman, wouldn't you?"

"There's so much I could do," he shot back. "John was right about the money for the Nickajack Expedition. If I could get Congress to appropriate that fund . . . and could collect some of my own money from Allison, enough to buy merchandise for another store . . ."

She gazed at him in awe.

"Andrew, you're going to be the busiest representative in all of Philadelphia!"

With what did a childless woman fill the rooms of this big house? she asked herself. It was the first year since their marriage that she and Andrew had been separated at Christmas, for he had been elected to Congress, and left for Philadelphia in November. In an effort to cheer the house with voices and laughter and good memories she planned a Christmas Eve dinner for the family: Mary and John Caffrey and their twelve children, Catherine and Thomas Hutchings and their nine, Jane and Robert Hays and their four, John and Mary and their eight, the latest of which was only a month old; Stockly, Leven, Alexander and Severn, still bachelors; William and Charity, newly married, as were Samuel and Polly Smith; John Overton and her mother.

Because it was really a children's party, Rachel used rock candy for the sauces; two enormous boards were covered with candied and spiced fruits, pickled walnuts, marmalades, honey and jellies, apple-mose and half a dozen different kinds of pie, along with pear and quince tarts. There was a gift for each of her nieces and nephews: ribbons, bonbons, gloves, rag dolls, embroidery equipment; for the boys: knives, shot pouches, moccasins, hunting shirts. Each child ran to Aunt Rachel to embrace her; the sight of the young ones, the children she so ardently wanted to bring into the world, made her cry out in hunger. When the families had bundled up their youngsters and piled them into the carriages and onto saddles, sometimes as many as four hanging on behind their father, she was alone again.

She lay awake in the high four-poster, the curtains pulled on all sides to afford her an island of warmth and security. But the weather had been raw and the wind had a penetrating quality which invaded the house, the shut door of her bedroom, even the closed-in darkness of the bed. Exhausted and let-down after the big party, she listened to the creaking noises of a new house solidifying itself against winter's attacks, wondering how she would endure the months that lay ahead. All the dictates of logic and expediency had made her agree that Andrew should go east to the Congress; but in the stark shivering clarity of the lonely night she knew that the more past business he settled the freer he would be to set up future business. All of his savings for eight years had been wiped out when David Allison's paper had gone bad; all of his work as well as profit from his store had been nullified when he had been obliged to sell hurriedly; and only that afternoon she had learned that the Blount paper for which he had traded his thirty-three thousand acres had become practically worthless because the Bank of England had suspended its specie payments and thrown the East into a panic. From his letter she could not tell whether Andrew was maddest at having lost his money or at learning that America was still controlled by the Bank of England. She thought of him on this Christmas Eve in some strange inn or boardinghouse, separated from her by a thousand miles and weeks of hard travel . . . for what purpose?

There was no dawn, just an ash-gray light filtering through the windows. She got out of bed, went to the wardrobe and took out the blue silk robe Andrew had bought her in Natchez. The silk was ice to her touch. She went through the center hallway and out the side door, then stood very still: for the light had come up in the east now, and below her the river was frozen solid, the first time it had frozen over since the Donelsons had come west on the *Adventure*. She went into the kitchen building where George had left the fire banked, boiled some water in a pan for coffee, and drank the fluid as hot as she could. Its heat relaxed her; she went back to bed and fell asleep.

She was awakened by a considerable hubbub outside the house, and through the window saw the entire population of Hunter's Hill gathered about a highly polished black carriage with red wheels and a pair of matched iron-gray horses.

She dressed as quickly as she could and descended to the front porch. As she walked toward the carriage she saw that it was empty, then in an unbelieving flash a brilliant red monogram on the door: R.J. George opened the door with a flourish and bowed Rachel in. She put her foot on the little iron pedestal. George closed the door behind her. Only then did she realize that Andrew had ordered this carriage for her and had given instructions that it be delivered on Christmas Day. She remembered how hard pressed he had been for cash before leaving for Philadelphia, how he had manipulated and exchanged lands and paper; yet he had thought of her alone on Christmas morning.

Tears sprang to her eyes. She sat as warm and secure as though he were beside her, his arm gripped tightly about her shoulder. How weak she had been: as long as she loved her husband and he loved her they would not be separated. Love was a mighty bridge which crossed frozen rivers and frozen hours: it enabled a man and a woman to walk hand in hand across a sunlit field even when a thousand miles separated them and the field was snow-covered under a leaden sky.

In his next letter Andrew told how the moment he had reached Philadelphia he had ordered a black coat and breeches to be made by a tailor.

They fit me quite well, and I thought I presented a handsome figure. But when I got to the Congress to be sworn in, I found myself the only one with a queue down my back tied with an eelskin. From the expressions of the more elegant nabobs about me, I could see that they thought me an uncouth looking personage with the manners of a rough backwoodsman.

She sensed how this must have galled him, for his manners were courtly; recalling her father's friends from the Virginia House of Burgesses, she knew that Andrew's manners were as gentlemanly as theirs.

In addition his very first act in Congress had antagonized not only a considerable portion of the legislators, but Tennessee as well. This news she learned when she went on a Sunday to her mother's home for dinner; as she came into the big room she perceived several sentences dangling in mid-air like the wool threads of an unfinished coverlet. She said in an impersonal voice:

"Very well, my husband has done something you don't like. Let's get it over with and not spoil Mother's Sunday dinner."

"Let's don't," replied Jane. "You're not responsible for your husband's political ideas."

"My dear Jane, the newspapers will reach me tomorrow."

Samuel lifted his head.

"You remember President Washington's farewell speech to the Congress? The House drew up an elaborate eulogy to make in return. Andrew voted against giving it, said it was a blanket approval and that some of Mr. Washington's acts sorely needed criticizing . . ."

Her eyes swept the room in a quick ring. "Has someone had a letter?"

Robert Hays pulled a paper out of his pocket, then read:

"*. . . Every day's paper proves the fact that the British are daily Capturing our vessels, impressing our seamen and Treating them with the utmost severity and brutality, but from the president's speech it would seem that the British were doing us no injury.*"

"I suppose it's all right for him to hate England so intensely while he's here at home," commented William, "but he has no right to make it appear that that's the way everybody in Tennessee feels. If he's not careful he'll get us into a war with the British."

Jane took the letter from her husband's hand and gave it to Rachel, murmuring, "The last paragraph is for you."

Rachel's eyes went quickly to the bottom of the page:

I make one request that you attend to my Dear Little Rachel and soothe her in my absence. If she should want anything get it for her if you can and you shall be amply rewarded.

She returned the paper, a smile on her lips.

During the latter weeks of January the cold intensified until one morning she found ice on the ground and her plants and young shade trees frozen. Moll was missing at breakfast. Rachel knew that she must be very sick indeed if she remained in her cabin. George too was ill. Rachel put her hand to Moll's forehead.

"You've got fever."

106

Moll leaned up in bed, her teeth chattering. "Sampson and Silvey is bedded too, and Winnie and James and their Orange. Must be the fluenzy."

She made a quick tour of the cabins: the grippe was of epidemic proportions. Among the older folks only one family had escaped, and Moll's niece Mitty. She sent them to bring blankets from the big house and to stack up the logs beside the fireplaces, then dispatched one of the younger boys to Nashville for the doctor. She herself went into the kitchen to brew the bitter tea of herbs and marshmallow root which her own mother used to fight the grippe. She and Mitty carried the steaming pot from cabin to cabin, plying the sick ones with the liquid.

For the next week she nursed her people night and day. She had always respected Andrew for his attitude toward their "black family." She had never seen him deny one of them a pass to visit friends, he never rationed their food or fuel, he refused to separate members of a family, gave them individual kitchens.

"I can't be as easygoing as you are, Andrew," she had once told her husband. "You're not responsible to anyone but yourself, but when you go away and set me tasks to do, I'm responsible to you."

"I think they understand that," Andrew answered; "in any event they accomplish more for you than they do for me."

No sooner had she been able to leave off making night rounds among her sick than she was awakened one midnight by the sound of a horse coming heavily up the road, and by someone pounding on the front door. She opened the window and called:

"Who's there?"

"Mrs. Jackson, ma'am, beggin' ya pardon for wakin' ya this hour at night, it's Tim Bentley, ya neighbor over beyond Willow Spring."

"What can I do for you, Mr. Bentley? What's wrong?"

The man shouted up at the window, the words coming in a frenzied jumble.

"It's the wife, Sarah, and the baby . . . I mean it should be the baby but it just won't get itself borned. I think Sarah's going to die, ma'am, the baby and she both . . ."

"Go around the side to the kitchen house and wake George; tell him to saddle me a horse."

In a matter of minutes she was racing downstairs. In the yellow glow of the porch lamp she saw the face of Tim Bentley. He could not have been more than twenty, but his skin was sallow, he had weak eyes and a chin that vanished at a precipitate angle under his lower lip. She told George to saddle another horse and bring along soap, blankets, sheets, towels, candles and food.

It required little light to indicate the ramshackle nature of the Bentley cabin: the notching was of such an uneven character that one end of the roof had begun to sag; inside, the logs that made up the floor

107

showed gaps of cold damp earth beneath, while the one window had been pasted over with successive layers of brown paper drenched in bear's oil. There were two pots hanging over the fire, a small table stood near the hearth . . . and in the corner a wooden bed with a young girl lying in it, covered by a ragged blanket. The only preparation for the expected baby appeared to be a crude cradle on which rested a linen christening gown they had apparently brought from the East.

Rachel said, "Hello, Mrs. Bentley, I'm your neighbor, Mrs. Jackson, from up on the hill. I'm going to stay right here with you until your baby is born. Why didn't you call someone before?"

"We was hopin' to see it through by ourselves. But it's lasted so long . . . the pains was so hard . . . The minute I heard your horses I felt better." She hesitated. "Are you *the* Mrs. Jackson, ma'am?"

"Who is *the* Mrs. Jackson?"

"The one they talk about so much? But you don't look at all like that kind. That Mrs. Jackson wouldn't come help me."

Rachel stroked the girl's hair soothingly.

"I want very much to help you. I've never had the good fortune to have a baby myself, but my sisters have, dozens of them, and I've helped them. So you see, everything is going to be all right . . ."

While speaking, she had slowly lifted the blanket. Now she glanced down and saw one of the baby's feet protruding. She recognized it as a breech birth; the baby had failed to turn to the proper position so that the head could emerge first. Her sister Mary's first child had been a breech birth; Mary had had the services of the competent French *sage femme* who delivered the youngsters in their county, since women were never attended by male doctors. Rachel remembered the birth vividly, for the midwife had commented that these cases were rare, and that many of the breech babies died in delivery. She spoke to the girl with considerably more calmness than she was feeling herself.

"Your baby is beginning to show itself, Sarah. Before another hour you will be holding it in your arms."

She wiped the girl's face with a cold cloth; every few moments she raised the blanket, watching the baby's second foot emerge, a little later the buttocks, then the two shanks. She recalled the midwife saying that it was best not to try to help the baby at this point. Between times she had the father build up the spindly fire until there was a good blaze. When George arrived with the supplies she washed her hands with hot water and soap, then fixed a basin of water for use at the bedside. She removed the old blanket under Mrs. Bentley and replaced it with a clean sheet; she lined the crib with the quilt George had brought. When she lifted the cover again the baby's hips had fought their way out.

"You're doing fine."

After she was able to take a deep breath, Mrs. Bentley replied, "I can tell I am."

108

With the next pain the baby's navel appeared. Rachel grew tense. Mrs. Bentley grabbed the sides of the bed, making a strong effort, and with that the baby emerged to the shoulders. Remembering how the midwife had done it, Rachel released the arms and hands, picked up the two feet and held them so that the trunk was perpendicular to the bed and at right angles to the mother; then with her free hand she applied pressure to the lower part of the mother's abdomen.

A minute passed, then two. Nothing was happening. Soon the pressure on the cord would stop the flow of blood to the infant. Rachel doubled her hand into a fist and threw her whole weight on Mrs. Bentley's abdomen. At that instant the mother let out a scream . . . and the baby was born. It was a girl.

Rachel tied the umbilical cord in two places with string, then cut between. Next she spanked its buttocks, hard; and it cried. She sponged the infant, wrapped on a tight bellyband to protect the navel, dressed her in the christening gown and lay her in the cradle before the fire. About twenty minutes had elapsed. She washed Mrs. Bentley with warm water, put her in one of her own white gowns, covered her with the blankets from Hunter's Hill, gave her a cup of coffee and some of Moll's apple cake.

It was some forty hours later before she finally reached home, having installed Mitty in the Bentley cabin. She went into the parlor, sank into a chair in front of the cold hearth. She knew that she should be cold and numb and exhausted; but she wasn't feeling cold at all. Or tired. Or alone. She had not been able to bear a child of her own, but that baby, it would have been dead without her help. This too was a way of creating life. She could feel the infant in her arms, its blood racing against her blood, warming it, warming away the dull ache that had settled in her when she had heard, "Are you *the* Mrs. Jackson?"

6

As long and severe as the winter had been, just so quickly was it gone, with the sun bright overhead and the grass growing green on the hillside. The hickories began to show their fine leaves, the buds opened on the honeysuckle and dogwood; the pelicans came flying in long trains, lighting on the surface of the river below. Andrew had said, "My ambition is to become a gentleman planter." Hunter's Hill had the makings of a rich plantation, the land a fine black mold lying on a bed of limestone; if they farmed it diligently it would not be long before he could build his racecourse and train thoroughbreds. Then he wouldn't have to ride fifty miles, or a hundred, every time he heard there were going to be blooded horses raced somewhere in this county or the next.

At that moment her first real interest in Hunter's Hill was born. The hands worked hard to clear new fields, and their crop this year would be a big one. Even her fear of the former Robards land vanished; it was good earth that could help them create a great plantation here, perhaps the biggest and best in the Cumberland. If that was what was needed to keep Andrew happily at home, then she must go about her plowing and planting with ardor.

She was out in the fields in a short-sleeved cotton dress with a wide skirt, her hair piled in a knot under the wide-brimmed straw hat, when John Overton brought her the news that Andrew had persuaded the Congress to reverse the War Department, legitimatize the Nickajack Expedition and pay back every dollar that Sevier and the rest of the militiamen had invested out of their own pockets.

"At last," she exclaimed, rooting her feet deep into the earth, as though she were a tree that grew there, "something good has happened in Philadelphia!"

On one of her visits to the Bentley cabin, carrying hyson tea, sugar and ginger for Sarah and lightweight cloth for the baby's gowns, she learned that Sarah had served a three-year apprenticeship as a seamstress in Baltimore. Since it was apparent that Tim would have trouble providing for his family, Sarah came to Hunter's Hill one day a week, bringing the baby with her, and sewed draperies of the loose-woven material Rachel had loomed for her spare bedrooms. Rachel passed Sarah along to Jane, who gave her an occasional day's sewing, and also introduced her to a friend in Nashville who was delighted with the way Sarah could fit the fashionable new styles.

Hunter's Hill was fully planted by the time Andrew reached home on April 1. He had not enjoyed his session in the Congress, but as far as Rachel could make out his feeling was more of bafflement than disappointment.

"I just don't feel comfortable in Philadelphia, Rachel. Those Federalist nabobs, I think they've never stopped regretting they admitted us as a state. The House is so crowded, and there were so many spouters. It's for men of a certain temperament, men who like to work with large groups, with plenty of persuasion and debate and compromise. I'm not good at that kind of thing. I like to work alone. Just between you and me and the front hitching post, I'd still like to master one field . . ."

"Say, the state militia?"

He grinned, "Yes, the militia. I assembled a library of military books in Philadelphia. I'll take this plantation off your hands now, darling. From the look of it we're going to be rich come next November."

"Well, not rich," she said smilingly, "but I do think we'll eat good."

He put his arms about her waist, which was as slim as when he had met her, and held her lightly, studying her face. Despite the wide brim of the straw hat she wore in the fields her skin was tanned almost as deep as the brown of her eyes.

"I like you when you make jokes," he said. "And you're going to have your husband home for good. I'm free of all involvements. No more politics, no more circuit riding, no more stores, no more debts. From now on I'm going to be a domesticated animal."

The house that had been so empty these many months was now crowded with visitors from all over the state; not only the foot soldiers who had received their long-due pay, but also the young officers who had been compensated for the money they had laid out for ammunition and supplies came to express their thanks, and remained for serious discussions of what was needed to revitalize the state troops. Rachel had never traveled circuit with Andrew and had not known the relationship between these men and her husband; now she saw that they looked to him for leadership. Many of them brought their wives. They came as friends, enthusiasts, admirers, their loyalty discernible in every word and gesture. She welcomed them all: there was food and drink and entertainment; when the bedrooms were filled in the main house there was always a guest cabin that could be requisitioned, and for the single men an emergency cot in Andrew's study. Strangers who came for an hour, diffidently, knew by the heartiness of their reception that they could stay as long as they liked. What they did not know was that a considerable part of her emotion was gratitude: for here at last was a circle she need not question or doubt, friends who would be her stanch defenders. To them she was Mrs. Jackson, ma'am, and not *the* Mrs. Jackson.

Andrew had carried home Caesar's *Commentaries* in his saddlebag, reading at night before snuffing the candle. Now his boxes of books arrived: military engineering, books on military discipline, on fortifications. But the studies he seemed to take the greatest pleasure in were the ones on the Revolutionary War: David Ramsay's *The History of the American Revolution,* Joseph Galloway's *A Short History of the War in America.* When she saw him reading in these volumes with such intentness and relish, she found herself perplexed. Basically her husband was a gentle soul. How then could he become so intrigued with the art of organized destruction? War meant people killing each other; she hated every aspect of it. Stumblingly, she tried to tell him of her feelings.

"But my dear, you know I'm not bellicose by nature." There was an injured note in his voice. "I wouldn't take a first step to encourage war with England or Spain. But if you could be in the Congress for a little while and see how close we actually are . . ."

He paced the floor and made a wide gesture with his arm to include every new military volume in the room.

"The good general does not lose men in war; his campaigns are so well planned and provisioned that he crushes the opposing army with a few swift blows. But if the commanding officer is untrained, stupid, commits his men needlessly, they butcher not only their own troops but those of the enemy. Only the strong, the equipped, the prepared can keep out of war or, if dragged in, end it quickly and without great loss. The weak are set upon and attacked by every passing bully."

"You make it sound very logical and humane. But do you mind if I just pray for peace . . . among my other prayers . . . ?" She burst into tears. "Oh, husband, how I wish we had a child!"

He took her in his arms.

"Darling, God knows what to give, what to withhold."

"Somewhere in the back of my mind I had given myself until my thirtieth birthday . . ."

". . . and that's tomorrow, June thirtieth!" He released her, strode to the door and began bellowing for George. "You wait here, and don't go out no matter what commotion you hear in the hall."

She sat in Andrew's work chair, her hands folded in her lap, hearing his muffled orders, the movement of feet. After a considerable amount of hammering he came back to the room, his coat off, a smudge across his forehead and his shirt ripped just inside the elbow.

"Andrew, what in heaven's name have you been doing to yourself?"

"Come along, but close your eyes." He led her through the hall, then released her hand. "All right, you can open them now."

In the center of the formerly empty music room was a shiny black pianoforte, smaller and squarer than any she had seen before, standing on four delicately carved legs in front and two at the rear. She went to it, breathlessly ran her fingers over the keys.

"Oh, Andrew, it's beautiful. We couldn't bring ours from Virginia, it would have filled the entire cabin of the *Adventure*."

She played a few chords. From behind her she heard strange sounds. She whirled about in astonishment.

"Why, it's a flute! You never told me you could play a flute."

He lowered his arms, gazing raptly at the ebony instrument.

"I couldn't. There was a man living at Mrs. Hardy's boardinghouse who used to practice in the parlor every night. He offered to teach me. I thought how pleasant it would be if we could play duets."

She jumped off the little bench and flung her arms impetuously about his neck.

"Andrew Jackson, you are the strangest and most improbable creature God ever created! And I am the luckiest of wives."

She had never seen his joy at being home or working in his own fields so great; nor had she ever seen him more effective. Watching him run the big plantation, she decided all over again that he was really a first-rate farmer: she was a conservative farmer, unwilling to try anything new; but time and again she was amazed to find how free and open Andrew's mind was: if he read of a new tool or an improved seed, he would send away for it; if he learned of a breeder who was raising a higher-quality stock, he would experiment in the hope of improving his own breed. He said that most men farmed by intuition, and that that was good if their intuition was good, but farming could become a science if a man would take the trouble to make himself expert at it.

In the early evenings after supper Rachel ran slow scales for him while he practiced the ascending notes on his flute, then they would try the songs they had learned together, *Within a Mile,* and *As Dawn in the Sunless Retreats.* Afterward they would go into his office where he worked on one of his military books, drawing up his own battle maps as he read *The Art of War* by Chevalier de la Valiere. She sat quietly by, reading in the New Testament or one of the volumes of Virgil which Samuel had given her for her last birthday. They retired late, yet frequently when she was awakened by the first rays of the sun she would find Andrew long since risen and reading by candlelight at the little mosaic table under the window.

"Andrew, you shouldn't get up in the middle of the night. You should sleep until dawn."

"Sleep? It's a pure waste, when you're as happy as I am, and interested in as many things." He paced between the window and the bed. "The trouble with that first store was that it was too small to maintain itself; it couldn't have amounted to much even if the Allison paper hadn't gone bad."

His voice became excited as he stood looking down at her.

". . . what I'd really like to do this fall is set up a trading center on the Stone River. I'd build a landing so the boats could bring us everything we wanted; we could run our own ferry. We wouldn't sell just to single customers, we'd make it a real trading center, the biggest between Philadelphia and New Orleans; we'd ship our crops to the highest bidder, North or South, and in return we'd take from them whatever was needed here in the Cumberland. We'd build our own whisky still and lumber mill . . ."

She did not answer. The more he built the busier he would be . . . and the surer to stay home.

7

Out of her bedroom window she saw coming up the road a carriage with two women in it. When they alighted at the front door she recognized them as Mrs. Somerset Phariss, president of the newly formed Nashville Culture Club, and Miss Daisy Deson, secretary of the club. The group was composed solely of Nashville ladies; she had heard about the organization from Jane, who had commented:

"They blackballed Hilda Hinston because she's not from one of the *old* families. Why do they have to start by being snobbish? Why can't they just grow into it gracefully over the years?"

She took a quick look in her dressing mirror, combed into place the loose ends of her hair, straightened the collar of her dress and went down the stairs.

Mrs. Phariss was the cultural leader of Nashville. Married to the wealthy third son of an English peer, and herself a graduate of one of the best girls' academies in Boston, she was still using her impeccably preserved New England accent to express her opinion of everything she found uncouth or provincial on the frontier. She was a big woman, with an enormous bosom, yet modishly dressed. Her companion, Daisy Deson, was a slim attractive young woman of thirty-five who came from one of the best-liked families in the Cumberland. She had charm and talent, but in the midst of being sweet and delightful could suddenly lash out with a single sentence of such penetrating cruelty that everyone in the room would wither under the blow. She had been losing prospective husbands by this method for a full twenty years.

The two women accepted Rachel's offer of a cold drink with hearty thanks. Mrs. Phariss then went about inspecting the house.

"What an interesting pianoforte. It's one of the new Zumpe's isn't it, made in London? This is a double Belfast damask, you can tell by the precise way the flower figures stand out. But perhaps you wondered why we drove out?"

"I think it was most friendly of you." Rachel's voice said only words. Precisely what did these ladies want of her?

"Mrs. Jackson," said Mrs. Phariss, "it's my feeling that town society should join forces with the country society. By working together we can throw off the primitive aspect of our backwoods life, and have our community's social and cultural affairs resemble the finest of the eastern cities. We would like you to join our Culture Club, and attend our meetings every Tuesday. Each week there will be a different attraction: a literary reading, a musicale, an inspirational talk . . . In our membership, which already totals thirty, we have only the *crème de la crème,* I assure you."

Rachel blanched at the thought of walking into a room filled with thirty strange women.

"But I never go out . . . I'm not at all social."

"Come now, Mrs. Jackson, you're being too modest," said Miss Deson, glancing about the large, elaborately furnished parlor. "We've heard about the dinner parties you've given here at Hunter's Hill for the young militia officers, and Mr. Jackson's political friends from Philadelphia . . ."

"No, no," Rachel interrupted; "people just drop in, that's all. And everybody who comes is welcome."

"Well, I know you will want to join the Culture Club," said Mrs. Phariss firmly as she rose from the settee. "The wife of our congressman has a public obligation."

After the women had bid her adieu, telling her they expected her for tea at Mrs. Peter Huygen's house the following Tuesday, Rachel wandered down the hall and into the study. Sitting at the walnut desk covered with Andrew's books and papers, she could see her father sitting before this same desk in the Virginia home, writing letters, drawing his survey maps. She felt the reassuring presence of both men, and a warm glow crept over her. It was kind of Mrs. Phariss and Miss Deson to invite her to join the Culture Club, even though the invitation had sounded more like an order; it was an act of espousal.

Tuesday morning she rose early and set out the new costume she had prepared to wear to the meeting, her town outfit she had called it the evening before when she had modeled the soft brown twill skirt and pelisse for Andrew. The color suited her eyes and sunburned complexion, and the styling gave her added height. The skirt needed a bit of rehemming, but Sarah would do that when she came by. Rachel wondered if all women were as exacting as she, when dressing for a group of other women; she couldn't remember ever having been so finicky.

Sarah arrived while Rachel was at breakfast and went quickly to the sewing room. When Rachel joined her she saw that the girl's eyes were red, the lids damp and swollen. The new skirt lay across her lap but she had given up all pretense of sewing. Rachel stared for an instant, then put a hand on Sarah's shoulder.

"What's wrong, Sarah? Are you ill?"

"No, I'm not sick, Mrs. Jackson, ma'am, unless it's my heart is sick. I can't sew on your skirt for the tea party today, because I can't let you go to that meetin'. They don't want you, really. All day yesterday I sewed at Mrs. Phariss's house; about ten of the ladies was there, and they was fighting over you something awful."

Rachel took the skirt from Sarah and handed the girl her own linen handkerchief.

"Oh, Mrs. Jackson, you're so good, you came to help me when you didn't even know me, and you saved my baby, and found me work. You take care of Mrs. Krudner and her young ones when they be sick, and she's just a poor widow woman. We love you here in the country, you don't belong with them . . . city folk. They say you are a bad woman."

The blood drained from Rachel's face; her fingertips felt like ice.

"Go on, Sarah."

"That Martha Dinsmore, she said she knew you when your husband sent you home to your mother from Kentucky for misbehavin'; Mrs. Quincy said she heard all about you in Harrodsburg, and the trial where they accused you of wrongdoin' . . . and your divorce . . . and she wouldn't belong to any club that let you be a member."

Rachel was too stiff to sink into the chair beside her, much as she ached to relieve the weight on her legs. For a moment Sarah's voice faded out; then she was listening again, intently to every word.

"A couple of ladies said if that was the case they didn't want to associate with you, and that no divorced lady could be considered respectable, and they was surprised at Mrs. Phariss to suggest you come in. Mrs. Phariss said her husband thinks Mr. Jackson is going to be a very important man in Tennessee, maybe even governor someday, and that in the East where she comes from it's considered important for a club to have the wives of men in politics, and that all your furniture come from Philadelphia, and your house would be elegant for big balls . . . When I left Mrs. Phariss's at four o'clock they was still arguin' and fightin' . . . Oh, Mrs. Jackson, ma'am, you can't go to that meetin' with those ladies who think you're sinful."

She looked up at Rachel pleadingly. Rachel would have liked to comfort her; but what good to explain to this child that she was already married to Mr. Jackson when they came up the Natchez Trace with Hugh McGary? What good to explain that she and Mr. Jackson had been married for two full years before they learned that Lewis Robards had never actually divorced her; and that she couldn't go into the Harrodsburg court to defend herself?

Out of the bedroom window she saw George bringing her carriage up the drive. He had spent hours shining and polishing it. She lifted Sarah from the chair.

"You go ahead home, Sarah; we won't do any sewing today. And when you get downstairs, tell George I shan't be needing the carriage."

She took the unfinished skirt, folded it and set it in her big cedar chest. Then she went into her own bedroom and pulled the cord to summon Moll. Perhaps some hot coffee would warm her, dissipate the chill.

8

There had always been the chance that when the moment came Andrew might change his mind and decide to go back to Congress; yet the only politics that interested him during the summer were the troubles of his friend and sponsor, Senator Blount, who had been expelled from the Senate for conspiring with the English to drive the Spaniards out of Louisiana and Florida. He had even rejected the overtures of Blount's friends and political backers who had arrived from Knoxville to inform him that he was the unanimous choice to finish out the unexpired senatorial term.

But most of the crops had been brought in; his yield of seventy-six bushels of corn to the acre was the top figure in the valley; the market was good and the crops sold for high prices. Andrew became restless. She recognized the symptoms. There was a time to cultivate one's fields and raise the crops and harvest them, and this was the time for home and hearth; but there was also a time to be out in a man's world, fighting for the things one believed in. All this was in his character, and had been from the beginning. When the Blount delegation urged him to reconsider the senatorial job, she saw that he was carrying their offer around in his pocket, taking it out every few moments to gaze anew at its contour and complexion.

"Actually it's not so bad an idea as it seemed at first," he offered tentatively. "I think I might like the Senate better than I did the House. I might be able to arrange a new Indian conference, and get back the land we lost under the Holston Treaty. Besides, if we went up to Philadelphia for the Senate, we could buy the merchandise for our new store . . ."

The fear that she would have to remain alone at Hunter's Hill for another long period turned into near-panic as she thought of facing Philadelphia society.

". . . no, I couldn't . . . I have to stay here to manage . . ."

"We can afford an overseer now that we've had such a good season, Rachel. Why shouldn't you want to go out and see the world?" There was a tinge of impatience in his voice. "You're happy when the world comes to you."

Silently she cried, All who seek us here are on our side, they have committed themselves, they believe in me. But when I must go out to meet strangers I become frightened, I withdraw. No, Andrew, I can't go with you.

He left for the Senate on a Friday, in the midst of a torrential downpour, complaining that it was the wrong day to start a journey; but since he was due in Philadelphia on November 13, he could wait no longer.

The rain continued for several more days; even when it ceased the skies remained leaden and the prospect dismal. She thought what bad luck it was always to be left at the most disagreeable time of the year. Or was it simply the most disagreeable because she was alone? Surely she would not have given up the magnificent spring and summer days with Andrew when they rode over the fields in the bright sunshine, or sat out on the porch during the warm evenings watching the countryside bathed in the light of the full moon.

No, she would not change that; but the Senate term probably would extend into the beginning of next summer; that could be seven or eight months without Andrew. She wished she could somehow fall asleep and not wake up until the following spring, the way grizzly bears did. Then she remembered that her father would disapprove of this thinking: for Colonel Donelson had believed it a sin to wish away the days of the short life God had granted one.

A few days later Jane came to visit and to read Rachel a portion of Andrew's letter to Robert Hays:

"I beg of you to try to amuse Mrs. Jackson and prevent her from fretting. The situation in which I left her—(Bathed in Tears) fills me with woe. Indeed, it has given me more pain than any event in my life, but I trust She will not remain long in her dolefull mood, but will again be cheerfull. Could I learn that was the case I could be satisfied."

"I'm not doleful," protested Rachel. "I'm just plain miserable."

She went to bed as soon as Jane left, slept long and deeply. When she awoke her mouth and lips were dry, and the heat she felt could not be the warmth of the room on this raw autumn day.

"You all right, Miz Rachel?" asked Moll with a troubled face. "I'll bring some coffee."

As always when she was alone, her despair at remaining childless returned to grip her. Women had children after they were thirty, but these were generally added to a long line. Her line seemed to have ended before it began. Why? Her sisters all had children; her brothers' wives all had children. Even Lewis Robards and his wife Hannah now had a son. She alone had never borne a child, to know its love and companionship.

She closed the curtains around her bed. Her mind went back to the first days Andrew had lived in the Donelson stockade. He had said, "I think the greatest thing a man can have is a family." Of how much was she depriving her husband by remaining childless? Last summer he had told her, "Darling, God knows what to give and what to withhold," but she knew that he was not a religious man, resigned to the dictates of God's will. He had said those words to comfort her. The stores he opened, the politics in which he professed not to be interested, the numerous business affairs in Philadelphia, could these be justifications rather than real desires? If there were half a dozen youngsters at Hunter's Hill could he have torn himself away? This was her failure, that she could not perpetuate his name.

Was there another, more serious failure? Was she a different woman from the one with whom Andrew had fallen in love? From that instant she had heard the news of Lewis Robards' Harrodsburg divorce, and learned that she was hopelessly trapped, her gay, warm, demonstrative nature had undergone a change, been replaced by the figure of the woman on horseback, riding across the fields alone at night to visit a cabin where someone was sick. The inescapable engulfment had turned her inward, banked the fires of her open, cheerful spontaneity, and in her self-consciousness made her search people's eyes to see if they thought her innocent or guilty. Would Andrew have loved her if she had been like this when he had first met her?

She grew thin and pale and, after a time, unwilling to distinguish between the gray darkness of night and the gray darkness of day. Only Jane knew that she was ill, and helped her, giving the Donelsons highly plausible reasons why Rachel was not coming to the Sunday dinners. She did not keep track of how long she lay abed torturing herself with self-reproaches, the victim of twisted and poisoned images, but at length the cycle wore itself out. She awakened one morning to find a warm November sun flooding into her bedroom. She groped at the head of the bed for the bellpull, shocked at the white boniness of her hands. When Moll came running she managed a little smile; Moll stopped short in her tracks, clasped her hands between her deep breasts and exclaimed:

"The Lawd be praised, Miz Rachel's come home again!"

"Moll, I'm actually hungry . . . for the first time since I learned that Mr. Jackson was going to the Senate."

Jane came in while she was sitting in her big iron bathing tub, splashing herself with warm water.

"As Moll says, 'The Lawd be praised.' For a while there I thought you had renounced all the pleasures of the flesh."

Rachel gazed down at herself, shaking her head despairingly.

"Doesn't look as though I have much flesh left."

"Moll will put the weight back on your bones; my only worry was that your spirit was getting a little thin."

"Almost to the point of vanishing, my dear. But I think I'm all right now: a great discovery has just come to me."

"Good, I'll leave you alone with it. Get some sunshine on that peaked little face of yours."

"Oh, Jane, I haven't become ugly?"

"No, darling, you could never be ugly; you have a light inside you that shines out warm and bright, and that light will keep you beautiful all your life."

Moll helped her to dress, selecting a warm woolen cape and a bright red knitted coverlet, and Rachel sat on the front porch with her face in the sun, thinking that she had not been joking with Jane when she had told her sister that she had made a discovery. She had thought that her love for Andrew was as great and full as it was possible for a woman to know. Now she realized that she had been cheating him, hoarding, holding back the love and devotion she was reserving for children.

It would be different now. There were no reservations in her mind, no more locked compartments. How much greater her love would be. Nor could she ever be really lonely or unhappy again; the important thing was to know the full extent of one's love and to give oneself to it. She would be able to face the calendars, accept her responsibility and do her work. She would not only survive, but be happy in that survival.

Her father had been right: the days vouchsafed to one were so precious and so few.

She had not thought very much about her looks since they had come to Hunter's Hill; she had had to be out in the fields in the strong wind, in the rain, in the hot biting sun. Nights she had been routed from her sleep by neighbors, had gone out in the snow and slush, sat up until dawn in cramped cabins, returning home in time to see the sun rise and to begin the day's work. Andrew had told her she was beautiful, spoke of the velvet quality of her eyes, the softness of her skin, the richness of her long dark hair, the gracefulness of her figure. Had she become an old woman at thirty? Had she thrown away whatever attractiveness she may have possessed?

That afternoon she dressed in her prettiest winter costume over which she wore a heavily lined capote, and had George drive her into Nashville. A good many houses had been erected, both on the main street and along the river, some of them of brick. In the public square she found the Methodist church, the first real church Nashville had known. From the outside the courthouse looked exactly the same as it had when she and her mother and Samuel had gone in to watch Andrew and John try their cases.

She headed directly for Lardner Clark's store and bought some new hairbrushes, a skin cream, some French cologne and a soft scented face powder. Then, a little guiltily, she picked up a small pot of rouge, wondering if she would ever have the daring to use it. She remembered Andrew telling her of the law that had been passed in Pennsylvania decreeing that a marriage might be annulled if it could be proved that during the courtship the wife had "deceived and misled" her prospective husband by the use of cosmetics. But there was nothing in the law that made it illegal for a married woman to hold her husband through a tiny touch of artifice!

She had George carry her purchases out to the carriage, then drove back to Hunter's Hill as fast as she could get there. She sat down before her dressing mirror, and her face shone back at her from the mirror. My hair will need considerable brushing night and morning, she thought, and some of that liquid soap Jane uses. Next she looked for the beginnings of crow's-feet about her eyes. But her skin was firm. Her mouth was full and red-lipped. Her face was thinner, the cheekbones showed slightly, the plumpness was gone from under her chin.

She felt young again, almost like a young girl waiting for her lover to return.

9

Few visitors came to Hunter's Hill that winter of 1797 while Andrew was away. To the people of the neighborhood who had learned that she was available no matter what the nature of the illness or adversity, she became Aunt Jackson. They borrowed a plow horse, an ax, seed for planting, meat and meal. There was not a cabin for miles around where she had not tended the sick, comforted the afflicted, helped bury the dead. She became a familiar sight riding alone through the fields and woods, bringing medications and a rapidly growing knowledge of the illnesses of the Cumberland. She went where she was called, not asking who it was or what the trouble, passing no judgment and wanting no return.

From Andrew's letters, the senators were doing little but sitting in their big red chairs with their binoculars trained on the war between England and France. He had ordered a handsome brown outfit with a velvet collar and vest, and had had his hair cut short. He was staying in a comfortable hostelry where he had attended a dinner party given by former Senator Aaron Burr. Apart from trying to get a raise for John Overton, who had been appointed inspector of revenue, and a job as marshal for Robert Hays, his only important effort was convincing the Senate that an Indian treaty conference should be held in Tennessee.

By the end of January, when both Houses and President Adams had consented to the treaty, the signs of his restlessness began to multiply: he sent home specifications for the store he wanted her to build, and bought six thousand dollars' worth of stock for their new trading center. She was to inquire among her young nephews to see if there was one who would like to come into business with them. Her sister Catherine's boy, John Hutchings, a mild-mannered lad of twenty-two, was delighted at the prospect.

She was sleeping soundly one soft spring night when she awakened to find Andrew standing above her. He had left Philadelphia on April 12 and accompanied his stock of goods to the Ohio Falls, riding the last hundred and eighty miles in three days and nights. He was completely done in.

"I've been drenched by sleet and rain every day for a week; my first horse went lame, the second took sick and died. Some of the cabins I stopped at were the poorest I've ever seen; once the spaces were so wide between the floor logs that I woke up to find a snake in my bed."

"Serves you right. Stay home with your wife."

She was rewarded with a smile, his first. She put on a robe and went to her dressing mirror to comb her hair. After a moment she raised her eyes higher on the mirror and saw Andrew kneeling behind her, gazing at his own countenance.

"You send me away looking clean and fat and sleek and see how I come back to you: I look twice my thirty years. I could hang my rifle on either cheekbone, my eyes are sunk so deep they're coming out the other end. Good thing you didn't marry me for my beauty."

She turned, cupped his rough bearded face in her hands and replied in a gentle voice, "Oh, but I did. And you never looked better to me than you do this very instant."

He put his arms about her and kissed her on the lips.

"Oh, Andrew," she whispered, holding her cheek against his, "to maintain one's love amongst the difficulties of living . . ."

". . . is like maintaining one's life in the midst of a war."

She had been under the impression that Andrew had quit Philadelphia because the Senate had adjourned; a few days later she learned that the Senate was still very much in session. She came upon him in his study, writing his resignation to Governor Sevier.

"I simply had to get out. When our people see the results of the Indian Conference, and all the lands that will be restored to Tennessee, they won't be angry at my resignation. That's what I went up there for, and I came home when my job was done."

He became a whirlwind of activity: the new store proved successful; with the first cash that came in he built a landing and flatboat to serve as a ferry; he worked with the overseer in the fields from dawn until noon, bought a cotton gin he had seen in Philadelphia, and rode over the countryside explaining to the planters how fast the gin worked, offering to process their cotton on a percentage basis. He hadn't bought his first thoroughbred yet, but every time he crossed into Sumner County he managed to find his way to the Hartsville Course for the races. While in Philadelphia he had bought an extensive law library, and was again riding into Nashville to handle a few of the matters that old clients were urging him to take.

"I'm very glad to see you interested in the law again, Andrew," she commented. "I never could understand why you should want to be through with it."

"A lawyer can never be through with the law."

Her hours with him were sweeter than they had ever been: this was what she had; this was what she would always have. Sometimes, watching him carry on the tasks of half a dozen men, she realized that he was not only her child but a whole brood of children; and that to keep him happy and working would require all of her strength and devotion.

One evening late in the fall John Overton rode out from their Nashville office with Andrew. Both men were deep in talk as they entered the house.

"What is it, Andrew?"

"Well, there's a vacancy coming up for the state Superior Court. The legislature has to elect a new man in December. Mr. Blount, General Robertson, Governor Sevier too, they think my name should be put up."

"I agree with them," she exclaimed heartily. "Tell me more about it."

"The appointment is for six years, pays six hundred a year . . . in cash. It's an independent office, outside of political factions and quarrels.

I'd have to ride circuit, same as I did when I was attorney general, but I'd still be able to run the plantation and the store . . ."

Rachel pushed back the hair from her brow, and smiled broadly. This is good, she thought. This is secure. Judges are above . . . gossip; no one would ever dare talk against a judge . . . or his wife . . .

10

She did not wait for the legislature to elect Andrew, but spun, dyed and wove some linen cloth. The prospect of six years without change, and a steady routine, kept her making lighthearted jokes as she draped the black material over Andrew's shoulders.

"Judging by the amount of material it takes to cover you," she teased, "you are going to be a very big judge. Pun me no puns."

"But can we afford all this drapery?" he asked as she swathed the material around him, "on a mere six hundred dollars a year?"

"Do you know what I like best about this job? That I will know what to expect tomorrow. Does that seem monotonous to you?"

"I'll draw you a chart for every day in the year. Undrape me now, lady, I've a heap of things to do."

He always had a heap of things to do; he could not abide inactivity: he had built a distillery; he had bought property at Gallatin and Lebanon and was erecting cabins to serve as branch stores. The cotton gin had arrived from Philadelphia and cotton was coming up the river to their landing on flatboats and over the dirt roads in oblong wagons. After the planters had delivered their cotton and bought their supplies Andrew invited them to Hunter's Hill for a visit, a drink and a meal. She found that if she set the noonday table for twenty, the same number her parents had always set for, she would not miss by more than a couple, one way or the other. These men liked Andrew and had confidence in him; in the same sense that his success in the Congress for the Nickajack Expedition had made him the leader of the young militiamen, so his bringing in of the first cotton gin and his successful marketing of the cotton had made him their business leader.

He was formally elected to the Supreme Court on December 20, 1798. John Overton came frequently to discuss the impending cases and to theorize about the law.

"Now John, you know I have no gift for abstract thought. Give me a set of facts between two contestants and I'll reach a fair decision."

"But that decision has got to emerge from a universal principle of law."

"And so it will, John, when you are sitting on the Bench; for my own part I'm still going to try to do what is right between two parties. That's what the law means to me."

123

John paced the study, idly inspecting a group of books stacked on a side table. "What are these military tomes open for?" he asked. "I thought you were reading Blackstone?"

Rachel too had noticed that Andrew was again studying military science. He had a deep-rooted respect for the law and for the position of a judge, but when she saw him consuming the military books with his eyes sparkling, his body poised tensely over the desk, every particle of him vibrantly alive and excited, she could not help but perceive that this was the field in which he had the greatest hunger.

"Andrew, I do believe you would like to become a professional soldier. I mean, a permanent officer of the Federal Army."

"What army?" he snorted. "We have none! Congress, the President, yes, the voters too, they're all deathly scared of a standing army . . . because the armies in Europe were always used against the people."

"That *is* something to be frightened about, Andrew. Even Mr. Jefferson is against . . ."

"Yes, where governments are ruled by monarchs. We could use our army to protect ourselves. England has never really given us up. She'll be back with her troops one day . . . just as sure as you and I are sitting at this desk together."

Looking down at his maps on which he had drawn troops and cannon and horses, it seemed like a game he was playing; yet the ringing conviction in every taut line of his figure portrayed a passion so strong that it at last convinced her too.

Dr. Henning sent a message that her mother had come down with pneumonia. Rachel went immediately to nurse her, and as soon as she was able to travel Andrew brought her to Hunter's Hill. Rachel thought her mother at seventy-six still beautiful; the lines had deepened about her eyes but there was no trace of white in her hair. Andrew fussed about her, saying, "You're going to stay with us permanently now."

"You're very kind, Andrew. But Colonel Donelson and I built our station together, and when it comes time for me to die I want to die at home and be buried there."

Mrs. Donelson watched her daughter's routine with approval.

"You remind me of myself, Rachel . . ."

". . . and Andrew reminds you of Father?"

"Yes. His activities here can no more keep him content than our plantation in Virginia was ever big enough to hold your father. But it was that same will to do things that made me fall in love with him in the first place . . . and kept me in love with him always."

Rachel leaned forward, her elbows on her knees and her face cupped in her hands.

"I used to pray, 'Dear God, make my husband happy here, so that he will want to stay home with me.'"

"And now?"

124

"Now I pray, 'Dear God, let him find a task and a mission that will be big enough to justify his talents and his energy.'"

Contrary to her expectation that Andrew's elevation to the Bench would put their private lives beyond petty gossip, she found that his becoming a judge had caused the disparagement to be directed against him as well. For the next ten years they would live their lives in the poisoned atmosphere of rumor: every action, every thought would be colored and influenced by it. How easily it spread, how quickly it was absorbed into the blood stream and became a near-truth! Even the brief happy days of respite, when they were free of attack, proved to be in themselves periods for the storing up and creating of material for the next siege. How unerringly rumor fastened onto the vulnerable facts, and sucked its sustenance from them, twisting and perverting until the character lay dead. Despite the fact that Andrew won praise throughout the state for getting rid of weak and crooked sheriffs, for buttressing the authority of the local officers of the court and instilling a rigid respect for the Bench wherever he sat, there were those in Nashville, many of the women of the Culture Club, who set out to prove that Mrs. Jackson was a backwoodswoman who was at home only among the poor and ignorant newcomers to the area, and that Mr. Jackson did not have the dignity or decorum required of a judge. They kept alive his criticism of George Washington, and in particular used him as a whipping boy in the encomiums when Washington died. They accused him of having represented the militia in the House rather than the whole state of Tennessee; and of having left his work unfinished when he walked out on his job as senator. They resurrected stories of his quarrels, one with Judge McNairy, caused by McNairy's brother carrying unfounded tales, which Andrew and his old friend had patched up; another with Senator Cocke, who claimed Andrew had been illegally appointed by Governor Sevier to replace him in the Senate, and which had almost ended in a duel; a third with Governor Sevier three years before, when the first major general of the Tennessee militia was to be elected, and Andrew had defeated the governor's maneuver to delegate the power of military appointments to men of his own choosing. The two men had called each other some unsavory names but in the end had apologized and resumed their friendship.

Rachel thought that John Overton and Samuel looked at her rather strangely when she urged them not to discuss these tales with Andrew; weeks later she learned that her husband was working equally to suppress the whispering campaign against her. Picking up the first of the talk outside his store one day, he had sent a friend to try to locate the source, and to see if the center of the activity was not in the kitchen of Betsey Harbin. The friend had been obliged to write back:

I can't learn that Betsey has said anything injurious of Mrs. Jackson.

Andrew had then inquired if a certain Mrs. Ball was the talebearer. The investigator had replied:

I pledge you that Mrs. Ball did not either directly or indirectly say anything intending to injure the reputation of Mrs. Jackson.

Rachel was shattered at the thought of Andrew devoting his time and energy to combating kitchen gossip. This matter of the unceasing talk about their past had never been discussed by either of them; it was too painful. Each had borne his own burden and pretended he knew nothing of what was going on. Now she sought her husband in his study.

"Andrew, I just can't let you waste your time and energy trying to fight gossip; it's a Hydra-headed monster. Not all the combined armies in the world can stop women from talking."

"But why should they want to hurt us?"

"The fault has been mine. I did not obey Mrs. Phariss's demand that I join her group. I'm going to become a member of the Culture Club, go to their meetings and give parties for them here . . ."

The declaration took all her strength. She sought shelter in his arms. He sat on a corner of his desk and held her close.

"Rachel, make no mistake about it, if they can conquer you with these methods you will not only be their slave but you will be at the mercy of every last person who stoops to slander to gain his ends. We've committed no crime, we've broken none of the commandments, we've hurt no man or woman, and we've helped a good many. We've got to be strong inside ourselves."

She was startled at the grim tone of his voice.

"All I want, Andrew, is for people to stop talking about us."

"We have stanch and loving friends all over Tennessee. In Knoxville and Jonesboro I have been asked again and again, 'Won't you bring Mrs. Jackson with you the next time you come?' By the Eternal, Rachel, you are going with me!"

It was her first trip with Andrew since they had come up the Natchez Trace. For this journey into society she would need traveling dresses, gowns for tea with the ladies of Knoxville and for visits to the courts; cloaks and shawls, slippers and gloves, hats and extra ivory combs. She would make the clothing, the accessories would be bought at Tatum's or Clark's in Nashville. She took inventory of the bolts of cottons and heavier linens stacked on the sewing-room shelves, then estimated how much lace, velvet and sheer linen batiste she would need for the three-month circuit. Sarah Bentley came every morning to sew. Rachel peered over her shoulder at the measurements; no question about it, striding the furrows of newly planted fields had added two inches to her hips!

She filled her hatboxes and Andrew's two aged trunks, then sent to Jane's for another. Her scented handkerchief was clutched into a tiny ball by the time she and Andrew drove down Hunter's Hill in their carriage.

In Knoxville Governor Sevier gave them an official banquet to which everyone in the government was invited. The Blount family held a magnificent ball; William Blount, the former senator, had died a few months before, but Willie, his half brother, was equally devoted to Andrew. At Hartsville they were the guests of honor for the opening of the racing season. She had not realized how many families she had entertained at Hunter's Hill, but every stop on the circuit was the occasion for a gala party. Her trepidation lessened, her natural buoyancy and gaiety rose as she found herself surrounded by old friends from early morning until she and Andrew could escape to their bed late at night. Lying by her husband's side she would close her eyes and think of the most gratifying picture she would take back to Hunter's Hill: Andrew presiding over the Knoxville court, handsome in his black gown, his tall lean figure towering over the courtroom, his face serious, his eyes somber, treated with vast respect by officers, lawyers and clients alike. She knew that he always had his brace of pistols resting on a little table out of sight but within immediate reach, for there was considerable brawling and turmoil in the courts, particularly in those closest to the newly established Indian frontier.

She was constantly amazed at the growth of Tennessee. When Colonel Donelson had ended his *Adventure* journey and the family had put up their tents on Clover Bottom, his group combined with Colonel Robertson's had made up about two hundred people. Now there were more than a hundred thousand people living in the state, with immigrant families pouring in so fast that in some places on the main road their carriages could not move because of the solid stream of wagons coming west. The wilderness through which she and Andrew had made their way on the last leg of the journey up the Natchez Trace was dotted with thriving settlements, the Trace was a tol'able road and on every side she saw cabins, barns, cultivated fields of corn, cotton and tobacco. Where she and Andrew had slept on the ground, cooking their supper over an open fire, there were now comfortable inns, county seats, courthouses, churches.

There was also a mail service to carry news home to her mother and Jane. From Jane she learned that the reports of the many banquets and balls with which she was being honored had had the effect of silencing her detractors.

Hunter's Hill and the stores were running at a profit for the time being.

"It's a good thing," groused Andrew. "I've been working for the county, the territory, the state and the nation for some twelve years now and I've yet to make my first dollar over expenses. You sure can't get rich working for the government."

"You're not supposed to, Andrew. Generals don't get rich, either. But they did name that new district Jackson County, after you."

Their serenity was frequently interrupted by outside events: John Overton lost the girl he was courting to a rival; Stockly, who had cleared some two hundred thousand dollars on gigantic speculations, was indicted along with his father-in-law by North Carolina for land fraud, though Governor Sevier refused to honor the request for extradition; in June their stillhouse burned down, consuming upward of three hundred gallons of whisky and rendering the still useless by melting down the caps and worms. At the end of the summer Mrs. Donelson died and was buried on her own plantation as she had requested. Severn, the sickly member of the family, promptly married Elizabeth Rucker, nineteen years younger than himself.

At the turn of the century practically every one in Tennessee voted the Republican ticket for the election of Thomas Jefferson and Aaron Burr, both of whom were sympathetic to the western states. When by a technicality Burr received the same number of electoral votes as Jefferson, the election was thrown into the House, where the defeated and disgruntled Federalists, who hated Jefferson as a revolutionist, did everything in their power to subvert the election and put Burr into the presidency. Aaron Burr was loved in Tennessee because he had been one of the leaders in the fight to have the state admitted to the Union, but even the Tennesseans wondered why he did not step up to the dais of the House and make the simple declaration that he had run for the vice-presidency, an act of forthright honesty that would have put an immediate end to the paralyzing controversy.

They made a new friend, John Coffee, a captain in the militia and the only man who, in Rachel's estimation, dwarfed her husband physically. Andrew had the determined strength of the man of will and grit, but Coffee wore his easily; powerfully built, he was gentle as the lamb she had raised at Poplar Grove, and so enormous he filled any room he entered. Andrew asked:

"Jax, I try to tell the truth most of the time but it seems to me that I frequently miss by a fraction. How do you manage to drive the center every shot?"

Coffee's face was round and full; his skin sunburned from his outdoor life as a surveyor and from running his own flatboat containing casks of salt to outlying river settlements.

"I'm not clever enough to distinguish between the various kinds of truth," he replied. "They all look alike to me."

Andrew was again plunged into state politics. Governor John Sevier, having served three consecutive terms, was obliged by the constitution to step aside for one session. Up to this time Tennessee politics had been controlled by the Blounts and Sevier on a friendly basis; now the Blount faction, to which Andrew belonged, decided to form its own party and elect its own governor. At a caucus in Blount's home early in the year they selected Andrew's friend and colleague, Judge Archibald Roane. Andrew resisted the considerable pressure put on him to stand for the Congress again.

"I don't want to leave the state," he confided to Rachel. "Major General Conway is ill; within a year I think our militia is going to need a new commanding officer . . ."

Major General Conway died. The election was posted for a new commanding officer. John Sevier immediately announced his candidacy; just as promptly Andrew was nominated by a group of militiamen. Knowing how passionately he wanted this post, Rachel imagined he would resign from the Bench to fling himself into the campaign. Instead he told her:

"I've always believed that the office should seek the man and not the man the office. I'm not saying a chap hasn't the right to be ambitious for a job, to study and prepare himself for it, yes, and even to let people know that he has mastered the field . . ."

"Then you really believe you have a chance?"

"Yes, a good one."

Among the officers of the militia seventeen cast their votes for Sevier, seventeen cast their votes for Andrew Jackson. According to the state constitution the deciding vote had then to be cast by the newly elected Governor Roane. Former Governor Sevier, chagrined at the tie, sent a message to Andrew requesting that he withdraw. Andrew replied that he would not walk out on the men who had supported him, and that he thought the properly constituted authority should make the decision. Bitterly angry, Sevier announced:

"What has this redheaded upstart ever done that entitles him to be military commander in chief of Tennessee? His whole warlike experience and service may be summed up in leading fifteen or twenty men on the trail of about a dozen Indians. He has the reputation of a fighting man, his friends say. Fighting whom?"

Governor Roane cast the deciding vote for Andrew. He was jubilant. Rachel said:

"I thought you were a small boy chasing rainbows."

Andrew laughed. "I'll not let anybody call me general until I win some battles. Nevertheless, the whole discipline of the militia has deteriorated during Conway's illness, and my first task is to rebuild the fighting spirit. The state of Tennessee is going to know they've got a new commanding officer. I'll never rest until it is a first-class fighting force."

She felt his eagerness to begin; yet how could it be possible for a man to sit in the Supreme Court and at the same time be a major general of the militia?

For his first general muster in Nashville in May, Andrew had a uniform made, the first he had ever owned. The collar was high, coming up just under his ears, with a long double-breasted coat, a row of buttons down either side, gold-braid epaulets and a broad brightly colored sash.

He tried to persuade Rachel to come with him to the muster, which was the grand event of the year for Nashville. All officers were dressed in their gayest trappings, the soldiers in fringed hunting shirts; the best marksmen in the state would be present for the shooting match. In many aspects the muster was actually a county fair, ringed by peddlers, farmers with horses, cows and pigs to trade, housewives selling their prize preserved fruits, cake men selling ginger cakes, the potters and ironmongers displaying their finest handiwork. It was Andrew's duty to supervise the inspection of the foot soldiers, making sure every commissioned officer had side arms, that every private was provided with either a musket, a cartouche box with nine charges of powder and ball, or a rifle, powder horn, shot pouch, spare flint, one picker and worm. With the horse troop he had to ascertain that every soldier had a good mount at least fourteen hands high, with a serviceable saddle, bridle, pistol, sword and cap, shoe boots, spurs, cartouche box and cartridges. The men received no pay and provided their own horses, uniforms, guns and ammunition, a situation which Andrew was determined to remedy as soon as he could wangle funds out of the state legislature.

He had ridden his fastest horse to the muster, but the bad news reached Hunter's Hill ahead of the returning general. Captain John Coffee brought it, his usually amiable face set in grim lines as he explained:

"The reason I'm here is I'm afraid Mr. Jackson will do something rash. You must calm him. It seems there was a young fellow at the muster, Charles Dickinson, a friend of Sevier's. They say he's the most brilliant young lawyer in Nashville. Trained by John Marshall. Dickinson was standing with a group of friends when the general rode onto the parade ground. Someone asked:

" 'What great military exploit has Mr. Jackson performed that entitles him to such exalted rank and gorgeous trappings?'

"Dickinson had been drinking; he replied in a voice loud enough for everyone to hear:

" 'Why, gentlemen, he has done a most daring exploit. He has captured another man's wife!' "

Rachel placed her weight against the mantel, trembling.

"Dickinson has a reputation as the best shot in the Cumberland Valley, ma'am," continued Coffee. "Andrew's a great commanding officer, but I can outshoot him ten to one. Don't let him challenge Dickinson to a duel; if there's going to be shooting, I want to be at the other end."

She thanked Jax for his offer to fight in her behalf, then ran up to her room and threw herself face down across the bed. She wanted sufficient time to quiet her pounding heart before she had to cope with her husband.

It was unbelievable to her that a gentleman could make such a coarse joke because Andrew had defeated his friend in an election. He had been drinking, Coffee said, and that was some mitigation; but how close to the top of his mind their story must have been if it could spring to his lips so spontaneously.

She thought, Andrew and I have been married a full ten years now. Would they never forget? Charles Dickinson's remark would be repeated all over Tennessee, in every home and shop and tavern . . . her name the loose thread in the idle talk.

Suddenly she sat upright in the center of the bed, for Andrew was winding his way up Hunter's Hill. Her head cleared: bad as Dickinson's remark had been, it had merely intimated that Andrew had won her away from her husband. She would have to make Andrew accept this and allow the affair to pass over. Not that he would forget; but he must not provide the community with further fuel to keep alive their bright fires of scandal.

Reluctantly, Andrew agreed.

12

She sat at the walnut desk with her ledger spread out before her. Andrew came quietly behind her, leaned over and kissed the top of her head.

"A lucky thing your father taught you to figure in that arithmetic book: Hunter's Hill is now supporting all our other activities."

She turned about at the seriousness in his voice, ill concealed under the banter.

"I'm having problems at the store," he confided. "John Hutchings is fine as a clerk, but I've been involved in so many things that the management has fallen on his shoulders . . . and he's just too green."

He also was having considerable trouble with Thomas Watson, whom

131

he had taken in to handle his huge cotton operation, and from whom he had been unable to get any accounting.

The unfortunate incident at the master muster proved to be the start of a series of disturbances. What had appeared to be a friendly break with former Governor Sevier now began to look like a political fight to the finish. After several years in which Andrew's opinions as a judge had been accepted with confidence, two new decisions brought condemnation upon his head. The first was one in which he was sitting with the two other judges of the circuit as a court of appeal involving a case which he himself had tried under Judge McNairy while he was attorney general. Now, as an appeal judge, he reversed himself; and was charged with being inconsistent, changeable, unreliable.

"I can't see that I had much choice," he expostulated to Rachel as they sat over their supper table scanning the criticism in the Knoxville newspapers. "I could have agreed with my reasoning of ten years ago and be called consistent, or decided according to what I thought was legal and proper for today."

The second outburst followed shortly after. Finding that a petitioner was one with whom he had been on unfriendly terms, Andrew summoned the petitioner's lawyer and urged him to ask for a postponement so that the case could be brought before another judge. He was immediately accused of being unable to decide a case on its legal merits. The probability that these attacks were politically inspired was of little comfort to her.

John Sevier, now qualified to run again for the governorship, announced his candidacy. Governor Roane announced his candidacy also. Sevier and his political followers let loose a thunderous blast, accusing Roane, Jackson and their supporters of double-dealing. Andrew maintained that Sevier was no longer fit to be governor.

"I can prove that he was deeply involved in that Glasgow land-fraud case. I'm going to expose him by showing how they changed the sale price on the warrants and falsified the dates. Why, they've stolen almost a sixth of the state of Tennessee."

Rachel was shocked: wasn't this the same affair in which Stockly had been involved several years before?

"Andrew, won't people accuse you of doing it for political purposes, to defeat Sevier in the election? Can't Governor Roane be re-elected without this exposure?"

"No. Sevier is too good an actor. He'll stump the state with that saber rattling at his side and relive the thirty battles he won during the War for Independence."

And he'll win, Rachel thought. His group will come into power again, and Andrew's group will go out. If he wants to stay on the Bench, they'll defeat him.

But she found herself unprepared for the clamor caused by Andrew's

132

accusing letter in the Tennessee *Gazette* of July 27, 1803. Everyone in the state read it or had it read to him; and they discussed with equal avidity Sevier's defense in the *Gazette* of August 8. Andrew left Hunter's Hill to hold court in Jonesboro, took ill on the way and was so racked by diarrhea he was hardly able to remain on his horse. He had no sooner reached the inn than a mob of Sevierites threatened to tar and feather him. Andrew stood with both pistols cocked. The crowd saw "Shoot!" in his eyes; it melted away.

The contest was no longer between two governors; people now asked, "Who are you siding with, Sevier or Jackson?" A few weeks later they elected Sevier by a full one-third majority.

"Who do you suppose had the worst time," Rachel asked Jane, "the Christians who were in the Coliseum being devoured by lions, or their sympathizers in the stands, watching them be devoured?"

"The sympathizers," replied Jane; "they had to wake up the next morning and remember what they had seen the day before."

I'm in an even worse position, thought Rachel; I feel as if I were in the catacombs . . . waiting my turn . . .

On Saturday, October 1, 1803, after the adjournment of his court, Andrew made his way toward the front door of the Knoxville courthouse. In the sunshine he saw John Sevier standing on the top step with a crowd below him. Before he could turn away he heard Sevier say:

"Judge Jackson is an abandoned rascal, a man whom the people have made a judge and thereby promoted to the unmerited status of a gentleman." He shook his cavalry saber in its scabbard, then continued, "I won independence for this state, I drove out the Indians, I formed your first government . . ."

Andrew strode to the top of the steps; he stood face to face with the fifty-eight-year-old Sevier.

"I do not contest your past services to the state of Tennessee, Governor. But by the same token I believe that I have performed public services too, and most of them have met with the approval of my fellow citizens."

"Services?" cried Sevier in a thunderous voice which carried to the other end of the public square. "I know of no great service you have rendered to the country except taking a trip to Natchez with another man's wife!"

Murder sprang into Andrew's eyes.

"Great God! Do you mention *her* sacred name?"

Sevier drew his sword. Andrew swung his heavy walking stick. Shots were fired in the crowd. A bystander was hurt. Friends intervened, carrying Andrew off in one direction and Sevier in another.

Andrew instantly challenged Sevier to a duel.

The remark made by Charles Dickinson had been uttered by an irresponsible young man who had been drinking and who later had denied having made it. But this charge by Governor Sevier in a public square

133

could never be denied or retracted. The passage of the years would not matter now; the length or extent of Andrew's service, or her own years of hard work, simple living, of neighborly kindliness would never wash away the sin of having lived a troubled youth.

For Governor Sevier had accused them before the world of wanton, deliberate adultery . . . John Sevier was the best-known and most influential man in Tennessee; as governor of the state he was its first citizen. If it were acceptable for him to heap calumny upon her character, what reason would there be for anyone, ever, to keep silent on the subject of Rachel and Andrew Jackson? Her personal life had become a political weapon.

When the ache had passed into a pulsating numbness her thoughts returned to Knoxville and to Andrew. The illegality of dueling in Tennessee would not stop him; the two men would meet across the border of the Indian country. The governor of the state, and a member of the Supreme Court, dueling on the frontier; what further scandal this would create!

Travelers and friends came in from Knoxville bringing news. Sevier had ignored Andrew's first challenges, confiding to his friend that his advanced years and large family should make it unnecessary for him to satisfy Jackson's demand. When Andrew's friends urged him to drop the challenge out of respect for his judicial robes he offered to resign immediately. When Sevier failed to answer his challenge, he placed an advertisement in the *Gazette*.

To all who shall see these presents Greeting. Know ye that I Andrew Jackson, do pronounce, publish, and declare to the world, that his excellency John Sevier, Captain General, and commander in chief of the land and naval forces of the state of Tennessee, is a base coward and poltroon. He will basely insult but has not courage to repair.

ANDREW JACKSON

Andrew left with his seconds for Southwest Point on the Cherokee boundary. For five days he awaited Sevier's arrival . . . and for five days Rachel plodded through her tasks, dreading the news, yet unable to believe that the two men would seriously injure each other. Surely they had been friends too long to fire for a kill? Many duels were fought but few had serious consequences, at worst a leg wound; adversaries frequently fired into the air, their pent-up anger spent with the bullet.

At last word came: just as Andrew was leaving Southwest Point, Sevier rode up with his party. In the melee Andrew drew his pistols and so did Sevier, advancing on each other with epithets. Members of both parties made overtures, the principles damned each other still once again, but put up their arms.

It was the end of the duel. But not of the strife.

134

On November 5, Governor Sevier pushed two bills through the legislature, the first of which split the Tennessee militia into two districts; the other provided for a second major general, to have equal status with General Jackson. The next morning Governor Sevier appointed former Senator William Cocke head of the eastern division of the militia, and dispatched him to Natchez with five hundred militiamen to make sure that Spain did not interfere with the transfer of the Louisiana Purchase to the United States. After rigorously training his troops and bringing them to peak form, Major General Jackson had been left twiddling his thumbs at home, his men of the western division deprived of the mission for which they had prepared.

When Rachel walked into his study she found Andrew slumped in his chair, his arms dangling lifelessly to the floor, his face ashen and his usually clear, determined eyes lost in some obscure mist. She had seen him through all manner of complication, adversity and despair, but she had never seen him so completely beaten. What disturbed her most was not that there were no words on his lips, but actually that there were no words being formulated anywhere in his brain. The final victory had been Sevier's; the ultimate defeat Andrew's . . . and hers.

13

On New Year's Day of 1804 they sat alone in their big room before a banked fire. It took no complicated profit-and-loss system or surrounding pile of ledgers for them to know where they stood after their years at Hunter's Hill. They had extended considerable credit at their stores, but a drive to collect the money owed them had been fruitless. The furs and pelts, salt, wheat, tobacco and other merchandise he took in exchange in the stores had been shipped out blind, for he could no longer get prices quoted in advance, and when the merchandise reached the port of New Orleans, or Philadelphia, it was sold for whatever it could bring. Most of the cotton crop in the Cumberland Valley had failed; there were now twenty cotton gins operating in the countryside, and Andrew was getting little outside cotton for processing or sale. In addition he had been obliged to bring suit against his former partner, Thomas Watson. His personal notes were piling up in New Orleans and Philadelphia, with the interest charges mounting; and he had the immediate obligation of paying back one thousand dollars in cash which had been loaned to him in Pittsburgh.

"There's no help for it, Rachel, I simply must resign the judgeship and devote my full time to getting us straightened out financially. Money, money, money! The deeper we get into business, the larger our stocks and transactions and sales, the worse off we become."

"Ah, the agonies of getting rich," she replied in a light tone; but he was not to be diverted.

Though he still held the title of major general, his command had virtually disappeared. Many of the officers were blaming him for being robbed of their expedition. It also was apparent that he had lost considerable prestige as the result of the personal feuds. The fact that he had quarreled only after his wife had been publicly slandered was lost in the ensuing embroilment.

Because of the investigation his charges against Sevier had started, the title to a considerable portion of their own lands, particularly those in the Indian country, had fallen under a shadow. All of their lands around Nashville were worth more than when he had bought them, and he should have been able to take a sufficient profit to quiet his most demanding creditors; but no one had any cash with which to buy and all he could get were other people's personal notes.

"It looks almost hopeless," he confessed in complete dejection. "We've got to get a fresh start."

She was shocked to learn a few weeks later that his "fresh start" might include shaking the dust of Tennessee from his boots.

"I think we've had enough of the Cumberland Valley, Rachel."

"But where would we go?"

"Now that Louisiana has been turned over to us, President Jefferson has to appoint a governor. Our congressmen in Washington are on my side; they think I have the proper qualifications: the legal training to help write and enforce the laws, the military experience to set up a militia. It's a great opportunity. Spain is angry at the transfer and she'll fight if she can. England is still searching our ships and impressing seamen; if war comes she will bring her troops in through Louisiana just as sure as she will go through the northern lakes . . ."

What an odd solution to our problems, she thought; Thomas Green urged us to stay right there in Natchez in the first place. How much turbulence might have been avoided; how pleasant life might have been.

". . . as governor, everything would be provided: a home, servants, carriages, military staff, and the salary would be clear cash." He came to her and took her in his arms; his voice was low and caressing. ". . . I remember how much you loved those beautiful homes in Natchez. We'd meet new people, make new friends. There'll be plenty of opportunity for a military man down there; we'll make Sevier eat his words about us."

It was not until this moment that she saw clearly why he wanted to go: to leave behind them the incessant talk, the insults to their love and marriage. It was not that he felt defeated, nor that he lacked the stamina to fight back; he had all these requisites and more. He was simply removing his wife from the battlefield.

She took his head between her hands and pressed her lips to his; she felt the tense bony strength of him.

"You'll be the First Lady of the territory," he murmured. "Remember

136

what I told you at Poplar Grove? We've got to get to the top, then no one will be able to climb up high enough to attack us."

There was no word from Washington about the appointment during February. A load of iron which he had ordered from Pittsburgh and which was supposed to constitute half a cargo was sent on alone; when it arrived in Nashville the boatman demanded three hundred and seventy-five dollars for freightage in cash. Andrew tried for days to collect enough to release the cargo, but could not gather anything beyond the little pile of English, Spanish and American coins which John Coffee dumped onto their dining board, obviously his lifetime savings, and the few dollars that John Overton found himself able to contribute.

"Think of it, Rachel: we own a plantation worth ten thousand dollars. We have thousands of dollars' worth of merchandise in the stores, and other thousands already shipped north and south. The total value of all the lands in our name must be a hundred thousand dollars . . . yet after trying desperately for a full week to find three hundred and seventy-five dollars in cash, I cannot raise that insignificant sum."

"Can't you make a quick sale of the iron and use part of the payment for the freight?"

"I've already tried. The only 'ready' available is the two hundred dollars due me in judge's salary."

Toward the end of February, in an effort to recoup their losses by one bold stroke he instructed John Coffee to make the trip north to the Illinois where a fabulous salt lick had been discovered, and to offer fifteen thousand dollars, if necessary as high as thirty thousand, for it . . . in their personal notes.

Rachel was staggered by the move, even though Jax accepted the instructions without question; how could Andrew be planning to spend another fifteen to thirty thousand dollars when he couldn't raise three hundred and seventy-five dollars to cover a freight charge?

During the next weeks her amazement grew. By that time Andrew had gone to Washington City en route to Philadelphia. The Secretary of War received him in a friendly spirit, confiding to him that the War Department would need two boats built within the next six weeks, to be used in the transportation of troops down the Mississippi. The Secretary also wanted chains for the ferryboats across the Tennessee River; could Andrew provide them?

John Coffee brought Andrew's letter up to Hunter's Hill where Rachel read it a dozen times, shaking her head in disbelief.

"A fabulous man, my husband. The War Department wants boats? He'll build them. They want chains? He'll make them. I'm sure he hasn't ten dollars in his pocket, nor are there more than ten dollars in our strongbox. That's either magnificent folly or magnificent wisdom. Which do you think, Jax?"

"Must be wisdom, Mrs. Jackson," Coffee replied with a slow smile, "because when Mr. Jackson orders me to repair the boat that was damaged at the mouth of the Spring Branch, and have a second one ready in six weeks, he knows I'm going to have them ready. When things got to be done, money's no help, it only gets in your way."

"Surely if Andrew provides these boats, the Secretary of War will let him fill them with his own troops and command the expedition?"

"Couldn't say, Mrs. Jackson; it seems likely."

She did not know when Andrew received the news, but one of the Philadelphia papers brought her the account of President Jefferson's appointment of William C. C. Claiborne as governor of Louisiana. Andrew's scheme of flight, of creating a new life for them, the rebuilding of his pride and prestige, had gone the way of most political appointments. They would have to stay home now and cope with their difficulties as best they could.

14

Andrew reached Hunter's Hill on June 19. They both knew that they would have to sell everything they owned for whatever price they could get. Andrew gazed lovingly at the pianoforte and the walnut desk.

"We'll keep those for our new home," she said.

"What new home?"

"Wherever we are going. Where are we going?"

"I don't know. There are one or two tracts we might save, that Hermitage land, for instance, across the river."

"What's it like?"

"Well, it's a fine piece of land, gently rolling, with abundant springs. There are beautiful trees, one cleared field. I bought it from Robert Hays's brother. The deed hasn't even been recorded yet."

"And a house? Is there a house on it, Andrew?"

"No, just an old blockhouse that was turned into a trading post. Hasn't been used for years. And a couple of smaller cabins close by."

"Could we go see it?"

He ran his hand through his hair, traced the boniness of his face and laid his palms across his troubled eyes.

"I can't move you there. It hurts . . . my pride. A crude, half-decayed cabin on a wild piece of land, just as though we were . . . poor settlers. How low I've brought you."

She stood before him, her feet anchored firmly, determination in her soft brown eyes and in her low musical voice as she said:

"Andrew, ask George to saddle our horses."

After crossing the Stone River they rode for two miles, then took a trail that curved around a burnt summer meadow. Andrew told her she

138

was now on the Hermitage land. They walked their horses through a cool stand of hickory, soon coming upon a bubbling spring and a branch which ran into the adjoining woods. Close by were a group of four log cabins, shaded by catalpa trees. They dismounted.

She stood for a moment before the former trading post. It was already a number of years old but the men who had constructed it had done an expert job: the logs were well matched, the notches evenly cut. There was a look of sturdiness about the two-storied, almost square building, an appearance of pride and independence.

"Could we go in, darling?"

He lifted the heavy leather latch and stood aside for her to enter. She walked in, the sun streaming over her shoulder. It was a single room, twenty-four feet wide and twenty-six feet long; the puncheon floor was as clean as though someone had broomed it the night before. The logs had been fitted with a master mechanic's skill, and the passage of the years had polished them to a high sheen, a luminous silver-gray which threw light upward, illuminating the massive beams. The mortar between the logs had mellowed to the same shade of warm silver. She walked to the fieldstone fireplace which could consume a cord of wood on a cold day; the stones had been selected with care and shared in the silver-gray luminosity of the rest of the room. She stood before the fireplace, deeply moved.

"Andrew, it's beautiful."

"It's just a log cabin, like all the others . . ."

"Oh no, my dear, it's not like any of the others. That name, Hermitage, doesn't it mean . . . a place of refuge?"

Book FOUR

AT THE END OF AUGUST 1804 they wound their way down the hill, Andrew in the lead wagon, Rachel in the carriage transporting their personal possessions, silver, clothing, linens; with Moll, George and the Negro families they had retained following with the dishes, cooking utensils, farm equipment and stores; the livestock was shepherded at the rear. Hunter's Hill had been sold with all its furnishings except the big four-poster in which they had slept since returning from their honeymoon at Bayou Pierre, the pianoforte Andrew had brought her from Philadelphia, the clock and desk inherited from her parents, the bookcases and books from Andrew's study.

That afternoon Rachel stood in the center of her big room, amidst the blanket-wrapped furniture, surveying her domain. At hand were Andrew, Samuel, John Overton and John Coffee ready to set things where she directed. After sending the heavy bed upstairs, she had the men place against the right wall the brocade satin settee which had arrived direct from Philadelphia, and facing it three mahogany chairs. This would be the sitting room. Along the back wall of the big room she placed her pianoforte, Andrew's music rack and flute; this would be the music room; and farther down the same wall Andrew's desk, and behind it the bookshelves for his books. In the corner by the settee she stood the big clock from the Donelson dining room; before the fireplace she left room for the dining-room table and chairs which they did not yet have. She had not curtained the windows because Andrew had promised to triple their size. Moll and George had set the gleaming copper and iron pots on the hooks by the fireplace and were cooking the first dinner at the Hermitage.

"What's the date today?" asked Rachel. "I want to note it down in my calendar. August twenty-fifth? Why Samuel, it's your little Andy's fourth birthday. You ride right over home now, get Polly and the three youngsters, and we'll celebrate our move-in supper and Andy's birthday at the same time."

Samuel was pleased; he went off at once for his family, returning before dark. It was eight years since their marriage, but golden-haired Polly of the symmetrical figure, laughing blue eyes and vivacious spirit was prettier and merrier than ever.

Rachel propped Andy high up on pillows at the end of the long boards which they had set up for a table. The boy was such a close reproduction of Samuel, and hence of herself, as to be almost a caricature: smooth olive skin and round face, with its slightly plump chin, warm, sensitive brown eyes and thick head of black hair, worn low on his neck. Rachel managed to rustle up a few presents, Andrew opened a bottle of his best French wine and everybody drank to long life and good fortune for the youngster and the new home.

The effect of the retrogression in the Jackson fortunes, of Andrew's resigning his judgeship and taking himself out of politics, was immediate: friends were sorry they had met with reverses, enemies were glad they had got their comeuppance. After everyone had said, "You know that the Jacksons had to sell Hunter's Hill and move into an abandoned store over on the Hermitage?" all interest vanished. To Rachel this was God's most beneficent gift; she had an instinct for measuring how much talk was going on about them. From the moment she moved into the Hermitage she found the air sweet and good.

Their expenses and responsibilities at the Hermitage were cut to a negligible fraction; although Hunter's Hill had been difficult to sell because of the omnipresent lack of cash, an old acquaintance by the name of Colonel Ward had advanced five thousand dollars in Virginia currency which had enabled Andrew to meet his most pressing debts. He became easygoing, full of laughter and good will, and had an inner quietude. He avoided the more rabid Sevier clique in Nashville, in particular young Charles Dickinson, but recaptured many of the friends he had alienated during the late quarrels. His chief pleasure was fixing up the Hermitage as Rachel wanted it, putting in big window lights in the main house and guest cabins, building a springhouse and buttery. Late each afternoon when his work was finished in the fields, or in the newly planted peach and apple orchards, or at the office-cabin he had built for himself just below the house, he would come to the door and call for her and they would walk hand in hand across their gently rolling land, stopping to inspect the trees and meadows and to follow the brook which flowed from their copious spring.

Occasionally on a warm morning during the colorful fall and the unusually mild winter they rode their horses into Nashville. In the evenings they sat before the fire, reading, had dinner with John Overton at Travellers Rest, or entertained themselves by playing duets. To Rachel it seemed as though ten heavy years had fallen off Andrew's shoulders; and when he had the opportunity to buy a race horse he had long admired, Indian Queen, and won his first race with her for a hundred-

141

dollar side bet, he looked once again like the twenty-two-year-old boy she remembered standing at the front door of the Donelsons', asking if he might be taken in.

"I'm going to build a stable around Indian Queen," he told her.

"Of wood, or of race horses?"

"Both. I've already picked a site where they will have good grazing and plenty of water. By the way, I hear that the Anderson brothers don't have enough money to finish their racecourse in Clover Bottom."

They were standing on a knoll of the Hermitage lands which commanded a view of their little group of cabins. She caught the note of excitement in his voice.

"And we do!"

"Are you encouraging me to buy? You're supposed to be the conservative member of our family."

"I'm only conservative when it comes to making money. When it comes to making fun I'm as radical as any man who signed the Declaration. One of the first things you ever told me you wanted was blooded horses and a racecourse of your own; I think we ought to try to get the things we want originally, instead of all the ones that crop up along the road that we have no real use or desire for."

He gathered her up and kissed her quickly, delighted with her approval.

With the privacy in their lives and the constant companionship, their love flowered fresh and vital; she felt almost as though they were just married and had moved into their first home here on the Hermitage. She found herself adding a bow to the neckline of her dress, an ornament in her hair, an extra row of eyelet-hole embroidery to her nightcap. When Andrew walked to the wall which separated their bedroom from the small room beyond and, rapping on it with his knuckles, said, "I could take this wall down if you like, and give us a really large bedroom," she became suddenly aware that she had been guarding this little room next to her own. She was in robust health, just thirty-seven, and only the other day she had heard of Thomas Hutchings' cousin who had borne her first baby at thirty-nine. The hope she had imagined to be extinguished would never die.

"Could we leave it . . . for a while, anyway?"

"Oh sure, it was just for your pleasure."

At the beginning of March, while she was working in front of the house preparing the garden she had planned all winter, she saw a rough emigrant wagon coming down the trail, escorted by a procession of silent horsemen. At the rear she recognized John Coffee, slouched over in the saddle, his head down. He spurred his horse, dismounted and asked quickly:

"Where is Mr. Jackson?"

"In his office. What has happened, Jax?"

"Please let me get Mr. Jackson."

His long strides ate up the twenty feet separating the house from Andrew's cabin. None of the riders dismounted, or met Rachel's eyes. Andrew came running, took her by the arm and led her into the house.

"Darling, it's . . . Samuel."

She could only stammer, "Sam . . . Samuel . . . but what . . . ?"

Andrew looked at Coffee supplicatingly. The big fellow said as gently as he could, "A surveyor friend of mine . . . found him . . . quite a few miles out on the trail. We don't know how long he had been there . . . or what happened."

"But he isn't . . . Jax, Samuel's not dead!"

"I'm afraid he is. Shot. We don't know how, or why. He's been dead for at least twenty-four hours."

Andrew lifted her, in a state of shock, onto the settee, and covered her with a warm quilt. Samuel, her closest and dearest brother. She had known it would be Samuel of all her seven brothers who would make the long trip to Harrodsburg for her. She saw before her now the pained concern in his warm brown eyes as he brought her down the Kentucky Road toward home. He had been so happy with the law, and his Polly and their three beautiful boys.

Samuel was buried the following day, next to his mother. They never learned who had shot him, nor even what he was doing out on that remote trail. His death was like their father's. Polly returned to her parents' home, but asked Rachel if she would like to take Andy to the Hermitage. The little room beside their bedroom was quickly furnished for him. He was a frolicsome boy, quick to laughter as well as tears, with a winning smile and a bright mind. His arrival filled the Jackson home with movement and play; and filled Rachel's heart with the kind of love for which she had yearned.

She and Andrew would take Andy upstairs to bed, kiss him good night and watch him fall asleep with the suddenness of a rock dropped into a pond.

"The room is filled," she said softly, "and with a child. But hardly in the way I wanted or anticipated." After a pause she asked, "Andrew, do you think we could keep Andy . . . raise him as our own son?"

Andrew put his arm around her shoulders.

"I'd be most willing. We'll speak to Polly."

2

Andrew officially purchased a two-third interest in the Anderson racecourse; John Coffee, who had become a partner in the Jackson, Hutchings store at Clover Bottom, put up his personal notes for the other third. Andrew was wild with joy.

143

"We'll build a tavern and stalls for farmers and merchants who come on racing days. And when we learn how to train the fastest horses, there's money to be made on the betting."

Work was resumed at once on the beautiful meadow with the rising hill on which a large crowd could stand and watch the races. Early each morning, after Rachel and Andy had breakfasted together, they walked to the corral to see Andrew train Indian Queen. In the afternoons they rode over to Clover Bottom, the boy on a white pony, where Andrew was dividing his time between the building of the tavern and timing the young jockey, Billey Phillips, for he had already added a number of quarter horses and fast mares to their stable.

The spring races had already been scheduled for Hartsville, but by fall they were to inaugurate the Clover Bottom course. At the end of April Indian Queen was to run against Greyhound, Lazarus Cotton's champion gelding. Andrew bet a thousand dollars in notes on Indian Queen to win. They set out for Hartsville the day before, since the thirty miles by carriage would take eight or nine hours, even though they crossed the river at Hendersonville on Hubbard Saunders' ferry. The road led through level valleys of pasture, grainfields and young orchards, crossed shallow creeks whose clear water flowed over pebbly beds, and then climbed the grass-covered uplands.

There was a large crowd gathered by the time the Jackson carriage reached the course. Rachel bet everything she had on Indian Queen, then wagered her pair of gloves against the walking stick of Lazarus Cotton, owner of Greyhound. Theirs was not the important race of the day; the big one came later when Greyhound was to race against Truxton, one of the most famous horses out of Virginia; nevertheless, interest was high in the Jackson entry. Suddenly, seeing their rather small mare against the famous Greyhound, Rachel had her first doubts.

"Are you sure Indian Queen can win?"

"Now, don't worry," said Andrew. "All Greyhound is going to see of that Queen is the dust coming up from her hind hoofs."

But it was Indian Queen who ate dust the first time around the track; and if the second time around she ate no dust, it was because it had already settled.

"Think of the fun we've had training her," Rachel said consolingly as she saw Andrew's disappointment. "It was worth every cent we lost."

It was Greyhound's day; the big gelding went on to beat Truxton as handily as he had Indian Queen. In the din she heard Andrew saying against her ear:

"Let's go round to the stables."

Truxton was an enormous bay stallion with white feet. Andrew put his arms up slowly, bringing the horse's head down onto his shoulder.

"This is the greatest horse I've ever seen on a racecourse. He should have beaten Greyhound."

"Why didn't he?"

"Because he was poorly trained. If I could take him home to the Hermitage with us for one month, he would beat Greyhound by ten lengths."

"But Andrew, he's not our horse . . ."

"You wouldn't like to place a small bet on that, would you, Mrs. Jackson? There's his owner coming toward us now; have you ever seen an unhappier man?"

Mr. Verell approached his horse with reluctance. "I had everything I owned on him, and quite a lot of money I didn't have. They'll be seizing Truxton for debt, twelve hundred dollars' worth."

"I'll make you a fair offer, Mr. Verell: I'll assume that debt and pay you three geldings in addition, worth over three hundred dollars. If Truxton wins an important race for me this year, I'll pay you two geldings as a bonus."

"That is indeed a fair offer, Mr. Jackson. I'll take it."

Andrew's eyes sparkled with excitement. Rachel saw him snap his head as he made a fast decision. He turned to the crowd clustered in front of Greyhound's stall.

"Mr. Cotton, I've just bought Truxton. I have five thousand dollars' side money says he can beat your Greyhound one month from today on this same course."

Rachel gasped; five thousand dollars! In paper, of course, like the land sales; but even so it was a lot of money. She heard Mr. Cotton say:

"Done! June twelfth, right here. Five thousand, side bet!"

The month that intervened was the most hectic they had ever known. There was considerable plowing and seeding to be done at the Hermitage, but the better part of their time was spent at Clover Bottom working with Truxton. The horse had power and speed; the one thing he lacked was stamina.

"That's because they treated him too delicately," Andrew explained. "They were afraid to work him hard for fear of exhausting him. We'll get him trimmed down until there's nothing left but pure fighting horse."

Rachel turned to Andy who was standing beside her.

"Truxton doesn't know it yet," she said, "but your Uncle Andrew has just inducted him into the militia."

Toward the end of May Andrew rode into Nashville to preside over a dinner being given for Aaron Burr, whose term as vice-president of the United States had recently been concluded, and to bring him back to the Hermitage. He rode his finest horse into town, taking along a milk-white mare for Colonel Burr. Rachel went about preparing the largest of her three guest cabins. As she worked with young Mitty, replenishing the candles and soap and putting a number of the latest journals on the table, she knew that Colonel Burr would be considered the most important visitor, socially, to have come to Nashville. She had an uneasy feeling that if Colonel Burr rode to the isolation of the Hermitage straight from the Nashville dinner, their newly acquired peace might be strained.

Returning to the main cabin she stood looking at the long, highly polished dining-room table of cherry wood and the dozen curved-back chairs that had arrived only a few days before. What if she were to give a dinner party for Colonel Burr the following Sunday, inviting a number of Andrew's friends and a few of the less rabid Sevierites? It might be a good idea to include as well Mr. and Mrs. Somerset Phariss, and Miss Daisy Deson.

In the midafternoon she and Andy went out to gather dogwood, forsythia and violets for the cabin; as they walked among the blossoms she thought of the strange career of the man who would shortly be her guest. Colonel Burr had been a resourceful commanding officer in the Revolutionary War; Andrew was not disturbed by the fact that he had been sent down from General Washington's staff and was frequently in conflict with his superior officers. He had been a brilliant and prosperous lawyer in New York, then United States senator during the time Andrew had been in the House, when the two men had first become acquainted. Rising from comparative obscurity to become Thomas Jefferson's running mate in the 1800 election, he had half destroyed his political career by allowing the House to wrangle and vote for days as to who should be president. The previous July he had shot and killed Alexander Hamilton, first Secretary of the Treasury, in a duel in Weehawken, been indicted by the state of New Jersey for murder, and obliged to flee south. However he had returned to Washington at the beginning of the year to finish out his term as presiding officer of the Senate. The chief topic of conversation in the days preceding his arrival had been:

"What is Aaron Burr doing in Nashville?"

Andrew and the colonel reached home at dusk. Rachel was surprised to find Burr a small man, slight of form; yet he was a striking figure, holding himself with military erectness and superb poise. She thought him handsome, with dramatically curved eyebrows, all-consuming jet-black eyes, a sensuous mouth and slender oval face that looked as though it had been carved out of pale ivory. His full sideburns had a fringe of pure white, making him seem older than his forty-nine years. Though she was captivated immediately by the warmth and enveloping quality of his voice, she thought she detected, in the first moment of their meeting, a touch of bitterness.

Sunday dawned clear and warm. By one o'clock when the first guests began arriving, a refreshing breeze was stirring the branches of the catalpa trees. The servants, dressed in immaculate white, circulated with trays of sherry for the ladies; the men gathered about Andrew's liquor chest, plunging at once into a discussion of politics. Rachel wore a filmy pale pink batiste, and her eyes glowed with excitement; both Mrs. Phariss and Daisy Deson had considered her invitation an important one: they

146

were richly gowned in silk and lace, with brilliant fans and very large hats.

Rachel had spent a number of uneasy hours on her menu, then realized that she was being foolish: she would offer the same simple and abundant hospitality that she had begun in Poplar Grove and which actually had changed little in character whether dispensed in a one-room log cabin or a large and beautiful mansion. The guests had barely finished their appetizer when she knew that this was going to be the most successful dinner party she would ever give. She watched Colonel Burr with the gratitude of a hostess who senses that her guest of honor has the entire table entranced, for Aaron Burr's magnetism leaped out to capture everyone. John Overton turned to her and said softly:

"The colonel has the most agile mind I've ever encountered."

Colonel Burr in turn complimented Judge Overton on the recording of his decisions, telling him this would be the beginning of codified law in Tennessee. Colonel Burr expressed himself with utter clarity on any subject, his voice captivated everyone who came within its aura as a beautiful woman does with a subtle perfume. Jane Hays tipped Rachel the tiniest wink from the end of the table, while Robert Hays accepted eagerly when Colonel Burr offered to take their seventeen-year-old son Stockly to New Orleans and train him for the law. The color stood high on Daisy Deson's cheeks.

Yet underneath Aaron Burr's charm and brilliance she thought she perceived . . . could it be? . . . death? But surely this was only because the blood of Alexander Hamilton was still so fresh on his hands? Old General Robertson, who had accepted her invitation reluctantly, said as much.

The most important part of Colonel Burr's talks with Andrew had concerned the Spanish in Florida and Texas: Andrew and his guest agreed that they must be ejected. Rachel had assumed that this was the answer to Colonel Burr's future: he was heading south to investigate the situation in Florida and prepare the way for American occupation. However, as he now talked to the various people around the dinner table she became a bit confused: to Mr. Phariss, who was interested in new settlements in the South, he intimated that the purpose of his present trip was to recruit settlers for a colony on the Ouachita River in Louisiana; to John Overton's brother Thomas, who had only recently settled in the Cumberland, he dropped a hint that one of the purposes of his trip was to prepare for the invasion of Texas; to Thomas Eastin, editor of the Nashville *Impartial Review,* he intimated that he was on unofficial business for the United States government, preparatory to taking over the governorship of Louisiana.

Andrew enjoyed himself thoroughly, and was particularly pleased when Colonel Burr assured him his wines were as fine as any he himself had served. For Rachel the day was successful because the Culture Club ladies had been enchanted with the colonel.

It's so easy this way, she thought. Why didn't I do it before?

3

It was hot the mid-June morning the Jackson caravan started for the Hartsville course. Rachel took her beautiful thirteen-year-old niece Rachel Hays with her and her nephew Sandy Donelson. Andy sat on John Coffee's lap; in a dozen other carriages were their friends from the neighborhood who had wagered everything on Truxton that could conceivably serve as a medium of exchange.

But when they reached the racecourse, jammed with a thousand spectators, she found that only their particular group had any faith in Truxton. Andrew plunged deeper and deeper; he bet the equivalent of fifteen hundred dollars in wearing apparel, and a number of his best six-forties. When the wife of one of the Greyhound backers said to Rachel:

"I understand Mr. Jackson has Truxton so exhausted the poor horse may not be able to run the whole course," Rachel caught the fever and replied:

"I'll wager my carriage and matched horses against yours, Mrs. Sitgreaves, that you've been listening to the wrong judges of horseflesh."

At last Truxton and Greyhound were led to the starting line. Andrew's face was pale under the bushy red-orange hair, his eyes the deepest blue she had ever remembered them.

"I just had a brief talk with Truxton."

"And what is the latest word from the horse's mouth?"

"He says not to worry about his being overtrained."

"I think it's us who are overtrained: if we lose we are going to have to walk home."

"In our long underwear," he agreed. "But if we win, I'll get back all of my grandfather's legacy that I lost in Charleston."

"Andrew, I'm happy." She folded her hands in her lap and looked up at him serenely from under the beribboned bonnet that cast a warm light on her olive skin. "I like to win because it's more fun that way, but if we lose we don't lose anything important."

The crowd suddenly went still, then the starter gave the signal. Greyhound took an immediate lead, setting a killing pace, though it was not too much of a margin as they came down the stretch after the first time around the course. Rachel turned to Andrew questioningly. Andrew, who was sitting tense but quiet, said:

"We're letting Greyhound set the pace. Wait till they round the curve."

The horses began the long straightaway opposite the spectators. Truxton seemed literally to shoot through the air, his flying hoofs making a continuous white blur against the landscape. He finished a full twenty lengths ahead of a thoroughly tired Greyhound.

"Too bad the race wasn't three times around the track," gloated Andrew, "that poor overtrained turf nag of ours would have passed Greyhound a second time."

She said impulsively, "Now Andrew, be charitable in your victory."

"Oh, I'll be charitable," he cried; "in fact I'm even going to give Lazarus Cotton a chance to recoup his losses by selling me Greyhound. Let's go back to the stables. He can be had mighty cheap right now."

Greyhound was bought for only a portion of their day's winnings. Rachel sold back to Mrs. Sitgreaves her carriage and horses at a modest figure so there would be no hard feelings. When they added their winnings the sum was sufficient to pay off the remainder of their indebtedness in Philadelphia. Rachel considered it ironic that after having worked very hard for so many years and rarely been out from under a burden of debt, their retirement had made them prosperous. Andrew set out to travel the state looking for a dozen more horses to add to his stable.

Captain Joseph Erwin, who owned two of the fastest racers in the West, Tanner and Ploughboy, posted notice that he would run Tanner against any horse in the world at the opening meet at Clover Bottom for a five-thousand-dollar side bet. Andrew accepted the challenge for Greyhound. Rachel heard about it with regret, for Captain Erwin was Charles Dickinson's father-in-law, and Mr. Dickinson had half his father-in-law's bet.

After a summer of training, Greyhound beat Tanner in three straight one-mile heats. It was a gala day for the Jacksons, who now owned not only the finest string of race horses in Tennessee but also its finest course. To Rachel's intense relief Captain Erwin took his defeat gracefully, paying the five-thousand-dollar bet, while Andrew's tavern, crowded for several days before the big race, dispensed free cider and ginger cakes.

Captain Erwin made only one request, that Andrew give him a return match at the end of November, this time with Ploughboy. The side bet was to be two thousand dollars, and eight hundred dollars in forfeit money to be paid if either withdrew from the race. Andrew accepted the match for Truxton. Charles Dickinson again had half his father-in-law's bet, and also was half owner of Ploughboy.

When the hour arrived for Truxton and Ploughboy to go to the post, Captain Erwin announced that Ploughboy had gone lame and that he would pay the eight hundred dollars. Rachel waited in her carriage while Andrew went back to the stables to collect the forfeit. Considerable time elapsed before he returned, his face the color of the red earth around Nashville.

"Why, Andrew, what's happened?"

"Something strange; the captain is too honorable to have done it intentionally . . ."

"Done what?"

"Well, you know we agreed on a list of notes to be used for payment, all notes due and payable on demand. However Captain Erwin offered me paper that's not due until next January. I told him I had to have half the forfeiture in due notes, as I had agreed to give that much to the trainer, who is leaving Nashville . . ."

"But you settled everything amiably?" Her voice was anxious. "You and Captain Erwin have known each other for a good many years."

Andrew hesitated for a moment, then spoke to the driver. They started on the way home.

"Charles Dickinson stepped in and offered his own due notes for four hundred dollars."

Two days after the forfeit, Thomas Overton rode out to the Hermitage. They heard him come riding up with the breakneck speed of a courier from Washington City, and went to the door of the springhouse where they were turning their cloth-wrapped cheeses.

"Why is he always in such a desperate hurry?" Rachel asked.

"It's his way of creating excitement."

Thomas was the exact opposite of John, his younger brother: red-faced, heavy-built, a hairy man with bristling rust-colored eyebrows, a beard which began just under the circle of his eyes, and an enormously thick head of rust-brown hair. He had been a valuable officer in the Revolution, and a general in the North Carolina militia: a fierce fighting man who became restive and unhappy when there was nothing to fight about. The Jacksons were hard pressed to understand how he could be John's blood brother.

"That has always puzzled Thomas too," John once told them wistfully; "but the answer is really a simple one: growing up in his shadow I developed an organic dislike of loud voices and bellicose arguments."

Thomas flung himself out of the saddle to the ground.

"What's the hurry?" asked Andrew with a laugh.

"Hurry! I'm already two days late. John gave me this message to deliver to you at the racecourse two days ago; then the race wasn't run, and I hung around the tavern . . . Guess Dickinson did too. He's a loose talker when he's imbibed too much . . ."

Rachel sat down on the edge of the cheese press, thinking, It's going to start all over again. That first time he attacked us it was because we won the militia election; now it's because we won a horse race.

"Was it something about the forfeit notes?" asked Andrew.

"No, it was something Mrs. Jackson said at the races."

Rachel jumped up.

"Something I said? But I never laid eyes on Mr. Dickinson . . ."

"It was when Captain Erwin announced Ploughboy couldn't run. Seems like you turned to your nephew Sandy Donelson and said, 'It's just as well, for Truxton would have left Ploughboy out of sight.'"

Rachel stared at Thomas in dread. He continued:

"One of Mr. Dickinson's friends heard what you said and repeated it to him. Dickinson shouted, 'Yes, about as far out of sight as Mrs. Jackson left her first husband when she ran away with the general.' Begging your pardon, Mrs. Jackson, ma'am . . ."

Rachel was shocked at how surely she had known what was coming. She flashed Andrew a look of despair.

"Oh, Andrew, this time the fault is mine. Why did I have to make such a prideful boast? It wasn't good manners on my part. I struck at Mr. Dickinson with my bragging words; and now he's struck back at me."

"Struck back is right: with a sharp-edged sword, a weapon of war."

"Apparently Mr. Dickinson is at war with us," she said helplessly. "But Andrew, I can't understand: what injury have we ever done him? Why does he hate us so?"

"It has nothing to do with you. It has only to do with his ambitions: he wants to become the political leader of Nashville, and he thinks I stand in his way."

"But you're no longer in politics, Andrew."

He made a ducking, deprecatory gesture of a shoulder.

"True. But I still have friends . . . and influence. Dickinson thinks I'm bad for Tennessee: that I'm a crude, ignorant backwoodsman who might have been all right in the days of the Indian raids, when the Cumberland Valley was still a wilderness, but that the state has now outgrown me and my kind; and we have to be put out of the way in order for Tennessee to become respected in Washington."

"He has actually said these things about you?" she asked, incredulous.

"Yes."

"And you have never confronted him with them?"

"No. He has a right to attack me politically."

She linked her arm through his.

"I'm proud of you, Andrew."

"Well, I'm not so proud of myself. I've kept the peace, but the only result seems to be that Mr. Dickinson is beginning to think me a coward. If I had stopped his talk earlier he would never have dared to bring up our marriage again. I wonder how many lives he thinks he has?"

The whole timbre of his voice had changed. She searched his face and saw that it was dark, his lips set firmly over the clenched teeth.

"Andrew, you won't fight him?"

He smoothed the worried lines in her forehead.

"No. I'm going to Captain Erwin's tonight and ask him to use his influence over his son-in-law. I'll tell the captain that I want no quarrel with Dickinson, and that he must stop trying to pick a quarrel with me."

She took his hand and held it against her cheek.

They rose early and prepared to receive company: Captain Erwin had promised he would bring his son-in-law out to the Hermitage that morning. Rachel thought how strange it was that she would now meet Charles Dickinson for the first time; how could it be that a man would set himself up as her mortal enemy without ever having laid eyes on her?

"I have great hopes for this meeting," she confided to Andrew; "I always think it difficult for people to hate each other once they have met and shaken hands."

She had been given many descriptions of Charles Dickinson by her friends and family: Dickinson was one of the best-looking men in the Cumberland Valley, with finely molded features and enormous eyes set wide apart; he was young, only twenty-seven, carried himself with a flashing poise, and even at this hour of the morning was immaculately garbed in royal-blue nankeens, an Irish-linen shirt and a handsome broad-brimmed hat. There had been stories of his excessive drinking, yet none of it showed on his smooth light skin.

It was apparent to Rachel that Mr. Dickinson had hated every foot of this journey out to the Hermitage, but it was also apparent that he would obey his father-in-law, a man half his size and twice his age, with a small mop of white hair standing straight up almost in the middle of his head, and twinkling eyes set deep under bony brows. Captain Erwin shook hands with Rachel, then turned to his son-in-law and said:

"May I present Mr. Charles Dickinson?"

Mr. Dickinson bowed low without looking at her. She had wanted to welcome him warmly, but the very remoteness of his bow made it impossible.

"Won't you sit down, gentlemen?" she asked. "You'll have a stirrup cup after your ride?"

Dickinson sat rigidly at the end of the settee, took the cup from Moll, touched it to his lips without drinking, then set it on the table beside him.

"Mr. and Mrs. Jackson, I have been accused of making a personal remark about you. I do not believe I passed that remark, for I have no memory of it. However, I had been drinking . . . Captain Erwin insists that I owe you an apology even if I can't remember having given offense. I herewith offer that apology."

How clear he had made it that he was offering this apology to satisfy his father-in-law. Andrew stood, legs apart, in front of the fireplace, his piercing blue eyes devouring every movement in the room. She waited for him to say something, but apparently he did not feel anything was expected of him. To fill the painful silence she said:

"Thank you, Mr. Dickinson; Mr. Jackson and I genuinely hope that we can be friends."

Mr. Dickinson rose. He advanced a few steps toward Andrew, then said in a cold voice:

"Mr. Jackson, I wish further to state that if I did make any derogatory remark, I was amply provoked."

"In what way, sir?"

"I have been informed that you accused Captain Erwin and myself of deliberate trickery over those forfeit notes."

"That is not true, Mr. Dickinson. I have known Captain Erwin for many years and consider him one of the most honest of men. I think the misunderstanding arose when Captain Erwin thought he had the right to pay the forfeit out of any notes of the stake, while as the winner I believed I had the right to choose the due notes. As for yourself, you did pay me in due notes."

Rachel felt chilled, as though the temperature had fallen twenty degrees. It was clear that Mr. Dickinson was not the slightest bit mollified by Andrew's explanation.

"I have it on excellent authority that you did make these statements."

"Then, sir, your informant told a damned lie. Who is he?"

"Thomas Swann, a friend of mine and a lawyer in Nashville."

"Very well, let us summon him."

"That I cannot do; it might lead Mr. Swann to think I want to throw the burden off my shoulders onto his."

Captain Erwin came to his son-in-law's side.

"Mr. and Mrs. Jackson accepted your apology even though you prefaced it by saying you did not believe you made the remark. Mr. Jackson now tells us that he merely said a different list of notes was offered by me, though not by you, and that he has never thought the difference in my list was premeditated. I think this amounts to the same kind of apology you proffered the Jacksons, and I for one am going to accept theirs. It behooves you to do the same."

He turned to Rachel, took her hand and smiled in the most friendly fashion.

"My wife and daughter are expecting us home."

When they left Rachel asked, "Who is this Thomas Swann?"

"One of Dickinson's toadies. He thinks that if he caters to the Dickinson crowd he can get some of their law work, maybe even a political office."

"Well, I'm glad it is settled."

4

She had underestimated the piercing power of trouble. Two days later Andrew received a letter from Thomas Swann telling him that Mr. Dickinson had informed him that Mr. Jackson had called him, Mr. Swann, a damned liar. Rachel read aloud:

"The harshness of this expression has deeply wounded my feelings; it is language to which I am a stranger, which no man ac-

quainted with my character would venture to apply to me, and which I shall be under the necessity of taking proper notice of.

"I am, sir, Your obt. servt.,

"Thos. Swann

"Mr. Dickinson should not have gone to Thomas Swann with this," she said gently.

Andrew was angry, but this time stone-cold angry.

"I've suspected for a long time he does not want this quarrel ended, he wants it to continue and to grow. I shall answer Mr. Swann in a day or two."

She did not see the letter that Andrew sent to Thomas Swann but she knew it was aimed at Dickinson. When she heard that Charles Dickinson had departed on a flatboat voyage to Natchez she was relieved; but the next day a letter reached them which he evidently had written just before leaving. The last of it cut across her eyes with the sharpness of a sword's tip.

As to the word coward, I think it is as applicable to yourself as any one I know, and I shall be very glad when an opportunity serves to know in what manner you give your anodynes, and hope you will take in payment, one of my most moderate Cathartick.

Yours at Command,

Charles Dickinson

She studied the words *anodyne* and *Cathartick*; all she could figure was that both words were being used as synonyms for ammunition. She hoped that Mr. Dickinson would have a long and pleasurable stay in Natchez, long enough to let this hopelessly tangled hullabaloo die down.

Rather, it grew apace. Andrew would no longer tell her the details, and she assembled the facts through her usual fragmentary sources. With Charles Dickinson gone, Thomas Swann was keeping the fire burning. He "demanded the satisfaction which as a gentleman he was entitled to receive." Andrew replied that if Swann challenged him he would be obliged to cane him. The next day Swann challenged; whereupon Andrew returned to Winn's Tavern and hit Swann over the shoulder with his cane.

Her consolation during these cold months was little Andy, who was now almost six. The weather was too raw to take him to school in town each day, so she undertook the teaching herself, training him from the same family arithmetic ledger and books from which she and Samuel had been instructed by their father. They walked a little each day, but the trees were bare and the earth heavy with rain. Everything was lying fallow. It was her frank opinion that the whole Swann dispute was due to the fact that they were in the deep of winter, with too little work that needed doing. She prayed for spring to come early, for the sun to get warm and the land to dry so that the men could throw their energies once again into their many tasks.

At this point General James Robertson, founder of the first settlement in the Cumberland, intervened. He was a solidly built man who stood with his head inclined a little forward, his white hair brushed down as a bang and cut square across his forehead. He was quiet, thoughtful, with forthright eyes, his once-fair skin darkened and reddened by exposure. He had been like a father to Andrew, backing him in the militia and helping Blount to push him along politically.

"Andrew, I've been watchin' you squabble with that young Tom Swann. I rode out here to beg you: don't fight."

"Swann's doing most of the fighting, General."

"Son, your courage and reputation don't require you to duel. If you lose your family suffers; if you win it will be a pyrrhic victory. Duelin's got to go, Andrew, it's nothing better than murder."

"There are times when dueling is justified."

"No, my boy." The general's hands were trembling a little, so he spread them out flat on the table before him to keep them still. "You can't take the life of a fellow mortal. If you kill young Swann, you might be miserable as long as you live . . . just like Aaron Burr. You know he was indicted for murder?"

"He will never be tried; but anyway I give you my word: under no circumstances will I duel with that puppy, Thomas Swann."

Rachel had remained silent during this exchange, deeply grateful to the older man for making this long trip to protect her; for she knew that he was thinking of more than Andrew's physical well-being.

With the beginning of February the dispute left the realm of semi-private, oral argumentation and broke into public print. Thomas Swann published a long and detailed attack on Andrew in the Nashville *Impartial Review*. Andrew published an even longer defense, documented with affidavits by friends who had overheard any part of the discussions. John Erwin, a relative of Mrs. Dickinson, inserted a third statement in the paper, urging people to reserve their judgment until Mr. Dickinson returned and could present his case. The only one who appeared to be enjoying the row was Thomas Eastin, owner of the *Impartial Review*: he charged for all of these articles at regular commercial rates.

Spring came at last. The sun dried the ground, the plows turned over the earth, the men went to work . . . Andrew returned to Clover Bottom to train Truxton for the big race against Ploughboy. And as Rachel had suspected, everybody dropped the discussion of the forfeit-note quarrel, transferring their excitement to the April contest. The betting was extraordinarily heavy.

It was overcast the morning of the Truxton-Ploughboy race, but the somber grays of the outdoors could not match Andrew's gloom; two days earlier Truxton had injured his thigh, and the swelling would not yield to massage or liniment. They left for Clover Bottom early. The crowd of spectators was already tremendous.

"This is the largest number of people I ever saw assembled," commented Andrew. "I would sure hate to disappoint them by calling off the race."

"But Andrew, if Truxton has a swollen thigh . . . ?"

His long bony chin set stubbornly.

"I'm just not convinced that a swollen thigh would keep Truxton from winning."

The men who had helped to train the horse, and had large sums of money bet on him, John Coffee, John Verell, Sam Pryor, all began speaking at once: Truxton would have to exert himself to the utmost to beat Ploughboy, even when in perfect condition.

"I never saw a horse more eager to win," said Andrew. "Gentlemen, I will gladly assume any part or all of your bets."

The two horses were led to the starting line. The word was given, and they shot forward. Truxton took a slight lead. The spectators were still, watching the two great animals circle the meadowland. Now as they came into the stretch, Truxton forged steadily ahead.

Their big stallion won the first heat easily; but he was limping badly. One of his front legs also had gone lame, the shoe having sprung. Captain Erwin's supporters were shouting that the race was over.

"It's too late to forfeit now, isn't it, Andrew?" Rachel asked.

"Yes. We either have to run the second heat or withdraw and pay the full amount of our wager."

To herself she thought, We may lose our money, but it's just as well: Truxton's opening win will satisfy Andrew, while Captain Erwin and Charles Dickinson will get their money back and also have the right to claim a victory.

But she had bargained without her husband.

"Truxton's going to run," he announced. "If he can beat Ploughboy with one bad leg . . . he can do it with two."

And Truxton did, by a full sixty yards, in a sudden heavy rain, running the two miles in one second short of four minutes. Andrew and his friends had won ten thousand dollars; Captain Erwin and his supporters were utterly crushed. It was the most humiliating defeat in the history of western racing. Rachel's heart pounded as she left the course.

5

If Andrew had experienced any despair over the reversal in his fortunes or the need to sell Hunter's Hill, his regrets now disappeared completely as his victories with his race horses established him as the top turfman

156

of Tennessee. Captain Erwin paid his debt, congratulating Andrew on having infused a great fighting spirit into his horse. Swann's diatribes had been silenced by the state authorities in Knoxville, who apparently had threatened to suspend his attorney's license, in which act Rachel was certain she saw General Robertson's influence. Reports filtered back to them that Charles Dickinson had engaged in considerable pistol practice on his way down the Mississippi, but Rachel dismissed this as gossip.

One night toward the end of May, Andrew came home from the store upset. Shortly after sundown Thomas Overton reached the Hermitage. Rachel, working on the small loom in her bedroom, heard the men's voices downstairs, Overton's high, almost querulous, Andrew's low and vibrant. He came upstairs after about twenty minutes, told her he had to go into town on urgent business, and that he would not be back until the following evening. She searched his face for some clue to the matter, but he kissed her, completely preoccupied, and left the room.

The next day passed quickly, for she had a number of chores: preserving fruits for candied desserts and appetizers, cleaning the heavy winter bedclothes before putting them away, sewing a light-weight suit for Andy. A neighbor returning from Nashville brought the message that Andrew would not be back that night. The following noon George brought her a copy of the *Impartial Review*. In it was an article by Charles Dickinson; she had not even known that he had returned to Nashville. She scanned the first part, finding it to be a long review of the quarrel over the forfeit notes. Then she read:

> General Jackson states that Mr. Swann has acted the puppet and lying valit, for a worthless, drunken, blackguard, scoundrel, etc. etc. Should Andrew Jackson have intended these epithets for me, I declare him (notwithstanding he is a major general of the militia) to be a worthless scoundrel a poltroon and a coward. A man who, by frivolous and evasive pretexts, avoided giving the satisfaction, which was his due to a gentleman whom he had injured. This had prevented me from calling on him in the manner I should otherwise have done; for I am well convinced, that he is too great a coward to administer any of those anodynes he promised me in his letter to Mr. Swann.

She sat on a hard dining chair, unable to move or even think until she heard Andrew's horse coming across the field. She ran to the open door, shading her eyes from the midday sun. He alighted in the yard, gathered her in his arms for a moment and, glancing at the newspaper she still held, murmured:

"Bad news travels fast because it has so many helping hands."

He led her into the house. Moll was cooking supper. She took a quick look at Rachel's face, then left, soundlessly.

"That's why you went into Nashville Thursday night: you had heard that Charles Dickinson was back."

"I went to see this article before Eastin set it up in type. Well . . . I saw it."

"Andrew, you didn't challenge!"

He took her hand in his.

"I had to. I wanted the whole thing settled this morning . . . before you could learn about it . . . but Dickinson's seconds had a lot of excuses."

"You are going to duel with him," she said numbly. "When . . . and where?"

"A week from today, at Harrison's Mill, Kentucky."

The air in the room became still. She felt something on her cheek, reached up and found tears: he would be traveling the Kentucky Road, the one on which he had brought her home from the Robards' fifteen years before, when her old life had ended . . . and her new life begun. How closely these two journeys were bound; and how inescapable was the past!

"Darling, you're not going to let this hotheaded boy shatter our lives?"

He walked away from her.

"I have no choice."

"This is not going to be like other duels, is it? You are both going to shoot to . . ."

"Yes."

She felt faint. Andrew brought her a mug of cool water. She took a sip, then looked up at him and cried, "For the dear God's sake, why must you do this? Do you no longer love me or care what happens that you can risk your life without reason or purpose?"

He took the water from her, dipped his fingers into it and ran them over her forehead.

"I do love you, my darling. I'll love you until my dying day."

"If he kills you, Andrew! There will be nothing left for me of love . . . or life."

He walked to the sideboard, cut a piece of loaf sugar and ground it in some whisky, downing the mixture in a swift draught. When he turned back to her his face was pale.

"If I ignore these insults men will spit on me when I walk down Market Street. My name will become a laughingstock. I will be the butt of derision throughout all Tennessee."

"Dueling is savage. Everyone who respects the law would respect you for declining to fight. General Robertson told you in this very room that your courage and reputation did not require this kind of vindication. He said that if you lose your family would suffer, and if you win it would be a pyrrhic victory . . ."

158

She watched him make his way almost blindly to a big chair and slump into it, holding his face in his hands.

"Oh, Rachel, I've tried so many things, and I've failed at so many. The one thing that has sustained me has been my sense of honor. This is what I live by. Take that away and it would be like severing a tent pole with an ax. I've never run away from anything or failed to fulfill my obligations. Make me do so just one time and you have destroyed me. What would you have left? I would no longer be a man."

"It would take far more courage to ignore this braggadocio letter and face the men on Market Street than it would to stand at Harrison's Mill with an almost complete stranger, both of you determined to kill each other."

"Perhaps so; but it's a kind of courage I don't possess. If Dickinson had sent this letter to me privately, then perhaps I might have found some way to answer him privately. But there won't be a man, woman or child who won't have read this article. I'm still a major general of the militia, and there are hundreds of militiamen who will read it and know instantly that I must fight Dickinson. If I fail I'm not the only one who stands in disgrace: the whole militia does, for if their leader is a coward, so are they. I fight, or I resign. I fight, or I stop racing our horses. I fight, or I sell our store and tavern, yes, and our home too. I fight, or I lose everything."

She waited for a moment, then asked quietly:

"Andrew, are you dueling with Charles Dickinson over the disputed forfeit notes . . . or the ugly things he has said about us and our marriage?"

"How can I say? If Charles Dickinson did not hate me so terribly he would never have made those attacks on you. By the same token, if I did not hate him so much for his slanders, this quarrel over the forfeit notes might not have gone so far."

"But if you know this, others will know it too. They will say the duel was fought over me."

"There is no way to stop the loose talk so long as we leave that man free to blacken us. I must close his mouth once and for all."

"It will be the end for both of us . . . and what a dreadful end to our love, and our hopes for each other."

"No, it will be a good end: we will have fought for our love. But if we let this go by we will die every hour and every day of our lives: die from bullets of gossip and vile charges." He paced the full length of the room. "Dickinson wants to be the great man of Tennessee. Everywhere he turns it seems I somehow thwart him." He could not restrain a wry grin. "Even his great Ploughboy is humiliated and disgraced by our Truxton."

She went to him, took his hands in hers.

"He's the best shot in this part of the country. He can hit a coin three times in the air before it falls, sever a string at twenty yards."

"He's gone to great pains to have these stories circulated."

159

"Then . . . he can . . . miss you?"

"Not totally. But I give you my promise I'll not miss him either."

"Oh, Andrew, I don't want you to be guilty of killing another man. Think of his wife . . . and their baby son."

He stood staring at her for a moment, then turned away, went to the door and called out:

"Moll, would you be so good as to serve dinner now? And ask George to bring up a bottle of wine from the springhouse."

She had expected to find some change in his routine in the days that preceded his departure for Harrison's Mill, some final preparations he would make or instructions he would leave, papers he might straighten out, accounts balanced. But he did none of these things. He went about his day's work in the fields, spending the early mornings at the stables on Clover Bottom exercising the horses; in the evenings they sat before the fire, reading or talking with friends who had come in for supper. He never again alluded to the oncoming duel.

He was to leave Thursday morning at five. They went to bed early the night before. Andrew fell into a sound sleep. Rachel did not close her eyes. Through her mind went all the happiness they had known, the successes and failures; and how wonderful Andrew had been: his soft, gentle love at Bayou Pierre, and at Poplar Grove; the big house he had built on Hunter's Hill to make her the great lady of Tennessee; the carriage he had had delivered to her on Christmas Day when they were so hard pressed for funds, the gifts he had brought back from Philadelphia when he had been deep in trouble and anxiety.

He awoke at four. They breakfasted together. There was so much she wanted to tell him: how much she loved him, how fine their years together had been, and how dear their love; yet she realized she could not utter one word, that she must not indicate by a single gesture that she feared she might never see him again. Instead, when it was time to go and they had clasped each other fervently, she said:

"Don't ride too hard; get some rest after lunch; and be careful . . ."

He smiled wistfully at her, said, "I'll be careful."

"Come home as quickly as you can. I'll be waiting for you. I'll have a whisky ready, and a hot supper on the fire."

There was gray light in the east by now. She stood at the doorway waving as he went across the fields. Then she turned back into the house. It was dark and still.

6

She went about her chores for the day, feeling strangely suspended in both time and space, as though she were standing above the world and

160

watching a woman by the name of Rachel Jackson desperately trying to fill redundant moments and hours with unthinking physical activity.

Jane arrived at midday with a small portmanteau. She said nothing about the duel or Andrew's abence: she was simply there as she always had been when Rachel was in trouble. The Hayses were in trouble too, Rachel knew; some of Robert's investments had gone bad and he had had to sacrifice most of his holdings. There was even some talk of their losing their plantation.

Jane slept with her that night. Several times Rachel fell into a nightmare, racked by throttled screams. She felt Jane's arm about her, comforting her. At the first sign of the sun Rachel looked over at her sister, saw that she was sleeping, got out of bed quietly, dressed and left the house. It was already warm but after she passed the springhouse and went into the woods she found the air closed in and cool.

She walked a very long time, having no way of telling when it was precisely seven o'clock and the shots would be fired, but feeling in her heart that if anything serious were to happen to Andrew she would sense it. The woods were like a series of walls within walls, through which no human eye or voice could penetrate, giving her privacy and seclusion. It was dark, yet the trees were friendly, as though they knew she needed protection against a cruel and chaotic world. She moved over the soft moss-covered earth as effortlessly as though she were floating in still warm waters in some nascent period before it had been necessary for her to think or struggle.

The sun had risen fairly high and was beginning to clear the treetops. She took her bearings and after a time found the trail that led her home. It was ten o'clock when she reached her cabin. Jane was sitting out in front knitting, with Andy playing at her feet. She looked up, made a swift appraisal of Rachel's face, then said:

"For a time there I thought you'd gone to Harrison's Mill to fight the duel for him."

"There's been no news, Jane?"

"No. How could there be? It's still a number of hours before Andrew could reach home, no matter how fast he rode." Jane rose, linked her arm through her sister's. "You need rest. It must be several nights since you really closed your eyes."

"I believe I *could* sleep . . . for an hour or two."

She put her head on the pillow, remembered Andrew's boyhood chum telling her, "I could throw Andrew three times out of four, but he would never stay throwed," and fell into a bottomless slumber. It was late afternoon by the time she awoke. Downstairs she could hear Moll humming and Jane's voice as she read to Andy. She poured some cold water into the bowl on the dresser, washed quickly, combed her hair and slipped on a white linen dress, wearing her pearl brooch, the first gift of jewelry Andrew had given her. Even as she descended the stairs she heard the noise of fast-moving horses, and by the time she reached the door she saw Andrew coming down the trail flanked on either side by Thomas Overton and Dr. May, whom she recognized as a Nashville surgeon. She was at his side as he lifted himself gingerly off his horse.

"Thank God, darling! Are you all right?"

"Oh, he pinked me."

"And Mr. Dickinson? How is he?"

"Well, I don't know precisely. He was hit. I sent Dr. May over to offer his assistance, but it was declined."

The men followed Rachel into the house and to the bedroom upstairs where they helped Andrew off with his coat and shirt. His chest was bandaged, but the blood had soaked through.

"I tried to get Mr. Jackson to stay at David Miller's tavern on the Red River for a couple of days until this wound healed," Dr. May said, "but he insisted he had to get home to prove to you that he was alive."

"How bad is it?"

"Painful, but not dangerous: the ball broke a rib or two and raked his breastbone."

She sat beside him, holding his hand while the surgeon cleansed the wound and redressed it. Andrew gritted his teeth, saying to her between gasps:

"Mr. Dickinson had not been bragging. His aim was perfect. He shot for exactly where he supposed my heart was beating. But you know how loosely that blue frock coat fits me? Standing sideways, as we did, it billowed out in front of me. I never thought it would do me any good in this world to be skinny, but it sure enough saved my life . . . by a half inch."

Dr. May took a handkerchief out of his pocket and wiped the perspiration from his face. "Right now I think we all could do with a good strong whisky. Mr. Jackson will have his in bed."

"Just one word to you, gentlemen, before you leave," said Andrew, leaning up on one elbow. "When you report this wound in Nashville, please be so kind as to use my words: 'Mr. Jackson was pinked, nothing more.'"

The men agreed, then accompanied Rachel downstairs. Thomas Overton had two fast drinks, then plunged into a recital of the duel.

"On our ride out to Red River the general and I discussed how the duel should be fought. As you know, the pistols were to be held downward until the word was given, then each man was to fire as soon as he pleased. It was scarcely possible that both pistols could be discharged at the same instant, therefore the one who was the quickest might end the duel with one shot. Should we try to get the first shot, or should we permit Dickinson to have it? We agreed that Dickinson would be sure to get the first fire . . ."

". . . please, Mr. Overton . . ."

"I'm telling it fast as I can, Mrs. Jackson. Well, when I gave the word 'Fire!' Dickinson raised his pistol like lightning and fired. I saw a puff of dust fly from the breast of the general's coat, watched him raise his left arm and place it tightly across his breast. Dickinson fell back a pace or two, saying in a faltering tone, 'Great God, have I missed him!' 'Back to the mark, sir,' I cried . . ."

"Mr. Overton, do you mind . . . ?"

"The general took aim at Mr. Dickinson and pulled the trigger. The gun neither snapped nor went off, it stopped at half cock. The general drew the trigger back, took second aim and fired. He did not miss, I assure you. That will be an end to Mr. Dickinson's challenging men he is positive he can kill at twenty-four paces."

Rachel took a supper tray upstairs to Andrew, propped him against soft pillows and, when his arm hurt, fed him.

Before long he fell into a quiet sleep. When Robert Hays came for Jane, Overton and Dr. May left with them. Rachel undressed and climbed into bed gently, not wanting to wake Andrew. She slept only intermittently, knowing she could not rest until she had had reassuring news about Charles Dickinson. She had never hated him, she had only considered him ungallant in attacking a defenseless woman. If Mr. Dickinson were fatally wounded, the responsibility would be as much hers as it was Andrew's; she did not want any man to be killed because of her.

The news came soon enough, out from Nashville.

The following morning before Andrew was awake, Moll summoned her quietly from the bottom of the stairs. Rachel put on her dressing gown and slippers and descended to find a militiaman waiting. He asked to see General Jackson. When she insisted that Andrew could not be awakened, the officer said:

"I have been sent to tell the general that Charles Dickinson died last night at nine o'clock."

She reached for a chair to steady herself. When the man left she fell to her knees on the floor.

"Oh, God, have pity on the poor wife; pity the babe in her arms." Then, from deep in the recesses of her mind, there came the whispered words, "And have pity on us too."

Book FIVE

RACHEL brooded over the death of Charles Dickinson. She watched with anxiety as the Cumberland Valley people reversed the roles of the duelists: somehow in their grief Andrew Jackson had become the invincible marksman who had mercilessly killed a younger and less experienced opponent. Captain Erwin's letter in the *Impartial Review*, stating that although Andrew technically had been within his rights in pressing the trigger a second time he had actually violated the unwritten code of dueling, found credence in Nashville; and the honor for which he had risked his life was being seriously tarnished. Among the women, Mrs. Somerset Phariss, who was a cousin of Charles Dickinson, now charged Rachel with having egged on Mr. Jackson because of Mr. Dickinson's two attacks on her, insinuating that Charles Dickinson's blood was on Rachel Jackson's hands. When Nashville turned out for Dickinson's funeral the sentiment ran so strong that a mass protest meeting was called.

It was no longer necessary for her to set her table for twenty; they ate alone. Even those friends who had believed the duel inevitable had been distressed by young Dickinson's death; their remaining away from the Hermitage was a confession of repugnance. Rachel understood this, for had not she too been repulsed by the all-too-fresh blood on Aaron Burr's hands? Her understanding lengthened her despair as Andrew's clients, his associates, his cronies from Nashville, the throng of admirers from the racecourse and the men who had come from all over the state to counsel, make land deals or swap horses vanished like morning frost. His friends who controlled Tennessee politics also dropped him, no longer seeking his advice or patronage. By dying, Charles Dickinson had obliterated Andrew's political position and influence far more effectively than he could have by staying alive. Only his young aides in the militia of West Tennessee remained loyal, riding out to the Hermitage for a handclasp and a drink, outlining campaigns by means of which they

164

could drive the Spanish from Florida. To them the duel had been an affair of honor, necessarily fought and resolved.

Andrew was allowed to leave his bed after noonday dinner, but he had to spend the afternoon reclining on the red settee, waiting for his broken ribs to mend. Rachel dressed the wound carefully, but it did not heal as the surgeon had predicted. Thomas Overton and Dr. May kept their word, telling no one that the Dickinson bullet had missed Andrew's heart by less than an inch.

Rachel pleaded, "Andrew, you've got to let Dr. May give an accurate report of your wound. A lot of the people who are angry with you because they think you are unscathed would feel differently if they knew how close Dickinson came to killing you."

"Where or how badly Dickinson hit me is my private affair," he answered abruptly; "there's no need for me to share that knowledge with those short-memoried folks who have turned against me."

"Be generous, Andrew, let them salvage their pride. Perhaps it would make Mr. Dickinson's family feel a little better."

Pain twisted Andrew's mouth as he sat up.

"He had no generosity for you; he struck at you in public. He had no generosity for me; he went to that dueling ground absolutely certain that I had no chance of emerging alive. He laid bets in Nashville that he would kill me at the first fire."

"Yes, Andrew, I know. But the air around us is black with hate, and with talk . . . the old talk . . . of Lewis, and our first two years together, and how I did not defend myself in Harrodsburg, and the jury's verdict against us . . ."

She felt Andrew's hand in hers; his face was pale, gaunt.

"Darling, you must trust me. I did what I had to do; I could no longer have lived with you or asked you to love me if I had let Charles Dickinson continue to humiliate us. We'll be vindicated."

She took his face in her hands and kissed his bloodless lips.

"All right, Andrew. Whatever you did, we did together; and whatever you must suffer we will suffer together." She hesitated for a moment, then added quickly, "That mass meeting got up a petition to have Editor Eastin put the next issue of the *Impartial Review* in mourning 'As a tribute of respect for the memory, and regret for the untimely death of Mr. Charles Dickinson . . .'"

"The paper in mourning, eh," he interrupted harshly, "with a nice official black band. By what right? If only I could ride into town . . ."

She rose from his side and went to the window, where she stood with her back to him, ostensibly straightening the curtain.

"Why not write a letter of protest? Eastin will be going to press tomorrow. I will take it in."

The next morning she waited in the outer office of the newspaper until the sandy-complexioned young man came forward from the composing room, a black apron covering his trousers, his hands smeared from the type he had been setting. She handed him Andrew's letter. He read it, leaning on his elbows behind the counter, his head bobbing.

"Now, Mrs. Jackson, you know we don't take sides on our paper. We make every effort to live up to our name, *Impartial Review*."

Rachel's eyes flashed fire.

"Your *Review* would have been a lot more *Impartial* if you had never run any of those letters by Thomas Swann, the Erwins, Mr. Dickinson, Mr. McNairy or General Jackson."

The editor's ink-smudged mouth dropped open with shock.

"But Mrs. Jackson, when a gentleman hands us a statement and pays the prevailing rates, we've no basis for refusing him. Any more than we can refuse seventy-three of our leading citizens the right to buy a black band around one issue of the paper."

She had no liking for the subtle or devious; this young newspaper owner was being clever with her.

"I assume you will list the names of all seventy-three of the men who are paying for the border?"

". . . well . . . no, there had been no mention of that."

"Then put on your coat, go out to your seventy-three purchasers and tell them that General Jackson insists you publish their names. We cannot have it look as though the *Impartial Review* were taking this stand editorially, can we?"

Eastin flushed.

"It's not common practice, ma'am, but I'll do what you say. We strive to please everybody."

Twenty-six of the mourners withdrew their names; the rest stood firm. To stress his impartiality, Eastin ran Andrew's letter without charge. The black border caused the controversy to heighten in intensity, while her own trip into town provided further ammunition for those who were charging her with complicity.

It was the hottest summer she could remember; the cattle lay panting under the trees, the hogs stood waist-deep in the pond and the dry clay earth became gray dust on the roads. Dr. May forbade Andrew to train his horses for the fall races. He promptly withdrew his entries.

It was a gratuitous withdrawal, for the Nashville Jockey Club claimed that people would no longer go to a track owned by Andrew Jackson. All races were to be transferred to Hartsville.

Despite her unceasing efforts to bring him back to health he remained thin to the point of emaciation. In the fall she went into the fields to supervise the bringing in of the crops; the earth was a caldron and the dust choked her. When she came in from work she went directly to the springhouse where Moll set out tubs of the cool water. Discarding her dust-caked bonnet and dress, she bathed and washed her hair, and piled it high on her head with the gold combs Andrew had given her. Then

166

she donned a white or pale yellow cotton, low-necked and short-sleeved, and went to the main house to drink a glass of cool wine with Andrew before their dinner. In the evening they sat under catalpa trees, using their fans to keep off the dry-weather flies.

Judge Overton visited as frequently as his arduous duties permitted, John Coffee came to spend the week ends. Of the Donelson family they saw Jane, who rode over in the afternoons, bringing her young daughter Rachel, while Mary and Catherine usually drove out on Saturday with a carriage full of grandchildren. William disapproved the duel; Johnny was silently protesting the further trouble Andrew had caused the clan; Alexander and Leven were too indifferent or too lazy to come or to send a sympathetic word. Only Severn, with whom neither she nor Andrew had been on intimate terms, sensed what they were suffering in their isolation. He bought the piece of land immediately adjoining the Hermitage and insisted that the Jacksons visit him frequently.

As soon as the doctor said Andrew could ride in the carriage he went over to Clover Bottom to his store. After three trips he stopped going and Rachel did not need to ask why: she had known that the store stood empty. She had also managed to conceal from her husband that Colonel Ward had defaulted on his second-half payment for Hunter's Hill. To add to their problems their last flotilla of seven boats of produce for New Orleans had been hit by a storm, three had been totally lost, and because of damage to the others they had arrived at the market too late to earn back their cost.

Rachel accepted these financial upsets philosophically, convinced that they were an inescapable part of their life pattern. But in the dark sleeplessness of the nights she murmured over and over, Oh, Andrew, if only you had raised your pistol high into the air that second time and fired at the sky, how great a man you would have been! You would have emerged as the merciful victor who had been too big to extract your pound of flesh! Yet in the few seconds that had passed between the click of Andrew's trigger and the recocking for a second shot, he had known he was seriously hit. Could a man wounded, perhaps dying, take pity on an opponent whose one grim determination had been to destroy him? And who was she to pass judgment? She who had reached out for love, gone quickly into a second marriage, knowing it was an unheard-of thing she was doing, that divorce was unknown in Tennessee and the frontier, that Lewis Robards would never allow her to become totally free . . . that the stigma would make her forever the source of contention and strife.

2

One night toward the end of September they heard a rider come up the trail. Andrew got out of bed, went to the big window which stood open and exclaimed:

"Why, it's Colonel Burr."

He put on his dressing gown and slippers. Rachel sat up in bed. "Andrew, can I go down with you?" she asked.

He glanced at her, her braids wound tightly about her head, her eyes excited by this unexpected visit.

"Come ahead," he said with a grin; "if the colonel feels so friendly as to break in upon us late at night, that means we can be *en famille.*"

Colonel Burr's face lit up with an affectionate smile when they opened the door to him.

"How wonderful to see you and the general again, Mrs. Jackson. I've been looking forward to it for days. That is the only excuse I can offer for my bad manners in intruding upon you at this late hour."

"Indeed, Colonel, I would have been deeply hurt if you had not," boomed Andrew.

Rachel gathered about her the folds of her voluminous flannel robe and made her way to the springhouse where she secured a cold fried chicken, a loaf of Moll's bread, some chilled butter and a bottle of white wine. She found her husband and the colonel deep in a discussion of the hostilities with Spain; Andrew was never more intensely alive. Only now did she realize how dormant he had lain all summer, how terribly he missed being at the center of the happenings in Tennessee. As she spread a cloth over the table and set out the dishes and glasses she listened to Colonel Burr report that Spain's armed forces, operating inside American territory, had imprisoned five United States citizens and had cut down an American flag flying over a friendly Indian nation.

"By the Eternal," Andrew exclaimed, "it looks as though our moment has come!"

"I have purchased a tract of two hundred thousand acres on the Washita," continued Burr, "and several hundred young fighting men have already signed to settle there with me. When the war breaks with Spain we'll be a self-constituted army, ready to move on Texas and Mexico."

"All of Nashville will be glad to hear your news, Colonel," said Andrew eagerly. He turned to Rachel. "My dear, I want you to invite to dinner all the people who were at our first dinner for Colonel Burr."

Rachel shrank as the two men looked toward her. Would anyone come? Did she dare to ask the Pharisses, Daisy Deson and her father, the others who had helped to pay for the black border? Should she risk their rejection for this chance to bridge the gap of coolness and hostility that had sprung up since the duel? John Overton could help her; he was in close contact with Nashville. She would have to speak to him first.

John was one of the managers of the Nashville Dancing Assembly, whose first ball was to be held that Saturday night at the new Talbot Hotel. Rachel asked if the Dancing Assembly would like to invite

Colonel Burr as its guest of honor. John considered the proposal, decided it would lend social importance to the occasion, and sent announcements to all subscribers of the Assembly.

The next afternoon he returned her visit.

"Seems as though I acted without my usual judicial calm in inviting Colonel Burr for Saturday night."

"Has there been objection?"

"Yes. Several men have come to my office to say they did not think we should honor Colonel Burr. It seems the colonel is charged with engaging in a number of questionable activities."

"Such as?" she asked uneasily.

"Such as: Mr. Daviess, attorney for the United States at Frankfort, is arraigning the colonel in Federal Court on charges of planning to injure a power with which the United States is at peace."

"Oh, you mean his preparations for a war against the Spanish. Andrew approves . . ."

"Such as: at Cannonsburg, Ohio, he told Colonel Morgan that the Union would not last, that the fumbling and imbecility of the Federal government was so great that a separation of the states could not be more than four or five years off; and that with two hundred men he could drive Congress, with the President at its head, into the Potomac."

"But that's treason!" She was dumfounded. "Do they have proof of these charges?"

"No proof. All bottomed on rumor . . . In any event we've reached a working compromise: Colonel Burr will be ticketed but he's not to be our guest of honor . . . And of course you and Andrew will attend the ball."

Colonel Burr went to Nashville on Friday to stay at the Talbot Hotel. Andrew donned his uniform as general of the militia, but Rachel was more timid. She thought it the better part of discretion to wear her simple black gown.

John greeted them, turned to Rachel with a wistful smile and said, "As manager of the ball, madam, may I have the great honor of taking you in?"

She flushed with pleasure; this was John's way of showing the hostile world precisely where he stood. Almost a decade and a half before he had demonstrated his belief in her innocence by coming to the Donelson stockade from Harrodsburg and asking to be taken in as a boarder. How many times in the intervening years had he had to renew that show of faith?

She had a single moment of uneasiness when Andrew entered the ballroom with the colonel on his arm and began presenting him to the members of the Assembly. To her relief they were received cordially; for the most part, Burr's efforts to instigate a war against Spain were looked upon with favor in Nashville. The colonel had a firm handclasp

169

and a brilliant smile for everyone. Rachel followed Andrew with her eyes; how wonderful to see him talking and laughing with friends whom he had not seen since the duel. She observed that Captain Erwin and his family, as well as a nucleus of Charles Dickinson's friends and relatives, had not attended.

At the beginning of November Andrew received from Burr a packet of three thousand dollars in Kentucky bank notes, with an order to build five flatboats and to outfit them. By the same messenger he asked Andrew for a list of men whom he could recommend to the War Department for commissions. Andrew turned the money over to Jax with instructions to start building the boats, then joined General Robertson in drawing up a list of able soldiers.

A few days later a handsome young man knocked at the door, took off his military cap to show a head of tight blond curls, introduced himself as Captain Fort, a friend of Colonel Burr. He was invited to stay the night. After dinner while the two men were smoking their pipes in front of the fire and Rachel was sitting behind them on the settee knitting a cap for Andy, the conversation took a strange turn. Though Andrew had not moved, she had seen his back stiffen and felt his intense concentration upon the glowing bowl of tobacco.

"This separatist movement is the best thing that could have happened," Captain Fort was saying smoothly. "It will give the western states a focus and a capital, and people to run the new nation."

Rachel recognized the deep calm which characterized Andrew's conversation in moments of crisis.

"And where is this new capital to be?"

"New Orleans. We will seize the port, then move on to conquer Mexico. This done, we'll unite the western part of the Union to the conquered country."

"And how is this to be effected?" Andrew's tone had risen slightly in warmth, but the captain was too absorbed to notice it.

"By the aid of Federal troops, with General Wilkinson at their head."

Andrew knocked out the gray ash on the hearth, straightened up and looked fiercely at Fort.

"Is Colonel Burr in on this scheme?"

"My information comes from a high officer who is well acquainted with Colonel Burr. General Wilkinson is one of our leaders."

All doubt had fled from their minds at the identical instant. There was a betrayed look on Andrew's face. He controlled himself with a determined effort, dismissing Captain Fort curtly. When he was gone, Andrew closed the door and bolted it. He was trembling.

"My God, is Burr really a traitor?"

"Sit down, my dear, before you fall into the fire. Now, tell me: is such a scheme to separate the West from the East really treason, or is it the foolishness of an overwrought mind?"

170

"I gave him military lists! Jax is building boats for him, and buying provisions!"

He turned and, with his eyebrows raised high, said, "Do you know what can happen if these charges are true?"

"Not . . . altogether."

"Aaron Burr has put me in a position where I too can be charged with treason!"

The news came by courier from Frankfort that Aaron Burr had been arraigned in Federal Court. That same morning they received a letter from Burr. Andrew read it aloud:

"MY DEAR GENERAL,

"I give you my most sacred pledges that I have never held any views inimical or hostile to the United States and if anyone should charge me with the intention of separating the Union they must charge me with insanity at the very same instant.

"And so I do," declared Andrew emphatically. "If he shows up at the Hermitage again, he'll be turned away."

Immediately after Burr's release from the Frankfort court because of lack of witnesses to testify against him, he arrived at the Hermitage, his smile warm and charming. Rachel planted herself squarely on the threshold.

"I'm sorry, Colonel Burr, but General Jackson is not at home."

"I'm indeed sorry to have missed him. Would you permit me to wait for his return?"

"The general has gone to Sumner County."

"Then could you perhaps give me some information about the five boats I ordered, and the provisions that were to have been laid in?"

"I can give you no information."

She saw Burr flinch, and felt her own distress: it was the first time she had ever denied anyone hospitality.

"If you are concerned about those absurd charges, Mrs. Jackson, I think I should tell you that I was completely exonerated in the Kentucky court."

"Colonel Burr, there is nothing I can do. Might I suggest the tavern at Clover Bottom? I am sure they can make you comfortable."

Burr pulled himself up to his full five feet four, bowed in imperious fashion, turned, mounted his horse and disappeared across the fields. Rachel watched him until he was out of sight.

When Andrew returned he rounded up John Coffee and Thomas Overton and rode over to the Clover Bottom Tavern for a final accounting, taking along some two thousand dollars, the balance of the Kentucky bank notes not expended. He returned several hours later, dropped into a chair and threw a batch of papers onto the table. His eyes were of many opinions. Rachel asked:

"What happened, Andrew?"

He ran his hand through the papers, said with a smile that had as much awe as bewilderment in it:

"Frankly, I don't know. He very nearly convinced me that those charges were pure nonsense. Do you know what he has in his possession? A blank commission, signed by President Jefferson." He looked down between his widespread knees, studying the carpet pattern. "If Governor Sevier gave me such a blank commission for my militia I could name any officer to any rank. But what does a blank commission from President Jefferson mean? That Burr can write himself in as a general?"

"Did you see the President's signature?"

"Only a quick look . . . Anyway we gave him back his money and told him he could take delivery of the two boats we finished. I don't know how far he can get in them, without provisions. I wouldn't be surprised if Stockly Hays came walking home within a week."

"Surely Jane and Robert are not going to let Stockly go with him after all that's happened!"

"Robert says it's a matter of honor; he gave his word to Burr that Stockly would go along. If he were my boy, I'd keep him here. But I think there's no danger on the voyage down the Mississippi. I've told Stockly to leave the flotilla at the first sign of anything suspicious."

Burr departed with his two boats at dawn on December 22. Five days later the explosion came in the form of a proclamation from President Jefferson which had been more than a month in transit. The people were warned that an illegal conspiracy against Spain had been set in motion; all military and civil officials were ordered to seize the conspirators. Everyone around Nashville read the separatist movement between the lines.

Rumors flew into the Hermitage faster than feathers in a high wind: Burr's army of invasion was assembling where the Cumberland River met the Ohio; he had a hundred boats and a thousand men under arms with vast stores of guns and ammunition stashed on Blennerhassett Island. Rachel worried about Stockly Hays; Andrew worried about the treachery of General Wilkinson in New Orleans; and Nashville worried about Andrew Jackson.

General Robertson came out to the Hermitage to report that the Dickinson clique had written to Governor Sevier demanding Andrew's removal as a general of the militia: in times of crisis any officer involved in an insurrection could be court-martialed. When Aaron Burr was burned in effigy in the public square, the figure looked more like gangling Andrew Jackson than it did the short-statured Burr. Rachel asked herself why it was that some men and women were storm centers all their lives, while others lived out their years in comparative quiet.

172

Then the insurrection collapsed: General Winchester informed General Jackson that when Burr left the mouth of the Cumberland he had only eleven boats and one hundred and ten men; Captain Bissell reported from Fort Massac that Colonel Burr had nothing on board his boats that a man could not be taking to market; Andrew's scout sent back word that Burr had no arms. Burr surrendered to the authorities just above Natchez and was returned north as a prisoner.

3

They were returning from a day of early spring hunting, with Andy riding his Indian Princess between their two horses and trying to contain his pride over the deer slung across his saddle, when Rachel saw Polly waiting for them under the trees. As she drew close it was evident from Polly's expression that her sister-in-law had reached a moment of decision and wasn't liking it too well. Had she come to take Andy away? But what reason could there be? The boy had flourished, learning to ride and shoot; according to the young tutor they had hired for him, he was making progress in the books.

The reason was quickly forthcoming.

"Rachel, I'm going to marry Colonel Saunders," declared Polly. "Pappy advised it, he thinks it's best for me and the boys."

Rachel stood with her head lowered. How lonely the house would seem without Andy. Despite their preoccupation since the duel, she had moved about her work or gone to bed at night always conscious of the boy in the next room. So many times he had pulled them out of a momentary despair with some foolish antic or pressing need. She had already been dreading the fact that he must go off to the academy next autumn, and she would be deprived of his companionship during the week. She looked at Andy, wondering how he would adjust himself to the middle-aged Colonel Saunders, a prosperous but dour man whose nickname was Johnny Dry.

Her question got itself answered two days before the wedding: along the trail came Polly and Andy. The boy slid off Indian Princess and ran to Rachel. Polly dismounted wearily.

"It just won't work . . . because neither of them want it to work. Andy has been misbehaving frightfully. He organized all sorts of annoyances, like cutting the stirrups off the colonel's saddle. The colonel whupped him; it's more than the poor man can endure."

She glanced toward her son, who had his arms wrapped tightly about Rachel's neck while she ran her fingers through his hair. Polly smiled, and her eyes were resigned. "I know he was only trying to get back here. He loves you both."

"We love him too."

173

"Yes, you do; and that's why I guess this is the best arrangement for everybody. I want Andy to be happy; but I also want the colonel to be happy. So he's yours . . . to raise . . . and keep, as long as you want him." The color drained from Polly's cheeks; she was still, very still.

Rachel went to the younger girl, put her arms around her. Polly began to sob.

"If the time ever comes . . . if I should need him . . . want him . . ."

Rachel answered quickly. "He'll always be your son, Polly. We won't ask to adopt him; he'll be our nephew. We'll just raise him, and teach him, and love him . . . as Samuel's boy."

At the beginning of May when they were in the midst of planting Indian corn in a newly cleared field a subpoena arrived from the Federal court in Richmond, summoning Andrew Jackson to appear and testify in the trial of the United States versus Aaron Burr. Andrew sent immediately for John Overton; he was considerably upset.

"I'm being called a traitor; that's the dirtiest word in our language!"

Rachel picked up the subpoena. She shook her head vigorously as if to say, Shame on you!

"Andrew, they're only asking you to come to Richmond to help carry on the trial and convict Aaron Burr . . . if he is guilty."

John arrived in response to their summons. Andrew turned two dining chairs to face the hearth. Both men stretched their legs toward the banked ashes.

"I know this is a bad season for you to leave," started John; "I'm also afraid that the trial may drag on considerably. You are not legally obliged to go to Richmond. But in all good conscience, is there any way for you to ignore this subpoena? After all, you've been a judge, and you must assist the Federal court in Richmond to function."

"If war with Spain had started," countered Andrew, "Colonel Burr would have been a hero instead of a villain."

"Ifs don't count," replied John tartly. "There'll be no hysteria in Chief Justice John Marshall's court. When you get on that stand, you stick to the facts: precisely what Burr said or wrote to you, what he ordered, paid for. Leave your opinions home with Rachel, who will take tender care of them in your absence."

There was no mistaking the stern warning in John's voice; Rachel saw Andrew's face go red as he bolted up from his chair and stood glaring down at John.

"Since you sent for me," said John coolly, "I assumed that you wanted my advice; and having ridden eight miles in very much of a hurry, you are going to get it whether you like its flavor or not."

"Oh, I always intended to go," growled Andrew, deflated.

The two men burst into laughter. Rachel sat quietly listening to their discussion of the impending trial, and what they knew about similar

174

trials for treason; whether or not Aaron Burr's copious but ambiguous talk would be sufficient to get him convicted.

"Andrew, John, do you think it's at all possible . . . that you two could go into the law together again someday? It isn't too late, is it?"

"I'd be willing," said Overton, his eyes bulking up like warm gray granite. "How about you, Andrew?"

"Frankly, I don't know. I must have forgotten most of my law by now."

"But you haven't forgotten how to shoot."

A silence fell. At the sound of the word "shoot" all three of their minds went back, not to the rough-and-tumble days when Andrew had had to carry his guns to enfore respect for the law and the courts, as John had intended, but to the Dickinson duel. Rachel felt hollow at the bottom of her stomach: the unfortunate little joke had answered her question better than an hour-long discussion: it was too late.

Andrew left for Richmond in the middle of June. Standing in the cornfield talking with Andy, she thought how more than half the time she was left to manage the plantation alone. Andrew had the energy to manage a dozen farms as big as the Hermitage, while the need to pace the work in the fields left her exhausted; but somehow there was always something to keep him from it. The penetrating sun was burning her face as deeply red as John Coffee's, the skin on her hands was becoming parched, a furrow deepened between her brows, pale, crinkling lines appeared about her eyes where she squinted to gaze over the expanse of work still to be done, or to the horizon to judge the next day's weather. Despite the sunbonnet she draped about her head like the other laborers in her fields, her hair was baked dry by the omnipresent heat. She was obliged to wear big boots while striding the rows; to her consternation she found that her shoes were almost impossible to get on.

She thought of the time at Hunter's Hill when she had become ill because of Andrew's absences, and had feared that she had lost so much of her attractiveness that her husband might no longer love her. Now she was forty; her figure was beginning to thicken at the waist. She sent in to Tatum's for the new French creams, rubbed oil through her hair in the mornings when she found it dry and brittle, ordered field gloves in which to work.

And, as ever, their separation served no purpose. During the solid month that Andrew spent in Richmond the case had not come to trial. He returned disgruntled.

"The first twenty days we sat there doing nothing because General Wilkinson refused to obey his summons. Then Chief Justice Marshall tried to get President Jefferson to testify, and Mr. Jefferson refused to come. There we sat, trying to convict one man of treason because he put together a few flatboats, while the English warship *Leopard* raked our ship the *Chesapeake,* killing and wounding twenty-one of our seamen on the flimsy pretext that we had a couple of English seamen aboard. That broadside was fired so close to the capital it must have rattled the dishes right off Mr. Jefferson's dinner table. But does he get mad? Does he protest to the British? Does he promise to blow their ships out of the water if they don't stop waging war on us? Hardly! He turns to polite diplomacy . . . which the British love. I made an hour's speech on the courthouse steps, best darn speech I ever made in my whole life. 'Mr. Jefferson has plenty of courage to seize peaceable Americans and persecute them for political purposes,' says I, 'but he is too cowardly to resent foreign outrage on the Republic. Millions to persecute an American,' I told that crowd, 'but not a cent to resist England.'"

Rachel shook her head at him in amused despair.

"My, my, that's going to make you popular with the Administration."

An article in the *Impartial Review* informed her that Mr. Andrew Jackson had been indicted for trespass, assault and battery against Mr. Samuel Jackson, no relation, charged with having attacked Samuel Jackson with a sword cane, on the premises where he had a shop and living quarters. The trial was to take place in four weeks.

This was the first time her information service had failed her. It was strange, for the brawl had taken place right out on Market Street with rocks being thrown, the two men fighting with their fists and then being separated be spectators.

Acting on an impulse she went back to Moll's and George's cabin.

"George, did you know that Mr. Jackson had a fight in Nashville with Samuel Jackson?"

"Yes, Miz Rachel, we all knowed it. Miz Jane says be sure not to mention it."

The now elderly couple dropped their eyes. Rachel walked back to the house, her feet dragging. This quarrel which had been so studiously kept from her could only mean a new outburst of gossip. Who was this Samuel Jackson, a newcomer to Nashville? Was there perhaps a Mrs. Jackson, a new member of the Culture Club, who had come in from Kentucky with a fresh re-reading of the record that Rachel Robards had been declared by a jury, "Guilty as charged"? How virulent this new outburst must be if Andrew had again taken to violence to combat it: Andrew, who had cried at the time that the record would live to plague them.

Gazing moodily out a side window she recognized the coal-black mare that Robert Hays had given his daughter several years before. Eighteen-year-old Rachel came into the house, draping her capote over a chair in front of the fireplace. The ride had brought high color to her cheeks, but her green eyes, so like her mother's, were red-rimmed. Rachel poured some milk into a copper boiling pan from the large leather jack, then stirred in a little chocolate and maple syrup. The girl turned the mug of

176

hot chocolate in her hands, staring into the flames and stalking the right moment to begin. Rachel sat across the dining table, watching the light of the fire through the youngster's soft blond hair, thinking how much she would have liked to have a daughter.

Suddenly her niece burst into tears, folding her arms over her face as a child might. Rachel went quickly around the table and stood before her.

"What is it, Rachel?" she asked softly.

"George Blakemore and those ruffians he goes about with: Shadrach Nye, Benjamin Rawlings . . . they're saying the most dreadful things." The girl raised her head; her eyes were thoroughly frightened. "I know you will help me, and Uncle Andrew will make them stop . . ."

"There's nothing we'd rather do than help you, darling."

"That George Blakemore, at the tavern last night, he told a lot of men, 'Like aunt, like niece.'"

Rachel quivered.

"Oh, Aunt Rachel, they've said so many ugly things about you. And now they're saying them about me. I know I like pretty clothes, and spend too much of Papa's money . . ."

"That's purely a family matter, my dear, and of no interest to an outsider." She tilted the girl's head upward until their eyes were on a level, then said firmly, "Now you must tell me what they are accusing you of."

"Of having a baby!"

The words had shot out. She averted her head and began weeping again.

"Of having a . . . ?" For a moment Rachel was too stunned to grasp the implication of what had been said. Then she murmured, "Oh, my dear," and took the girl in her arms, feeling as utterly sick as she had that day so long ago when Andrew had brought home the news that they had not been legally married.

"Who could start such a malignant rumor?"

"I don't know. A wagoner who was hauling Joel Childrips' property over to Forks Camp saw the Hudson boy and told him he'd heard Rachel Hays had a fine son. George Blakemore told Boyd, 'Have you heard the news? Miss Rachel Hays had a child; Davis told me he saw her with the child in her arms, about to suckle it.'"

"Oh, Rachel, there's been some dreadful mistake. Go on home, dear. Your uncle and I will handle it."

Andrew had already heard the rumor.

"Andrew, who could possibly start a story like that? Do you know?"

"Yes, I traced it down. Samuel Jackson's wife."

"Samuel Jackson! The one you . . . fought with?"

"Yes."

"And that was the reason for your quarrel?"

177

"Yes. I wrote him a note telling him to silence his wife or I would hold him responsible. He refused."

"Oh, darling, I thought it was about us. Jane thought so too. She tried to protect me."

"I'll go into Nashville first thing in the morning, and make every last one of those men sign an affidavit that they are liars. Where are my pistols?"

And so he did, bringing six signed statements home to Rachel to put in her strongbox. The talk dried up instantly, no one wanting to share Charles Dickinson's fate. What Andrew had never been able to do for them, he had swiftly accomplished for young Rachel Hays.

4

She had never seen him so irascible or depressed. He had troubles enough, she knew, for most of them were too close at hand and too familiar to be concealed; he had to sell his racecourse at a loss; he and Jax closed their store, and not even their desperate dunning succeeded in raising any appreciable part of the twenty thousand dollars owed them by customers. No purchaser could be found for the store, the tavern or the boatyard. Jax gave Andrew his personal notes for half the debt, then went back to surveying for a living. Her own account books showed that there was no use farming the Hermitage except for their own food: the merchants were taking all the profit, leaving them no return for their year of hard labor except swollen feet, a sore back and the glory of having raised a crop.

Though Aaron Burr had been acquitted in the Richmond court, most of the Cumberland Valley felt he had committed no treason only because his conspiracy had been discovered in time. Andrew incurred additional disfavor by defending Burr and damning his accusers. Enlistments in his militia ceased altogether; interest in the musters fell to such a low point that not enough soldiers assembled on drill days to warrant a review. When the presidential election rolled around Andrew canvassed the countryside for James Monroe in an effort to defeat Secretary of State Madison, whom Jefferson wanted as his successor. If his effort earned no votes for Mr. Monroe, it earned for himself a renewed vote of hostility from the government in Washington City.

And now, after seventeen years of marriage, a strangeness fell between them; Andrew went about his chores silently, glumly; even little Andy's company could not raise him out of the doldrums. He glowered when she made little jokes, and when she once timidly suggested that they try a few of their duets he put her off with a curt wave of the hand. He rarely talked to her: she moved quietly through the hours, saying little, waiting for the opportunity to bring their common problems into the open. It was a considerable time before she grasped that the basis of his melancholy was that nothing interested him any more, and consequently he had nothing to do. When in desperation she persuaded him to race one of their two-year-olds he heard a last-minute rumor in the stables, dashed out to the starting line and held up the race at the point of his pistols. He began going into town to spend his afternoons at the Nashville Inn, word seeping back to the Hermitage that he was drinking too much, pounding his fists on the table and getting red of face.

She had always imagined that her most unhappy periods were those of Andrew's long absences; but this was worse. No matter what she might have suffered in terms of personal loneliness she had had the reassurance that he was doing an important job, that they were building for the future, and that her husband loved her. But where was the mighty soaring bridge which enabled them to meet and clasp hands when they were together in the same house yet separated by a chasm of despair? How could it be that a man who had done the work of a dozen men, with energies enough on the side to be a student of all that went on, how could that same man only a month or a year later have insufficient energy or interest to take care of his simplest duties? Every day was Friday now; lucky Tuesday had disappeared from the week. In their early days he had said that their love was a fortress, impregnable from without. Had it decayed from within?

She knew intuitively that talk with an unhappy man was dangerous: it could flare into argument or angry retort, words which would be difficult to forget. Yet surely there was something even more dangerous than the possibility of provoking Andrew: the possibility of his doing himself irremedial damage. She did not believe him to be quarrelsome by nature; he liked people, was loyal to his friends, wanted to be loved. But circumstances seemed to combine in an infinite variety to rob him of his tranquillity, to violate his innate sense of justice. Was this too part of their life pattern? Must it always be so? Or did men go through cycles in their lives, just as the earth did? Now he was lying hard and barren beneath a winter snow; but surely if the soil was good, and the proper season came, it would yield?

In her need she found company and friendship with her brother Severn. His cabin, just beyond the Hermitage spring, reminded her of Poplar Grove. It was small but cozy, with an adjoining lean-to similar to the one Johnny's Mary had used for her prayers, big enough to hold the large bed in which the four older children slept. The baby's trundle was kept in the main room.

It was strange about Severn: Rachel had never been close to him, his illness had made him shy and he had kept himself apart from the family. He looked like no one Rachel had ever seen, bearing not the slightest resemblance to his parents or to any of his brothers or sisters. Now that they had won each other's confidence she learned that Severn read in the Bible for an hour upon awakening and also before going to sleep at night. Perhaps that is the source of his tranquillity, she thought; anyone who grows up hand in hand with death must have a feeling of intimacy with God. When she listened to Severn speak with reverence of God's will she knew that of the eleven Donelson children, he alone had inherited his father's religious nature; and that seemed doubly wondrous to her; for Severn not to have inherited his father's eyes or chin or voice or wilderness fever but precisely the one thing he needed to sustain him: devoutness. In her confused and frightened frame of mind, when Jane's cool asepticism would have been unacceptable, she had found a brother whose very nature fitted her need.

In return she was able to help Severn, whose wife Elizabeth was growing increasingly unable to cope with her brood; she had borne five children in the eight years of their marriage, not a staggering amount by Donelson standards: Johnny's wife Mary was about to have her thirteenth, Mary Caffrey had twelve: but Elizabeth had had a bad period after the birth of each child. During Andrew's frequent absences, that now began to extend from the day in town to several days on the road, Rachel and little Andy walked over to Severn's bringing a lunch basket and sweets; sometimes she took the four older youngsters back home with her. When Elizabeth was with child again she cried to Rachel:

"It isn't that I don't love them, but I just don't have the strength to bear them and nurse them and keep them out from under my feet."

Rachel thought, Oh, Liz, if you could know how terribly I have wished that God would bless me with just one. She recalled Jane's saying shortly after she had moved into Poplar Grove, "For some women they come a little too fast, for others a little too slow, but we Donelsons all seem to get our share." Jane, how wrong you were!

Andrew had been away for a week when she received word that he was on his way home after working with a group of Sumner County folks who were planning to move down to the new Mississippi Territory. She heated a tub of water, dressed in a soft brown muslin with the full skirt which she preferred to the newly fashionable narrow ones, and hung her pearl brooch on the end of her silver chain. She had Mitty polish the large candelabrum and put it in the center of the white huckaback-linen board cover, set the dining-room table festively, placing a vase of riotously colored autumn leaves at one end. The papaws were ripening, and she piled some in a pewter bowl on the sideboard next to Andrew's decanters. When he arrived home shortly before dark and saw the special preparations, he asked:

"Party?"

"For two."

"I see." Then with a wry smile, "Welcoming home the prodigal son?"

"The prodigal husband."

"I guess you could call me that; and it would be the kindest thing that has been said of me in quite a while."

"You should stay home more often and listen to your wife. I can think of all sorts of nice things I would like to say if I thought you were interested."

"I'm always interested in anything you have to say, Mrs. Jackson."

"Not for the past few months you haven't been, Mr. Jackson."

He walked over to the table and selected a pickled walnut from a pewter porringer. Then, slowly, almost apologetically, he moved toward where she was standing, took her in his arms and kissed her.

"Darling, you haven't kissed me for so very long, or taken me in your arms."

"I know, I've been too unhappy; when you hate yourself and the whole world around you . . ."

"But Andrew, you've always been so strong, so sure of yourself."

"I don't know. Everything just seems to have . . ."

"Could one of the reasons be that you are quarreling so constantly with Mr. Jefferson and President Madison? What would you do if you were in their shoes? Each section of the country has its special problems, and its separate demands. With the war still going on in Europe each foreign country has its demands too."

"I'll admit poor Mr. Madison is beset by everyone . . . including me." He grinned, the first sign that the good soil of Andrew Jackson was sprouting life again. "God help anyone who has to be president!" Then he waved his arms high above his head and brought his fists plunging through the air. "But by the Eternal, I'd be tougher with the British; I'd kick them out of those forts in the North . . ."

He picked up one of his clay pipes, filled it with tobacco, then crouched on the hearth, lighting it with a small live coal. "Those families over in Sumner County have reports that the land is fertile in the Mississippi Territory, and that a man can own as much of it as he can survey. There's a Federal judgeship open down there; if it paid only a thousand dollars a year, I'd take it."

He looked up into her face. "I think we can get the appointment this time; it's not a big enough job for Mr. Madison to bother about. Well, my dear, what do you think?"

What could she think? The last time he had wanted "to shake the dust of the Cumberland Valley from my boots," he had thought to go in splendor as governor of the new and vast Louisiana Territory, with a governor's mansion, and high social standing. Now, only five years later, he was content to plunge into the wilderness, swing an ax to level the fields and build himself another log cabin . . . if only he could get a thousand-dollar-a-year judgeship!

Two events, one political and one personal, brought them great pleasure: the election of their old friend Willie Blount as governor; and the marriage of John Coffee to Johnny's daughter Mary. The wedding party at the Mansion was the happiest reunion the Donelson family had known in a long time. Rachel and Andrew were pleased to have their good friend Jax a member of the family; by way of a wedding present they took from their strongbox Jax's notes for his portion of the store debts and tore them up.

When Severn's Elizabeth was ready to be delivered, Rachel hired the best midwife in the neighborhood and went herself to assist in the nursing. The child got itself born without difficulty, but there was a complication which the midwife did not explain. A half hour later it resolved itself in the form of a second child, a twin boy. Elizabeth burst into tears.

"Why does it have to be two when I have barely the strength to nurse one?"

One of the twins began to cry. Rachel took the baby, wrapped him in a soft blanket and put him on her shoulder with his head nestled against her neck. She was standing this way when Severn and Andrew came into the room. Andrew stood above her, gazing down at the infant in her arms, sensing how her heart ached with the need to keep this newborn babe right where he was. Then, suddenly, Elizabeth called from the bed:

"Keep that boy. We only expected one. We wouldn't be losing anything."

Rachel turned her head slowly.

"Yes, Rachel, keep that boy you have in your arms," said Severn softly; "we know how you've longed for a child, and he'll be well off."

Rachel looked about her, managing to bring Andrew's face into focus. His eyes were bright. Weak with expectancy, she sank into a chair, still holding the child.

"You can't be serious, Liz. This is your child. You just bore him. Wait until you recover your strength before you make such an important decision."

"If we could bring some happiness to you, Rachel and Andrew," said Severn, "and at the same time help Liz and the boy . . ."

Andrew's expression left little doubt about how he felt.

Elizabeth asked: "Do you have a woman at home who can wet-nurse him?"

"Yes. Orange has a little one."

"Then take him right this instant. Andrew, you go into Nashville tomorrow and file adoption papers."

When they reached the Hermitage, Andrew drew a chair up to the fire for her. She sat holding the baby in her arms and looking down into its face. Andrew watched her silently. Her eyes were fathomless, all the mystery and magic of life reflected in them. The years had fallen away.

They named him Andrew Jackson, Jr. Andrew brought her the adoption papers, signed and approved by the court, to put into her strongbox. Jane brought her the Hays trundle, which Rachel placed beside her bed. She had trouble falling asleep at night because she was listening so intently to the child's breathing; if a twig fell on the roof she was out of bed and leaning over the crib before she was awake. He was a long lean baby, with a thatch of black hair and pastel blue eyes; he cried little, except in the early morning when he was hungry. Rachel kept the fire roaring in the cabin to make sure he did not catch cold; Andrew could hardly breathe for the heat.

One day George reported that Mr. Jackson would not be home to dinner. When Andrew reached the Hermitage later that evening he was excitedly leading a new filly across the yard. Rachel ran up to him and examined the little roan race horse. Her eyes sought Andrew's, a small smile playing about her lips: could it be her husband's nose had been put out of joint?

The filly was so small and light in weight that it hardly seemed she could last out a long race.

"That's why I got her cheap," said Andrew gleefully as he came in from the yard where he had been training her. "I've entered her in the big race on Saturday with a thousand-dollar side bet against the course champion."

To everyone's astonishment except Andrew's, the little roan won handily, streaking around the course so fast her hoofs hardly seemed to touch the turf. Rachel could not tell from Andrew's chuckles whether his pleasure came from this renewed proof of his sense of horseflesh, or the fact that he had won what would have been a year's salary from the Mississippi judgeship . . . which had just been given to someone else.

"You know what I'm going to do with this thousand dollars?" he asked.

"No, what?"

"I heard of a stand of arms for sale in Hiwassie, and I'm going to use this money to buy them. I'm starting out tomorrow to see and talk to every militiaman who's ever served under me; if I can't persuade them back into the ranks, or convince them that we'll be training for an actual war, then I'll simply have to bribe them with whatever it is they need: a horse, or a sword, or a gun. I've got to build that militia from inside myself; there is no other place it can come from."

He was gone all day now, touring the countryside. Rachel would watch him leave the Hermitage a little after dawn, when she rose to tend the baby. It's so important that he be happy, she repeated to herself, for when he is unhappy he tears himself apart, and then the seamside of his fabric shows through.

For herself the baby had an annealing effect; a buoyancy permeated her outlook and her actions. She felt light on her feet, running the hundreds of errands needed for the child, and light of heart as she

183

played the pianoforte after dinner. She was happy and grateful; she no longer turned inward, wondering what people knew or thought about her. She met strangers as easily as she did friends. Her sanguinity coincided with Andrew's renewed faith in himself, his own return to patience and lightness of touch. She realized that therein lay the curse and the genius of a good marriage: that what happened to one member happened equally to both.

She was the only one who knew that Andrew was spending his own money on the militia. He told her, "We should never count pennies on this subject," yet she was amused to see that he brought home the record of every dollar spent, asking her to post it in his militia account book.

"So you really think we'll be paid back, Andrew?"

"If war comes, every dollar will be returned; if not, it'll be like coming in second in a horse race."

As a result of his new fighting spirit, and Governor Blount's espousal, Sunday was once again open house at the Hermitage. A group of bright young aides-de-camp came for the afternoon and supper: Thomas Hart Benton, a law student, Robert Butler, recently married to Rachel Hays, John Reid, a bank clerk, William Carroll, who owned a successful hardware store in Nashville, and William B. Lewis, a neighbor. Eight years had passed since Andrew had taken command, so that he was able to draw a whole new generation of subalterns from among Rachel's nephews. When the weather was warm she spread long tables under the catalpa trees; when it turned cool she served inside, using her cherrywood dining table as a buffet, with some thirty men standing in groups eating and discussing military problems. Andrew, Jr., learning to walk, made the adventuresome journey from one military leg to another as though he were wandering through a forest of young trees.

For the first master muster the following spring Rachel rode in her carriage to the drill grounds. There formerly had been some two thousand members of the militia, but surely, she told herself, there could not be more than two hundred assembled here? Few of the townspeople had bothered to come, the wrestling matches had disappeared, there were only a few old women selling ginger cakes. Yet even to her inexperienced eye it was clear that there were many new guns in evidence, as well as fine horses and considerable of what Andrew called *accouterments*. Andrew was pleased.

"Wait till word gets around about the new spirit and the new muskets," he told her; "the volunteers will start drifting back of their own accord."

It seemed only a few months before a visiting officer declared General Jackson's militia the most perfect of its kind in the country. Rachel found herself thinking, If war must come, let it come now so that Andrew can prove he has been right.

184

And so he was. On June 21, 1812, Billey Phillips, their former jockey and now a presidential courier, brought the news from Washington to Nashville: the United States had declared war on Great Britain!

Rachel was swept by a hundred inner gales. War, then, as Andrew had predicted that first night at supper at the Donelson stockade, more than twenty years before. She thought of the line he was so fond of quoting: someone had spoken to Benjamin Franklin of the Revolution as the War for Independence, and Mr. Franklin had replied, "Sir, the war for independence is yet to come!" Well, it was here now, and she knew that whatever might happen to the country, the government or the army it was a war that Andrew Jackson would never abandon until it had been won.

The weeks of July 1812 passed in a fever. Andrew rose at dawn and tried to supervise the farming of the Hermitage, but he was so preoccupied with military affairs that the effort was galling to him. Once again she made her way into the fields, releasing him for the thousand tasks involved in getting his troops armed and trained: for there was no help forthcoming from either the state or the Federal government, and he had to send out his own purchasing agents to places like Newport in Kentucky to bring back the necessary muskets and ammunition. To Rachel, who had watched him drawing up his maps, he explained:

"If President Madison approves, I can move my militia to Canada within ninety days and take Quebec. The British forces there are still feeble. We could sweep straight through Canada before they'd have a chance to reinforce their garrisons."

Since the Creeks, now heavily armed and incited by British agents, had already begun their war at the Tennessee border, Andrew stood poised with his men, ready to move in either direction upon receipt of an order. Then, late in July, the message arrived. Andrew was away, so Rachel tore open the sealed envelope. She read:

> *The tender of Service by Genl. Jackson and the volunteers under his command is Received by the President with peculiar satisfaction and in accepting their services, he cannot withhold an expression of his admiration of the zeal and ardour by which they are animated.*
>
> WILLIAM EUSTIS
> *Secretary of War*

The news of Secretary of War Eustis's note had been released by Governor Blount, and with it the announcement that a general of the United States Army was to be appointed from the West and dispatched at once to Canada. When Andrew reached home he barely glanced at the note which she stood waving at him as he came across the yard to the house.

"The War Department has accepted my plan for a march on Quebec!" he exclaimed. "Rachel, remember at Hunter's Hill, when you said to me, 'Why Andrew, I do believe you would like to be a regular officer in the United States Army'? Well, my dear, it has come to pass."

"You've received the appointment?"

"It should be here on the next dispatch. I've alerted the militia. We'll be ready to move within a few hours."

The appointment came through the very next day, but it was for James Winchester, Andrew's second-in-command, who was made a brigadier general in the regular army and ordered to leave at once with Kentucky troops to join General William H. Harrison in Canada. Andrew sat on a bench outside their cabin, his face an earth-red in color, a dazed expression in his eyes, looking straight through Rachel.

"Perhaps it's because General Winchester had such a fine record in the Revolution?" she offered. When he did not answer, she continued, "Or it may be that they want you for the southern campaign? You've been telling the War Department for years that when the British struck they'd come in through Louisiana."

This helped a little; he gulped a few times and moved his head as though searching for the early August stars through the trees.

The first news of the war in the North was catastrophic: General Hull, who commanded the largest part of the American troops in Canada, had surrendered Detroit and his entire army. For days Andrew wandered about the Hermitage, unable to eat or sleep or discuss anything else. This time she did not try to bring him out of his gloom: it was too deep to be dissipated by any comforting word.

He did not find release from his lethargy for almost a full week, and then only because he learned that four hundred first-class rifles, of a better caliber than anything his militia had ever owned, were available on the Indian frontier. He secured twenty-eight hundred dollars from Governor Blount, signed his own personal paper for another thirty-two hundred dollars and sent the swiftest scouts in Tennessee to buy the rifles before anyone else could stumble across them.

At long last, in October, Governor Blount received seventy blank commissions from the War Department. Andrew assured Rachel that this was the authorization for which they had been waiting: if they could not push the British out of Canada, at least they would now be able to reach Louisiana before the British fleet could transport its victorious northern troops to New Orleans. She and Andrew were having a late supper after having taken Andy back to the Cumberland Academy, which had formerly been the Davidson Academy, when General Robertson came in from Knoxville. They could tell he was angry by the way he kept pushing back his bang of pure-white hair.

186

"I got bad news for you, son: the President and Secretary of War are ignorin' your militia. Governor Blount has been ordered to call out and equip fifteen hundred new volunteers."

Andrew sat stunned, his extraordinarily large mouth open and out of control, foam working in one corner. Rachel asked:

"But how can that be? They know that Andrew has twenty-seven hundred men trained and ready. They already accepted . . ."

General Robertson answered softly, as one does in the presence of a stricken man.

"Governor Blount is convinced that the President and the War Department don't want Andrew in their army."

"No," Andrew shot back, finding speech at last, "they want General Hull, who surrenders without a shot. I might fight, and embarrass them."

"Confidentially, son, the governor is afraid you won't take a subordinate position under General Wilkinson. But maybe I can find some way . . ."

"All I ask is a chance to fight; but to have to sneak into the war through the back door . . ."

Rachel sat quietly, her hands folded in her lap, half listening to the discussion, half hearing her own inner voices. The War Department had made it mercilessly clear that they were afraid of Andrew and mistrusted him. Why? Because of the Burr affair? Because of his early political quarrels with Sevier and Jefferson? Because he had had no real war experience? She would not let herself think what would happen to her husband if he were denied the right to participate in this war of which he had kept Tennessee aware these many years.

"Once you're inside the house, Andrew," she proffered, "the interior looks the same regardless of whether you came in the front door or the back."

He smiled at her wanly, said, "Agreed!" then turned to Robertson. "Just get me into the war, by fair means or foul, and nobody will ever get me out."

Her family reported that their every enemy in the state was working to convince Governor Blount that since the War Department had rejected Mr. Jackson, he must do likewise. Rachel watched Andrew grow thinner and jumpier with the passing of the days, but she knew that Willie Blount must be suffering equally: for he had now signed sixty-nine of the commissions, and had only one left. Would he abandon his old friend and commander of his western division? It seemed to Rachel that Andrew had not uttered ten words since the blank commissions had reached Tennessee.

On November 1, the governor's respect for Andrew conquered his fear of the War Department: Andrew was commissioned a major general of the volunteers, ordered to call a rendezvous of his troops and to move as quickly as possible to New Orleans to reinforce General Wilkinson.

Andrew brought home an overseer, an elderly man by the name of Dinwiddie, who did not look to Rachel as though he would be of much help. During the next ten days she showed Mr. Dinwiddie over the Hermitage and laid out her plan of work. She saw almost nothing of Andrew, who was trying to assemble a thousand horses for Colonel John Coffee's cavalry, a flotilla of flatboats to transport his militia down the Mississippi, muskets, powder and shot, medical supplies, blankets, tents and uniforms, of which there were almost none available except what the volunteers offered themselves. When he issued his order for the rendezvous in Nashville, Rachel asked:

"Darling, can you give me any idea of how long you may be gone?"

"No, my dear, only the British know the answer to that. They are in complete control in the North, raiding and burning all through New England, with no one to stop them. Their ships can move thousands of men southward to invade through the Floridas and Louisiana."

"Then let me come into Nashville and stay for the last days of your encampment? There's room for us at Tabitha's."

Tabitha was Johnny's daughter who had married Polly's brother, George Smith.

She awoke on the morning of the rendezvous to the most penetrating cold she had experienced in the Cumberland. She waited until the fire was crackling in the downstairs hearth before venturing to dress her son. Her sled had been brought out; she and the boy huddled beneath a big bear robe, while Andrew rode alongside on his black charger, man and horse sending up streamers of frosty breath. The Cumberland River had frozen during the night, a sight she had not seen since the unhappy dawn at Hunter's Hill when she had despaired of her husband's long absences. Andrew leaned over to tell her what bad luck it was to have this terrible cold on the day the troops were to rendezvous, and how glad he was that the quartermaster, Major William B. Lewis, had assembled a thousand cords of wood at the cantonment.

When they reached Nashville Rachel went directly to Tabitha's house. At four o'clock she put on a heavily lined capuchin, mittens and boots, and waited for young Thomas Hart Benton to take her to the cantonment. The ground was snow-covered, but the camp itself, where more than two thousand men stood stomping about the fires, had been turned into a slough of mud. Benton led her to Andrew's tent; he was writing orders on a crudely contrived table.

"Andrew, they're saying in town that it's going to be the coldest night in the history of Tennessee. Couldn't you billet the men in the homes and stores and taverns?"

"I have no authority to do that," he said. "Besides, if we can't survive one night of cold how are we going to stay alive through a whole war?"

It was pitch-black by the time she reached her niece's house. Little Andrew was asleep. Rachel sat before the fire reading in Psalms 91:5:

188

Thou shalt not be afraid for the terror by night; nor for the arrow that flieth by day.

The cold so permeated the very stones of the hearth that by seven o'clock she began heating the sheets of her bed with the copper warming pan filled with hot coals. She slept intermittently, worried about Andrew and the men who had insufficient blankets to lie in the snow.

The next morning Andrew sent her a message that his troops had weathered their first bout with adversity. At the breakfast table she asked her redheaded niece:

"Tabitha, is that artist, Josh Clenning, still painting vases and fans? Do you think he can catch a likeness on ivory?"

"I think so, Aunt Rachel. Why don't we go ask him?"

During the following weeks Andrew managed occasionally to come into Tabitha's for a cup of coffee late at night. He strode up and down the front room in his dark blue uniform, boots and sword, his red hair now graying at the temples, a cyclone of activity, telling Rachel of his problems. The two months' advance pay which the soldiers wanted to leave behind with their families had not arrived from Washington City. He was attempting to assemble provisions and boats on his own credit, and had used his own personal note for sixteen hundred dollars on urgent supplies; would she be sure to meet it when it came due in ninety days? He did not tell her with what.

Rachel went each morning for a sitting at Josh Clenning's, but apparently the artist did not think the general and his troops were going to leave Nashville; he only shrugged when Rachel tried to hasten his work.

Finally, in the first week of January, Colonel John Coffee rode off with his six hundred and seventy cavalrymen, heading down the Natchez Trace. Three days later she stood on the bank of the river, Andrew, Jr., in her arms, while she and the entire population of Nashville waved and cried their farewells to General Jackson and his fourteen hundred infantrymen. Andrew had said to her that morning as he kissed her goodby:

"Be of good heart, my dear, I can take care of myself. You know I'll be doing the one job I've wanted most in life to do."

Yes, she knew this; and she was resigned. She said, "Darling, he promised me he would have it ready. I wanted you to have it as my farewell gift."

"Oh, a surprise?"

"A painting of me, on ivory. I wanted you to carry it in your pocket."

"Not a chance. It'll go around my neck on a chain, and I'll never take it off, night or day. If it's finished within the next ten days send it by Dinwiddie to the juncture of the Cumberland and Ohio. It will be my good-luck piece."

She stood on the bank, watching the last of the boats shove off from

189

the shore in the cold gray January light, with Andrew's lead boat slowly pulling out of sight.

6

It was not until she had entered the front door and Moll had taken her cape that she perceived the change that had come over her home in the short time since she had left it; for this would be Andrew's first long absence from the Hermitage. When he had been away for a week or a month she had felt his presence within the rooms, heard his voice, seen his lanky figure moving about with that awkward grace of extraordinarily tall men. Now he was gone: his voice, his figure, his presence; and the room had become not only enormous but empty.

She sat on the edge of one of her parlor chairs while Moll took the boy upstairs, not tired physically yet pervaded by a sense of letdown. Did soldiers' wives gear themselves to be brave and cheerful, and never let their husbands see any of the trembling or fear? And when the men had gone, when they returned to the silence of their homes, having used up the grit meant to last a year or perhaps a lifetime, did they all suffer alike? Did they feel weak and hollow, not knowing how long it might take before they could stand on their feet again? And why was it that not even the presence of a beloved son could make up for the absence of a beloved husband?

Moll and the boy came downstairs; he was in his night clothes and ready for supper. Rachel read to him for a little while, then put him to sleep early, in her own bed, for he had been up since dawn. Moll was sitting in a little rocker by the fire when she returned to the big room. Her hair had turned white and her face had thinned considerably with the years, but otherwise she gave no sign that she had passed her seventieth birthday.

"You didn't have to wait for me, Moll; I'm not planning to eat anything."

"I know *you* ain't, Miz Rachel, but *I'm* plannin'. General Jackson, he tell me before he leave, I'm to take care of you. Remember up on the Hill how skinny you got 'cause you wouldn't eat? Now you come over to the table and have some of this here pot pie."

She ate a little of the veal to satisfy Moll, then felt better and warmer. She went upstairs, undressed quickly, put on a long flannel nightgown, not bothering to braid her hair or put on a nightcap. She moved the boy onto his pillow, tucked the blankets around his shoulders, then slipped into her old and badly worn blue silk Spanish robe. She was weary from the long trip, from the days of waiting and the constant anxiety that at any moment Andrew might be relieved of his command; but she knew she could not sleep, for her loneliness was wide awake within her.

190

Downstairs, she put fresh logs on the fire and sat very close to its heat, her elbows planted firmly on her knees, her palms extended toward the flames. The nights would be the worst; during the day she could placate time with her chores, she would have the company of her son, she would invite over several of Severn's children; yet the greatest burden a woman had to bear was to be left behind with so little to do beyond the repetitious and, when alone, meaningless chores of housekeeping. It was the fate of women, she reflected, never to be the doers in the sense that men were, but always to serve as passive instruments to whom things happened.

She rose and moved about the room, touching old and familiar objects: her mother's gridiron hanging by the side of the fireplace, the big wooden clock, her pianoforte and Andrew's flute lying in its case, her father's walnut desk. She opened it, saw one of Andrew's clay pipes lying there and beside it a wooden bowl of tobacco. Unthinking, she picked up the pipe, stuffed it with tobacco, then went to the fireplace, took the pipe tongs and lifted a small coal from the fireplace, holding it to the bowl as Andrew did. The smoke tasted acrid in her mouth; it had an almost insupportably heavy body. She spat it out quickly. After a few moments she puffed in the smoke again; the sensation was not so unpleasant this time. She sank onto her chair, drawing little bits of smoke and then blowing them toward the crackling logs. She felt closer to Andrew. The pain eased a little.

She fell into a reverie, her mind returning to her early years on the Virginia plantation, and to her father, who had begun each day of his life with prayer. One of the first things he had tried to teach her was that God was not an idea or a remote presence, but actually part of herself. She could hear his voice saying to her, "We are all integral parts of God." To her father, she knew, God had been very close. When she had come upon him praying silently and asked if he wasn't afraid God might not be able to hear him, John Donelson had smiled indulgently as he replied, "No, my dear, God hears what we think even clearer than what we say."

She had never fully accepted or even understood her father's concept of the Deity. To her, God had been the all-powerful ruler of the universe, the distant and frequently terrifying force which controlled her and everybody else, whether they liked it or not. She had never been able to achieve any sense of intimacy in her prayers, for He had seemed to her to live too far away, up beyond the heavens, to be able to see or even care about one solitary soul. She knew other people besides her father who walked with their hand in God's; her brother Severn was one of these. She had prayed when Andrew had been away, but it had always been with more fear than love, and to some remote omniscience in whom she had neither abiding faith nor genuine hope.

Now she found herself on her knees by the hearth, praying for her husband with more devoutness and humility than she had ever known. Her sense of the remoteness and untouchability of God fell away; she felt His presence not merely in her house, the simple log cabin on the Hermitage, but in her being, hearing her silent prayer:

Please, let my husband find his fulfillment . . . and keep him safe.

A few days later Josh Clenning sent her picture out to the Hermitage. She took the ivory from the cotton in which Mr. Clenning had wrapped it, then stood by the window with the sun beating down on her likeness. Her heart dropped when she realized that this was by no means the picture of a young or beautiful girl. Why hadn't she had a picture painted when she had first met Andrew, when her skin had been flawlessly smooth? Then she would not have had to send her husband this picture of a forty-five-year-old woman, slightly plump under the chin.

But that was foolishness; Andrew was no longer young either: the embattlements had put rings under his eyes, wrinkles at their corners, and deep lines starting on either cheek above his nostrils and curving their way down to the corners of his uneven mouth. Thanks to the heritage from her mother, her hair was still richly black, her skin kept its slightly pink glow, the brown of her eyes was as dark and vibrant as when she had been twenty-one. There was strain there, suffering and uncertainty; these qualities hovered about her mouth too. But there was nothing frightening about losing one's youth so long as one's love struck ever deeper with the passage of the years.

She turned away from the window, wrapped the miniature securely in a box, then wrote Andrew a letter. When she had finished she summoned Mr. Dinwiddie. He returned a few days later with a reply from Andrew. She mounted the stairs, curled up on the bed and took out the sheet of paper that was covered with his cramped but clear writing.

MY LOVE:
I have this evening received your affectionate letter by Dinwiddie. He has carefully handed me your miniature. I shall wear it near my bosom; but this was useless for without your miniature my recollection never fails me of your likeness.

I thank you for your prayers. I thank you for your determined resolution to bear our separation with fortitude. I shall write to you often. If I can get the arms on board tomorrow I shall sail early on Monday morning.

It is now 1 o'clock in the morning—the candle nearly out. May the angelic hosts that reward and protect virtue be with you until I return, is the sincere supplication of your affectionate husband.

She lay quietly for a considerable time, the letter held firmly at her bosom, thinking nothing, feeling all. Then she rose, went down to the walnut desk, took paper and pen and began to write.

MY DEAR HUSBAND:

Your letter of the 18th of January from the mouth of the Cumberland river came safe to hand. It was everything to me. I rejoiced.

Do not, my beloved husband, let the love of country, fame and honor, make you forget. Without you, I would think them all empty shadows. You will say this is not the language of a patriot, but it is the language of a faithful wife.

Our little Andrew is well. Pray, my dear, write me often. It's a cordial—it's a balm to my mind in my lonesome hours. I treasure them up as a miser his gold.

Think of me your dearest friend on earth.

The reports that filtered back to her were good; John Coffee's cavalry and Andrew's flotilla were making excellent progress toward New Orleans. It was the news from the North that was disastrous: Brigadier General Winchester, having been captured by the British in Canada and assured that if he would counsel his troops to surrender they would be well treated, had given up his two regiments. Most of the Kentuckians had then been massacred by northern Indians who had been fighting alongside the British. Old General Robertson, so calm and philosophical by nature, was in an absolute rage as he paced the floor of the Hermitage.

"What has happened to the American army?" he demanded. "First Hull surrenders, not only himself, but Detroit. Now Winchester surrenders, and his two regiments with him, and we lose all those fine boys. If we'd fought that way in the Revolution we would still be British subjects. By the Eternal, Rachel, if they'll only give Andrew Jackson a chance to fight . . ."

He broke off abruptly. She caught the innuendo in his "If they'll only . . ." She went to the old man's side, linking her arm through his.

"What has happened to upset you about Andrew?"

". . . well . . . He's being accused of having stated that the same county could not contain himself and General Wilkinson, that he has his dueling pistols with him."

She brushed aside the reference to dueling pistols. "When Andrew took his commission he knew he would have to serve under General Wilkinson. He said it was a bitter pill, but that he will obey like any other good officer."

Robertson ran his hand through his thinning white hair, sending it forward over his brow until it came on an even line with his eyebrows.

"We know that, my dear friend, but does the War Department?"

She told herself that it was futile to worry about what such stories might do to injure Andrew. Surely the Secretary of War was not going to dismiss an able general on the basis of sheer rumor, not after the other generals had been so sorely defeated and there were so few left to stand up against the British arms?

The first letter Andrew wrote her from Natchez told her that General Wilkinson had ordered him to remain there and not to go down the river to New Orleans. He had obeyed, pitching his tents four miles from the town in a handsome plain with wood and water convenient. He had also written to Governor Blount and to the War Department saying that he had followed Wilkinson's orders. His letter reassured her.

Then, less than a month after Andrew had left with his troops, a new Secretary of War took office in Washington City, Mr. John Armstrong. Almost instantly upon sitting down to his desk he wrote a dispatch to Major General Jackson, a copy of which found its way to the Hermitage:

War Department
February 5, 1813

Sir,

The causes for embodying and marching to New Orleans the Corps under your command having ceased to exist, you will on receipt of this letter, consider it as dismissed from public service and take measures to have delivered over to Major General Wilkinson all articles of public property which may have been put into its possession. You will accept for yourself and the Corps the thanks of the President of the United States. I have the honor to be Sir, With great respect,

Your Most Obedient Servant,

She was staggered by this development. Dear God, would it never cease? She studied the text a hundred times in an effort to make some sense out of it. *"The causes for embodying and marching to New Orleans the Corps under your command having ceased to exist . . ."* What could the new Secretary of War mean? The cause for Andrew's moving his troops to New Orleans could only cease to exist when the war was over!

Of all the things that might have happened to Andrew, she decided, this was the worst possible blow: after having taken two thousand men a thousand miles in the dead of winter, having almost bankrupted himself by paying out his own money to get whatever equipment and supplies were needed, he was now curtly dismissed! The War Department had not wanted General Jackson in the army in the first place, and now they had succeeded in booting him out.

7

Two weeks later Major William B. Lewis, Andrew's supply officer in Nashville, came to her with a letter he had received from Andrew in which he asked that transportation be sent down to the Tennessee River to afford passage for his officers and men, particularly for the sick.

194

"I can't send him even a single horse through army channels," Major Lewis told her. "So I've started taking up private subscriptions. I have about six hundred dollars, but Captain Erwin stopped me from collecting in Nashville on the grounds that I was aiding and abetting a mutiny."

"A mutiny!" She was thunderstruck. "On what grounds?"

"On the grounds that General Jackson was ordered to dismiss the corps under his command, but refused to do so, insisting upon marching them back to their homes."

She planted her feet firmly on the braided rag rug, stood with her legs apart as she did in the fields, and held her head high in the air.

"Well, good for General Jackson! What an idea of the War Department, to discharge all those soldiers so far from home, with no way and no supplies to get back."

Six weeks later, summoned by a courier, she rode her fastest horse into town to find the troops drawn up in the square. The men were gaunt and threadbare after their month trip up the Trace. Remembering the crowds that had turned out to bid them farewell three months before, how cannon had been fired, flags waved and speeches made, she now looked about the square to see that there was only a handful of onlookers.

As she walked toward where Andrew stood shaking the hands of his officers, she realized that she had not seen him so fleshless since his first return from Philadelphia, that hot June day in 1795 when she had come up from the barn to find him sagging on his horse in front of their cabin at Poplar Grove. But there was nothing thin about his spirit; he kissed her on the mouth, hard, the sharp bones of his body hurting her wherever they touched. As he stood there, his arm fiercely about her, watching his men leave through the many exits of the square, his emotion was not one of hurt pride, or even anger, but sheer grim determination that the War Department must not be so willfully stupid as to dismiss their fighting troops. As they rode home, their horses close together, he related how General Wilkinson had provided him with twenty days' rations, nothing more.

"I had to hire wagons and wagoners, and buy up whatever medicines I could find out of my own funds; when the food ran out or we needed additional horses I bought those too."

She looked at him quizzically.

"You bought, my dear? With what?"

"My personal notes. Drawn on Wilkinson's quartermaster."

A few days later they made a trip into town, Andrew to buy a dragon plow and a two-inch auger, Rachel to present her compliments to Sarah Bentley, who was opening a little shop to make gowns and dresses for the women of Nashville. Their carriage had no sooner entered Market Street than several people on the streets cried out, "There's General Jackson!" When Andrew had tied the horses in front of the Nashville Inn they were quickly surrounded by a group of young men. Someone called:

"Three cheers for Old Hickory!"

"Would this Old Hickory be you?" Rachel demanded, seeing him flush.

"Might. Let's go inside and find out why I've changed from a useless character to a hero overnight."

In the lobby of the inn she heard half a dozen stories at once: of how Andrew had walked all the way home, his mounts being used to carry the sick; of how he had turned over his share of the food to those who were weakened by the tropical fevers; of how he had nursed the boys and walked alongside the wagons, sometimes holding their hands, and bringing every last one home alive. Sandy Donelson said:

"Uncle ate less than anybody, walked farther, worked harder and slept the least; that's why we said he was tough."

"Sure," one of the soldiers added, "tough as hickory. We called him hickory for a considerable spell up the Trace, hating him for getting us into the mess. Then, when we saw he was going to bring us all in, we started calling him Old Hickory. We was proud to be serving under him."

John Overton pushed through the crowd, linked one arm through Rachel's and the other through Andrew's, escorting them to his office. He lifted a pile of law books and briefs from a chair, dusted it with his handkerchief. Then he turned to Andrew.

"That damned Wilkinson! He has refused to honor your notes. They've all been sent here to Nashville for collection."

Andrew's jaw locked. She watched him gulp.

"I guaranteed everyone from whom I took food, wagons, horses, medicines, that the United States Army would pay on demand, and that if they wouldn't, I would."

"How much does your paper amount to?"

"I don't know. Thousands of dollars."

"Thousands?" exclaimed Rachel. "Oh, darling, I had to sell a big part of last year's crop and much of our livestock to meet that sixteen-hundred-dollar note you left behind."

John said quietly, "I have some money put aside, it's yours for the using."

Andrew shook his head.

"How much easier it would have been for me to have dismissed my men at Natchez! I had money in my pocket, three good horses to carry me home. But could I be an obedient soldier? No! I gave Jax half my cash because his cavalry was starving, and then had to bring every last one of my men back here."

Rachel rose and stood beside him.

"And if the War Department refuses to honor the notes?"

He took her hand in his.

"Then we'll have to sell the Hermitage."

That night she heard the bleating of a young lamb. She went to the door and saw a little white animal, a few days old, which had strayed out of the barn. She picked it up and took it to Andrew, who was smoking before the fire.

"Remember that lamb we saved at Poplar Grove?" she asked. "This one looks enough like him to be his brother."

"His great-grandchild." He stroked the soft curly white wool. Rachel went to the desk, took one of his pipes and filled it with tobacco.

"I started smoking while you were away," she said. "When I was lonely I found it consoling."

He beckoned for her to come and sit by him. He put one arm about her shoulders and brought her head and cheek close to his.

"I leave you alone a terrible lot, don't I?"

She rubbed her cheek against his; he was unshaven and she found it pleasurable to feel her soft skin on the rough stubble of his beard.

"If I wanted to unboosom myself, I could tell you just how much."

He picked up a live coal in the tongs and held it in the bowl of her pipe. She sat looking into the glow of the ash, wondering where their next hearth would be. There was a brusque knock at the door. Andrew called, "Enter." Thomas Hart Benton came into the room, closed the door behind him and covered the space to the hearth all in one movement. He was thirty-one, a man of unceasing energies and ambition, handsome in a hacked-out fashion, with a powerfully made head, a great shock of hair, a huge jutting and crooked nose, devouring eyes, an orator's mouth, a massive chin. Benton said:

"General, I've come to say good-by, and to ask if you'll give me a letter of recommendation to the War Department. I'm going to apply for a position in the regular army."

"The regular army, eh? I don't think my recommendation will carry much weight right now, but I'll write them a letter telling them I think you were one of the finest officers in the corps."

"While you are writing that letter, why not restate the case of your promissory notes?" asked Rachel. "Colonel Benton can tell them the story."

The next day Andy came home, the spring term being over, and her family of four was together again. She let the two big Andrews teach little Andrew how to ride his pony and pretty soon her three men were riding across the fields, making for the river for a swim and a mess of catfish. She knew that there was a fire eating at her husband's vitals: for here he sat in enforced idleness while the war went from bad to worse, the American officers constantly being outmaneuvered and crushed by the more experienced English commanders, and no one in Washington willing to summon him or so much as let him fire a gun: yet he concealed all this from his son and nephew, giving them the companionship they so sorely missed during his absence and biding his time with more patience and fortitude than she had ever seen in him.

197

She returned from Severn's to find Andrew closeted with his brigade inspector, Major William Carroll, who had just been challenged by another of Andrew's officers, Littleton Johnston. From what she could gather, Carroll had refused to fight Johnston on the ground that the latter was not a gentleman, whereupon Jesse Benton, Colonel Thomas Hart Benton's younger brother and a friend of Johnston, had brought a second challenge; Carroll, assuming that Jesse Benton was willing to become a principal in the duel, had come out to the Hermitage to ask the general to deliver the challenge to Benton.

Rachel exclaimed: "Andrew, surely you are not going to let those two young men fight? Only we know how terrible . . ."

She broke off. Andrew replied quietly:

"I'll do everything in my power to stop them."

But when he returned home the next day she learned that in spite of his efforts he had been ineffective. Jesse Benton had decided that he must fight if he were to continue to live in Tennessee; while Carroll, instead of being dissuaded by Andrew's arguments, asked that the duel be fought at ten paces instead of the usual thirty. Carroll also insisted that his commanding officer serve as his second.

"I just couldn't find any way of saying no to him, Rachel. He's such a poor shot with a pistol, and Jesse Benton is a good one."

"But if you're on the dueling ground," she protested, "it will look as though you are condoning the affair!"

Monday morning, when Andrew came home from the duel, he was wearing a broad smile.

"Young Benton wheeled so fast he couldn't aim, and only hit Carroll in the thumb. Then he suddenly doubled up at the waist and exposed the broadest part of his anatomy to Carroll. And that's precisely where he got shot. He'll have to eat his meals standing up for a week or two."

On the Fourth of July they received a letter from Thomas Benton from Washington City informing them that the War Department had ordered General Wilkinson to pay General Jackson's notes in full. Rachel felt as though a hundred-pound sack of meal had been unlashed from her back. They were deeply grateful to Benton for his assistance; Andrew wrote thanking him. However, others in Nashville were reaching Benton with a series of inflammatory letters about the duel, charging Andrew Jackson with having been the instigator. Andrew explained the circumstances; Benton replied that Andrew had conducted the duel in a "savage, unequal, unfair and base manner." Friends brought word to the Hermitage that Colonel Benton was about to challenge General Jackson; Andrew became so incensed that he promised to horsewhip his aide on sight.

She was operating the churn in the shade of the catalpas, with both boys helping her, when Robert Hays appeared in view, his horse breathing hard.

198

"There's been a ruckus in town, Rachel; Andrew's got himself a little hurt. I think you best come in with me."

As they drove off, Robert linked his arm through hers, telling her as simply as he could what had happened: Tom and Jesse Benton had come from their home in Franklin the night before and put up at the City Hotel. Andrew and John Coffee had tied their horses at the Nashville Inn, then cut across the square to the post office. On the way back they had passed the City Hotel, and there in the doorway had stood Tom Benton, glowering at them. Andrew had raised his riding whip; Benton went into his breast pocket for his pistol; Andrew snatched his pistol out of his back pocket, pressing it against Tom Benton's chest and backing him down a long hall. Jesse Benton suddenly appeared behind them and fired, hitting Andrew in the shoulder.

Robert Hays led her quickly through the lobby of the Nashville Inn and up the stairs to Andrew's room. There were several men clustered about his bed.

"Please, ask them to leave," she said, feeling faint.

Only dimly did she hear Hays reply, "They're all doctors."

She went to the head of the bed. Andrew's face was lifeless, his lids closed tight over his eyes; he hardly seemed to be breathing. His left shoulder was heavily bandaged but soaked through with blood. She put her fingers lightly on his brow. His lids shot open.

"There's only one touch like that . . ."

Dr. May came to her side.

"I'm sorry, Mrs. Jackson, but the general is badly wounded: one bullet broke a bone in his shoulder, the second is lodged against his armbone. We've agreed, these other doctors and I, that the arm cannot be saved; if we do not amputate, gangrene . . ."

The room went black; the voices of the men became like sharp-beaked birds flying inside her skull. Then she heard Andrew say hoarsely:

"Thank you, gentlemen, but I'll keep my arm!"

The youngest of the doctors present, Felix Robertson, son of General Robertson, said:

"With all due apologies to my fellows in medicine, Mrs. Jackson, I don't think the arm needs to be amputated. I've applied strong pressure to stop the bleeding, and put poultices of slippery elm on the wounds."

By now she had regained control of herself. She thanked the doctors, dismissed them all except young Robertson, and sent Stockly Hays out to the Hermitage for sheets and food. With Andrew's great loss of blood had come a strong thirst; every few minutes throughout the night and following day she fed him sips of milk or tea. Though he was in bad pain he did not complain. Dr. Robertson bent the elbow and fixed his forearm to his chest with bandages. By the end of the second day he was able to take small quantities of solid food. Robert Hays came to report that Nashville was in an uproar, that the Bentons nearly had been mur-

199

dered by some of Andrew's former soldiers, and had left town hastily, promising never to return. Sentiment also had turned strongly against Captain Erwin and his group for inciting the quarrel.

"On the strength of that good news," said Andrew, "I think I'll go home."

She prevailed upon him to remain in the room for another two days, until Dr. Robertson had changed the poultice and assured them that the danger of infection was past. Then they returned to the Hermitage. Two of their field hands carried him into the house and up the stairs, his arm still tightly bound, his smashed shoulder useless. Dr. Robertson informed her that there would be a long siege, probably months before he could be up and around, or have the use of his left side.

She was able to keep him quietly in bed for precisely twenty-four hours: for the very next day news reached Nashville that the Creeks had attacked Fort Mims, on the southern border of Mississippi Territory, massacring four hundred men, women and children. A delegation including Governor Blount and John Coffee arrived at the Hermitage to inform General Jackson that the state militia was disconsolate because he could not take command. Rachel waylaid them downstairs.

"Governor Blount, you know the general is ill. He hasn't the strength to stand on his feet, let alone ride a horse for hundreds of miles, and fight a war."

No one answered her, for all eyes had turned toward the stairs. There, coming down slowly, his good right arm holding his shattered left one, was Andrew, his face long and bony, his lips set, his eyes bright as hot coals. When he reached the bottom of the stairs he walked across the room, put his arm about Rachel's waist.

"Gentlemen, it is no time for a patriot to be sick when his country needs his services. We'll be ready to march in a few days. I shall command in person."

She helped him into his uniform, made a sturdy sling for his arm. She took his hand, holding it against her cheek for a moment. How could he fight a war when he had to be helped into his saddle?

8

By vigorous training at Fayetteville Andrew again whipped two thousand recruits into a cohesive force. Hardly a day passed but that she had a visit from a friend or relative who had been sent up the long trail from his headquarters seeking beef and flour for the troops, for the provisions on which the army was to march never reached Fort Deposit. Despite this, an early dispatch carried the news that he had forded the Coosa River and the following dawn took the Creeks by surprise. Three hundred of the Indians were killed.

The victory-starved nation, defeated and humiliated so often in the past year and a half, was singing General Jackson's praises. After eleven years of fanatical preparation, this was his first actual battle; and he had emerged triumphant.

In spite of the exultation of the press, the flatboats on which his provisions from East Tennessee had been loaded were still stuck there, the river being too low for the boats to navigate; the officers and soldiers of the militia, who had been existing on squirrels and then acorns, decided there was no use starving to death; large segments of the troops threatened to leave. General Jackson lined the road with loyal men, promising to fire on all deserters, and actually had to execute one young mutineer. When General Cocke arrived with fifteen hundred troops, Andrew dismissed the mutinous regiment, only to learn that the new arrivals had but ten days further to serve. His command was reduced to a hundred and thirty cold, starved and ragged men.

All work on the Hermitage came to a standstill; Fields, the new overseer, was drinking and quarreling with the hands; the acreage that Andrew had asked to be cleared was still untouched. And for the first time in her many years as a farmer, Rachel did not care. All of her energy and her desire was concentrated on this war with Britain, for Andrew had written that the Creeks were armed with new British rifles, and that the British agents had made extravagant promises to the Indians if they would continue to harass the United States troops until British soldiers could arrive to defeat the Americans. Young Andrew was a solace to her in her anxiety, for he liked to talk about Papa, and she was humbly grateful to anyone who would let her talk about her husband . . . even her son!

Andrew made no effort to conceal his illness from her: the wounds inflicted by Jesse Benton's bullets had not healed; in the cold the pain was so excruciating that he could sleep for only a few moments at a time. He was stricken with diarrhea because he had no food beyond what he could grub from the fields by way of acorns and nuts. Sometimes for hours on end he could retain consciousness only by remaining on his feet, his arms dangling over a tree limb to hold him up. On certain aggravated days he lay prostrate in his tent, unable to twitch a hand or foot, and when it was necessary to march, moved along on sheer will power.

When Governor Blount ordered him to bring his troops home he replied, "What, retrograde under these circumstances? I will perish first!"

His plight was so admittedly desperate that she found herself unable to eat or sleep. The snow broke large limbs off the trees. After helping to control an epidemic of the grippe which swept the Hermitage, including little Andrew, she herself collapsed, running such a high fever that Dr. May decided to bleed her. He also gave her frequent doses of calomel. When she wrote to Andrew her hands shook as though she had palsy.

It was not the bleeding or calomel that put an end to her anxieties: it was Andrew's victory at Emuckfau. Reinforced by eight hundred recruits delivered to him in person by Colonel Robert Hays, he led his scant and greatly outnumbered reserves into action, charging the Creeks before they had a chance to charge him. Colonel John Coffee was seriously wounded, Sandy Donelson, Johnny's boy, was among those killed.

Once again a beaten Administration and a starved press hailed the victory, calling it the greatest ever enjoyed against the Indians. Andrew Jackson became the most exalted commander in the field. Five thousand volunteers poured into the Indian country to report to General Jackson.

Buoyed by the presence of a company of United States regulars, Andrew attacked the Creek bastion at Horseshoe Bend and fought the Creeks across their own exposed plain. In a ferocious hand-to-hand encounter he had lost forty-nine men, but by the end of the day only a handful of the Creeks survived, their leader had surrendered, all British guns were captured, the Creek war ended. The British would have to find themselves new allies in the South.

Early in May, some five weeks later, with the sun warm overhead and the peach trees a mass of delicate blooms, a courier brought a note from Andrew asking her to meet him the following noon, five miles out on the road to Nashville. She knew she wouldn't sleep, so she spent the early hours of the evening washing her hair, bathing, shaping her nails and selecting the costume she would wear. Since their troubles over the Dickinson duel she had done little sewing. She had always loved pretty clothes, but the enforced isolation, and Andrew's apparent disregard of what she was wearing, had discouraged her. Now she found her wardrobe dull, and she searched her memory for some clue to which gown he would find the most attractive. She finally selected a brown cambric with rows of trimming around the neck and hem because it seemed the gayest, and because they had had a happy time together when she had worn it last, at Jane's twenty-fifth anniversary.

It was ten o'clock when her carriage reached the designated spot on the route, having passed hundreds of Cumberland Valley folk who were lining the road waiting for a sight of General Jackson. There were two hours to wait, but as she sat quietly against the cushions of the carriage, her hands folded in her lap, and thought back to the illnesses, to the actual physical terrors of the past seven months, she felt as though she might like to sit for a very long time in this suspended state, recouping her strength and composure.

Then she heard a rushing clatter and her carriage was surrounded by a dozen mounted men. Before she could distinguish their faces her carriage door was flung open and Andrew was by her side, crushing her to him. She had time for only one swift look at his face, but even in that fleeting instant she saw that his eyes were more truly alive and fulfilled than she had ever seen them before.

9

In the hail of Indian bullets that had fallen, not one piece of lead had touched him. A week at the Hermitage, with food and warmth, saw the grayness disappear from his face. There were many guests during the day; the dining table was crowded with friends and admirers; in the warm June evenings they sat quietly under the trees, watching the moon pull up into the heavens on the first half of its journey. Their time together was doubly sweet because they knew it would be short; the battles against the Creeks had been but the barest prologue to what would happen when the British terminated their long war in Europe and were free to pour the might of their Empire against Louisiana.

John Overton came back from the court at Knoxville bringing word of what people were saying in East Tennessee and Kentucky. There were already those who were inclined to boom him for governor. Even Sevier's followers were speaking of him in terms of respect. What ill feeling there was, was confined to militiamen and volunteers who had abandoned him before the big victories, and who now maintained that they had only wanted to return for food and winter clothing, but that General Jackson's arbitrary conduct had prevented them from so doing. The family of John Woods, whom Andrew had had executed for desertion, was claiming that this was an illegal act; and General Cocke, whom Andrew had had court-martialed for failure to report with his troops, had supporters who were charging that Andrew Jackson's purpose in this trial was to hog all the credit for himself.

"But these whiners are few in number," John concluded. "I only tell you about them because I know they are going to try to irritate you and involve you in bickering, their aim being to lessen your fame. If you will pardon these hints, I beg you not to notice them but just to let them write or speak as they wish. And don't thank me to keep out of your private affairs!"

"I won't, Counselor," Andrew replied. "There'll be no more of those Benton shootings or Samuel Jackson fights. I'm not the same man who got into those controversies; I've got a real antagonist now, and I'm saving my ammunition for the British."

She and Andrew had a month's honeymoon. They were never apart, riding for the day into the cooler hill country, picnicking on cold chicken and buttermilk, gazing down on the river valley and the flatlands while they talked helter-skelter of the hundreds of things they had perforce stored up for just such moments of leisure and intimacy. In the evenings she read Cowper's poems to him, or Virgil, while he sat smoking his pipe; or she triumphantly took him to dinner at Jane's or Johnny's or William's. The already neglected Hermitage was further neglected.

Then one morning a courier arrived from the War Department with two sealed dispatches. The first ordered him to "proceed without delay to Fort Jackson and consummate a treaty with the Creeks."

"That's fine," he cried, "but hear this next bit for idiocy." He began pacing, his long legs eating up the modest distance from wall to wall.

If the hostile part of the Creeks is really broken down, if they are prostrate before us, and even begging from us the means of sub-sistence, why retain in service any portion of the militia?

JOHN ARMSTRONG

He tossed the letter into the air, as he did all communications that irritated him.

"Now you know why we've lost every land battle since this war began, why they captured Detroit without a shot, annihilated Winchester's troops at Frenchtown, defeated Van Rensselaer at Queenstown, chewed up Dearborn's detachments and made such a fool out of Wilkinson in Canada that he had to be retired."

"Maybe the other letter is better?"

He returned to the table, picked up the second envelope and broke the seal. This time he stood awkwardly, embarrassed and apologetic.

"I take back everything I said about the Secretary of War. He is a man of infinite wisdom and discernment. Listen to this:

"War Department, May 28, 1814.

"SIR,

"Since the date of my letter of the twenty-fourth, Major General Harrison has resigned his commission in the army, and thus is created a vacancy in that grade, which I hasten to fill with your name."

They both held their breath for an instant, then Andrew, his whole body surging with excitement, exploded:

"By the Eternal! After all these years, they've finally taken me into their regular army. You see, miracles are not impossible . . ."

She reached her arms up about his neck, and he lifted her until their lips were on a level.

"May I be the first to congratulate you, Regular Army General Jackson? And don't tell me I can't call you general until you've won some battles. Tell me just what the appointment means."

In the surge of his joy he kissed her harder than she had been kissed in years. Then he set her down and stood with his head cocked to one side, his smile composited of gratification, determination . . . and happiness for the both of them.

"I will have command of the Seventh Military District, which includes Tennessee, the territory of Mississippi and Louisiana. It will also

204

mean that you are not going to be left behind any more. As soon as I set up headquarters I'll send for you. Wherever I go from now on you will go with me."

"Please God! But what about the Hermitage?"

"It will go up for sale: lock and stock. My salary and allowance as a general will come to almost six thousand dollars a year."

They embraced again. This time they were joined by little Andrew, who had come into the room and tugged at his father's shirt, enviously. They picked him up and held him between them, kissing him and each other, all three laughing and crying in turn.

Toward the end of June news reached the Hermitage that the British were in Paris, and that Napoleon had fallen. The long war in Europe was over. Andrew was crushed by the defeat of his hero, but to Rachel he spoke only of the gigantic British fleet of a thousand vessels and the brilliant commanding officers and trained troops who would now be free to descend upon the United States in their full might.

She bade him good-by as he left for Fort Jackson. He had promised to send for her in a very few weeks.

"Darling, you told me I was to get a new carriage for my journey south, and travel in the style becoming to the wife of a major general of the United States Army. How about you stopping off at Murfreesboro and getting yourself a new uniform? Surely your shoulder will hold up an epaulet of the *regular* army?"

The little joke eased the moment of separation.

That very day she had the trunks and portmanteau aired in the July sun and brought up to her bedroom. If their permanent headquarters was to be in Mobile she might not need much in the way of stylish clothing, but if they were to settle in New Orleans, then her wardrobe would be inadequate. She decided to have Sarah Bentley sew her some new dresses.

Jane helped pick out the silks and satins, the hats and muffs and thin-soled slippers at the Nashville stores, spending many hours with her at Sarah Bentley's establishment while they pored over the color illustrations published in London, and discussed the latest fashion edicts.

"But Jane," protested Rachel, "you don't want me to arrive in New Orleans with these half-naked gowns. In the first place Andrew wouldn't recognize me, in the second he wouldn't approve, and in the third place, my dear sister, I'm a frontierswoman, slightly weather-beaten . . ."

"You're going into the most elegant city in America," said Jane. "Those Frenchwomen get their gowns direct from Paris, or at least their styles come from there. I'd like to see you give them a run for their money."

Time went quickly for her. She completed her packing and made her final arrangements. A courier arrived with a letter from Andrew:

Fortune that fickle dame, mars all my wishes—I have this moment received an express from Alabama Heights that will compel me to Mobile with all the regular Troops here. If I can spare Col Butler I shall send him to bring you down the river to me, at Natchez or New Orleans.

She re-read the line, "*Fortune that fickle dame, mars all my wishes,*" and smiled to herself as she heard Andrew's voice saying, "Pun me no puns." The Creek treaty must have been concluded to his entire satisfaction if he was in the mood to joke.

There was nothing amusing in the next intelligence: the British ships *Hermes, Carron* and *Sophia* had arrived at the Spanish town of Pensacola with land forces and large supplies of arms and ordnances; the *Orpheus* was also expected in a few days, with fourteen warships and transports carrying ten thousand troops. Fourteen more warships and transports had already arrived at Bermuda with Lord Wellington's army.

General John Coffee, and Rachel Hays's husband, Colonel Robert Butler, came to the Hermitage to say farewell. They had orders from General Jackson to leave Nashville as quickly as possible with one thousand cavalrymen. Andrew confided to her in a short note, brought to the Hermitage by an officer whom he had sent back to raise a battalion of artillery:

Before one month the British and Spanish expect to be in possession of Mobile and all surrounding country. There will be bloody noses before this happens.

The army that had smashed Napoleon was advancing rapidly on the shores of America, and Andrew Jackson was promising to bloody their noses! When she thought of the mass mutinies of the year before, of his abandonment in the wilderness fort with a hundred officers and men, and no supplies, she was staggered by his inner strength. At the same time she was admittedly frightened. It would be Andrew's will to win pitted against the might of the British army that had just captured Washington City, burned the Capitol, shelled Baltimore, plundered Alexandria, occupied the state of Maine, burned the eastern seaboard, captured Nantucket and all of Cape Cod. New England was so deathly sick of the war that a convention had been held in Hartford at which secession sentiments bulked large, and delegates were appointed to go to Washington City and insist on peace at any price. Between the seasoned British army and the surrender of the American government stood . . . her husband!

She learned from dispatches in the Nashville papers that Andrew, believing the British would first have to capture Fort Bowyer, guardian of Mobile Bay, in order to take Mobile, had sped there with a hundred and sixty men and spent twelve days in repair work, setting up his cannon just as the British fleet attacked. One British ship was destroyed, another blown out of the water . . . after which the rest of the fleet fled to sea. It was his first victory against the British. What the newspapers did not tell her and she had to learn from her husband was that when he next decided to move his three thousand troops on Pensacola and needed rations for eight days, he once again had been obliged to buy the supplies with his own money.

The Hermitage lands had found a buyer in Philadelphia for twenty dollars an acre. Rachel knew that Andrew would use every dollar of the sale to provision his men. She wished there were some way the War Department could be induced to supply its troops. It really wasn't Andrew's private war, though he would probably say it was. And if it was his private war, it was hers too.

In the meanwhile her trunks remained in her bedroom. "With a war on my hands," wrote Andrew, "would you mind waiting just another few weeks?" It was now three full months since he had left, after his promise that they would never be separated again; but how could she put the burden of her safety, and her son's, upon him, when he had drawn his troops up before Pensacola, and the Spanish governor was refusing to put the English out of Fort Barrancas or surrender the arms and ammunition within the town? The next word she received was that he had stormed the Pensacola fortifications in the face of heavy guns and British warships, capturing the city and forcing the British to blow up Fort Barrancas and once again put to sea. He had then moved into New Orleans.

She went to Nashville to buy a sturdy carriage and a pair of strong horses. Then suddenly the letters stopped.

The heavy rains started early in December; it would be impossible to use her carriage and team of horses. The rivers were rising rapidly and were already navigable; now she would have to go by river. Robert Hays engaged a boat for her and she stood like a fledgling on a limb, poised for flight. At last young Stockly brought her marching orders: he had been instructed to bring Aunt Rachel and Cousin Andrew down the Mississippi to New Orleans and General Jackson.

She paid four hundred and twenty dollars in cash for the journey, but not wanting the money to be wasted, she began loading the boat with their bacon, beef, oats and corn, all of which should bring a profit in New Orleans. Robert Hays set her departure for December 28. At the family Christmas dinner at Haysboro Jane took her aside and said:

"Sister, Colonel Anderson is leaving for New Orleans with several other officers on January tenth; Robert feels you should have that extra military protection. We simply can't risk having you captured by the British."

"Oh, Jane," she wailed, "I know you're right, but it's six months since

I've seen my husband. In the past year Andrew's been with me only four weeks!"

That there was a gigantic struggle pending near New Orleans she could not doubt; nor did she any longer care. Her patience was utterly exhausted. She remembered Andrew asking her, when they had come down the Kentucky Road for the first time, "Can you shoot?" She was so determined to join him that she would have been willing to shoot her way down the entire Mississippi. The Philadelphia purchase of the Hermitage had come to the signing point; Jane was keeping Moll, George, Mitty and Hannah until the Jacksons could find out where they were settling permanently. Everything else on the Hermitage was to be sold at the best price Robert Hays could get.

She was packing the last of her personal possessions in the big room downstairs when the door was opened and Jane with Robert and their daughter Rachel entered. She had been so preoccupied she had not even heard them ride up; now as she raised her head she saw that they were big-eyed. They sat down just as Severn and Elizabeth entered. She heard more horses coming down the trail, and still more. From the excited expressions, from the spontaneous cries of "It has happened, the great battle of New Orleans!" and Thomas Overton's "Only General Jackson would have had the unmitigated gall to surprise the British"; from the glowing look of Johnny Donelson, who arrived with his wife and daughter, Mary Coffee, and boasted, "If he had sat in New Orleans with his few troops, the British could have attacked from a dozen sides!" she realized that this was not a planned gathering. The next to arrive were Sarah and Tim Bentley, then her bachelor brothers Alexander and Leven, whom she saw only at weddings and funerals, followed shortly by William and Charity, who had apparently picked up Catherine and John Hutchings on the way. The last to arrive was John Overton, who had ridden over from Travellers Rest in his gardening clothes, needing a shave. Looking around the room, with every one of the seats filled, she saw that once again the Donelson family and its intimates had assembled in a council of war.

She stood in the middle of the floor, waiting, while a dozen excited discussions were crisscrossing the oblong room. She moved her hearing among them, trying to separate collisions and sort out phrases; but the din was tremendous:

". . . Kentucky militia arrived exhausted and without guns" . . . "captured his few little gunboats on Lake Borgne" . . . "shipment of rifles from the War Department that stupid contractor sent by slow freight to save money" . . . "British undiscovered only eight miles from New Orleans" . . . "good thing he broke into those warehouses . . . warm clothing" . . . "hadn't heard from Washington for sixty days . . ."

"Stop! Please, everybody! Be quiet!" She walked to the fireplace. "I understand there has been a major battle? Robert, won't you please tell me what happened?"

Colonel Robert Hays stood beside her, his massive shoulders squared back. She remembered that it had been loyal, loving Robert who almost singlehanded had assembled and delivered the troops with which Andrew had defeated the Creeks. He was the handsomest man anywhere in the Donelson family, and now his fine features were alight with pride as he fitted together for her the pieces of the story that had reached them an hour before:

The British, with a force of nine to ten thousand men, had landed at Lake Borgne, pushed through five miles of impassable swamp, then seized the Villere plantation, eight miles from New Orleans. Major Villere was captured, but escaped and reported the news to General Jackson. Though he had only one thousand regulars, and two thousand militia, Andrew summoned his aides, brought his fist down on the table with such force that it nearly smashed under the impact, and cried:

"By the Eternal, they shall not sleep on our soil! We must fight them tonight."

Within two hours he was leading his troops out of the city. At seven that night he surprised the British in their camp, gathered around their fires. It was hand-to-hand fighting, with Generals Coffee and Carroll leading the assault. The British were disorganized and hurt, but best of all, the British major who had burned the Capitol at Washington City had been captured. In the morning Andrew pulled his troops back of Rodriguez Canal, then built his defenses with every shovel, musket and able-bodied man from New Orleans pressed into service: for the British before him were constantly being reinforced. He fortified everything from the river to the swamp and woods, entrenched his few cannon, erected walls of baled cotton.

Two limited attacks were launched against him on December 28 and January 1. Then on the morning of January 8, the famous British General Pakenham fired a silver-blue rocket announcing the great attack. General Jackson was ready with his troops, deployed in a deep-dug defense arc. At seven in the morning the fog broke. Andrew, standing on his parapet above Rodriguez Canal, saw a field of stubble cane before him, frosted silver and, a little more than six hundred yards away, British soldiers by the thousands, white belts across red tunics, muskets at the ready.

They charged. Andrew gave his order: the twelve-pounders went off; then the first rank of men fired, stooped to unload, the second rank fired, then the third. They were all woodsmen, dead shots; the close-packed British lines fell. Others came on; Andrew's men and cannon, protected by their defenses, poured in more fire. The Highlanders attacked, but the Americans reloaded so fast the Scots went down without even shooting their guns. The British commanding officers were being eliminated one after the other: Generals Pakenham and Gibbs dead, Colonel Dale dead, General Keane injured. Fewer than a hundred English soldiers ever reached Rodriguez Canal, a few lived to scale the embankment . . . and died. After only an hour and a half of fighting the British withdrew, their morale shattered, their fighting force spent. Seven hundred British soldiers lay dead on the field before Andrew as he again mounted the parapet to survey the result of the battle. Fourteen hundred more were wounded, disabled and dying. When he saw some five hundred Britons rising from the heaps of their dead comrades and coming forward to surrender, he said:

"I never had such a grand or awful idea of the resurrection."

Moments later he learned that he had lost but seven men, and that, incredible as it seemed, the British army had inflicted wounds on only six others. The Donelson family had particular reason to rejoice: their husbands, sons and nephews had fought doggedly and well, and not one had been hurt. Rachel's memory reached back to the library at Hunter's Hill where Andrew had sat poring over his military books, where he had proclaimed, "The good general does not lose men in war; his campaigns are so well planned he crushes the opposing army with a few swift blows."

The British, beaten and broken, made their way back to their ships. Andrew chose not to pursue them. He received a note from the British commanding officer, General Keane, on board his ship, offering remuneration for his beloved battle sword, lost on the plain before Rodriguez Canal.

"Did Andrew have the sword?" asked Rachel excitedly. "I hope he returned it? It could be a symbol for that other sword that cut his head so cruelly when he was a boy."

"Oh yes, he returned it," said Robert Hays. "And sent with it a letter expressing his feeling for the misfortunes of all the brave English soldiers who had fallen in battle."

"Now his victory is complete," she murmured to herself, an ache of joy in her heart, "over the British . . . and over himself."

After a pause, Johnny said, "Perhaps Andrew will be home soon? Maybe you don't have to leave for New Orleans in the morning."

"I'm going!" she announced with a finality that silenced all further discussion. She turned to her brother-in-law. "But this does change one thing. If the war is really finished, Andrew will want a home to come back to. Don't sign those Hermitage papers when they come through from Philadelphia."

They ate and drank and told family anecdotes until the winter sun moved reluctantly over the horizon. Then they rode into Nashville and to the river landing. An icy wind whipped up whitecaps on the river. As Rachel took little Andrew firmly by the hand and walked across the loading plank she suddenly stopped in the midst of her passage and stood with her head bent, time and the years dissolving; she was a young girl again, only twenty-three, her brother Samuel had brought her to this very same landing to put her on board Colonel Stark's flatboat bound for Natchez. Unmoving, not hearing the cries of farewell from her family, she saw with memory's eye the tall, redheaded, twenty-three-year-old Andrew Jackson emerge from the Starks' boat to take her portmanteau and welcome her on board. What an arduous, troubled voyage it had been; but Andrew had said, in Tom Green's home, when he had brought her the report of her divorce and the news that they could be married:

"Our love shall be a fortress."

She turned to wave her last smiling farewells to her family on the riverbank, then continued up the gangplank onto the boat.

And so it had been.

Book SIX

SHE SAT out in the blue flagstone courtyard, the morning air filled with the scent of cape jasmine and crepe myrtle. The breakfast table was placed next to colorful flower beds and a trickling fountain. As she looked up she saw the graceful curving stairs which rose from the courtyard to the roof, and the wrought-iron balconies of the second and third floor. Two *gardiennes* came out in calico gowns with gay madras handkerchiefs tied about their heads and held up by high combs. They carried freshly baked croissants and coffee. From outside the spiked iron fence she heard the vendors in the streets crying out their wares:

"Belles des figues! Bons petits calas! Tout chauds!"

It was her first big city and practically a foreign one; Philadelphia or New York, she thought, would have seemed less strange. The entire culture, from the small cakes at eleven o'clock coffee down through the performance at the Théâtre d'Orléans, was French. It was not only the exotic feel of New Orleans which fascinated her, it was the lush, tropical aspect, so diametrically opposed to the lean sinewy countryside of the Cumberland.

Dr. Kerr was Andrew's military surgeon; he had graciously turned over his home and staff to the Jacksons. Opposite her at breakfast sat thirty-year-old Major John Reid, who had been Andrew's secretary since the beginning of the Creek wars. Reid was a handsome chap with a mass of jet black curls falling over his forehead, heavy black sideburns and black eyebrows, one of which shot upward like an exclamation point. He seemed considerably thinner than when Rachel had last seen him at the Hermitage.

"Small wonder," he replied in a thin voice. "The general has me up all night and every night writing hundreds of dispatches."

Andrew came quickly down the outside stairway.

"Good morning, my dear," he said as he stood with an arm about her

212

shoulder. "This is the first time I've slept past five o'clock since I left home."

"You should have had me with you this whole time," she replied with a smile, feeling warm and happy inside herself. "Then Major Reid would have gotten some sleep too, instead of your keeping him up all night writing letters."

Andrew laughed. He dropped into a chair beside her as Major Reid excused himself. She poured him a cup of coffee. They sat with the sun on their faces, holding hands under the table. Rachel murmured, "New Orleans may be a bad place to wage a war, but it's certainly a wonderful place for love."

"I remember your saying that any place is a good place for love."

"This country takes me back to our honeymoon at Bayou Pierre. Remember Tom Green telling us we ought to stay?"

He leaned across the table, pressed his cheek to hers.

"Would you like to live down here? Andrew is wild about the place; he spent all day yesterday on the levee watching the ships. I could have permanent headquarters in New Orleans, we could buy a beautiful house like this one out of the Hermitage sale."

"There wasn't any sale."

"Oh?"

"I stopped it when the news reached me. I thought that your victory would make everything right again. Those crowds lining the streets of New Orleans yesterday shouting your name as we went by in the carriage . . ."

"That was yesterday," he interrupted grimly; "a temporary truce declared in honor of your arrival. Right now I have two wars on my hands, one with the British and the other with the merchants and legislators of New Orleans who want to get back to business as usual. Governor Claiborne is due at my headquarters right now."

"Isn't he the one who got the job as governor of the Louisiana Territory that you wanted so badly back at Hunter's Hill? Now you're his commanding officer."

"Governor Claiborne doesn't think so; the purpose of his visit this morning is to force me to lift martial law and let the ships sail out of the harbor with the cotton and tobacco that's been in the warehouses for two years. He's also going to order me to dismiss all the Louisiana militia and volunteers, and take myself and my own troops out of his jurisdiction. According to Claiborne, the war is over."

"Well, isn't it?" she asked anxiously. "Your friend Edward Livingston came back from the British flagship yesterday with news that a treaty peace with England had been signed at Ghent."

"He also brought news that the British had captured Fort Bowyer!" He snapped this out at her almost angrily, then apologized with a self-deprecatory smile. "Forgive me, but we are still in danger here and so few seem to understand it. The British are maintaining a complete spy system; they know how many troops we have, where they are stationed, where our big guns are located and the morale of our men. They may strike again at any hour."

"But why would they want to, my dear, if they know the peace treaty has been signed? What could they hope to gain?"

"They have never acknowledged Napoleon's right to sell us Louisiana; if they can drive me and my men out of here they will claim this country as their own in spite of any peace treaty with the rest of the United States."

He jumped up, having eaten nothing. She held herself against him.

"It wasn't a very long truce, was it, dear? Only one day and one night. But I'm so terribly grateful even for that." A melodious clock inside the house chimed eight times. "Would you drop me at Madam Livingston's on your way to headquarters? Sister Jane was right, I have no proper clothes for these elegant Frenchwomen. Mrs. Livingston is having the finest seamstress in New Orleans at her home this morning to make me a gown for the George Washington Ball on Wednesday."

Two days later Andrew handed her into their carriage. It had rained the night before and the streets were filled with puddles of mud. Andrew carried her dainty ballroom slippers, while she held the bouffant velvet skirt up out of the mud. Mrs. Edward Livingston, who was the social leader of both the French and American colonies of New Orleans, had turned her second-floor salon into a fitting room; for the better part of two days Rachel had stood on a raised platform in the middle of the floor while the best of the French couturières draped yards of material about her and a swarm of voluble French needlewomen fitted and sewed, then cut and resewed until the gown was precisely what Madam Livingston wanted.

"It must be the most exquisite gown at the Exchange Ball," she had demanded of her couturière. "General Jackson and his lady are our guests of honor; no one may outshine them."

And so it had been: for Louise Livingston had driven her sewing staff relentlessly and between them they had designed this luxurious deep violet gown of the softest velvet with its short-sleeved bodice of sheer lace. Draped over her dark hair she wore a mantilla of the same lace, while her evening bag was of the same shade of deep violet as the wide velvet skirt. There was a strand of matched pearls at her throat, with small opals around the clasp of her bag.

She did not know how Louise Livingston would look in her gown, in fact how any of the hundreds of gorgeous Creole women would look; but when she saw the delight in Andrew's face as his eyes devoured her, she knew that, for her own purposes at least, Mrs. Livingston had succeeded. What a joy it had been to gaze at herself in a full-length

214

mirror, and to see herself so elegantly gowned. She actually looked ten years younger, and twenty pounds lighter. How Jane's eyes would have flashed with pride could she have seen her. She was doubly pleased with herself for she had sold her bacon, beef, oats and corn for a sufficient profit to pay for the new costume.

As the carriage bumped slowly along the muddy streets Rachel thought of the woman who had given up her own role as queen of this ball so that she might be the center of attention. Louise Livingston was only thirty years old, yet she occupied the position in New Orleans society to which Mrs. Phariss aspired in Nashville; but Mrs. Phariss lacked the native charm, breadth of character and the innate love of people which Louise Livingston possessed so naturally. She had married at the age of thirteen in Santo Domingo, lost three infant children before being widowed at sixteen, and had then seen her father and two brothers killed in the uprising from which she, her mother, grandmother and infant sister and brother had escaped to Louisiana. The most beautiful of the New Orleans matrons, she was also a woman of the highest intelligence, giving Edward Livingston important help in the writing of his legal briefs. Rachel thought how companionable it must be to collaborate with one's husband in this capacity; she found herself wishing she had been born smarter so that she could have been of greater assistance to Andrew.

The members of the French Exchange had worked hard to transform their building into a glittering replica of a Parisian ballroom. The ground floor, on which the long dinner tables had been set up, was magnificently decorated with flowers, colored lamps, transparencies and the most brilliant crystal chandeliers she had seen since Tom Green's Springfield. She was escorted to her seat by Edward Livingston, a tall, slender, stoop-shouldered man with a genial disposition and an all-pervading sense of human dignity.

She found herself placed opposite the motto, *Jackson and Victory Are One*. There were gold hams on the table, and jeweled ornaments. In the center was a pyramid on the top of which was written *Vive Jackson* in large letters. So many toasts were drunk to Andrew as the "Hero of our country" and "Savior of New Orleans," that by the time they went upstairs to the second-floor ballroom for the dancing she felt a little dizzy. Everyone was very friendly. She found herself talking animatedly with handsome, impeccably garbed men and soignée women. She danced minuets and waltzes for hours. At the end of one dance Andrew linked his arm through hers and, smiling down from his tremendous height, said:

"You're beautiful, my darling."

"It's this velvet gown you're looking at; it does wonderful things for my eyes."

215

"No, it's you, your face, you are glowing with happiness. You're the loveliest lady here."

"Tell me, *General Jackson and Victory Are One*," she teased, "now that you've whupped the British, do you think you might be able to stay home for a while?"

"Forever."

"Can we go there soon?"

"How soon?"

"Tomorrow?"

"You sound just like the Louisiana militiamen. Wouldn't you like a few years of this kind of life, Rachel? Dinners and receptions and balls and new gowns and dances and laughter and music? Because you can have it now, if you wish."

"I've seen more already than in my whole life past. And I will cherish the memory of this night as long as I live. But now that I've had it, I'm content. I'm ready to go back to the Hermitage. That's what you want too, isn't it?"

He did not answer.

The weeks that followed were a phantasmagoria of band concerts, plays in the Théâtre d'Orléans, ballets and pantomimes in the Théâtre St. Philippe, dinner parties in the sumptuous homes of the first Creole families, trips to the battlefield with young Reid and Jax to show her where every company was placed, and how they had fought. She walked along the broad tree-shaded levee, inspected old Spanish forts, journeyed through the lakes and bayous, finding Italian-styled villas surrounded by gardens and magnificent wild-orange groves.

Her son Andrew spent all day at headquarters with his father, where he had become the pet of the staff. Headquarters was the elegant Daniel Clark residence at 106 Royal Street, one of the few brick buildings in New Orleans.

"I'm going to have to spend my time at headquarters too," Rachel chided her husband as she stood in the big front room which he used as his office. "My dear, do you know that every day for the past week you have worked from eight in the morning until eleven at night? Your face is so pale and thin."

"If only I could get word from Washington City that the war is really over . . . This whole city is about to rise up in mutiny: today there is a long article in the *Courrière* telling me to get out of New Orleans and let the Louisiana soldiers return to the farms for their planting. I've clapped the author of that article in jail as an *agent provocateur*. And if Federal Judge Dominick A. Hall insists on releasing him, I'll lock Hall up too. I'll lock up the whole confounded town rather than let this army disintegrate before official word of the peace reaches me."

"As a beginning, let's go home and lock ourselves up and forget about your troubles until morning."

They were awakened early by the noise of a crowd coming down the street shouting, "*La paix! La paix!*" Andrew sprang out of bed, donned a robe and went downstairs. From behind the batten blinds she watched him take a dispatch from a travel-stained courier, then heard the groan of disappointment that went up from the crowd. Andrew returned to her, flinging the dispatch onto the table top. She waited for him to explain.

"It's absolutely unbelievable. This packet contains nothing more than authorization by Secretary Monroe for me to raise the state troops that have been fighting with me for months."

The rains fell heavily, converting the city and the outlying country into a quagmire; provisions were difficult to get from the New Orleans merchants, and hundreds of soldiers came down with influenza, fever and dysentery. Andrew's portrait in the Exchange Coffee House was destroyed by an angry mob. Rachel learned from her nephews that the Hero of New Orleans had become the Villain of New Orleans, a dictator who was holding his military control over the city for his own gratification. Andrew had a birthday coming, on March 15, his forty-eighth; Rachel wanted to give him a party, but there was so much hostility and sickness that she hardly knew whether a celebration would be appropriate.

Then on March 13, 1815, official news of the ratification of the peace treaty at long last reached New Orleans. The British fleet departed for home. Andrew lifted martial law, dismissed the Louisiana troops and sent the Tennessee, Mississippi and Kentucky troops home. The sun came out, the throngs were in the street again shouting, "Jackson and Peace," and Rachel sent invitations all over the city, to relatives and aides and to the French people who had been kind to her, inviting them to a birthday party for the general.

After dinner when her guests were assembled in the second-floor drawing room with coffee and liqueurs, Andrew sat in a comfortable chair, his legs stretched out in front of him, surrounded by his officers and nephews, by John Coffee, Edward Livingston and Dr. Kerr. Rachel listened from across the room while he talked of his mother, telling how she had rescued him and his brother from the British prison at Camden thirty-four years before. Seeing that everyone was well fortified, she slipped out to her bedroom to adjust the combs in her hair. As she stood before the mirror which hung above the handsome Louis XIV chest her eyes came down to a letter on top of the chest where Andrew had put it. She recognized the signature of a cousin on her mother's side, John Stokely, who held an important government position in Washington City. Suddenly, as though the lines had been raised by use of forceps, the words stood out:

We are entitled to a President from the West, your activity and

217

uniform success has rendered you very popular amongst the American people and I do conceive that you ought to fill the chair of the Chief Magistrate of this Union.

She stood leaning against the chest, one hand clutched at her breast, too stunned to think articulately. After a time her mind returned to the Hermitage, with John Overton standing before her, his silver specs lying over the hump of his nose, saying, "He might just as well go right to the top, where he belongs. There is only one real and indisputable top in this country, my dear Rachel, and when a man rises that high he is freed from all petty bickerings, jealousies and quarrels."

She sat down on the edge of the gilt-backed French chair, her heart pounding high in her throat. If they had been plunged into a caldron of heated emotions and animosity when Andrew ran for comparatively modest offices, if they found themselves and their love and marriage embroiled in scandal, accusations, bitternesses, feuds, duels and killings, what in the dear God's name would happen to them if he should ever get involved in a campaign for the presidency of the United States? And what had been said at that family council of war in her mother's home when they first learned of Lewis Robards' impending Harrodsburg divorce? "Those records will be there forever, for anyone to use for his own purposes."

If Andrew ran for the presidency would not his enemies and opponents dig up those records and use them in an effort to defeat him? Politics was a lethal business. Whatever she had suffered by way of malicious gossip, invasion of privacy and willful traduction, at least it had been confined to the Tennessee country. Wouldn't the difficulties of her first marriage to Lewis Robards and the illegality of her Natchez marriage to Andrew Jackson now be spread over the entire nation, made a matter of public domain?

Her terror passed. In its place came a clarity amounting almost to prescience: the storms, the scandals, the accusations and denials, the revelation of her most intimate life, all of these things which had seemed so violent and omnipresent would be but passing winds compared to what she would undergo in the future. And yet, if it all were to come to pass, would she make any effort to stop it? What a glorious fulfillment for Andrew Jackson, the penniless orphan who had pulled himself up the perpendicular mountainside by his bootstraps, sitting in the Chief Executive's chair which had been occupied by such fine and highborn gentlemen as George Washington, John Adams and James Madison.

2

New Orleans showered gifts upon the Jacksons, the magnificent furnishings from their bedroom in the Kerr home, a set of topaz jewelry for Rachel, a diamond pin for Andrew. They had once again completed the cycle: hero into villain and back again to hero.

Only Federal Judge Dominick Hall did not join in the adoration; instead he issued an order for Andrew's arrest on a charge of contempt of court.

"Andrew, you don't have to obey that summons, do you?"

"Why, Mrs. Jackson, that's no way for the wife of a former judge to speak. I threw Hall into jail to protect our military position; he has a right to try to throw me into jail to protect the position of the courts."

She rode to court with Andrew and Edward Livingston. The room was so crowded that attendants had to clear a lane for them down to the defense table. Judge Hall refused to hear the Livingston defense, fining Andrew a thousand dollars for contempt. For the briefest moment she feared that Andrew might rise in anger against the fine, but instead he accepted it graciously; when finally they made their way through the cheering throngs and into their carriage the people of New Orleans unhitched the horses and pulled them through the streets to the square before the Exchange. As she listened to Andrew say his farewells to the thousand admirers jammed into the square, she thought:

My brother Severn was right: the identical qualities which led to his failures have also brought about his success.

They left New Orleans at the end of the first week in April 1815. The streets and country roads were lined for miles by every class of Louisiana society crying out their gratitude and benedictions. They went by water to Natchez, but from there on they had to travel by horseback and carriage up the Trace, following the route they had taken home from their honeymoon at Bayou Pierre, that fateful journey on which Andrew had quarreled with Hugh McGary over an imminent Indian attack, so embittering McGary that two years later he had been willing to go before a Harrodsburg jury and testify that he had seen Rachel Robards and Andrew Jackson sleeping under the same blanket.

The Natchez Trace was still deeply rutted; sometimes she felt as though her spine would be jarred through the top of her head; when she could stand the jouncing no longer she joined her husband and son on horseback. This trip took them several weeks longer than the earlier one, for every hamlet along the way had its population in the street for a tumultuous reception. For Rachel the best of all the parties was the one given them by the now greatly expanded Green family, in the room with the exquisite glass chandeliers under which she and Andrew had been married.

She had difficulty in understanding the almost frenzied crowds that took over their party at the Tennessee border: the families that had ridden in from every direction to shout their names; the enormous throngs that led them into Nashville as though they were a triumphal procession;

or the assemblage in the courthouse square, so tremendous that it seemed as if every last soul in Tennessee had come to pay homage. It was not until they had ridden out to the Hermitage, to be welcomed at the gates by their neighbors, and she had had the chance to read the first eastern newspapers she had seen since her departure from New Orleans and to study the details of the Treaty of Ghent, that she began to grasp what her husband had come to mean to the people of the country. Even to her untrained mind it was apparent that this peace treaty was a humiliating document, signed by the American negotiators after three years of continuous defeats. The British had not even agreed to end their seizure of American vessels or the impressment of American seamen! Andrew's triumph at New Orleans had actually come after the signing of the peace terms at Ghent and thus legally had accomplished nothing, yet it had accomplished everything, turning three years of defeat into victory, restoring the self-confidence of the American people and, as the eastern editors added, teaching the British a lesson they would never forget.

Sitting up in bed, propped comfortably with pillows and enjoying the tray Mitty had brought up to her, she pushed the journals aside and stared sightlessly out the big window overlooking the Hermitage fields. If what these editors said was true, would not the pressure on Andrew to run for the presidency next year be almost inescapable? She recalled how just a few hours before their departure their friend Edward Livingston had said:

"You know, General, the road north from New Orleans could lead directly to Washington City."

She had remained silent and, she hoped, expressionless; Andrew had laughed good-naturedly, thanked Livingston for the compliment, then said in terms of finality that the idea was absurd.

But was it? Nobody who came out to the Hermitage seemed to think so. The air was filled with presidential talk: the Federalist party, which had backed the Hartford Convention and declared for surrender in the war, was now passing from existence. Whoever the Republicans nominated was certain to be elected. James Monroe was the favorite, yet there were many who felt that the Virginia dynasty of twenty-four years, starting with George Washington, coming through Thomas Jefferson and James Madison, had reached its proper and logical conclusion. Another man was wanted, an outsider with a fresh face and a strong will and new ideas; who better fitted these qualifications, people were asking, than the Hero of New Orleans?

But if Andrew knew all this talk was going on he gave no sign of it; only once did he speak to her about the campaign which had already begun for his nomination:

"Don't worry, my darling, it would take a writ of habeas corpus to get me back into politics."

Twenty-four hours before she was to leave the Hermitage to meet her husband in New Orleans the Hermitage had been for sale. Now the Hermitage lands which had been so badly neglected the year before were teeming with activity, the forest cleared and planted in cotton by the new overseer hired by Robert Hays. As far as her eyes could see there were rows upon rows of young cotton plants showing healthy and green in the warm May air: for in the months following Andrew's victory at New Orleans his neighbors had come to the Hermitage wanting to do something for the general by way of showing their appreciation, and indefatigable Robert Hays had taken such good advantage of their offers that the barns had been repaired, the cabins chinked, the apple and peach trees pruned, new orchards set out from John Overton's stock of young trees. Pretty Jane Caffrey, one of Mary's daughters, had moved into the Hermitage to take care of the house. She had everything shined and gleaming for their return.

Rachel felt a little ashamed, as she wandered the fields, visited with the hands and neighbors, drank in the particular beauty of the Cumberland Valley, that she could ever have been willing to abandon this home. By what strange twists of fate were people's lives destroyed or saved by a mere matter of hours? After the Charles Dickinson duel Andrew had lost nearly every friend in the Cumberland; he had become despondent, quarrelsome, had drunk too much and made scenes in public. He had lost his joy in this fine plantation and even in his blooded horses, and she had wondered if life were over for them, if it were to continue to be a mud-rutted downhill road to some obscure end. And she, seeing him restless, frustrated, unable to find his place in the world, had been equally willing to leave the Hermitage, to go seeking a more fertile land in which Andrew might prosper.

How wrong that would have been for Andrew, who this very moment was attending a dinner being given to him at the Bell Tavern in Nashville, at which the most important men in the state had gathered to present him with a ceremonial sword sent as a gift from Mississippi; and where even Mr. Phariss and Mr. Deson would go out of their way to shake his hand. How wrong it would have been for her, who had never wanted to be anything but First Lady in her husband's affection and to live peacefully and happily on her plantation, surrounded by friends, relatives and neighbors as she was doing today.

The Hermitage once again seemed to be the crossroads of the West, literally hundreds of people pouring in: not only their countless relatives and the folk of the Cumberland Valley who wanted to thank the general personally, but all the political figures from the East who had business anywhere within several days' ride, and all of the army officers and officials and businessmen of the South making their way up the Trace toward the capital or New York. No one came empty-handed: each day saw dozens of gifts brought or delivered: for Rachel, a sewing box inlaid with mother-of-pearl, Chinese mandarin scent bottles, a beaded purse, rare laces, a guitar, a shell jewel case, initialed bedspreads, leather-bound Bibles, beautiful English bone china and glassware; and for Andrew, canes and swords and books, rare wines and fruits.

For herself Rachel maintained the pattern she had set at Hunter's Hill: all who sought her out were welcome, all who came were her friends. She received them graciously, gave freely of herself. But she rarely left the Hermitage grounds. She went into Nashville only when it was necessary, contenting herself with visits to the numerous Donelsons and their offspring, and to her long-time neighbors.

Moll and George had grown too old to handle the volume of work, so big Hannah took over the cooking, assisted by Mitty and Orange. Young Jane proved to be such a capable housekeeper and was so fascinated by the flow of celebrities to the Hermitage that she asked:

"Aunt Rachel, couldn't I just stay here with you permanently? I could take all the work off your hands and you could give your full attention to Uncle Andrew."

Andrew's health was by no means good. He had suffered six months of the almost universal military dysentery, and for weeks on end had gone with no more nourishment than the rice he could hold on his stomach. They had both assumed that all he needed was a regular routine and a lot of good solid food, but now, safely ensconced at home, he grew more rather than less ill. Even the special foods that Moll insisted she alone could prepare for him he was unable to retain. He had been holding himself together these many months by will power and now that there was no need to remain upright he suddenly collapsed and had to go to bed altogether. The flow of visitors was cut off. She sat by his bedside feeding him chicken broth, accompanying each spoonful with a prayer that he would be able to keep it down.

"You have simply used up the energies of six years in the past six months, Andrew. You need a great deal of rest. We are going to start from the beginning and raise you as though you were an infant."

"Sounds pleasant," he said faintly from his pillow.

"We have absolutely nothing to worry about," she reassured him. "Cotton prices are soaring and we are going to have a bumper crop."

"I wanted to go to Washington to make my reports . . . explain the Judge Hall affair, participate in the reorganization of the army . . . but it can wait."

"Of course it can. When the warm weather comes you must take your son fishing. And Andy feels badly that I insisted he remain in school instead of going to New Orleans with me, so you are going to have to spend time with him, riding and hunting. Major Reid will be here to begin his book about the history of your wars. And I must get

222

you strong and handsome again because you have to have a painting made to send to Congress for that medal they are awarding you."

He lifted the ivory miniature of her which still hung on its silver chain about his neck.

"Perhaps I'll send them this instead."

3

By October, after a lazy summer, he became restless. He decided he must go to Washington City: to designate the military posts that were needed in the wilderness; to explain why the Creek opposition to the land treaty should be disregarded; to secure permission to move all Indian tribes west of the Mississippi so that they could not again be armed and used by a hostile European nation; and to drive out the Spanish, who still held Florida, and were thus in a position to allow enemy troops to invade the United States.

She knew that the little group of would-be president-makers, John Overton, John Reid, John Eaton, a wealthy lawyer and planter of Franklin, William Lewis, William Carroll, were anxious that Andrew expose himself on all sides, thus increasing his chances for the nomination. She asked herself, Does he want the presidency? Is that why he is making this trip? Was he giving in to the urge that in the early years had led him to become a congressman and a senator?

And if Andrew asked her to accompany him, would she go? The reasons for which she had formerly refused to travel, the fear of meeting strangers, of being looked down at as *the* Mrs. Jackson, had been pushed deep into the background with Andrew's success and her own wonderful stay in New Orleans. Her problem was no longer whether she was willing to make the journey to Washington City, with its attendant dinners, balls and receptions, but whether she would not, by accompanying him, give evidence that she favored his drive for the presidency and was attempting to help her husband win both the nomination and the office of Chief Executive. In her heart she knew the answer: she did not wish to aid Andrew in this ambition. Yet if her husband invited her to accompany him, she would go; she had had enough of separations . . .

The inns at which they stayed each night were comfortable, but she was glad when they neared Lynchburg and the home of Major Reid's parents, where they were to rest for a few days. The elder Reids, genteel folk, were overjoyed at receiving the Jacksons. As Rachel and Andrew were about to descend for supper young Reid came running up the stairs.

"General, there's a delegation downstairs from Lynchburg; the town is tending you a formal banquet tomorrow. Thomas Jefferson is riding in from Monticello to preside!"

Rachel saw the flash of joy cross Andrew's face. She reached out a hand to him. He squeezed it hard. With his eyes brilliant he murmured:

"Mr. Jefferson would have reason to hate me, I've been a wasp stinging at him all these years; and yet he's so fine a gentleman as to ride almost a hundred miles to be at a dinner for me."

Yes, thought Rachel, you can forgive each other now that the war with Britain has been fought and won.

The tableau that presented itself to her eyes as she entered the ballroom of the hotel the following afternoon at three o'clock, her hand lightly on Mr. Jefferson's arm, was even more impressive to her than the Exchange Ball in New Orleans: their three hundred hosts stood at attention while she and Andrew walked slowly down the center aisle of the ballroom on either side of Mr. Jefferson. She had only a fleeting impression through dinner of the succeeding courses as they were placed before her and taken away, for underneath the quiet talk she felt a submerged tension, as though everyone were expecting something of critical importance and no one was quite sure what it would be. At last, when the tables had been cleared, the chairman rose, gestured for silence and turned to Thomas Jefferson. Mr. Jefferson got up slowly from his chair, stood with a wine goblet raised, the white hair falling thickly over his ears, his eyes luminous and infinitely wise, his face at seventy-two still patrician and beautiful. He extended his glass toward Andrew and in a low, carrying voice said:

"Honor and gratitude to those who have filled the measure of their country's honor."

The three hundred men rose in their chairs, extended their glasses toward Andrew and drank to him. Rachel's head began to spin: she knew quite well the importance of Mr. Jefferson's gesture; within a few days it would be in every newspaper in America and would be the chief topic of conversation in Washington City.

What did it all mean: merely that Mr. Jefferson was putting into words the thanks of the nation for Andrew's indestructible will to victory? Or was it, as indicated in the expressions of many standing above her, something of far greater significance: that Thomas Jefferson was putting his public seal of approval on Andrew Jackson as the next president of the United States?

But how could that be? James Monroe was one of Mr. Jefferson's oldest and dearest friends and had served Mr. Jefferson and Mr. Madison these last sixteen years in the most important governmental posts. It was inconceivable that Mr. Jefferson would jettison his old comrade whom he had trained for the presidency in favor of a man who had long been his adversary.

Her thoughts took but a few swift seconds. Silence filled the room, silence fraught with the deepest of drama. Everyone's eyes were fixed on Andrew: how would he respond to this toast? Would he use this banquet room as a political stump, making known his willingness to contest the presidency? Or would he let the moment pass, respond with routine courtesy, indicating nothing of what he felt or wanted?

Andrew rose on the other side of Mr. Jefferson. His eyes were masked. After what seemed to her an intolerable time, during which she could hear the silence adumbrating about the banquet hall, he raised his glass, smiled down at Mr. Jefferson and said:

"James Monroe, late Secretary of War."

The great hall broke into bedlam, with men waving their arms and cheering and crying out to each other across the length of the room: for in these six short words Andrew Jackson had bowed himself out of the presidential race of 1816, officially nominating James Monroe of Virginia. Everything that would happen between now and the election would be an anticlimax because there would be no one in all America to rise up and contest Mr. Monroe.

The picture of that moment was stamped forever on Rachel's mind: Andrew standing above the noise and the multitude, a half-wistful smile raising the left corner of his mouth, happy that he had at last committed himself and that the questioning and suspense were over; yet at the same time the tiniest touch sad that he had voluntarily given up this chance of becoming the first man of his country. And on Mr. Jefferson's face too she caught a strange expression: was it, she asked herself, one of not too completely disguised relief? Had Mr. Jefferson taken a long gamble? Had he, knowing his man, made the *beau geste* of riding the hundred miles, officiating at this banquet and paying the greatest honor to General Jackson, believing that in turn Mr. Jackson would make the *beau geste* of acclaiming James Monroe? But whatever had been Mr. Jefferson's thinking, there could be no doubt in her mind of his enormous pleasure: he had not wanted Mr. Jackson to be president, he had passionately wanted his friend, neighbor and protégé in that office.

Washington City had been the source of so much of Andrew's aggravation that in her mind it had become a place of evil. She therefore approached the city with considerable trepidation. The town itself was a frightful disappointment to her, with its deeply rutted, muddy streets and ugly brick houses standing unshaded and solitary amidst the fields and swamps. This impression of rawness, almost of desolation, was heightened by the damage that had been caused by the British burning of the Capitol, the President's House, the Treasury and Departments of State and War, only part of which had been repaired.

On their first morning in Washington City Andrew awakened at dawn; she found him pacing the hotel room looking nervous and constrained. She sat bolt upright in bed.

"Andrew, what's wrong?"

"It's just that I'm scheduled for a joust with the War Department to-

225

day. They, and the President too, have been receiving letters from New Orleans protesting my arrest of Judge Hall and Louallier, who wrote that inflammatory letter in the *Courrière*."

"But they know you were fighting a war!"

"It's always the people who never get near a battlefield who want you to fight according to gentlemen's rules."

That morning Major Reid took her and little Andrew for a tour of the city, but she insisted on being back early, before Andrew could return from the War Department. He came in in high spirits, exclaiming, "I did all that worrying for nothing! I had no sooner started to justify my use of martial law to Secretary Dallas than he said that explanations were not in order, that everything I did in New Orleans was quite all right, and the President as well as the heads of departments were happy and satisfied. I tried to get him to approve a fifteen-thousand-man standing army, but the best I could do was ten thousand."

Relieved, she said, "I'm glad you've come back in such good spirits because we are due at the Monroes' for dinner at three, and frankly I'm a bit nervous."

"Of the Monroes? Why? He is one of the most loyal and friendly men I've ever known."

"Oh, it's not Mr. Monroe I'm worried about, it's his wife. I've heard her called an aristocratic woman; they say she comes from the highest New York society and is very regal in her manner."

"You are going to be received as no woman has ever been received by any other woman."

"Why?"

"Because we are helping her to achieve her life ambition to become First Lady."

For Rachel the ugliness of the city was more than made up for by the tremendous cordiality of its citizens; it seemed that every last family wanted to entertain for them: there was a brilliant ball at McKeowin's Hotel, attended by every important personage in the government; President Madison entertained formally for them at the Octagon House, a sumptuous dinner to which had been invited the entire diplomatic corps, including members of the British Embassy. To Rachel's infinite amusement Andrew and the British Ambassador had a long and cordial conversation.

The following morning a well-known Washington artist, Anna Peale, asked Rachel to sit for her portrait. Andrew was flattered by the idea, and insisted that she do so. Rachel posed in a dark blue velvet gown, with a soft lace collar and matching lace cap.

That Saturday evening as they were retiring Andrew said, "I've planned a trip out to Mount Vernon for tomorrow. I've never been there and I thought it would make a nice day in the country for us." When she raised her eyebrows he rushed ahead with, "You're remembering how

226

I refused to vote for the encomium after Mr. Washington's farewell address. Even great presidents need criticism."

She looked up at him out of laughing eyes.

"A principle to which you have made a considerable contribution."

"Yes," he said sheepishly. "I have made life unpleasant for a few of them, haven't I?"

The day was warm for mid-December; their visit to Washington City had been eminently successful; they felt lighthearted and young as they left their carriage at the foot of the hill and by gentle ascent reached the summit which overlooked the Potomac River on one side, and on the other a superb panorama of the Virginia countryside. The Custis family received them with the utmost hospitality, showing them through the simple but beautiful home. They wandered through the flower garden laid out and trimmed with exactness, then walked down the hill on the far side of the house to the small vault, overgrown with cedar, where President Washington had been buried.

Later, after being served refreshments by the family of Washington's adopted son, Andrew and Rachel sat on the front porch overlooking the beautiful Potomac and the many craft plowing gently along its surface.

"Next to Bayou Pierre," Andrew murmured, "this must surely be the most beautiful prospect in the world."

"Yes, along with the view of our own countryside, from that knoll on the Hermitage."

He turned his face full to her, studying her meaning for a moment.

"My dear, we could build the equivalent of Mount Vernon in Tennessee: a lovely house and garden like this, overlooking the fields and forest, with the Cumberland and Stone rivers in the distance."

"Andrew, I had no such thought and you know it! I am completely happy in our cabin. I don't ever want to move."

"You won't be so happy when we get back in January and you feel that north wind come through the logs."

"I've survived that north wind for eleven years now; besides, I heard you ask Robert Butler to rechink the entire cabin."

He did not reply. She saw by his sense of inner excitement that he had not been dissuaded.

4

They sold their cotton crop for the highest price they had ever received, thirty-eight cents a pound; for the first time in years they were out of debt, with more than twenty-two thousand dollars to their account in the Nashville bank. The death of young Reid, whom they had left only two weeks before, was a severe blow. Andrew turned over the materials for the biography to John Eaton, with the proviso that all of

227

the proceeds from the book were to go to Reid's widow and children.

They had been home less than three weeks when Andrew announced that he had to make a tour of the Indian country: the Creeks were complaining about the harshness of the treaty he had given them, and were not only refusing to move off certain lands they had ceded to the United States but were rousing their neighbors, the Cherokees and Chickasaws, and threatening to resume fighting. Rachel felt there was no immediacy to the problem.

"I suppose it sounds wifely of me," she insisted, "but do you really have to go? Jax is surveying down there and surely he would let you know if trouble were brewing."

"As long as I am on salary," he replied stubbornly, "I'm going to continue doing the best job I know how. I can't bear to report unfit for duty while eating the public bread."

No sooner had he ridden down the trail to the Tennessee border than a virulent epidemic which the doctors called "cold plague" broke out, felling whole families. Once again Rachel became a familiar figure in the countryside, riding across the fields at night wrapped in a dark cape and hood, carrying provisions and medication and warm friendliness. Day after day she closed the eyes of friends and neighbors who died while she sat by their bedside, ignoring the doctor's warning that since six and seven members of a family were dying within hours of each other the disease was highly contagious.

By the time spring came, and an end to the plague, almost a third of the population of the Cumberland had been wiped out. Rachel took to her bed, her own strength gone. Desperately as she missed Andrew, she was glad that she would have a few weeks in which to recuperate.

He was gone five months in all, returning in time for their nephew Andy's graduation from Cumberland Academy. During the exercises the headmaster told the parents how badly the school needed a new dormitory. Rachel plucked at Andrew's sleeve.

"Remember back at Poplar Grove when you were elected to the board of trustees, you said you were going to help make it a great school. Did you ever do much for them?"

"A little free legal advice here and there."

"Then don't you think this would be a good time to fulfill your promise?"

"You mean . . . the whole building?"

"The headmaster said it would only cost a thousand dollars. Our Andrew is going to be entered in the fall . . ."

He stood up and, when recognized, said, "Mr. Headmaster, I'd like to announce that you now have your new dormitory."

The next day, during a party for Andy's classmates, an itinerant portrait painter appeared on the scene, a most personable young man with a sweet smile and a lovable manner. He introduced himself as Ralph

Earl, son of a Connecticut painter, and asked if he might have the pleasure of painting General Jackson's portrait. Rachel saw that her niece Jane was smitten at first sight; and since Andrew also liked the chap's air of inner quietude and confidence, she assigned him a guest cottage. He went to work at once, painting Andrew in his full-dress uniform.

The Earl sittings were soon interrupted however, for General Jackson received a formal notification from the new Secretary of War, William Crawford, that his treaty with the Creeks had been set aside, and that vast tracts of land had been returned to the Cherokees. Andrew was wild with anger, insisting that the news was the worst since the burning of Washington City; it put him flat on his back with an attack of diarrhea. When he was able to sit up and Rachel brought him his writing materials, he wrote Secretary Crawford a blistering letter. She feared that the strenuous effort and anger might bring on another attack, but instead it had a healing effect and by the next morning he was on his feet again, gaunt and concave of stomach, but ready to head the mass meetings of indignation that were being called throughout Tennessee.

President Madison named him as commissioner, with instructions to return to the Indian country and buy from the Cherokees the lands which he had taken from them and that Secretary Crawford had given back.

Once again they were separated. Once again she was alone. But the feeling of being only half alive when her husband was away was replaced by a feeling of complete bafflement when he returned to the Hermitage after several months and fell into a series of quarrels, disputes and conflicts that kept them in an uproar. She made no attempt to keep the details of the interlocking feuds straight in her mind; letters and episodes tumbled over each other in such fast sequence that it would have been impossible in any event.

He was still quarreling violently with Secretary of War Crawford, who was refusing to put the newly purchased Cherokee land on the market so that it could be bought by American settlers; with the Kentucky newspapers who were defending the Kentucky troops who had given way under British fire at New Orleans, and whom he had excoriated in his report to the War Department; and finally with the War Department itself, which had taken one of Andrew's officers off a topographical assignment and summoned him to New York without informing General Jackson of the transfer. Outraged, Andrew issued an order to his entire division instructing them to disregard all orders from the War Department unless they came through him.

In the midst of the cyclone, John Overton brought her the news that under the newly elected President Monroe, William Crawford was to become Secretary of the Treasury, and that the position of Secretary of War was now available to Andrew. It would mean leaving the Hermitage and settling in Washington City, probably for several years; and as a Cabinet member, a return to national politics. But then didn't all of Andrew's activities, including the winning of wars, end in political embroilments? Since he was always going to be involved, might it not be advisable to be at the center of the conflict? As Secretary of War he could issue the orders which would fulfill his life ambition: the solid settling of all lands between Tennessee and the Gulf of Mexico with American families. Tentatively, as they sat before the fire after dinner smoking their pipes, she suggested this line of reasoning to him.

He looked up at her in astonishment.

"You must be terribly upset by my difficulties, my dear, if you can make such a recommendation. I don't want to sit behind a desk; I want to march back south and send the Dons home from Florida."

And that was precisely what he did, leaving her for a fourth long journey within the period of two years.

The Hermitage was in the hands of a capable overseer; she no longer had to go into the fields, to be exposed to the hard labor, to the drying heat of the sun. Yet it seemed that each day brought its own misfortune: Severn took to bed with a hacking cough and died from it. John Overton became so ill he had to resign his judgeship and retire to Travellers Rest. Her nephew, John Hutchings, who had been Andrew's business partner for so many years, died at his home in Huntsville. Rachel brought his four-year-old son, Andrew Jackson Hutchings, now an orphan, back home with her. Only two pleasant things happened: her niece Jane and the portraitist, Ralph Earl, fell in love and asked her permission to be married. Rachel gave them a big wedding party at the Hermitage, and they moved into what had gradually become Earl's studio. Also that spring, 1817, the biography of Andrew was published, and enthusiastically received.

Andrew returned from the Seminole-Florida war after a half year's absence, though Rachel could not have said just how long it was; with her release from farming she had given up all calendars. His hands were shaking as though he had palsy and he had a cough as bad as the one that had killed Severn. He had a mysterious pain in his side which kept him from sleeping, and his left shoulder, broken by the Benton bullet five years before, had stiffened so severely that he had no use of the arm. She summoned Dr. Bronaugh from Nashville; John Overton rose from his sickbed to spend an hour locked in the upper bedroom with Andrew. He came downstairs shaking his head in mystification.

"That's quite a man you married yourself to: he doesn't think he can survive this illness but he's writing President Monroe that it's urgent for us to take St. Augustine and Cuba at once; and that all he needs is the President's order to lead an expedition southward."

"But surely no one would give him such an order!"

230

John studied her face for a moment, the silver specs down over the hump of his nose and his eyes frankly puzzled.

"Then you don't know what's happening?" he asked blandly.

Before a week was out she learned that her husband's seizure of Florida had caused an international scandal: Spain was demanding an immediate return of Pensacola, with indemnities and severe punishment of General Jackson. England was threatening war over his court-martial and execution of Lieutenant Ambrister of the Royal Colonial Marines, who had led the Indians in their fight during the Seminole war, and Alexander Arbuthnot, a Scotsman, also charged with spying and helping the enemy. Negotiations for the purchase of Florida, which had been progressing slowly, now collapsed. The press of America as well as of England and Europe cried out for General Jackson's scalp. It wasn't possible for her to keep the newspapers out of the Hermitage, nor to bar her gates to the loyal officers who were organizing to fight the movement in Congress which would impeach Andrew and relieve him of his command. Apparently the only two men in the country who were defending her husband's course were John Quincy Adams, Secretary of State, and someone using the pseudonym of Aristedes, who was publishing a brilliant series of pro-Jackson articles in the Tennessee papers. Only by accident did she learn that Aristedes was their own John Overton.

She had had Andrew sitting up in a chair for a few hours each day, but this fresh crisis put him back in bed again. There he remained for two solid months, neither his temper nor his health helped any by President Monroe's apologetic return of Pensacola and St. Marks to Spain, thus nullifying Andrew's second conquest of Florida.

Yet this was the very moment that he told her he was ready to begin building the fine house he had promised her at Mount Vernon; apparently he had been planning its details during the six months he had been away. They went across the fields one hot August day, Andrew walking with slow and faltering steps, leaning heavily on his cane; at the top of a slight rise overlooking their cabins, the spring and the deep woods beyond, he stopped.

"This has always been your favorite spot." Raising his stick and pointing with it, he said, "There's a better elevation over there, you'll get a wider view. Wouldn't you prefer to build on that highest level?"

She smiled to herself, realizing that by his oblique question he had taken the subject of the new house out of the realm of disputation. The humble Hermitage cabin, which satisfied her completely, was no longer adequate to his *amour-propre*. She had no logic on her side, only sentiment: they had plenty of money in the bank, and their little cabin was really inadequate for the amount of entertaining they were obliged to do. Since Andrew wanted the big home, she might just as well enter into the plan with enthusiasm. But she would hold out for the lower knoll.

231

"We have so many pleasant memories of this spot," she pleaded. "That other hill has a little too much . . . eminence . . . for me. You know . . . I get vertigo."

He chuckled softly, then with his stick began outlining the house he had in mind: it was to be a two-story brick building with a big hall downstairs, two good-sized rooms on either side, and four rooms upstairs directly over the four below. He had been his own architect; he would be his own builder.

The harvest season brought them another excellent crop, but when they found a limestone quarry on their own land she agreed that they should take several of their more skilled hands out of the fields to start the foundation work. They spent days together wandering over their acreage until they located a good bed of clay; when the topsoil had been removed and lime sprinkled over the deposit, they let their son ride the mule who was treading the lime into the clay to give it the proper hardness. They built their own kiln, experimenting with the fires in an effort to get the kind of brick they wanted, and rode through the forest, marking the best poplar trees for timbers and structural lumber. Then he received an order from Washington City to go back into the Indian country and arrange a treaty with the Chickasaws.

She was left with the actual building of the house. Because the responsibility was now hers, and she had to make decisions about the fireplace and the wine cellar, she found that she was building into her new home an ever-growing interest and emotion. It wasn't going to be too grand a place after all: just a square brick building with a little picket fence around it. There would still be plenty of seclusion, for the house stood a hundred yards back from the road, completely screened by tall trees.

When Andrew returned in mid-November, having been delayed by an excursion into Alabama where he had bought a large cotton plantation next to the one on which John Coffee now lived, he approved the way the building had taken shape. Six weeks later he started out for Washington City to be on hand when his enemies in the Congress started impeachment proceedings against him. He left on horseback in the midst of torrential rains, rejecting her suggestion that he take their carriage. Within a week she had a letter from Knoxville, telling her that she had been right after all; he had been unable to stay on his horse and had had to borrow a carriage for the journey.

She filled her days with the completing of the big house, building a separate kitchen just across the porch from the dining room and sinking a deep well which brought up cool water by windlass and bucket, staking out her first garden inside the low white picket fence. And as always when Andrew was away, the deepest tragedies struck: young Jane Earl died in childbed, just ten months after her wedding, and was buried in the family plot next to Mrs. Donelson, Samuel, Stockly and Severn.

Within a few days Robert Hays was stricken and died, and Rachel lost her dearest and most loyal friend.

Jane went to live with one of her sons in West Tennessee, Andy was at West Point, young Andrew was in school in Nashville, and Earl wandered off, heartbroken at the loss of his wife. Yet Rachel could hardly say she was alone, for the air crackled with news about Andrew: the Committee on Military Affairs attacked him for the executions of Ambrister and Arbuthnot; Speaker of the House Henry Clay of Kentucky stepped down from the dais to attack the Creek Treaty and the conquest of Pensacola, charging Andrew Jackson with being a military chieftain who would one day destroy the liberties of the American people.

Rachel mounted Duke, Andrew's favorite horse, the superb stallion who had carried his master through the Battle of New Orleans and the Florida wars, now getting old but still beloved of the family. She rode over to Travellers Rest, where she found Overton puttering in a greenhouse amidst his young trees.

"I simply can't understand the ferocity of these attacks, John."

"Mr. Clay wants to be our next president," replied John. "He'd kill his own grandmother if he thought she stood in his way. The same applies to Mr. Crawford. Each gentleman thinks Andrew Jackson is standing in his way."

"But Andrew has said he doesn't want the presidency."

Overton buttoned up his collar against the cool of the greenhouse.

"Messrs. Clay and Crawford remain unconvinced: neither one will have a peaceful night's sleep until Andrew is relieved of his commission and punished for taking Florida. But our side will have its turn. Let me give you some of these purple flags to take home; they'll grow wonderfully in your new garden."

For the next two weeks the Nashville papers were filled with the fiery defense set up by their friends, who described Andrew's every action as part of an over-all military strategy designed to safeguard the American people. When the final vote was taken Andrew was vindicated. Philadelphia gave him a four-day celebration, New York a five-day reception while he was on his way to visit Andy at West Point. In his letters Andrew assured her that during even the most tumultuous hours of the debate he had remained quietly in his hotel room and had not entered personally into the controversy; was it not natural then for a man who had just triumphed over his bitterest adversaries to glory a little in public acclaim? She was convinced that if Andrew's military career had not been attacked he would have remained a general and a gentleman planter; but would he be content to remain so now with the ovations of Philadelphia and New York fresh in his ears?

5

She had the house completed, with carpets in the bedrooms, draperies at the windows and her cherry-wood table installed in the dining room by the time Andrew returned from Washington in mid-April. Her settee and the chairs were on the worn side, the pianoforte needed a resurfacing, but she enjoyed the sense of continuity that the old pieces brought to a house still smelling slightly of paint. Despite the fact that she now had eight rooms instead of the three in which they had lived for fifteen years at the cabin, it nonetheless had for her a feeling of compactness; Andrew had designed it on a somewhat smaller scale than Hunter's Hill. The entrance hall and stairs were of dark polished wood; to the left as one entered was the front parlor and dining room, with a nice view of the hill which rolled gently down to the old Hermitage buildings. The rooms were almost square, about twenty by twenty. Across the hall to the right was Andrew's office into which she moved her father's walnut desk and two walls of bookshelves. Behind Andrew's room was a passage with a side door leading out, and just beyond that a bedroom for young Andrew, who could get up as early as he liked and slip out of doors without disturbing the rest of the family.

Andrew walked about for an entire day determining where they would put up the fine wallpapers he had brought back from the East and what furniture was needed to complete the rooms. They had their first supper that night under the many candles of the crystal chandelier; Hannah had done the cooking, but Moll and George insisted upon serving the food. After dinner they walked outside to look at the house against the night sky; it had a simple grace and dignity that made them proud. Andrew brought forth a box from his waistcoat pocket, then leaned over to kiss her.

"It seems I'm forever leaving you home to finish something I started."

Rachel opened the box to find a set of beautiful mosaic jewelry, a necklace, earrings and belt clasp. She took the necklace from the case and held it draped over her palm. Andrew stood behind her to fasten the catch, then kept his arms about her. He went away so often, and stayed away so long, yet he always returned to her completely, bringing his full self, his full spirit, his full love and desire. She turned in his arms, found herself clasped against him. He couldn't help what he did; he was driven. He had great spirit, vision, courage, leadership; half the time she knew him to be physically more dead than alive; but the fire never went out, the fire which fed on itself, creating its own fuel even while consuming it.

At the beginning of June they received a note from President Monroe, who was touring Georgia, accepting Andrew's invitation to visit at the Hermitage for a few days. Rachel took the news in stride. It did not seem to her extraordinary that she should be offering hospitality to the President of the United States; her father before her had entertained George Washington, Patrick Henry and the other leaders of the House of Burgesses; the Donelson stockade had been the stopping-off station for all important visitors from the East, and now it seemed only natural to her that Mr. Monroe should come to the Hermitage.

She decided that he must have the big front bedroom over the parlor, and went that day into Nashville to buy a sturdy mahogany bed with a canopy, a marble-topped table with a comfortable chair for the center of the room and a mahogany dresser that fitted nicely into the corner beyond the fireplace. The last of the white curtains and damask draperies were hung the evening before his arrival.

"We finished this house just in time," said Andrew, watching her preparations with approval. "It's more fitting to entertain the President here."

"Oh, I think I could have made Mr. Monroe as comfortable in the cabin."

James Monroe proved to be the most undemanding of guests. A deep and abiding affection between the President and Andrew was apparent in their every word to each other as they lingered over a late supper, the three of them in the cozy intimacy of the dining room. Mr. Monroe was to have only two or three free days before going into Nashville for entertainment by the Female Academy, and a grand ball; Rachel saw to it that he had complete relaxation.

But after Andrew had left to make part of the return journey with the President she found that apparently the only center of quiet during his stay had been inside the red brick walls of the Hermitage; the newspaper editors and politicos all over the country were asking just what were the implications of President Monroe's visit to the Jacksons? In one Washington City newspaper Rachel read that this visit was planned by the President to give official approval to all of General Jackson's acts, starting with the Creek treaties and going straight through the capture of Florida; from a second group she learned that the visit had to do with internal politics: Mr. Monroe had reasoned that if the Jacksons received him in their home as a guest they would not shortly thereafter attempt to wrest the presidency from him; that in fact General Jackson, in affording hospitality to Mr. Monroe, had taken this means of announcing to the country that he was supporting Mr. Monroe for re-election in 1820. Their own friends in Tennessee maintained that by going directly to the Hermitage before he visited Nashville, Mr. Monroe was announcing publicly that he favored the succession of General and Mrs. Andrew Jackson to the President's House in Washington City in 1824.

This was indeed news to Mrs. Jackson.

Andrew had been gone only a few days when a panic descended upon the West with terrifying force; it was not merely that there would be no market for their cotton or for anything else they might raise on the Hermitage, but that the three years of prosperity following the Battle of New Orleans, during which countless new factories had been opened and vast quantities of outlying lands put under cultivation, were now ended with the suddenness of a cannon shot. Local banks which had sprung up by the dozens, issuing credit on unbroken lands and unplanted crops, had their voluminous paper money called in by the Bank of the United States in Philadelphia. Fortunately for her, Andrew had done no borrowing and had been far too busy to buy or start planting new farms; in fact he had opposed the new paper-money banks as being financially unsound; but most of their friends and neighbors had borrowed heavily for their speculations.

From her bedroom she now saw them ride wearily up the road and turn into the Hermitage. Could Mrs. Jackson lend them five hundred dollars . . . a thousand? If they had that much cash they could hold off the banks . . . She had gone through several of these crises before, and was pretty well convinced that it would be throwing good money after bad; but she had lived with Andrew long enough to know that he too would want to help as much as he could.

She made substantial loans to twenty families; in a few cases the money saved their homes. But by the time she had loaned out half of her available cash she had also come to a realization that they themselves would be deeply involved in the depression. She stopped the lending until Andrew returned. He approved of what she had done, then continued to parcel out their money until he had not a dollar of cash left. After they had processed their cotton, and sold it at a pitiful price, he told Rachel:

"We now have cash loans out to a hundred and twenty-nine men; and are down to rock bottom. It's the fault of the Biddle crowd in Philadelphia that owns the Bank of the United States: if they hadn't forced the local banks to redeem their paper in specie, we might have worked out of this crisis. I really ought to get back to Washington City: Clay and Crawford are doing everything they can to scuttle our treaty with Spain for the purchase of Florida. But I need several hundred dollars for travel expenses . . ."

"I was never so happy to be without a sou," she said with a laugh. "And this is one time you can't borrow from John Overton: I think he's about to propose to Dr. May's widow. If she accepts he's going to have to build an extra wing for her five children. We're all hoping she will accept; after all, John is fifty-four now, and he's lived alone too long."

The Widow May did accept; almost the whole Cumberland Valley attended the wedding at Travellers Rest.

Spain finally signed the treaty. Rachel was happy because Andrew

236

would not be going off to war again. Instead there came a letter from President Monroe offering him the governorship of Florida.

"Doesn't this governorship come a good many years too late?" she asked.

"Admittedly the appointment is anticlimactic. However, President Monroe seems to think I'm the logical person to organize an American government down there, since I know the most about it."

"You could also be the illogical person: the Spanish governors hate you, and not without reason."

He chewed on this for a number of moments, then sighed deeply.

"You're perfectly right. I have neither the strength nor the appetite for the task. I'll sit down right now and write to President Monroe, refusing the office."

"You partially want that appointment, don't you?"

"That's my curse: I partially want everything. Wasn't it your father who used to say, 'Every man is his own jailer, and every man his own prison'?"

They slept late and were in the midst of a leisurely breakfast when a group of riders came up the road from Nashville. John Overton, Dr. Bronaugh and Felix Grundy were ushered in.

"We came to congratulate you on being the first American governor of Florida."

"Then you can take your glasses off, John, because you are not going to get a clear view of the governor through them; I sent a letter last night, declining the position."

"You didn't!" It was Dr. Bronaugh, Andrew's military surgeon.

"We think you should hold a few such posts in the government, preparatory to the presidency."

"And we're convinced that's why President Monroe made the appointment," added Felix Grundy.

She watched the dull brick color mount in Andrew's cheeks.

"Do you think I'm such a damned fool as to think myself fit for president of the United States? No sir; I know what I am fit for. I can command a body of men in a rough way; but I am not fit to be president."

They were silent for a moment, then John said quietly, "This is only further proof of your good sense, Andrew. Couldn't we go into the library?"

She went up to her bedroom and resumed work on the bedspread she was making for a guest room. It was noon before the meeting in the library broke up. One of the men went out the front door and rode rapidly away in the direction of town. Andrew came up the stairs.

"I told them that if my letter of refusal had not yet left the post office I would withdraw it and send an acceptance letter in its place." He grimaced. "But you know the mail leaves the Nashville post office at noon, and it's past that now. We are perfectly safe."

She wanted to exclaim, Andrew, it isn't like you to let a major decision hinge upon whether a messenger can reach the Nashville post office before the mails leave! It must be that he really wants to go, she thought, and with his own eyes and his own hands effectuate the transfer of Florida.

She was no whit surprised when the messenger returned, triumphantly bearing the letter. She sat quietly while he wrote an acceptance.

They descended the Mississippi to New Orleans by steamboat in eight days, their freshly painted carriage trimmed with morocco skins securely lashed in the hold. They brought with them their son, also Lieutenant Andy, just out of West Point, and as special company for Rachel, Narcissa Hays, Jane's twenty-year-old daughter. There were two hundred passengers on board where only fifty could be cared for comfortably. "I guess I'm old-fashioned," she told Andrew one midnight as they stood at the prow, wrapped in greatcoats. "I prefer Colonel Stark's flatboat." She turned to put her arm through his. ". . . particularly when you were steering it."

It seemed to her as though all of New Orleans had assembled at the pier to welcome them, with a full band of martial music. That night they were conducted to the Grand Theatre by a guard of honor, and when they entered their box the audience rose to its feet, shouting: "Viva Jackson! Long live the Jacksons!" Later a delegation came into the box to place a crown of laurel on Andrew's head. Rachel shrank from the gesture of worship and sat staring at the shiny green leaves uneasily: by some optical illusion the laurel had turned to thorns. When the lights were extinguished and the curtain went up she found herself unable to follow the play.

The next morning she rose early and went on a buying spree to accumulate the new bedsteads, sideboard and dining table needed to complete the Hermitage. Louise Livingston knew the finest shops, making sure that she purchased only the best materials. Andrew's salary as governor was five thousand dollars, and Rachel reasoned it was wise to put some of the money into furnishings which they would enjoy for the rest of their lives, including the wonderful new French mattresses. By the end of their week's stay in New Orleans she had bought seven packing cases of furniture, which Edward Livingston arranged to send north.

They took a boat on Lake Pontchartrain, crossed the Gulf and landed at Mobile Bay. When they were within fifteen miles of Pensacola, where Andrew was to set up headquarters and take over the government, he decided he would go no further, but remain at the home of a friendly Spaniard, Señor Manuel, to which he had been invited.

"You and the children take the carriage into Pensacola," he explained to Rachel. "There's a comfortable house waiting for us on Main Street. It wouldn't be proper for me to go into the town until Governor Callava is ready to deliver the province to me officially."

Assured that it would be only a matter of a day or two, Rachel gathered up her son, her niece and her nephew and they rode the fifteen miles into Pensacola. The town lay on the bay, and from her balcony she had a fine view over the water, with a sea breeze from ten o'clock in the morning until ten at night.

Before the sun became too warm she went for a walk about the town, flanked by Narcissa and her two Andrews. Pensacola lay in a perfect plain, the land nearly as white as flour, yet productive of fine peach trees, oranges in abundance, grapes, figs and pomegranates. The Spanish residents, expecting a change of government, had neglected their gardens, flowers were growing wild, and the many public squares were overgrown with thick shrubs, weeping willows and pride of China. The streets were crowded with the most amazing polyglot she had ever seen: Spanish, French, Negroes from the islands, Indians in native costume; there were so few Americans that she heard only an occasional word of English in the streets.

There were daily notes from Andrew telling her of the hundred difficulties in his way: he did not believe it proper to call on Governor Callava before the governor called on him; the ships bearing American troops were missing; the Spanish governor was insisting on taking the guns in the fortifications. He would join her in a few days.

Dawn in Pensacola was the loveliest time; she arose while it was still dark, had a cup of coffee, then sat out on the balcony watching the ships coming into the harbor, most of them now loaded with Americans seeking political appointments or business opportunities. It was only two weeks since her arrival, yet the town had become so jammed that it was no longer possible for her to take her daily promenade down Main Street or through the square. On Sunday morning she decided to hold services for her family in her own living room. The town was still in an uproar from its Saturday-night brawl. Instead of holding the services she sat down at her desk and wrote letters to friends in Tennessee asking if they might know of a clergyman who would be attracted to this heathen land.

It took another two weeks of exasperating negotiations before Andrew was able to make his entry into Pensacola, arriving in time for a six o'clock breakfast, to which Governor Callava had been invited, but which he had declined. At ten o'clock Rachel stood on her balcony watching the Spanish troops drawn up in the square, their flag still flying, and the Americans marching down the street to take a position opposite them. The Spanish flag was lowered halfway, then she saw Andrew give a command and the American flag rose in its place. At long last Andrew Jackson had made a bloodless and permanent conquest of Florida! The Spanish people below her burst into tears and walked disconsolately out of the square; her own exultation faded in the face of her sympathy for them.

Within a very few days her sympathy veered to her husband. While the Spanish residents were prospering under the influx of Americans, Andrew was encountering little but obstruction and aggravation: the men he had invited down from Nashville to take part in the government were stranded because President Monroe had sent his own administrative staff into Florida. Aside from such minor tasks as cleaning the drunks off the streets on Sunday mornings, he had little to do. The rains began to fall as though the heavens had burst; her son came down with a fever, so Rachel sent the boy home with Colonel Butler. Because he was idle and frustrated, Andrew got into a row over the archives with ex-Governor Callava: Andrew insisted that the records be handed to the new American government, Callava refused, Andrew had him arrested and seized the records in Callava's house. That night, closeted in their bedroom, he confessed:

"You were right, I should never have come. The whole thing's been a wild-goose chase."

"Not entirely," she replied consolingly. "If you hadn't come you might always have had an unfinished feeling in your mind about Florida. But if your job is done now, why don't we just pack our trunks and go home?"

6

They returned to the Hermitage during the first week of November, after having been gone eight months. They found that a large portion of their crop had been destroyed by freshets, hailstorms and a deluge of rain. The *National Intelligencer* carried further deluge; they read of the demand being made for a congressional investigation of Governor Jackson's official behavior in Florida, in particular his jailing of the former Spanish Governor Callava, and his seizing of the Spanish archives.

"It's Crawford and Clay again," declared Andrew. "They are still trying to eliminate me from presidential consideration. I'm going to write a letter saying that I admire the talents of Secretary of State John Quincy Adams, and that I shall support him for the presidency when Mr. Monroe retires. That will put an end to their hellish machinations. Can you understand that?"

"Yes, I can understand it. But can you write the letter?"

"Just find a comfortable position anywhere behind my shoulder."

He was right; the congressional investigation was dropped.

At the beginning of February 1822, Andy came home for a conference with his aunt and uncle; he was bored with army life and attracted to the law. Since his uncle was now convinced that the United States was safe from invasion, he consented to Andy's resigning from the army and entering Transylvania Law College in Kentucky. At the same time Ralph Earl returned; he had been wandering for several years, unable to reconcile himself to the loss of his wife. He asked if he might stay at the

Hermitage, since it was the only home he knew and he no longer could flee from his memories. Could he do a portrait of Mrs. Jackson, and several of Mr. Jackson? Rachel and Andrew assured him he could remain as part of the family for the rest of his days if he so desired.

With the coming of spring Andrew got out on the farm to supervise the planting. Rachel saw that he was in better health and in better spirits than at any time during the past ten years. With the passing months letters arrived from many states telling them how popular he was with the voters; there was an unending number of newspaper articles wondering when the wily Mr. Jackson was finally going to show his hand. He answered none of the letters which asked him to make political comments or commitments; the newspaper articles amused him. Each week saw a group of excited friends at the Hermitage estimating the popularity of various candidates, showing letters from their friends indicating that Pennsylvania would go for Jackson, or New York would, or he need only appear in Boston to assure himself of Massachusetts. If these presidential handicappers made any impression on Andrew, she could find no evidence of it. To Johnny's daughter Mary, who had married Jax and was living in Alabama, Rachel wrote:

I do hope they will leave Mr. Jackson alone. He is not a well man and never will be unless they allow him to rest. He has done his share for the country. He has not spent one-fourth of his days under his own roof. Now I hope it is at an end. They talk of his being President. Major Eaton, General Carroll, Mr. Campbell, Doctor Bronough and even the Parson and I can't tell how many others—all of his friends who come here—talk everlastingly about his being President. In this as in all else, I can only say, the Lord's will be done. But I hope he may not be called again to the strife and empty honors of public place.

However, it was a letter from her sister Jane that really upset her:

You will miss your fine farm and comfortable house for the city of Washington, when the General is elected President.

If sensible, hardheaded Jane had been convinced that Andrew would be the next president, then whom in all God's world could they ever persuade that they intended to remain by their hearth for the rest of their lives?

It would have been difficult for her to tell the exact moment at which Andrew began to grow restless. The action of the Tennessee legislature in officially nominating their favorite son for the presidency in July of 1822 could surely excite any man who was genuinely interested in the office. However, Andrew did not take the move seriously; he merely commented to her that the usual method of nominating presidents, that of a caucus of congressmen who dictated the party's choice, was now obsolete. Yet no matter what he did or did not do the papers found it significant: when he declined the post as minister to Mexico, this was interpreted as proof of his interest in the presidency; when he declined to go on tour through the Northwest, this was interpreted as a lack of interest in the presidency.

What actually caused the first real break in his resolution? she asked herself. Was it the information that President Monroe was supporting Secretary William Crawford? Was it the fact that the second of his personal adversaries, Henry Clay of Kentucky, was rapidly gaining adherents in such states as Ohio, Indiana and Illinois? Was it the disconcerting news that the man he was backing for the post, John Quincy Adams, was losing ground? Or was it, as she was coming more and more to suspect, that Andrew's interest had lain dormant simply because the election had been so far away?

Activity about the Hermitage increased: newspapermen, politicians, officers who had been disappointed at the cutting down of the army, old-time friends and that little clique of Jacksonians, Overton, Lewis and Eaton, were constantly closeted with Andrew, analyzing for him the newest developments, building on their one sure foundation: that Adam's strength was failing and that the next president would be either William Crawford or Henry Clay; and how would he be able to live peaceably and happily at the Hermitage with either of these two men as Chief Executive?

"I know I don't have the proper training or temperament for the presidency," Andrew confided to her late one Sunday night, after she had gone to bed exhausted from entertaining almost a hundred guests; "but certainly I have greater honesty and integrity than either of those two adventurers."

"Perhaps if you went on a tour at election time, urging everyone to support Mr. Adams . . . ?"

"Then I'd be in politics again, up to my scrawny neck. Either I am in . . . completely . . . or completely out."

The inevitable incident came in the fall after they had harvested their crop and then found there was no market whatever for the cotton. Perhaps if he had not been depressed over the lack of money he would not have reacted so volcanically to the attack unleashed against him by Senator Williams of Tennessee, a Crawford man who thought the moment ripe to eliminate Mr. Jackson permanently from the presidential scene. Senator Williams made his criticism of Andrew the major plank in his own platform for re-election. Andrew had endorsed his old friend Congressman Rhea for senator, and John Overton, John Eaton and William Lewis were at the capital fighting desperately to win votes for Rhea in the state legislature where the election was to be determined.

On the night before the senatorial election John Overton rode into the

242

Hermitage weary and disheveled, accompanied by one of Andrew's former generals. Rachel saw by John's paleness and by the angularity of his movements that it was a moment of crisis. She got the two men a cool drink, then sat stiffly on a straight-backed chair listening to every word.

"Andrew, we're licked. Rhea can't make it. You are going to have to take his place and run for the Senate; that's the only way we can defeat Williams and his anti-Jackson platform. If we defeat Williams, and you go to the Senate, we are in a perfect position for next year's presidential campaign." John's gray eyes had bulked up dark. "Gather together a few things and come back with us. It's going to be a difficult battle, and your presence will help."

Rachel found herself unable to breathe. Andrew turned to gaze at her. After a moment he murmured, "Excuse me, I wish to talk to my wife."

He came to her side, put his hand under her arm and lifted her from the chair. They left Andrew's office, went through the hall and into the parlor. He closed the door behind them.

They stood in the center of the room facing each other, very close, very intent, their eyes boring deep, touching one another neither by hand nor thought. Her only positive feeling at the moment was the need within herself to find out what, under the layers of years, wounds, ambitions, accomplishments and failures, was the real truth about what Andrew wanted. He grinned at her sheepishly.

"Everything would be simple, my dear, if only I knew what I wanted. I've never been happier than during the last two years living quietly here at the Hermitage, being a gentleman planter, enjoying your companionship."

She tried to keep all emotion out of her voice.

"There's a time to lie fallow and there's a time to bear fruit. If you want the presidency, Andrew, and I can understand how greatly a man would feel honored . . ."

"No, no, it's not honor that I would be seeking, I've had all of that any man could want. It's the chance for service that intrigues me. I'd fight for this country every minute of the day, just as hard as I fought at New Orleans."

"And just as well, too. If this is the thing you want, Andrew, then you must do everything in your power to achieve it. You must go tonight with John and General Coleman."

He opened his arms to her and at last they were clinging to each other, lonely and a little forlorn.

"And what of you, Rachel? What of the consequences?"

She left his side, walked over to the big front window, her head lowered, caught somewhere in the mysterious space between thought and reverie. What precisely did Andrew mean? The fact that she would have to leave the Hermitage which she loved dearly and move to Washington City? That she too would become a public servant, be obliged to enter

243

the world of protocol and society? Did she have the temperament for that kind of life after having sought seclusion these many years?

Her mind drifted backward, to New Orleans, and the birthday party she had given for Andrew when the peace with Britain had become official; to the letter from her cousin, John Stockly, which had said, "We are entitled to a President from the West," to the question she had asked herself then, If it all were to come to pass, would I make any effort to stop it? She had recognized the issue then; and nothing had changed. This could be the most important decision of her life, for the followers of neither Mr. Crawford nor Mr. Clay would hesitate to use her private affairs as the whipping post on which to flay the political aspirations of Andrew Jackson to death. The presidential campaign would be bloody and bitter.

Wasn't that what Andrew meant when he spoke of the consequences? Wasn't he asking for her permission to plunge her into this maelstrom?

They were so completely without cash that they would have to borrow money from John Overton to cover Andrew's expenses. She would have to remain at the Hermitage to get the cotton ginned, the foodstuffs stored, the tools and cabins repaired, the mill moved and the new gin house built. He would be gone for . . . how long . . . six months, a year? Once again she would be alone in a big house.

Our lives have come full circle, she thought. How impossible it is for any man to break out of his pattern. We have come through all these years and all this suffering only to be caught in the identical predicament at the end of our lives that we were in in the beginning.

She rose, walked to her husband, who had been standing awkwardly in the center of the room, trying not to intrude upon her decision. She reached up her face to be kissed, then said quietly:

"I will accept the consequences."

Book SEVEN

THE HOURS clung stickily to her fingers; yet this long separation after Andrew had been elected and gone to the Senate was not unpleasant. Andy, who had opened his law office in Nashville, was taking full responsibility for affairs at the Hermitage. He was selling their cotton for a good price and, at his uncle's orders, putting the money away for the trip the family would take with Andrew to Washington City the following fall. Andy had his father's rich black hair and big warm sensitive brown eyes as well as his voice and gestures; it was like having Samuel at her side.

The house was filled with her young nieces: there were seldom fewer than five or six of them visiting at one time and that meant their admirers and suitors as well. The evenings and week ends were gay with music and singing and laughter. It seemed to Rachel that she was never alone; she did not discover until spring that this was no accident, but rather an express order from Andrew in Washington City to Andy at home:

"Keep your aunt's spirits up."

In the Senate Andrew sat next to Thomas Hart Benton, and the two men had become friends again; he extended the olive branch to General Winfield Scott, with whom he had quarreled over the powers of the War Department; Henry Clay had come to dinner with him several times at O'Neale's Tavern.

At Christmas she helped decorate Johnny's house for the big family party, festooning the walls and windows with holly and berries and clusters of mistletoe. Johnny told her that from everything he could sense in the papers and the wind, Andrew would be the next president; he then added in a bemused tone:

"Your husband is a very surprising man; his nearest and best friends never found him out."

A strange way, thought Rachel, of saying, We never fully appreciated him.

After the holidays she was able to fulfill a wish she had been nurturing

245

for several years: to have a little church right on the Hermitage where their friends and relatives could come on Sunday morning for services, and one night a week for a good bout of preaching. She built it of brick, just a mile or so from the house; it looked like a New England schoolhouse, for it had no steeple or portico; on the inside there were forty unpainted pews standing on a brick floor. The building of the church and the hiring of a pastor absorbed most of her energies over the winter. In the spring she replanted her garden with hollyhocks, white and purple heliotrope, tiger lilies and white lilacs, many of the beds being edged with sage and thyme. At the entrance to the garden there was a rope tied to the limb of a hickory tree where the dozens of children who visited the Hermitage could swing. Some of the trees brought by friends from distant places were beginning to bloom now, the pink magnolia from Japan, the fig tree from the far South.

For years there had been twenty to thirty journals coming into the Hermitage, but Andrew had canceled all of these except the Nashville newspaper. How much more pleasant it was to follow the romance of the youngsters about her: for twenty-three-year-old Andy had been smitten by Johnny's youngest daughter, sixteen-year-old Emily, the red-haired, delicate-featured beauty of the Donelson crop. Her brother Johnny opposed this marriage because they were first cousins; Rachel gave them sanctuary at the Hermitage.

"I guess I'm a sentimentalist; I don't think love should be opposed."

One day late in March she perceived through a subtle change in the tone and manner of her family that something untoward had happened. She asked Andy to tell her what it was.

"Uncle has forbidden me to pass on any such information. It is not important."

"Darling, you never were any good at concealing, even as a child."

"But Aunt Rachel, Uncle says it is simply that the caucus people behind Crawford are growing desperate because they see his strength waning and so they are trying to arouse Uncle's anger." He hesitated, but there was no turning away from the command in her eyes. "John Overton has received a letter from Senator John Eaton asking for detailed information and proof about your marriage . . . so they can put an end to the rumors in Washington."

Rachel cried, "But surely John hasn't complied!"

"I don't know, Aunt Rachel. I haven't discussed it with him."

"Then I shall have to. Andy, have a horse saddled for me at once."

She did not bother to knock at the front door, for John was sure to be in his garden in this pleasant weather. She found him cultivating a new flower bed; to her precipitate question of what he had done about Eaton's letter he said:

"Nothing. These attacks should not be dignified with a reply."

She sat down abruptly on a log bench, begging his forgiveness for im-

246

agining that he could be indiscreet. He sat beside her, his arm about her shoulder, sharing her distress.

"Rachel, as your friend and family lawyer, I must counsel you not to pursue these matters. They should be no part of your life."

"John, isn't knowing better than conjuring up dragons?"

He walked a short distance from her and said in a voice so low she barely could hear:

"The truth is rarely as ugly as we imagine it."

"Then please, John, let me see Eaton's letter."

They entered his office through a side door. She could hear the sound of children playing in the upper rooms. He took the letter from a desk drawer and handed it to her. She read:

DEAR SIR:

Today I have written to Mr. Crutcher with the request that he and you should give me information of the circumstances of General Jackson's marriage. Now seemingly a most prominent rival, they are bringing all their batteries to bear against him; and yesterday I was told by a friend that they were preparing to attack him on this ground. They will doubtless make a very varnished and false presentation of the facts, and delicate as it may be to go into a man's family concerns, necessity demands that we should at least be possessed of the facts, that we may act defensively.

Rachel rested the letter on the desk. Her chest rose and fell rapidly; she seemed unable to get enough air into her lungs. She felt considerable pain about her heart. John poured some water from the heavy silver pitcher on his desk, self-reproaches tumbling from his lips.

"No, John, it's still better this way. Could you take me home?"

She remained in bed for two days, provoked with herself for feeling ill; troubles worked themselves out, given time enough. This one would too.

Andrew returned in mid-June with the news that he had engaged a suite for them at O'Neale's Tavern. He had even investigated the college there for young Andrew and found that it was supervised by a Baptist clergyman of considerable ability. He looked well, his skin bronzed, his eyes clear and peaceable. Rachel was delighted to find that for the first time politics was agreeing with him. Although he had not missed a single day of the Senate session he had risen to speak only twice, and even where he had been involved in controversial issues, such as pleading for internal improvements and for a "judicious tariff," he had remained calm. Straw votes being taken at mass meetings and militia musters indicated him to be a favorite among the people, but when stories came in about the weakening of his chances he appeared to be unperturbed, maintaining that he was neither burning nor running after the office the way Clay and Crawford were.

"Andrew, I must ask you, so that I will know how to plan: in your own mind are you returning to Washington for another session of the Senate, or to move into the White House?"

"According to our best reports the vote is going to be split between Adams, Clay, Crawford and myself. I doubt if anyone of us will get a majority of the electoral votes. The election will therefore be thrown into the House."

"What happens if the House should select one of the others as president?"

He wandered through the implications of her straightforward question as though it were a forest. After a few moments he came out the other side in the clear sunlight and smiled at her with a slightly deprecatory shrug of his left shoulder.

"We remain to congratulate the president at his inauguration, then put our trunks on top of the carriage and come home."

"With no ill will, and no regrets?"

"None."

"Not even if it's William Crawford you must congratulate?"

He clenched his fists at his side.

"My dear, you would have made a good prosecuting attorney."

She saw that he was hurt. "I'm simply trying to find out how we stand for the future," she said gently. "If any of these men is elected, we will be back here by the end of March, to stay?"

"Forever," he said grimly.

"What do you intend to do about the election?"

"Remain home and watch it. Maybe write a few letters. My advisers want me to attend a number of musters and barbecues to meet the people. They say it's a new form of campaigning, because this is the first time the president is going to be elected by the voters instead of the Congress. I'm not going, of course. But could we have open house on July Fourth? It comes on a Sunday this year."

Barbecues being the new vogue, she had a great pit dug down by their old cabin for the roasting of venison, beef and lamb. Four hundred of their neighbors came, spicing the roasted meats with peppered speeches and the reading of editorials. The one that aroused the greatest shout of derision was from a Louisville newspaper which reported that at a military muster in Ohio, where Andrew had drubbed Henry Clay in a test vote . . . "the rowdies, the very dregs of the community, had won the day."

Each week brought its important development, good and bad: John Calhoun decided to content himself with the vice-presidency, and threw his weight behind Andrew; however Andrew's stand on the tariff was losing him votes in the South. William Crawford suffered a paralytic stroke and some of his supporters were talking of shifting to Jackson; while Jesse Benton, no whit placated by the fact that Andrew and his brother had become friends again, issued a pamphlet containing thirty-two charges against Andrew, all of them widely reprinted in the opposition press.

Toward the end of September the family assembled at Johnny Donelson's house, the Mansion, for the wedding of Emily and Andy. The night before, Rachel went into Andy's room to tell him that he and Emily could have a honeymoon trip to Washington City if they desired it; Andy would serve as his uncle's secretary while there, and the young couple could move into the White House if Andrew were elected. Andy hesitated; he was beginning to get a few clients and he did not want to abandon his practice if he would have to start all over again in six months. Rachel tucked the covers around his shoulders, then sat on the edge of the bed and said:

"Andy, we are all gambling. Don't you think you ought to throw in your lot with the family? Uncle Andrew needs you very much."

"Well, I'd like to be the President's secretary . . . and Emily's never been out of the Cumberland. All right. Thank Uncle Andrew for me. And don't tell him that I even thought there was any gamble involved."

They were scheduled to leave for Washington City during the first week in November. Rachel found herself with a packing problem. How long was she to be gone: four months or four years? Did she take only winter clothes, or summer clothes as well? Should she have Sarah Bentley make an inaugural gown in Nashville? Should she keep the house open and running so they could come back to it at the end of March, or cover the furniture and put away the silver, china and linens? Did she interrupt her son's term at school and take him with her, or did she leave him behind?

There was no use going to any of Andrew's friends for information: they had already moved her into the White House, even the usually level-headed John Overton. But she had learned from experience that for the Jacksons fulfillment rarely came when anticipated; generally it was achieved later, when it had lost much of its meaning and savor. She recalled how eagerly Andrew had wanted to be appointed governor of Louisiana back in 1804, and how sure everyone was that President Jefferson would give him the appointment; she remembered how terribly he had wanted to be judge of the Mississippi Territory, and how certain he was that he would get it; she recalled how he had been kept out of Canada during the War of 1812 by an Administration that was desperate for commanding generals, only to be sent to Natchez and then dismissed without firing a shot.

When had he ever achieved anything the easy way? Why should they expect a smooth passage to this highest office in the land when even their

249

simplest ambitions had taken years of disappointment, frustration and defeat?

2

They left the Hermitage on November 7, 1824, in the morocco-lined carriage they had taken to Florida with them three years before. Rachel and Emily rode in the carriage, with Andrew and Andy alongside on their saddle horses. It would be a hard trip in spite of the fact that they were taking the road through Harrodsburg and Lexington, then over the new National Turnpike through Ohio. Rachel dreaded the moment she would reach Harrodsburg; but perhaps it was fitting that she should go over the scene of her early trials on her way to Washington City, for was not Harrodsburg the omnipresent obstacle in the way of Andrew's progress to the White House?

She hardly recognized the town, which had grown from a few scattered cabins to a good-sized village with a comfortable inn. Supper was served before the fire, but she had little appetite and listened instead to Andy and Emily speak excitedly about the ball to be given for them at Lexington by Henry Clay's followers, who had assured them that if Clay could not have the presidency Kentucky would support Jackson.

Later, lying warm under a huge *federbett*, with Andrew sleeping peaceably at her side, apparently unconcerned about Harrodsburg or perhaps even having forgotten that as a young man of twenty-three he had ridden up the Kentucky Road to rescue her, she remembered the smallest details, reliving them as the night wore on: her arrival as a bride at the Robards home, her early attempts to understand Lewis's moodiness and unwillingness to assume responsibility, the later jealous quarrels and their culmination in his announcement that he was casting her out, that he had written to her family for someone to come and get her; and her trip home with Samuel. She remembered her return to Harrodsburg, her hope for her marriage almost completely dissipated, but not knowing what other way of life she could pursue; and Lewis's red-eyed, mean-tempered reception of her. She saw her mother-in-law's thin face on the pillow, telling her to return to Nashville, that she would not be able to live with Lewis; and finally that incredible sight of Andrew in buckskin trousers and leather hunting shirt coming up the road to the Robards door. How much heartache and disillusion she had suffered here! Her brother Samuel had been only twenty years old then, and now his son Andy was twenty-four and sleeping in the next room with his bride; and Andrew was on his way to Washington, perhaps to the presidency . . .

As dawn grayed the bedroom window she felt Andrew stirring beside her. They were in high spirits at breakfast, Emily because she was heading for a formal ball; her husband and nephew because they were reasoning that this reception tonight would be Kentucky's official declaration of support for Andrew; Rachel because she was leaving Harrodsburg behind. As she was handed into the carriage and settled into the comfortable leather cushions she realized that the very name of the town had haunted her . . . haunted? That was the word Lewis Robards had used. Lewis was dead ten full years now, buried in the little cemetery they were passing even then.

A few miles beyond, as they reached the top of a steep and rocky hill, there was heard a splintering sound, then a sharp rending crack. The carriage tongue had broken. Andrew lunged for the lead horse but it was too late; down the hill went carriage, horses and passengers. Several times they teetered on two wheels; once they barely missed going over into a ditch.

When they finally stopped at the bottom of the hill and the two Andrews had lifted their wives out, Rachel said with a wry smile:

"I never did have any luck in that town."

At eleven o'clock on December 7 they crossed the bridge which led into Washington from Virginia. Rachel pointed out to Emily the Bulfinch Dome of the Capitol. They made their way up a dirt road called Pennsylvania Avenue. When they passed the White House Rachel said to Emily, "That's where Mr. and Mrs. Monroe live." Emily leaned out the window, gazing rapturously at the structure.

"And where the four of us are going to live!"

O'Neale's Tavern at the corner of Pennsylvania Avenue and Twenty-first Street had changed hands and was now known as the Franklin House. Rachel and Andrew had a comfortable suite of bedroom and parlor, while Andy and Emily had a considerably smaller one. Rachel was concerned over the fact that these two suites cost them a hundred dollars a week, including their meals.

"I've just found a good reason to hope you are elected, Andrew. The rent at the White House should be somewhat cheaper than it is here."

Andrew shook his head, smiling ironically.

"Not really. Mr. Monroe tells me he is going out poor and dissatisfied."

"And that's the office for which you, Mr. Adams, Mr. Crawford and Mr. Clay are battling so furiously!"

"Maybe it's part of the genius of this form of government that men want to serve in the highest offices, knowing that they will come out impoverished and tender from the many beatings."

Their rooms were crowded with a host of neighbors from Tennessee, officers from the Creek and British wars, the ever-growing clique of president-makers and the many eastern friends Andrew had accumulated since his first trip to the Congress in 1796. It wasn't until midafternoon of the second day that she perceived their callers were men only. No woman had so much as left her card at the Franklin House. Though there was a written invitation from President and Mrs. Monroe to a reception at the White House, Washington society, dominated by the wives of the higher officials, was pointedly staying away. That evening when she went in to bid Emily good night she found her niece in tears. At her feet she saw a newspaper which had obviously been crumpled in high anger. She picked it up, smoothed out the page and saw that it was the Raleigh *Register*. The offending article read:

> *I make a solemn appeal to the reflecting part of the community, and beg of them to ponder well before they place their tickets in the box, how they can justify it to themselves and posterity to place such a woman as Mrs. Jackson! at the head of the female society of the United States.*

Emily sought refuge in her aunt's arms.

"Oh, Aunt Rachel, they're saying the most terrible things about us: that we are vulgar, ignorant and awkward frontierswomen without breeding or decorum. But they have never even met us!"

Rachel had never made any pretension about her education or culture. The imputations against her background she resented more for her parents' sake than for her own. She held Emily at arm's length.

"Wipe your eyes, child. This is all part of what your uncle would call 'the consequences of politics.' As for my lack of social polish, neither Mr. Madison nor Mr. Monroe seemed to notice it."

Late that afternoon they had their first callers: the wives of two senators. Rachel wore a dress of pale brown cambric finished at the bottom by two rows of "letting-in-lace," embroidered between with muslin leaves and touched off by an apron of cambric trimmed with two rows of quilted muslin. She had refused the elaborate hair styling with curls which Emily insisted was the newest thing, saying that she thought the height of her hair on top of her head made her face seem a little less round. She had tea served in her parlor. Her practiced eye perceived that it was curiosity that had helped overcome the ladies' prejudice. She thought, I'll not let them know what I see; but neither will I make a great effort. They must like us for what we are.

It did not prove to be a difficult task: at the end of an hour the women had become friends and were exchanging stories about the domestic problems in different parts of the country. Nor would they leave until Rachel had accepted their invitations to tea.

That, and Elizabeth Monroe's party for them at the White House, broke the ice; Emily was the happiest girl in the capital because there were invitations for each day. The December weather was springlike in its warmth; Rachel paid calls, and went with Andrew to dinner with friends, but they turned down the hundreds of invitations for the evenings to the theater, to parties and balls, content to remain in their hotel sitting room before the fire, smoking their pipes and receiving a few in-

252

timates. On Sunday mornings they went to the Presbyterian church to hear Mr. Baker preach, and one night a week they went to the Methodist church for Mr. Summerfield's prayer meeting.

On December 16, the results from the last state to vote, Louisiana, reached Washington. Andrew had the largest popular vote, 152,901; Mr. Adams came second with 114,023; Mr. Clay 47,217 and Mr. Crawford 46,979. In the electoral votes by states Andrew had a decisive lead also: 99 to Adams's 84, with Crawford showing a surprising 41 to eliminate Mr. Clay from the race. Because no one candidate had achieved a majority the election would go into the House. Andrew's supporters were certain he would be selected: after all, the most people had wanted him, and the most states: he had the electoral votes of eleven states and needed only two more for a majority. With Mr. Clay out, the Kentucky legislature adopted a resolution recommending that their representative in the House support Mr. Jackson; the Missouri representative declared that since the people of his state wanted Clay first and Jackson second, he contemplated casting his vote for General Jackson; Ohio should be his, too, for he had received only a few votes less than Clay, with Mr. Adams running an unpopular third.

In January there were blizzards and snowstorms which brought Rachel down with a cold. The Senate was in session and Andrew attended faithfully each day. Old friends came in for dinner. Though Andrew refused to let them join politics with their food, they were nevertheless surrounded by intrigue: if he would make certain promises, commit himself as to whom he would name Secretary of State, the presidency could be his. There were rumors to the effect that Henry Clay had made such a bargain with John Quincy Adams, Mr. Clay to throw all of his influence and votes to Mr. Adams in return for Mr. Adams's appointment of Mr. Clay as Secretary of State. John Eaton was disturbed, but Andrew did not take it seriously.

"Mr. Adams is an honest man and a good man. He would not engage in a corrupt bargain. If he gets the majority of votes in the House, I will be content. He was my first choice, anyway."

They awakened on the morning of February 9, the day of decision, to find snow falling heavily. Andrew donned a greatcoat and boots and left the hotel in time to reach the Capitol by noon, so that he might participate in the senatorial count which would name John Calhoun as vice-president. When Rachel asked if he were intending to remain after the Senate adjourned and the House took its seat to vote for president, he replied that he did not think it proper for him to be in the House while the members were being polled.

He was back shortly after one o'clock, ordering dinner sent up to their room so they could avoid the milling crowds below in the tavern. The first course had just been set on their parlor table when Andy came in, the expression on his face clearer than any marked ballot: Mr. Adams had been elected on the first count! By prodigious efforts and brilliant maneuvering Henry Clay, singlehanded, had swung Kentucky, Ohio and Missouri behind Adams.

John Eaton stormed in, his face black with disappointment and chagrin, and proceeded to give Henry Clay a thorough castigation. Andrew heard him out, then said quietly:

"That's not altogether fair to Mr. Clay, John. He has a right to throw his influence to the man he thinks best for the job. You remember he once accused me, right on the floor of the House, of being a 'military chieftain who would overthrow the liberties of the people.'"

That evening they attended the last of President Monroe's regular Wednesday levees. Andrew congratulated Mr. Adams cordially. While riding back to the hotel in the Jackson carriage, John Eaton commented on how quiet the city was: no bonfires, no victory celebrations or cheering crowds.

"They wanted you, General," Eaton concluded morosely. "They feel cheated."

But nothing could shake Andrew's calm acceptance. For her own part, Rachel was content. On the whole it had been a decent election; the predictions that the Republic would fall into ruin because its Chief Executive was to be chosen by popular vote had failed to materialize; and so had her own fears of being pilloried by the opposition.

Back in their suite with a log fire crackling on the hearth, they had a hot toddy with Andy and Emily.

"How much longer do you think we will be in Washington, Uncle Andrew?" asked Andy anxiously. "I must be getting back to Nashville and starting my practice. I've got a bride to support, you know."

"Your uncle and I have a wedding present for you that will make things a little easier," said Rachel, knowing how disappointed the two youngsters had been at Andrew's defeat. "We are going to give you the Sanders plantation."

There were expressions of joy and much embracing before the young couple left for their rooms. Despite the fire, the room was chilly; Andrew wrapped a blanket about Rachel's legs, tucking it under her feet.

"Well, Rachel, my dear, I tried to make you First Lady of the land. You are not too disappointed, are you?"

She smiled inwardly, ran her fingers over the bony ridge of his face. "Whatever disappointment I may feel is for you."

"Well, then, I'll be happy to get back to the Hermitage."

"For how long?" she asked softly. ". . . until the next election?"

His eyes met hers. They were stern.

"I will be fifty-eight in a month. Mr. Adams is certain to serve the regular two terms. Surely you don't think at the age of sixty-six . . . ? This is *forever!*"

He used that word to me at home, thought Rachel, but this time he means it. Perhaps at long last he will be content to remain a gentleman planter.

Forever lasted five days. On February 14, President-elect Adams offered the post of Secretary of State to Henry Clay. All hell broke loose, in Washington and across the nation . . . and particularly in their two rooms in the Franklin House. People came and went continually, all passionately protesting against what now appeared to have been a swap of votes for office.

Every ounce of Andrew's calm and acceptance vanished. She knew from the sense of outrage that shook his long lean frame that nothing in his tumultuous career, always excepting the maraudings of the British, had ever made him so utterly determined to avenge a wrong. As he stood in the far corner of the room surrounded by his most ardent supporters, she heard him cry:

"So the Judas of the West has closed the contract and will receive the thirty pieces of silver? The end will be the same. Was there ever witnessed such a bare-faced corruption before?"

A dozen voices answered him at once.

"But surely Mr. Clay will know that the whole country is outraged?" "He can't be so stupid as to accept . . ."

"What, refuse his part of the booty?" Andrew's voice, as it penetrated to her, was shrill and cold. "But he must go before the Senate for confirmation. By the Eternal, gentlemen, I still have a vote there, and I pledge you my word that I shall unboosom myself. This barter of votes is sheer bribery, and if allowed to continue will destroy our form of government."

Three weeks later, in a slanting rainstorm, the family left the capital, all four riding in the carriage with the extra horses tied behind. Andrew was silent, his head on his chest, his eyes closed; he was still smarting from his defeat in the Senate where he had been able to garner only fourteen votes against the appointment of Mr. Clay. She had persuaded him that, as a matter of form, he should attend the inauguration. He had complained to her that Mr. Adams "had been escorted to the Capitol with the pomp and ceremony of guns and drums, which is not consistent with the character of the occasion." However he had been among the first to shake hands with Mr. Adams, and had administered the oath to Calhoun, the new Vice-President, in the Senate.

As the carriage passed the boundary of Washington City she felt him stiffen at her side. He turned in his seat, gazing long and hard at the capital. In his expression she saw the unshatterable resolve she had known so well during the years leading up to the Battle of New Orleans.

He brought his face around to hers.

"We'll be back."

3

They arrived at the Hermitage in the midst of a dry cold spring. The plantation had been well cared for, though both the corn and the cotton needed rain. She had brought home a lemon tree and a box of plants for her garden, and was eager to lay aside her city clothes, don her calico and get out onto the land. She pushed to the back of her mind the knowledge that this was an interlude, that she would have to go through the identical process yet again, enjoying the feel of the rich red earth between her fingers, the fragrance of the adjacent forest in her nostrils and the sight of the tree-covered rolling hills. But what a shame, she thought, that the contest could not have been settled permanently, one way or the other.

Their journey home had been more like a triumphal procession than the return of a defeated candidate; though Andrew had sent word ahead asking that there be no formal demonstrations, the crowds that assembled in every town to greet him were tremendous; at Louisville, in Mr. Clay's home state of Kentucky, they attended a banquet where toasts were drunk to General Jackson as the next president of the United States. It was abundantly clear that the election of 1824 was by no means over; every hour of the day and night between now and November of 1828 would be devoted to this struggle.

The Hermitage became not only the Jackson rallying point, with hundreds of people, letters, couriers, newspapers and broadsides arriving each day, but in actuality a frontier White House in which all elements of the opposition centered, where they looked for leadership. The dominating passion was hatred of Adams and Clay, and the conviction that the will of the people had been thwarted.

One evening, when a particularly torrid discussion filled her dining room and parlor, Rachel found herself unable to stand the intensity of feeling or the volume of noise. She went upstairs to the quiet of her bedroom, where the air was free of tobacco smoke, human odors and the restless movement of excited men. She pulled up a chair to the open window. The tempest in the downstairs of her house was no temporary reaction; the volume, the tone and intensity would rise with the passing weeks and months. Andrew was in deep now, up to the top of his bushy white hair; but would it not be the better part of wisdom for her to withdraw? To provide food and drink and beds for the travelers, and close her ears to what was going on? She had given her husband his freedom to pursue this ambition; was she also obliged to participate? Would it not be better to remove herself from the turbulence, to enjoy her garden, her ever-growing circle of nieces and nephews, to sit before her fire reading or working tranquilly at her loom?

The late summer rains revived the meadows. Their herds of cattle and sheep grew fat and sleek. The harvesting seemed to require more than its usual hard work, but now the cotton and corn were in the storehouse, and the market price was good.

In October of 1825 the Tennessee legislature formally nominated Andrew Jackson for the presidency. He persuaded her to accompany him to the capital at Murfreesboro where he accepted the nomination and officially resigned his seat in the Senate. From here they swung west to visit Jane. The hurtleberries were still abundant in the swamps, and the sloes, serviceberries and grapes were heavy on the vines. Jane's figure was trim, her hair had lost little of its blond light and her eyes were penetratingly clear. She too had taken to smoking a clay pipe. The two sisters sat before the fire talking nostalgically of the past, exclaiming at the vast extent of the Donelson clan throughout Tennessee, Kentucky, Mississippi and Louisiana.

When they passed through Nashville on their way home they found the town abuzz: someone by the name of Day, a seedy little man whose occupation was allegedly that of collecting bills for Baltimore and Pittsburgh merchants, had spent the past few days in Nashville asking endless questions about the Jackson marriage, and displaying a transcript of the Robards divorce records from Harrodsburg, legally copied out for him by the clerk.

On their return to the Hermitage John Overton told them that he believed the material was being collected to hold over Andrew's head in the hope of making him withdraw from the race. John Eaton thought the stories were being assembled for future publication in an effort to provoke Andrew to a violent outburst, perhaps even to a duel, thus reestablishing him as a man of uncontrollable temper.

Rachel went upstairs, undressed, got into bed and pulled the covers over her head. What good to withdraw from the turmoil of the politics about her when at any moment she could become the focus of its vehemence? They were still three years away from the election of 1828, but already some member of the opposition had sought her out as a potential weapon.

Actually there was only one way to avoid the torment: to go to Andrew and say, Andrew, I've made a mistake. I thought I could take the consequences, but I can't. I haven't the moral strength. You must release me. I've been a good and faithful wife to you for nearly forty years. I have given you everything in my power to give, and I've never asked that you forsake anything you wanted to do. I have aided you whenever I was able. We're going on fifty-nine. You know that I love you dearly. I know that you love me. Then, Andrew, sacrifice this last campaign. Fulfill your promise that we would live tranquilly at home and enjoy the companionship of our last years. This is no longer an ordinary political contest; it is war. Surely if you have to become president by placing me on the battlefield, you would refuse?

257

But several hours later, when Andrew came up to bed, she said nothing. Hadn't they undergone countless attacks since their difficulties in 1793; and hadn't they always managed to survive them?

By the spring of 1826 the Hermitage had become headquarters for an integrated political group which established its own newspaper, Duff Green's *Telegraph* in Washington City, and had enthusiastic organizations in nearly every state of the Union, its members comprising not only the westerners who were in favor of Andrew Jackson but also those who were left over from the now-defunct Crawford organization, those who hated Henry Clay, those who could find no sympathy for the temperamentally cold John Quincy Adams or his buffeted Administration, those who belonged to no party but felt that Jackson had been robbed; and lastly the masses of simple folk who never before had had the right to vote for their president and were convinced that General Jackson had earned them this right, that he alone would fight for their interests.

The New York *Courier* was pro-Jackson; nearly every major city had its pro-Jackson newspaper. When the results of the mid-term Congressional election of 1826 were tabulated it was found that most of the Henry Clay men who had helped put Adams into the presidency had been defeated; and that the Jackson supporters had been triumphant in New York, Ohio, Virginia, Georgia, Kentucky, Missouri and Illinois. Once again visitors to the Hermitage assured Rachel that her husband would be the next president.

Then, within a matter of weeks, a pamphlet reached the Hermitage, printed in East Tennessee by Thomas Arnold, who belonged in the camp of the defeated Senator Williams:

> *Andrew Jackson spent the prime of his life in gambling, in horse-racing; and to cap it all tore from a husband the wife of his bosom.*
>
> *Anyone approving of Andrew Jackson must therefore declare in favor of the philosophy that any man wanting someone else's pretty wife has nothing to do but take his pistol in one hand and a horse-whip in another and possess her.*
>
> *General Jackson has admitted that he boarded at the house of old Mrs. Donelson, and that Robards became jealous of him, but he omits the cause of that jealousy . . . that one day Robards surprised General Jackson and his wife exchanging most delicious kisses.*

Her first reaction was one of shame: shame that this assault should have sprung from her home state and from one of her neighbors. She told herself that she would be calm, that she would not become upset over these scurrilous lines; yet she burned inwardly at the implication of an illicit carnality; of a vulgar, behind-the-back deception which debased her motives as well as her conduct. Andrew grew silent and grim, but no word of the pamphlet passed between them. She burned her copy, resolutely putting it out of her mind.

She had underestimated the power of the printed word. Shortly after, Colonel Charles Hammond, editor of a Cincinnati newspaper, emboldened by the fact that he now had a published precedent, wrote an article for his paper based on the Arnold pamphlet, adding to it the stories collected by Mr. Day. The clipping was sent to her anonymously through the mail:

If the President be a married man, his wife must share the distinction of the station he occupies. Her qualifications for the station, her character, and standing, her personal defects, or excellencies, must all be drawn out, and made subjects of remark, and will be commended, caricatured or ridiculed, as they may furnish occasion.

If she be weak and vulgar she cannot escape becoming a theme for ridicule, a portion of which, and its consequent contempt, must attach to her husband . . . We must see a degraded female placed at the head of the female society of the nation, or we must proclaim and urge the fact as a ground for excluding her husband.

Wherever he was known, public rumor had circulated suspicions as to the correctness of his matrimonial alliance . . . It was no case of mere surmise against an unmarried female, arising out of possible indiscretion, and resting upon a peculiar freedom of manners. On the contrary . . . it was an accusation of gross adultery, in which outrage upon the rights of the husband was urged against General Jackson, and desertion from her husband to the arms of a paramour, was charged against the wife.

In September, 1793, twelve men, constituting a jury, after hearing proof, declared . . . that Mrs. Robards was guilty of adultery. Ought a convicted adultress, and her paramour husband, to be placed in the highest offices?

Her arms fell wearily to her side. The Cincinnati newspaper dropped to the floor. There it was at last, the dread and awful word that had pursued her all of her married life, that had changed her from a gay and happy young woman into a wounded prisoner within her own walls: *Adulteress.*

4

That night a group of tight-lipped, white-faced men sat in Andrew's study behind the closed door and spoke in voices so low that no sound escaped the room. The meeting lasted late, but she remained rigid and wide-eyed before the parlor fireplace, waiting for Andrew to come. It was in this very room he had sought her permission to run for the Senate and the presidency. He had asked, "And what about you, Rachel?" She had said, "I will accept the consequences."

It was midnight when he came into the room. He explained quietly: "There is a cloud collecting and I must endeavor to burst it before it bursts upon us."

". . . yes . . . but by what means?"

"By making our position impregnable. We are going to get testimonials from the Reverend Craighead's widow, and Polly's mother, General Smith's widow. They've known us from the beginning."

"Testimonials . . . about what?" she asked numbly.

He leaned down, put his arms about her and raised her from the chair, kissing her cool cheeks and tired eyes.

"I know how hard it is on you, darling, but we must defend ourselves at every point where we are attacked. There's no part of my life that they are not trying to falsify and degrade, but we will meet them head on with documents and affidavits, and we will beat them every time."

She wanted to say, That is all right for public matters having to do with your work! How can it help me to prove that Colonel Hammond is a liar when he accuses me of "gross adultery"? To admit still more people into our private affairs, and spread the controversy ever wider?

The letters written by the Reverend Craighead's widow and General Daniel Smith's widow were loving tributes. They told the story of her difficulties with Lewis Robards, of her several attempts to reconcile with him, of his going before the Virginia legislature for a divorce. These testimonials would be enough to convince any man of good will; but word now arrived from their friend Sam Houston in Washington City that Hammond was in Henry Clay's service.

The testimonials were no sooner locked in her strongbox than Editor Hammond made his next move. He informed Senator John Eaton that Rachel and Andrew Jackson had never been married in Natchez! Rachel dropped her gardening tools, thrust her hands into the deep pockets of her earth-stained, heavy muslin apron. If she had married Andrew Jackson in 1791 when convinced that Robards had been granted his divorce by the Virginia legislature, then any sin or crime she had committed during the next two years of living with Andrew had been of a technical nature. Surely most people would understand her predicament, and would not hold that unfortunate situation against her. But if Editor Hammond convinced the country that she had not been married to Andrew Jackson in Natchez, that she had lived with him openly in an unwed state for more than two years until Lewis went into the Harrodsburg court and secured his divorce, then that would appear to have been bold concupiscence.

They had no written document of their marriage in Natchez. The ceremony performed at Springfield had been considered legal and binding by the Americans living in the Spanish territory, but to whom did they go for proof after thirty-six years? Old Thomas Green was long since dead, many of his descendants and friends also were dead, the rest widely scattered. Andrew dispatched William Lewis down the Mississippi to find and bring back any written record he could trace.

Taking this attack on a Tennessee woman as a personal affront, the members of the Culture Club, now known as the Nashville Ladies Club, went out of their way to express their vote of confidence. Many letters came through the mail to the Hermitage; three of the ladies came to call. Rachel received them in her parlor and served tea. It was a heart-warming hour for her.

By way of further buttressing their defenses a mass meeting was called by Andrew's closest friends at the Nashville courthouse. Andy attended and rode home to bring news of hundreds of people gathering in the square to pledge their support to the Jacksons, resolving:

"*To detect and arrest falsehood and calumny by the publication of truth.*"

A committee of eighteen of the most respected citizens of the state, among them their former friend Judge John McNairy, Colonel Edward Ward, former Ambassador George W. Campbell, Thomas Claiborne, a relative of the governor of Louisiana, Justice John Catron of the United States Supreme Court, two members of the highest court of Tennessee and a number of others who had long disagreed politically with Andrew, was set up to examine all materials relative to the relationship and marriages of Rachel and Andrew Jackson. John Overton was to head the committee.

He came directly out from Nashville to the Hermitage, joining them for dinner. Andrew poured a drink from the sideboard, saying as they clinked glasses:

"John, this is one time I'm not going to ask you to stay out of my private affairs. I want you to get in just as deeply as you can and see that the committee obtains the full truth."

John picked up a spoon from the sideboard, using it to stir the sugar around in the bottom of his whisky glass.

"I'll be as strict and objective as I ever was as a member of the Tennessee Supreme Court. No material will be accepted that can't withstand the most relentless scrutiny; witnesses will state for the record only what they know; and we will publish only what we can prove. The language of the report will be kept calm and judicial; nothing will be allowed that won't hold up as the authentic truth when looked at a hundred years from today."

There was a moment of silence in the dining room. The men turned to Rachel. John's eyes bulked gun-metal gray. She gave him a quick nod of approbation, happy that he was undertaking to head up her defense;

he had been her friend at the Robards house in Harrodsburg even before she had met Andrew.

"I haven't approved of any of these methods of defending ourselves, John, but I think this one is right. I know you will do a fine job. Let us publish our story to the world, once and for all, and then rest content."

The full report of the Overton committee, as well as the testimonial letters from Mrs. Craighead and Mrs. Smith, was published in the *United States Telegraph* on June 22, 1827, and widely reproduced throughout the country. Reluctant as Rachel had been to expose her intimate relationships to the eyes of thousands of strangers who had known nothing about them before, she found that the report had an immediate and salutary effect. Letters came to the Hermitage from Washington City, Philadelphia, New York and New Orleans offering congratulations "on the vindication of your innocence," and assuring her of continued friendship.

She locked away the newspapers, letters and reports, going through the automatic gesture of washing her hands of them. "I'll read no more charges and I'll participate in no more answers. They've done me all the harm they can. With God's help, I've risen above it."

She had reckoned without her own family. Emily called one morning when Rachel was in the dining room having breakfast. She pulled up a chair to the dining table and placed upon it a paper she held in her hand.

"Aunt Rachel," she began, straightening out the paper, "have you seen this copy of Hammond's latest pamphlet? We can't let them say this kind of thing about you. After all, we Donelsons have our pride!"

Rachel thought, She surely is Johnny's daughter!

"We've got to release our own statement," continued Emily. "The honor of our family is at stake! When you have read it, I'm certain you'll join with us in issuing a Donelson answer."

Filled with an almost ineluctable dread, Rachel's eyes went down the tight-packed column:

It is an insult to common sense to say that Overton's narrative does not place the seduction and adultery in as prominent and reprehensible a light as it is placed by the legislative and judicial proceedings themselves.

Mrs. Jackson was unfaithful to her marriage vow with Robards. No man of the world can believe that she would have been guilty of the great indiscretion of flying beyond the reach of her husband, with a man charged to be her paramour, were she innocent of the charge.

It would be as rational to give credit of innocence, had they been found at midnight, undressed, in the same bed.

262

When they assumed the open relation of husband and wife, it was an illegal and criminal act. They are the mere creatures of passion. General Jackson and Mrs. Robards . . . voluntarily, and for the gratification of their own appetites, placed themselves in a situation to render it necessary that Mrs. Robards should be convicted of desertion and adultery . . .

Those then, who believe that an adulteress, who has become, after a time, the legal wife of her paramour is not a suitable person to be placed at the head of the female society of the United States, cannot with propriety, vote for General Jackson . . .

The small print swam before her eyes. She dug her nails into her palms, then drank the last bitter dregs of the coffee in the bottom of her cup. When Emily left she sat frozen in the chair. Had the country gone insane, that the campaign should be waged on whether or not she had lived in adultery with Andrew? What had those two years so long ago got to do with his accomplishments or capacity for being president? He had been a lawyer, an attorney general, a congressman, a senator, a judge, a general, a governor; he had served his country long and well.

She did not hear him come into the room and stand behind her. When his hand touched her shoulder she turned, saw that his face was ashen. He held in his hand a copy of the same publication that had stirred Emily to action.

"Sit down, my dear. I'll get you a cup of hot coffee."

He sank into the chair Emily had used, staring at her with rout in his fierce blue eyes.

"Do you know that this is the most difficult task of my life, to be forced to sit here, impotent, while they call you foul names, debase our love and our marriage? I've never wanted anything so much in my life as to go to Cincinnati and shoot that slimy creature in his tracks. When I realize that I let myself get into a position where, no matter what they say about you, I cannot rise up in your defense . . ."

"Andrew, we knew this would happen. I fully expected it during the first campaign. It seemed to me a miracle that it didn't happen. But it was only a postponement, and the storm is doubly violent now because it's been so long in the making. Surely you knew that this would be part of what you called 'the consequences'?"

"No. I . . . didn't . . . It's unprecedented! They've never attacked a defenseless woman . . ."

He stopped, sat in silence for a moment, his misery hovering about him like a cloak. Then he drew a letter from his pocket. It had just arrived from John Eaton, who was serving as senator in Washington and directing the Jackson campaign. "You hear what Eaton says? 'Be cautious, be still, be quiet. Avoid all issues and controversies. Weigh and bale your cotton and sell it; and if you see anything about yourself just throw the paper into the fire, and go on to weigh the cotton. All you have to do is remain quietly at the Hermitage and the people will sweep you into office.'"

He rose, went to the window and stared out moodily, his back to her. ". . . sweep you into office." He turned around abruptly. "I saw it as a chance for service. There's so much I thought I could contribute to the growth of our country. But now that they're crucifying you . . . is it worth it?"

To herself she murmured, It's too late for this kind of questioning.

5

She found herself living in two diametrically opposed worlds. The first concerned itself with the normal routine of her everyday life, and most of it was pleasant; the dining table she had bought in New Orleans was always set for its full capacity of thirty guests for dinner. There were acquaintances from Louisiana who were passing through Tennessee on their way north; a honeymoon couple whose family had known her family in Accomac County in Virginia; newly made friends from New York and Pennsylvania, traveling south: all roads appeared to lead through the Hermitage. The flow of visitors constituted a heavy drain on their purse; an obscure disease had hit their livestock and they had lost three thousand dollars' worth of horses in the last eighteen months. Although they had brought in a good cotton crop, the market was so low as to leave no measurable profit. In addition she had never found anyone to take the place of Jane Caffrey as a household manager, and so most of the unending duties fell upon her shoulders.

But these difficulties were supportable, for they represented a sane workaday world; and no matter how great the problem or disappointment, as when their young grandnephew, Andrew Jackson Hutchings, was expelled from Cumberland College, or her son got into some irresponsible scrape from which his father had to bail him out, she could cope with them because they were part of a normal pattern.

But there was a second world that engulfed her like a black, noxious cloud, a world filled with hysteria and insanity, with which she found herself unable to cope. There was no tiny segment of her husband's personal or professional life that was left unraked: he had tried to kill Governor Sevier in a public brawl, had murdered Charles Dickinson in cold blood, had conspired with Aaron Burr to destroy the Union, had executed loyal militiamen during the Creek wars, had robbed and maltreated the Indians, bullied and outraged the Spanish, had been in flight from the British when stopped by Monroe, had fought the Battle of New Orleans stupidly, stolen thousands of dollars of military funds, flouted the civil law and set himself up as a military dictator . . .

Andrew's advisers prevailed upon him to make the trip for the January 8, 1828, anniversary of the Battle of New Orleans on the grounds that such a celebration would receive national attention that would serve as an excellent starting point for the final push to the presidency. Andrew asked Rachel to go with him, assuring her that the steamboat *Pocahontas* could actually make its way up the Mississippi against the current.

They stood on the prow watching the snow-lined banks of the Tennessee give way to the semi-tropical verdure of the Mississippi, much of it country they knew so well. She had been reluctant to leave the Hermitage, but she enjoyed the sight at Natchez where the heights above the river were filled with spectators cheering their arrival. At New Orleans there was a picturesque forest of masts rising from the water as the fleet of steamboats came to escort them; and at ten in the morning the thick mist that covered the water began to rise, and the city with its many steeples became visible. They stood on the back gallery of the *Pocahontas,* while the thousands of people on the banks and in the boats cheered and the artillery kept up a constant fire.

They were met by Edward and Louise Livingston. When Andrew realized how much the two women liked each other he promised Rachel that if he were elected president, Edward Livingston would be given a position in the government and Rachel would have Louise by her side in Washington City to help with the arduous social life.

But even as they were returning to the Hermitage the opposition launched its answer to the victory celebration in the form of *Truth's Advocate, A Monthly Anti-Jackson Expositor* published in Cincinnati by Colonel Charles Hammond, the material being promptly reproduced in all of the Clay newspapers.

There was no respite. Each week saw deadlier charges hurled, elaborations on a theme that fed on itself, until Andrew Jackson had "torn her from her nuptial couch and seduced her"; they had "indulged their unbridled appetites" during all the time she was married to Robards; she had not gone down the river with Colonel Stark and his wife, but had followed in a second boat on which she and Andrew had lived alone. Her relations with Andrew had been a "standing jest for nearly thirty years"; she was even today an adulteress, for there never had been any marriage ceremony performed between Rachel and Andrew Jackson, not even that second time in 1794.

. . . adulteress . . . Adulteress . . . ADULTERESS . . .

The attack was so sharp and so virulent that the walls of the Hermitage were not thick enough to hold it out. It was mixed in the air she breathed and the food she ate; at night when she went upstairs while Andrew remained below at his desk frantically writing hundreds of letters of defense and justification during the dark hours, not even the act of locking her door and closing her windows could keep out the malignant wind. She lay rigidly in bed, every bone and muscle in her body aching, her eyes wide and staring, hearing the word reverberate hollowly about the room, encompassing her, possessing her.

The election approached; the tension mounted. The Adams press now joined the hunt, referring to her as "the woman they call Mrs. Jackson." They accused her of having caused the early death of Lewis Robards; and at long last, thirty-five years after she and Andrew had been forced to remain quiet and allow Lewis Robards to convict her of adultery, the record from the Harrodsburg court as copied out for Mr. Day was splashed across the press of the nation. Seventy thousand dollars of the government's contingent funds were used to print the anti-Jackson, anti-Rachel material; fifteen thousand pamphlets a month containing the charges against Rachel and Andrew Jackson were being franked by the Adams and Clay supporters in Congress and sent through the mails.

When she was the most soul-sick she went for comfort to her little church. She had been praying for a cessation of the attacks; now her clergyman, Dr. A. D. Campbell, taught her that instead of praying for herself she should be praying for her traducers, for they were the ones who would need her prayers on Judgment Day. That night she knelt by the side of the bed and prayed:

"Forgive them, O Lord, for they know not what they do."

Summer came on. Hundreds of test ballots were taken throughout the land. In most of them Andrew emerged triumphant by landslide proportions. She thought, Perhaps now, if not from compassion, then from fear of retribution, the vehemence will cease. But there were still several months before the official casting of the ballots; crude caricatures were being distributed showing her as an ignorant backwoodswoman, ribald songs were chanted about her in the streets of the big cities, obscene poems were printed by the thousands.

William Lewis returned from Natchez, having been unable to locate a record of their first marriage. She listened to his report to Andrew with half an ear: there was nothing further they could say of her. Besides, it was growing increasingly difficult for her to breathe, and she was almost never without pain in her chest. Merely to get through her daily tasks was taking all of her energy and concentration.

She was no stranger to the insidious power of rumor and gossip; she had lived with it a very long time and knew its many faces. And so she was only mildly startled when John Eaton and William Lewis came to her and suggested that perhaps it would be better advised for her not to join the triumphal procession to Washington City, or the inaugural festivities, since tempers were high and any show of violence would necessarily endanger her. She knew that her friends truly believed her innocent of wrongdoing, nevertheless the opposition had at last succeeded in making even them consider her a liability and a burden. That night as she was preparing for bed she said to Andrew:

266

"My dear, if you should be elected I think it best that you go to Washington City alone. I'll come on later, after you've been installed in office, when the election hysteria has died down. Then I can slip in quietly, without causing comment."

He was both angry and hurt, though she could not judge which emotion predominated. He jumped to his feet and stood towering above her.

"Don't you see how wrong that would be! If you remain at home you admit that you are frightened. Even worse, you would make it look as though I didn't want you. Or that you are not qualified to serve as First Lady. This will be as much your triumph as mine; we'll go to Washington City together. You'll be by my side when I take the oath of office. And then God pity those wretches who have made life so miserable for you. I know you pray to God that He forgive your enemies; I never can."

On November 24, Governor Carroll of Tennessee rode up to the Hermitage in great excitement. Rachel received him in the parlor. The governor's face was shining. He bowed low, kissed Rachel's hand, exclaimed:

"I would let no one else bring the news. I wanted to be the first to tell you that Andrew Jackson has been elected president of the United States."

It was over. She had survived. She stood before the governor in silence, hearing only the tremendous pounding of her own heart, which felt as though it would burst through her chest. When Andrew came into the room she put her arms about his neck, kissed him on the lips and said:

"I'm happy for you, darling."

Nashville went wild with joy. A huge celebration banquet was planned for December 23. It seemed to Rachel as though the entire Cumberland Valley came to the front door of the Hermitage to shake Andrew's hand and then hers. The Nashville Ladies Club was having a beautiful and costly wardrobe prepared for her. Yet she observed that there was not much of rejoicing or exultation in Andrew. He seemed subdued. She asked herself, Is it because he has suffered so terribly these past two years, suffered for both himself and for me? As she watched him accept the congratulations of throngs that came out from Nashville, heard the crowds cheer him when they rode into town, the picture flashed into her mind of Andrew in New Orleans after his great triumph, when the Louisianians had lined the streets and the roads crying out his praises, and he had doffed his hat awkwardly as though his spirit were humbled and abashed.

Only now did she realize how much burden there was in every victory; Andrew would become Chief Executive of a torn, almost shattered country, with whole classes of its society loathing him and predicting that he would bring the mob, the canaille, into government, that the

267

day he took office would mark the end of the great American Republic. She found herself pitying her husband for the terrifying task that lay ahead of him.

And what of herself? What of the vast responsibility that faced her as mistress of the White House? The scandalmongering would die down, but was it possible that these years of vituperation could ever wholly be forgotten? Where in all of Washington City would she find privacy from the probing eyes of strangers who wondered what part of the story might be true? She had no choice; she could not refuse to go to Washington City with Andrew. The law might question her Natchez marriage, but there was no question in her own heart. There, under Tom Green's glowing chandelier, she had inextricably tied her fate to Andrew's . . . and would today, if she had it to do all over again.

6

There was much work to be done. This time she did not have to ask her husband whether they were going for a few months or a few years. He told her that if they were fortunate they might get back to the Hermitage for a visit in the summer of 1830, but that she was not to count on it. The plantation would be well run; but what of the house itself? Should they cover the furnishings, batten down the blinds? Or should they leave it as it was with perhaps a niece or nephew installed so that their friends could continue to stop over? And for that matter, how completely furnished was the White House? Knowing Andrew's propensity for keeping his home full of guests, had she not better take along large quantities of silver, dishware, linens?

December was hectic; when she found herself growing increasingly tired and tense she called Dr. Samuel Hogg, their family physician, who bled her, relieving the pressure. Several times when she was supposed to go into Nashville for fittings or to buy what they needed for their trip she could not summon the energy to get out of bed. They were scheduled to leave the Hermitage for Washington City immediately after the holidays.

On Monday, December 17, she received an urgent message from Sarah Bentley: if she did not come in for the final fitting on her inaugural dress and reception gown she could not possibly have them ready by the time she left for Washington City. Rachel knew how disappointed Sarah would be, and Andrew too, if she did not take these clothes with her; digging deep into her reserves, she dressed and was driven in the carriage to Nashville.

The fittings were long and exhausting, for Sarah was determined that her gowns should reflect credit on Tennessee. When they were finished, Rachel said:

268

"Sarah, when my boy comes for me, please tell him I will be at the Nashville Inn; I'll rest there till time to go home."

She walked a block down the street, entered the inn, found the small back parlor deserted at this hour, and with a sigh of relief sank into a big comfortable chair in a corner hidden from the larger lounging room just beyond.

She had fallen into a half sleep when fragments of conversation drifting through the open doorway from the next parlor awakened her. Two women were talking; the voices sounded familiar . . . she had heard them before: loud, haughty, metallic; but there were differences too . . . she could not be sure . . .

Then she stopped listening to the intonations and began to hear the words. The women were discussing the election and the imminent departure of the Jacksons. The one with the deeper, chesty voice asked what would become of the country now that the lowest and most ignorant class of society had come into power, with a drinking, gambling bully and murderer sitting in the White House. The voice that was higher and shriller said she shuddered to think what Washington City's international society would make of his dumpy, pipe-smoking illiterate backwoodswoman who was now to become First Lady of the land.

"Lady?" exclaimed the first. "How can you call her a lady . . . ?"

Rachel gripped the arms of her chair and raised herself up. She knew what was coming next. She planted her feet firmly on the carpet, her legs a little apart, digging her toes into her shoes, her back arched, her arms rigidly outstretched to catch and hold the heavy weight.

". . . it's just as the newspapers kept asking: shall there be a *whore* in the White House?"

She was totally unprepared. A sharp, knifelike stab of almost unendurable pain went through her heart and down her left arm. She sagged, fell into the chair behind her. Had she thought it was over? It would never be over!

To her lips came a prayer:

No, no, dear God, not here . . . in a strange hotel parlor. Please let me get home . . . to my own roof . . . my own bed . . . my husband . . .

With an intense effort she dragged herself to her feet once again, walked stiffly to the entrance.

Her carriage was waiting. The boy helped her in. She leaned back against the cushions. Her left arm felt useless . . . paralyzed. Her head was heavy, her thoughts cloudy; there was only the one determination remaining: to hold on until she got back to the Hermitage.

Halfway home the road paralleled a creek. The sound of the clearly flowing water was refreshing. Perhaps if she bathed her face a little in the cold water it would revive her? She did not want to reach home in this state; Andrew would be so frightened and upset . . .

She asked the driver to stop, laboriously descended from the car-

269

riage, then pushed her way down the shallow bank to the water's edge. She took off her hat, loosened her coat, dipped her handkerchief into the stream, held it against her eyes and brow.

The coldness was good. She leaned farther over the water, cupping handfuls of it and patting it back through her hair. She felt relieved; the intense pain in her heart was lessening. Into her mind flashed another journey home, another stream where she had run water through her long black hair and cooled her fevered thoughts: she had been ordered out of the Robards house and had stopped by a little stream to make herself presentable before facing her family, resolved to hold her head high, secure in the knowledge that she had done no wrong.

How surely the end was implicit in the beginning!

Andrew was completely distraught. He sat by her bed clasping her hand in his, unable to speak. The neighborhood doctor bled her at once, saying to Andrew: "Spasmodic affection . . . muscles of chest and left shoulder . . . irregular action of heart . . ." Dr. Heiskell arrived from Nashville, found that the first bleeding had not caused an abatement of the symptoms, and bled her again. It was night before Dr. Hogg reached the Hermitage; he bled her a third time, and now all her pain seemed to vanish. Andrew placed a pillow behind her and raised her a little in the bed, then seated himself in a chair beside her.

She did not know how much time passed; at least twice it was night, then twice it was day. Andrew never left her side. Dimly she heard the doctors telling him that he must get some sleep or he would collapse: there was the celebration banquet in Nashville the next day which he must attend, and it was not right that he should receive this acclaim from his neighbors looking like a death's-head.

She raised herself slightly and managed a little smile. She felt no pain; in fact she could not feel her body at all.

"I'm so much . . . better," she said slowly. "Could you put me in that chair . . . in front of the fire? We'll visit for a little while . . . you'll have a night's sleep."

He put a fresh log on the fire, then lifted her out of the bed, covers and all. He sat on the floor before her, his long thin arms holding the blankets securely about her knees, his devotion carved deep in every line of his face.

"Andrew, you must prepare to go to Washington City without me. I'll follow in a few weeks . . . as soon as I am strong enough."

"No!" He rose to his knees. "I won't go without you! I can't face it . . . I can wait . . . I have time to wait. We've endured so much, we can conquer this too. Your love is the most important thing in my life. I'll not set foot out of this house until you are able to stand by my side . . . as you always have."

She took his thin, seamed face in her hands, remembering the first

270

time she had seen him, when he had knocked on the door of the Donelson stockade and she had stood smiling as she gazed at the bushy red hair, the piercing blue eyes, the overly large mouth and the powerful chin. Well, his hair was snow-white now, his lips taut, his brow and cheeks deeply furrowed. But he had earned his age; and now he would go on to the highest position in the land. How richly his life had been fulfilled; and in the doing, how richly it had fulfilled hers!

She kissed him on the forehead, murmured:

"That's what I wanted to hear you say, my darling. Everything's all right now. Go to bed and get some sleep. I will be here in the morning. And I'll go to Washington City with you."

He kissed her good night. She watched him go out the door, across the hall to the guest bedroom.

She sat watching the flames light up the fireplace and the room . . . then felt herself slipping . . .

She fell. In the distance she heard the sound of running feet. Someone picked her up. Was it . . . ? Yes, it was Andrew. That was good. That was the way it should be.

With the last of her consciousness she felt herself put into bed. Her head was on her own pillow. She felt Andrew's tear-stained cheek on hers, heard him say over and over:

"I love you, I love you."

Somewhere within herself, at a great and receding distance, she smiled. And then she knew nothing more.

7

He left Gadsby's Hotel with a small group of friends and walked up Pennsylvania Avenue to the Capitol. There were patches of snow underfoot. Cannons boomed, the thousands of people lining the avenue cheered lustily; he heard neither. He entered the Capitol through a rear basement, made his way to a roped-off portico where Chief Justice Marshall administered the oath while the enormous assemblage roared its approval. His mind was back at the Hermitage; he had told Rachel that she would be by his side when he took this oath of office, but she lay buried in her beloved garden in the Cumberland Valley. The Reverend Hume had said, "The righteous shall be in everlasting remembrance." And so it would be.

He mounted his horse and rode to the White House. Long tables had been set up in the beautiful East Room, laden with orange punch, ice cream and cakes. This was to be his first reception; yet he hated the thought of it, walking the horse slowly, his head lowered. Protocol had dictated who might be invited: the highest-ranking members of Washington society: the friends of John Quincy Adams and Henry Clay, who had branded him an ignoramus, a thief, a coward, a bully, a liar, a revolutionist who would destroy the Republic. Aside from a few personal friends and his adherents in Congress, there would be no one at the reception he wanted; none of his followers or the people who had elected him. No, the White House and the East Room would be filled with the bejeweled women and the socially and politically important men who had despised his wife, called her every foul name they could conjure up; and had ended by murdering his beloved Rachel. These were the people he must receive!

But he had reckoned without the mob of his followers who had come to Washington City from every part of the Union to witness his inauguration. They poured down Pennsylvania Avenue, streamed through the gates of the White House, fought their way into the East Room, devoured the ice cream and cakes and orange punch. They climbed on the furniture to catch a glimpse of Andrew, soiling the damask chairs with their muddy boots, staining the carpets, breaking glasses and china, shouting and surging and pushing, all thousands of them, wanting to reach Andrew, to embrace him.

He stood at the back of the room, imprisoned, yet feeling the first glint of happiness since Rachel's death. These were the people; they had stood by him. They had loved Rachel, they had vindicated her. For that, he loved them, and would fight for them the rest of his days.

BIBLIOGRAPHY

RACHEL JACKSON

There is only one biography published about Rachel Jackson, *General Jackson's Lady*, by Mary French Caldwell (privately printed by the Ladies' Hermitage Association, Nashville, Tennessee, 1936). This is indispensable source material. There are chapters on Rachel Jackson in *Some American Ladies*, by Meade Minnigerode (G. P. Putnam's Sons, New York, 1926), and *First First Ladies*, by Mary Ormsbee Whitton (Hastings House, New York, 1948). There are two chapters on Mrs. Jackson in *Andrew Jackson and Early Tennessee History*, by S. G. Heiskell (Ambrose Printing Co., Nashville, Tennessee, 1918), Vol. I, Chapter 21; Vol. III, Chapter 11. There is a pamphlet, *Rachel Jackson*, by Nellie Treanor Stokes (printed by the Ladies' Hermitage Association, Nashville, Tennessee, 1942); a *Saturday Evening Post* article (July 25, 1925), "Jackson and his Beloved Rachel," by John Trotwood Moore, and she and Andrew are the main characters in Alfred Leland Crabb's excellent mood and atmosphere novel, *Home to the Hermitage*. Important material on the Hermitage and Rachel's family is to be found in *Emily Donelson of Tennessee* in two volumes by Pauline Wilcox Burke (Garrett and Massie, Inc., Richmond, Virginia, 1941); *Andrew Jackson's Hermitage*, by Mary French Caldwell (Ladies' Hermitage Association, 1933); *The Hermitage*, by Stanley F. Horn (Greenberg, New York, 1950); *The History of Pittsylvania County*, by Maude Carter Clement (J. P. Bell Company, Inc., Lynchburg, Virginia, 1929).

ANDREW JACKSON

The seven volumes of Andrew Jackson's Correspondence, which also include most of Rachel Jackson's correspondence, were edited by John Spencer Bassett and published by the Carnegie Institute, 1926-35.

(Listed Chronologically, According to Date of Publication)
The Life of Andrew Jackson, John Reid and John Eaton (1817)

Biography of Andrew Jackson, Philo A. Goodwin, Esq. (1832)

The Life of Andrew Jackson, Amos Kendall (pamphlet form, Library of Congress, apparently published in 1843)

Life of Andrew Jackson, James Parton, 3 vols. (1860)

Andrew Jackson, William Graham Sumner (1897)

The Jacksonian Epoch, Charles H. Peck (1899)

The Life and Times of Andrew Jackson, A. S. Colyar, Vol. I (1904)

History of Andrew Jackson, Augustus C. Buell, 2 vols. (1904)

The True Andrew Jackson, Cyrus Townsend Brady (1906)

Andrew Jackson and Early Tennessee History, S. G. Heiskell, 3 vols. (1918)

The Reign of Andrew Jackson, Frederic Austin Ogg (1919)

The Party Battles of the Jackson Period, Claude G. Bowers (1922)

The Life of Andrew Jackson, John Spencer Bassett (1925)

Andrew Jackson, An Epic in Homespun, Gerald W. Johnson (1927)

The Cavalier of Tennessee, Meredith Nicholson (novel, 1928)

Andrew Jackson, The Gentle Savage, David Karsner (1929)

The Life of Andrew Jackson, Marquis James, 2 vols. (1938)

The Age of Jackson, Arthur M. Schlesinger, Jr. (1945)

Home to the Hermitage, Alfred Leland Crabb (novel, 1948)

SOURCE BOOKS ON TENNESSEE

Civil and Political History of the State of Tennessee, John Haywood (1823)

The Annals of Tennessee, J. G. M. Ramsey, A.M., M.D. (1853)

Old Times in Tennessee, Josephus C. Guild (1878)

History of Davidson County, W. W. Clayton (1880)

Dropped Stitches in Tennessee History, John Allison (1897)

The Backward Trail, Will T. Hale (1899)

Old Tales Retold, Octavia Zollicoffer Bond (1900)

History of Tennessee, W. R. Garrett and A. V. Goodpasture (1903)

Historic Sumner County, Tennessee, Jay Guy Cisco (1909)

Historical and Beautiful Country Homes Near Nashville, Tennessee, Mrs. James E. Caldwell (1911)

A History of Tennessee and Tennesseans, Will T. Hale and Dixon L. Merritt, first 3 vols. (1913)

The Conquest of the Old Southwest, Archibald Henderson, Ph.D., D.C.L. (1920)

Economic and Social Beginnings of Tennessee, Albert C. Holt, Ph.D. (Dissertation submitted to George Peabody College, Nashville, Tennessee, in partial requirement for Doctor of Philosophy degree, 1923)

Tennessee, the Volunteer State, John Trotwood Moore, editor (1923)

Early Travels in the Tennessee Country, Samuel Cole Williams (1928)

From Frontier to Plantation in Tennessee, Thomas Perkins Abernethy (1932)

History of Homes and Gardens of Tennessee, Mrs. John Trotwood Moore, collaborating, Roberta Seawell Brandau, editor (1936)

Tennessee, Federal Writers Project of Works Progress Administration of Tennessee (1939)

Tennessee: A Political Study, William H. Combs and William E. Cole (1940)

The Tennessee, Donald Davidson (1946)

Farming and Progress, Published by Department of Agriculture, State of Tennessee, 37th Biennial Report (1947-48)

SOURCE BOOKS ON PERSONALITIES

Memoirs of Aaron Burr, Matthew L. Davis, 2 vols. (1837)

The Life and Times of Aaron Burr, James Parton (1858)

Life and Times of Henry Clay, Samuel M. Smucker (1860)

James Madison, Sydney Howard Gay (1884)

Memoir of Mrs. Edward Livingston, Louise Livingston Hunt (1886)

Thomas H. Benton, Theodore Roosevelt (1899)

Henry Clay, Carl Schurz (1899)

Thomas Hart Benton, William M. Meigs (1904)

Thomas Hart Benton, Joseph M. Rogers (1905)

The Life of John Marshall, Albert J. Beveridge, Vol. III (1919)

Autobiography of Martin Van Buren, John C. Fitzpatrick, editor, Vol. II (1920)

Aaron Burr, Samuel H. Wandell and Meade Minnigerode (1927)

An Epoch and a Man (*Martin Van Buren and His Times*) Denis Tilden Lynch (1929)

Great American Personalities, Paul Perigord (1936)

Thomas Jefferson, Claude G. Bowers, 3 vols. (1936)

Henry Clay, Bernard Mayo (1937)

Aaron Burr, Nathan Schachner (1937)

Edward Livingston, William B. Hatcher (1940)

Men of Spine in Mississippi, Clayton Rand (1940)

James Madison, James Brant, 2 vols. (1941)

They Also Ran, Irving Stone (1943)

The Complete Jefferson, Saul K. Padover, editor (1943)

James Monroe, W. P. Cresson (1946)

GENERAL SOURCE BOOKS

History of the War between the United States and Great Britain, J. Russell, Jr., editor (1815)

State of Louisiana, William Darby (1817)

History of the Discovery and Settlement of the Valley of the Mississippi, John W. Monette, 2 vols. (1846)

Thirty Years View, Thomas H. Benton, Vol. I (1854)

The Memories of Fifty Years, W. H. Sparks (1870)

Seven Decades of the Union, Governor Henry Alexander Wise (1872)

Mississippi as a Province, Territory and State, J. F. H. Claiborne, Vol. I (1880)

Colonial Dames and Good Wives, Alice Morse Earle (1895)

A History of Jessamine County, Kentucky, Bennett H. Young (1898)

Home Life in Colonial Days, Alice Morse Earle (1899)

New Orleans, Grace King (1899)

Narrative and Critical History of America, Justin Winsor, editor, 8 vols. (1889)

Social Life in the Early Republic, Anne Hollingsworth Wharton (1902)

Harper's Encyclopaedia of United States History, 10 vols. (1906)

Men Women and Manners in Colonial Times, Sydney George Fisher, 2 vols. (1908)

Historic Dress in America, Elisabeth McClellan (1910)

The Complete Poetical Works of William Cowper, H. S. Milford, editor (1913)

A History of Travel in America, Seymour Dunbar, 4 vols. (1915)

Making the American Thoroughbred, James Douglas Anderson (1916)

The Frontier in American History, Frederick Jackson Turner (1920)

History of Mercer and Boyle Counties, Mrs. Maria T. Daviess (1924)

A History of the Presidency from 1788 to 1897, Edward Stanwood (1926)

The Capture of Old Vincennes, Milo M. Quaife, editor (1927)

The Spanish American Frontiers: 1782–1795, Arthur Preston Whitaker (1927)

Fabulous New Orleans, Lyle Saxon (1928)

Costume throughout the Ages, Mary Evans (1930)

The Outlaw Years, Robert M. Coates (1930)

The March of Democracy, James Truslow Adams (1932)

The Rise of American Civilization, Charles A. and Mary R. Beard (1936)

The American Language, H. L. Mencken (1936)

Dictionary of American Biography, 20 vols. (1937)

The Biography of a River Town, Gerald M. Capers, Jr. (1939)

The Trees, Conrad Richter (1940)

A History of American Foreign Policy, John Holladay Latané and David W. Wainhouse (1941)

Lower Mississippi, Hodding Carter (1942)

Atlas of American History, James Truslow Adams, editor (1943)

Album of American History, James Truslow Adams, editor, 2 vols. (1945)

The American Language, Supplement I, H. L. Mencken (1945)

A Treasury of Early American Homes, Richard Pratt (1949)

Historic Madison County, Emma Williams (1946)

Natchez on the Mississippi, Harnett T. Kane (1947)

The Wilderness Road, Robert L. Kincaid (1947)

The Unhurried Years, Pierce Butler (1948)

The Western Country in 1793, Harry Toulman (1948)

The Romantic New Orleanians, Robert Tallant (1950)

MAGAZINES, NEWSPAPERS, PAMPHLETS

United States Telegraph, June 22, 1827

A Letter From The Jackson Committee of Nashville, In Answer to One From Similar Committee at Cincinnati Upon The Subject of General Jackson's Marriage, 1827, pamphlet, 30 pp.

Execution of Tennessee Militiamen, 1815, 1828, Number II in series of sixteen anti-Jackson pamphlets

Truth's Advocate, series of 10 anti-Jackson pamphlets published monthly, January through October, 1828

American Historical Magazine, Vol. III, 1898; Vol. IV, 1899; Vol. V, 1900; Vol. VI, 1901; Vol. VIII, 1903

A Traffic History of the Mississippi River System, Frank Haigh Dixon, 1909

Seventh Annual Report of the Director of the Department of Archives and History Guion Letters, 1797–1799, Dunbar Rowland (director), 1909

The American Historical Review, J. Franklin Jameson (editor), Vol. XV, 1910

The Draper Manuscripts as Relating to Tennessee, John Trotwood Moore, 1919

The Horse and Its Heritage in Tennessee, Tennessee State Department of Agriculture, 1945

Rayon Yarns, April 1946; October 1947; January 1949

Tennessee Historical Quarterly, Vol. VI, June 1947, Number 2

The Hermitage, Mrs. Mary C. Dorris (compiled by) (no date)

Journal of the Illinois State Historical Society, Jessie Palmer Weber (editor), Vol. VIII (no date)

Tennessee Historical Magazine, Series I, Vols. I, II, III, VII, VIII; Series II, Vol. I (no date)

UNPUBLISHED THESES

The Life and Activities of John Coffee, Gordon Thomas Chappell (submitted to the faculty of Vanderbilt University, Nashville, Tennessee, 1941)

The Life and Activities of John Overton, Frances Clifton (submitted to the faculty of Vanderbilt University, 1948)

MANUSCRIPTS

LIBRARY OF CONGRESS: Andrew Jackson Papers; Henry Clay Family Papers; Newspaper Files (*United States Telegraph*, June 22, 1827)

TENNESSEE HISTORICAL SOCIETY AND TENNESSEE STATE LIBRARY: Andrew Jackson Papers; John Overton Papers; John Coffee Papers; Donelson Family Papers; Political pamphlets, broadsides, newspapers and magazine articles

PRIVATE COLLECTIONS: Mrs. Mary Hooper Donelson Jones (Mr. P. T.); Joseph L. Mann McHenry

DAVIDSON COUNTY COURT RECORDS: Andrew's land transactions; Donelson family birth and death records